ANGELS AND APOSTLES

A DARK TIDES THRILLER

TONY HUTCHINSON

CHESHIRE CAT BOOKS LTD

The book is published by Cheshire Cat Books Ltd
Suite 50-58 Low Friar Street, Newcastle upon Tyne, NE1 5UD.

ISBN 978-1-9164457-5-8

To Saphron.
My very own guardian angel.

CHAPTER ONE

Thursday 11th December 2014

'SCREAM as much as you want nonce.'

The voice wasn't raised, the words softly spoken.

'No one outside can hear you and no one in here gives a shit.'

The interrogator in the blue boiler suit and steel toe-capped boots was on his haunches, peering into the dark and dust of the vehicle inspection pit, torch pointing into the captive's face.

The other two stood silent, gloved hands gripping their own black machined aluminium Maglites, staring down at the man whose arms stretched backwards, hands tied around an old green oil drum, the thick rope useful again after years left coiled in a cobweb-covered heap.

The steady beams illuminated decades of neglect in the desolate garage, discarded needles and rusted metal Castrol signs from conflicting times; what was once a busy petrol and MOT station reduced to a foul-smelling junkies den, a relic like some broken beast left to rot by poachers on a bone dry African plain. For poachers with rifles and night sights read cheap supermarket fuel and shiny vehicle service centres, all testaments to so-called progress.

'You know why you're here?'

The interrogator's voice remained quiet, soft almost. He was too experienced to raise it. Conversational and controlled was always more threatening.

'I don't,' the man shouted, his desert dry mouth fighting to release saliva. 'I really don't. I've done nothing. I'm retired. All I did was try to collect my television.'

'Well let's see if we can jog your memory.'

The interrogator turned to one of his accomplices. 'Pass the petrol.'

'No!' the man's ragged voice ricocheted around the pit, heels scrambling for leverage, his back pushing against the drum.

The interrogator stood up and tipped the can.

Petrol flowed over the captive's hair, streaming into his blinking eyes, into his mouth, his convulsing body sending the viscose liquid down his torso onto his cheap brown trousers, the smell and taste making him retch.

'Please no,' he screamed.

Back on his haunches the interrogator took out a cigarette, struck a match and lit up. He inhaled, slow and deep, then spoke as he exhaled.

'Now then Jeremy,' still with that unnerving calm. 'The little boys in your school. How many?'

'None! I swear. I didn't do anything. I was acquitted.'

The interrogator shook his head, shook it slowly.

'We both know an acquittal just means your defence barrister was better than the prosecutor, a bit sharper. It's got fuck all to do with truth and justice.'

He inhaled again.

'But in here it's different. There are no legal tricks, Jeremy, no loopholes or laws about inadmissible evidence. The whole system's not weighted in the defendant's favour. This is a fairer courtroom. Here, truth prevails. Justice is served. Everything is admissible. Everything.'

Capturing Jeremy Scott had been easy. A promotional 'claim-your-prize' letter from a fictitious company, the bait of a 52" flat screen TV, and a request the retired schoolteacher be at home on the given time and date with proof of ID. The police had deployed the same tactic to round up people for years. Play the greed card and reel them in once they bite.

When the interrogator had arrived he had asked Jeremy to help carry the TV from the van. Greed made some people so gullible. When the back doors had opened, he was quickly shoved forward and four arms had yanked him into the van.

'Jeremy.' The voice remained soft. He struck another match and waved it towards the pit.

Jeremy Scott sagged and let his head drop to his heaving chest.

'It was a lifetime ago,' he said, as if somehow time was his saviour, his get out clause. 'Who remembers?'

The interrogator turned to look at the two others, held their eyes for a moment, and then moved his gaze back. The torch beam burning through tiny motes of drifting debris had never wavered.

'The innocent boys remember Jeremy, the ones who came forward and others the police don't even know about. They all remember even if you pretend you don't.'

Head bowed, Scott's lips moved but the words were half-formed and too mumbled to hear.

'Please look up Jeremy, look at me...that's better.'

His voice was more like a counsellor than an interrogator.

'Now, it may have been a lifetime ago for you, but for those boys every single day has been full of memories as fresh and horrific as the moment you made them. Do you know genuine fear Jeremy?'

Scott nodded, almost hypnotised by the voice.

'Oh, I'm not sure,' the interrogator said. 'I'm not talking about the fear of a parent when they lose a child in a busy department store or the fear of a hard working single mum when another bill drops on her mat and she knows she won't be able to feed her kids. I'm talking real down-deep fear. The fear I want you to feel now...an overweight, retired, never-been-married-teacher in a badly-fitting brown suit stinking of piss and petrol.'

'Please don't,' he muttered.

The interrogator moved the beam up and down Scott's rope-bound body, silent until he centred the light back on his face.

'Did you listen to those little boys when they said that? Did you hear their fear when you walked into their dorm in the middle of the night, terrified and not knowing if it was going to be their turn? Did you stop when they begged you to leave them alone? When they cried out in pain? Did you stop?'

Scott's voice rose again, his frantic mind grasping for a new escape route.

'Alright I did it,' he shouted. 'There. Is that what you want?'

The interrogator paused as if he was contemplating his answer. 'No,' he said at last. 'What we want is justice. Society's spent a lifetime watching people like you, people everyone knows are guilty but who still walk free, people whose slick barristers get important evidence kicked out and bully victims in the witness box, victims who are already emotional wrecks, middle-aged men now but still carrying the scars a piece of shit like you inflicted.'

He stood, dropped the cigarette, and stubbed it out with his boot.

The movement made Scott jerk and his eyes began to dart from the interrogator to the others.

He struggled again against the rope around him.

'Just let me go,' he said quickly.' You've got your admission. You've got the fear you wanted.'

The interrogator let the words drift through the specks of dust floating lazily in the torch-light, watching the trembling mouth and the man that spoke them.

He was right about the fear, but the admission? Hand him over to the police and even a z-list lawyer would have that kicked out once they discovered how the confession came about. All lies dished out under 'duress' to save his skin from the bad men. That's how it would play.

The interrogator lit up again, turned his back, and

smoked the cigarette, the smoke curling towards the grime-covered skylights.

'One last thing,' he said, turning back towards the pit, flicking the cigarette in the air.

Jeremy Scott watched wide-eyed as the glowing red end arced over the inspection pit and dropped safely on the other side.

'Do you go to the dentist regularly?'

Realisation came in a flood and the screams that returned sounded more like wails.

'I think he understands,' the interrogator shouted over his shoulder. 'Not lost that public school brain.'

Then the voice dropped and was quiet again as he turned back.

'After you're found, the victims will need to know it's definitely you,' he said. 'That's where your teeth come in. Believe me, there'll be nothing else.'

The interrogator picked up an empty milk bottle, filled it with petrol and stuffed a rag into the liquid.

'No!' Scott screamed. 'Please. I'm begging you!'

The interrogator lit the rag with a steady hand and hurled the bottle.

'Too late for begging,' he said as the glass shattered in a fireball of searing heat and flame. 'Burn in hell you piece of shit.'

He and the men walked away in silence. There was nothing to be said. The screams would die long before the flames.

Detective Chief Inspector Sam Parker, hands deep in pockets, walked amongst the late evening Christmas crowds on Seaton St George's High Street, Ed Whelan, her Murder Team Detective Sergeant, alongside her.

'So you've got absolutely no idea what you want to buy your wife for Christmas?'

'That's why you're here,' Ed said, a Baker Boy flat cap

protecting his bald head from the cold air. 'I'm counting on you for some inspiration.'

'Bloody hell Ed, Sue doesn't even like me,' Sam looked up at the Christmas lights hanging above the road. 'If she thought I was helping you buy her present she'd probably kill us both.'

Ed grinned: 'Which is why I'm not going to tell her.'

Sam stopped to take a Marlboro Gold from her pocket, glanced up and down the street, and lit up. 'What if she sees us?'

'She won't,' Ed said, standing next to her, sounding more confident than he felt. 'So...any ideas?'

Sam inhaled on the cigarette and exhaled slowly, hoping somewhere in the breath a light would shine.

'I don't know. Underwear?'

Ed felt the bones in his neck crick as he snapped his head sharp right to face her.

'Underwear? Are you having a laugh? If I gave her underwear she'd think I'd bought it for my bit-on-the-side.'

'I didn't know you had one of those.'

'Ha ha. Look I haven't got a clue what to get her, that's why you're here. The daughter normally does this sort of thing but she's not speaking to me at the moment.'

Sam inhaled again, waiting for Ed to continue.

'All I asked was whether she watered her new boyfriend every day because he seemed to have the IQ of a plant.'

Sam raised her eyebrows and smiled. Ed Whelan and his lost career as a diplomat.

'You haven't met him,' Ed protested. 'Thick as pig-shit and recently had his personality surgically removed, I swear.'

'Well I can see why she's not doing your Christmas shopping,' Sam muttered. 'You want some help picking out a present for him?'

'Who? Jasper?'

'Jasper?'

'Exactly. Bloody dog's name, and just as smelly. '

'Alright Ed?'

The voice from behind was one Ed immediately

recognised, the Devon accent as slow and pronounced as the rising bubbles in a glass of cider.

Sam and Ed turned around.

'Alright Ray. How's it going?'

Ray Reynolds, thick jet black hair swept backwards, was an inch bigger than Ed at 6'6", and not looking much older or fatter since he retired over ten years ago.

'Good. And this is?' the raised eyebrows an attempt to send Ed's cheeks strawberry red.

Ed recognised the look, the unspoken question...'colleague, affair or both?'

At least Reynolds hadn't seen them shopping together, especially for underwear.

Jesus, just imagine. Ed winced inside.

He smiled. 'My boss. Sam Parker. Sam, this is Ray Reynolds, retired Detective Super.'

Ray Reynolds extended his hand and shook Sam's.

'Delighted. I've seen some of your TV performances. Very accomplished.'

'Thank you and I've heard the stories about you.'

Reynolds shook his head.

'Don't listen,' he told her lightly. 'War stories always sound better with the passing of time. Anyway I must crack on. Pleasure, Sam. Take it easy Ed. Might catch up with you at the Pensioners' Party.'

Reynolds walked into the crowd, hair visible above the throng.

'He's never changed,' Ed said. 'Not everybody's cup of tea but fiercely loyal if you were loyal to him.'

Sam watched the impressive hair get smaller in the distance.

'He'd see a few changes if he came back now.'

Ed shrugged, remembering different days.

'The Ray Reynolds of this world wouldn't cope with all the politically correct crap today. A man's man, no time for pussyfooting. Job first, beer second, upsetting people not even on his radar. But all our yesterdays isn't getting the shopping done.'

Sam stubbed the cigarette onto the top of a bin before flicking it inside. 'Perfume? A nice scarf? New gloves?'

What would it be like if you were buying them for me?

'Genius. A scarf sounds good.'

'Right I know just the shop. Nice and expensive.' She glanced at her watch. 'Then you're buying the coffees and a slice of Christmas cake.'

CHAPTER TWO

THE DARK BROWN leather armchair was so big William Skinner looked like he was on a Hollywood film set auditioning for Land of the Giants or The Borrowers, his stumpy legs barely able to touch the floor. The ice in the gin and tonic had long since melted, a casualty of his wife's love affair with central heating and a nod to the time in their lives when they could have food or warmth but not both. In those days he'd still be drinking pints at 8pm, but not now. He looked around. He loved the living room with its sunken sitting area, the dark wood flooring and Chinese pale blue rugs, the pool table, balls racked, on the raised area.

The smell of garlic drifted from the kitchen. When they first married he'd made the mistake of telling her he liked her spaghetti bolognaise. Now it was a 'treat' she cooked every Thursday. He couldn't even remember why it had to be a Thursday. Thirty-three years of bolognaise and the nearest he had ever been to Italy was watching Liverpool beat Milan on the TV. Even his sons did their best to be somewhere else on a Thursday.

Still she was fiercely loyal and plenty tough. She never succumbed to police threats, kept a clear head whenever he was arrested and turned a blind eye when his own eyes wandered.

'Won't be long,' she shouted from the kitchen.

He stood up, walked to the timber-framed patio doors and looked across the carpet-bowls lawn and the borders full of plants and colour. The monthly cost of the gardeners was more than the rent on their old two bedroom flat but the two acres resembled Augusta. Not that he played golf.

Growing up the only green he saw in his concrete jungle was the school football pitch and that was often more mud than grass. He smiled, remembering his mother running out of money for the electric meter. He'd go to bed in the dark more often than not, no sheet on the mattress, brothers lying alongside, coats piled on top. Only rich people had blankets.

Now he had the best cotton on every bed and enough electricity to light up his garden like a football stadium, power the nine feet high security gates and service CCTV cameras that blinked red like dragons' eyes 24 hours a day.

'It's on the table,' his wife shouted.

He turned away from the garden and walked to the kitchen, by-passing the formal dining room.

'Looks great,' he said, pulling the stool closer to the kitchen table.

Marge bent down to kiss his head. 'You'll say 'owt but your prayers Billy Skinner.'

The mobile started to dance around the bench.

'You eat. I'll get it.' Marge answered the phone. 'Yeah, I'll tell him.'

Billy looked up from the spaghetti covered in so much Parmesan it looked like snowfall.

'Stuart's on his way.'

Billy nodded and slurped the pasta.

Stuart McFadden parked next to the fountain, a must-have for Marge the moment she saw the Trevi on a friend's hen trip to Rome and fell in love. Walking across the gravel, Stuart eyed the marble mermaid surrounded by spouting water flumes from her sculptured rock and shook his head. He remembered the bloated monstrosity had been installed after the weekend break in Copenhagen.

It was true what people said: money couldn't buy class.

He rang the bell and listened to something that would have given Big Ben a run for its money.

'Come in Stuart. Do you want anything to eat?' Marge asked.

On a Thursday? Not bloody likely.

'I'm fine thanks.'

He followed her into the kitchen and pulled out a chair.

'Don't get comfy, I'm coming.' Billy stood up, dropping the linen napkin on the table. 'We'll see you later Marge.'

She walked over, kissed his cheek and told him: 'Okay.'

A minute later Billy had settled into the tan leather of the BMW Seven Series and stretched his legs as Stuart started her up.

'Pussycats?'

Billy Skinner nodded.

Skinner had opened Pussycats, a lap dancing club, in the mid-nineties on an industrial estate on the outskirts of town. There had been the usual protests over the years, do-gooders demonstrating about the exploitation of women, but it was well run and the police were never called.

Stuart pulled up outside and threw the keys to one of the doormen.

Inside, the lights were as low as the bikini tops. Suits sat around tables, talking to the beachwear or watching even slinkier numbers glide up and down the pole.

Stuart followed Billy across the blue carpet into the back office.

'Anything?' Billy looked at the manager, a forty something with no convictions, the Pussycats front man.

'Councillor Elgin's in.'

He zoomed the CCTV onto the tall, dark haired, fifty-year-old with the looks, but not the wealth, of a 1950s movie idol. The navy suit, so shiny it looked polished, reflected the spinning stage lights; the grubby pink tie had been out of fashion so long it was a museum piece. Milk bottle white fingers squeezed the shoulders of the two girls sitting on his knees.

Billy pulled out a chair. 'Tell Zara and Chloe to look after him. I'll sort their wages. Tell them to say it's on the house.'

'You're the boss.' Forty-something left the room.

'Stuart, I want him videoed shagging them two. Nothing concentrates your mind more than being caught with a couple of young fillies, especially when you're married to a battle-axe like he is. The woman's scary.'

'No bother. The Green Room's all ready.'

'Great. The boys will be here soon. I want to run through the figures.' He walked over to the free-standing safe, opened it, and took out two £1000 bundles.

'Give that to Zara and Chloe, and send a bottle of cheap fizz to their table. No point wasting the good stuff on Elgin.'

Billy's three sons walked in, Mathew, Mark, and Luke. People called them The Apostles, but only behind their backs. They were all short and squat, like their father, and each was wearing an expensive suit with an open necked white shirt.

'All done?' Billy asked.

'All good,' Mathew said, the oldest of the brothers and the one with a cigarette permanently sticking out of his lips. 'Half a kilo dropped off at all of our establishments, all couriers safe, no thefts.'

The couriers were young, female and drove non-descript family hatchbacks provided by Billy. Most importantly they were all of previous good character, their job being to collect and deliver the packages to the trusted managers of each establishment. The family had twenty pubs and clubs throughout the north east and the Skinners controlled the supply of cocaine within them.

None of the delivery girls had ever met Billy Skinner. Each went to a public pay phone at a specified time, was told where to collect the packages and where to deliver them. The phone boxes continually changed, and the girls were given their location by text twenty minutes before the call. None of them had ever opened a package and were never told what they contained, although at £200 a drop they must have worked out they weren't delivering bar snacks or bingo cards.

The Skinners bought loyalty with two things: cash and the

threat of violence. The price of disloyalty, on an escalating scale, was a limb rendered useless through to death itself. Billy had been the enforcer years ago, but his sons had taken over that role and Mathew, not the luckiest when the brain cells were being dished out, was darkly imaginative when it came to punishments. He revelled in striking fear into people, loved being called Iron Man. A cruel streak ran through his DNA like the hidden metal in reinforced concrete

Billy opened a ledger. He didn't trust computers; if hackers could slip inside the computers of NASA and the FBI, what chance did he have?

'Takings seem to be down at 'Scaramangers'. Why?'

He loved James Bond, 'The Man with the Golden Gun' his favourite.

'Sound the doormen out. See if trade's dropped off the last few weeks. The bar's down, the food's down, and we haven't had the return we should have had on the coke. Don't go in all guns blazing, especially you Mat, but let's make sure no one's taking the piss.'

Mathew looked at the floor. Being rebuked in front of his younger brothers was bad enough, but having that ingratiating Stuart there really nauseated him.

'Harry Pullman's been with me for years. I can't believe he would skim but he's hit the bottle big time since his wife died. Drink does funny things to men.'

He closed the ledger. 'After that and before you hit the clubs, go and see your mother.'

He looked at each of them and smiled. 'You never know, there might be some spaghetti left.'

Everyone in the room laughed except Mathew. He was shooting daggers at Stuart McFadden.

Who the fuck are you to laugh at my mother?

'Right,' Billy said, 'Where's Pixie?'

'Cellar,' Mat tried to hide his anger.

Billy stood up. 'Best go and see the little fucker then.'

Peter 'Pixie' Carlton, slumped and tied to a wooden chair surrounded by kegs, raised his head when the metal door swung open, the draught from the corridor a small reprieve from the stale air that had built up over the three hours of his incarceration. His whole body was shivering, a combination of fear and nakedness.

'Pixie. How are you?' Billy, smiling, sounded as if he was greeting a welcome guest at a family wedding.

Tears rolled down Pixie's face. The nickname had stuck since his first day in secondary school when the older kids saw the gangly 6' plus 11-year-old for the first time. He finally stopped growing when he reached 6'8" and the nickname had remained.

'Please Mr. Skinner.'

'Now now Pixie,' Billy said, his voice light. 'A bit late for please and thank you.'

He walked behind Pixie and looked for an unmarked patch of skin on his back. There wasn't any. Various red, long, linear marks in the early stages of bruising would eventually join together to form a solid black and blue mass. His sons had always been accurate with pick-axe handles. He'd taught them well.

The Skinner sons and Stuart stood leaning back against the wall. Each would do whatever Billy asked.

Billy grabbed Pixie's blond hair, pulled his head backwards and spat on his face.

'You are not here to supply coke to your estate agent mates and play the big-I-am.'

He slapped Pixie around the back of the head, then walked around the chair and stood in front of him.

'I trust you with the product which I expect you to sell and give the profits to me. You get yours for free, but obviously that's not been enough.'

He bent down. His face was inches from Pixie's although his wasn't shaking and decorated with a trembling blob of saliva. Billy put his hands in his trouser pockets, took out four sovereign rings, and put one on each finger of his right hand.

'I'm sorry Mr. Skinner it won't happen again,' Pixie gasped, his wide eyes flashing between Billy and the others.

'You're right there Pixie. It won't. In Saudi they chop off a thief's right hand. Did you know that? Safest country in the world.'

Billy Skinner had dished out plenty of punishment beatings, but he doubted he'd seen anybody's eyes stretch as wide as Pixie's were now.

'Please.'

'No seriously. In Saudi they chop your right hand off so you can never sit at anyone's table. That's because they're very clean. Wipe their backsides only with their left hand. Nobody will eat with someone who uses their left hand at the table.'

'Please Mr. Skinner.'

A river was now flowing freely down his face.

'Relax. I'm not chopping your hand off. Well not this time anyway. But you have to be punished. Can't have people thinking I'm going soft. Where would that leave me?'

'Please Mr. Skinner.'

'If you don't stop bleating on like a little girl I will cut your bloody hand off. Understand?'

A nod.

'Luke, Mark. Untie this piece of shit.'

Seconds later Pixie was upright towering over both Skinners.

Luke and Mark grabbed his arms, arms that had never seen a gym.

'Now this can be as quick or as slow as you choose,' Billy said. 'I can take a bolt cropper to each finger on your right hand and snap them off neatly below the first knuckle.'

Pixie struggled but was forced back into the chair by Luke and Mark.

Billy Skinner punched him on the face, the sovereign rings slicing his skin quicker than a tin opener cutting through a can.

'Or,' Billy continued, his voice like a businessman chairing a meeting, 'we can put your fingers in the doorframe and kick it shut.'

Pixie spluttered blood, his voice childlike and desperate.

'Please, I'll pay it back.'

Billy nodded. 'You'll pay it back anyway, just with fewer fingers than before. Count yourself lucky. If you had really upset me, you'd be a dead man. Instead you'll be the walking reminder if you fuck with Billy Skinner, you get fucked.'

Mat laughed. 'You never know they might change your nickname from Pixie to Fingers.'

Or Miles O'Toole he thought, staring at the 20 year old's cock.

Billy glared at his son, then turned back to Pixie.

'So, hand in door and it's over quickly or one at a time with the bolt croppers. You decide.'

Pixie stared at the floor, said nothing.

'Okay,' Billy said. 'We'll try the door first. If you move your hand there is no second chance. It will be the bolt croppers and we'll do your fingers one at a time…over the next twenty-four hours.'

Billy moved away. 'Take him to the door.'

CHAPTER THREE

Friday 12th December

DECLAN DOHERTY HAD one hand on the wheel, the other on a cigar. The road noise from the A1 northbound buffeted his ears, more to do with the driver's window being open than the twin-axle caravan being towed behind the big Mercedes.

He had a couple of hundred King Edwards in his van. Each wedding guest would get one, at least the ones he knew.

He gripped his with his teeth, fiddled with the in-car computer: average speed, average fuel consumption and distance travelled. The miles were clocking up, every minute putting Newark another mile behind him. That's why he liked driving at night. Much easier; roads clearer, less police.

His wife, daughter and two granddaughters were asleep in the van. He thought that might be illegal, but since when did that bother Travellers like him. It was more important that his girls got a good night's sleep. Besides what was the difference between sleeping on the road and sleeping in those posh trains?

The sting of the smoke was blinding him.

'Bollocks,' he muttered. He took the cigar from his mouth and threw it out of the window then rubbed his stinging eyes while he steered with his knees.

He contemplated where to exit the A1 to get to Seaton St George. There were so many choices. At 2am it didn't matter whether he drove past Middlesbrough, Darlington or Hartlepool. He wouldn't get stuck in traffic, unlike a couple of days ago when he'd driven up with a few of the lads.

Suddenly he leaned so far forward his nose almost touched the windscreen. He rubbed his eyes again but this time there was no smoke. Ahead in the quickly closing distance he saw a naked man walking along the roadside, the Mercedes' powerful beams leaving no room for illusion or a trick of the hard-shoulder shadows.

These fucking stag parties.

Declan braked, pulled into a lay-by, and waited for the man to catch up.

As he got nearer, Declan could see the man's back was stooped and he had his right hand stuffed in his left armpit as if it was seeking warmth and protection.

'Jesus,' Declan said, as the naked stranger collapsed on the verge. Declan saw the bruising on his back, the missing fingertips on his right hand.

He rushed into the caravan and woke the girls and together they helped the man inside.

Declan saw his granddaughters' wide-eyed shock. Whether that was down to the stranger's injuries or the size of his private parts, Declan wasn't sure.

Sam Parker pulled up the fur hood of her military-style coat as she walked across the forecourt of the disused garage. The uniform PC, his breath visible in the cold night air, nodded at her as he lifted the blue tape to allow her and Ed Whelan to duck underneath, writing their names in the scene log as they walked towards the doors and the Senior Scenes of Crime Officer.

'What have we got Julie?' Sam asked, burying her hands in her coat pockets.

Julie Trescothick pulled down her paper mouth mask. She was wearing a white paper suit and white paper overshoes.

'Come in and see for yourself. The plates are already down.'

She bent and picked up two clear plastic bags - a white suit and a pair of overshoes in each - and handed them to Sam and Ed.

'Extra large I hope,' Ed said. He hated fighting to get into the Teletubby suits when they were too tight but at least this time there was no crowd to watch him struggle.

Suits zipped they followed Julie into the garage, the interior lit by freestanding floodlights powered by a noisy diesel generator.

'Evening boss,' the two other SOCOs said in unison.

Evening? It's bloody two am.

'Info from a druggie, Curtis something or other. He's down the nick with uniform. Came to shoot up, saw this and rang us,' Julie said.

The charred figure was on the floor of the inspection pit, feet near an oil drum, burnt pieces of rope close by, one piece on his left wrist. His jaw was clenched shut, his fingers curled like claws, his crisp blackened skin stretched tighter than fresh cling-film.

The smell was like putting your head into a coal fire after it had gone out.

'Male or female?' Sam asked.

'Male,' Julie said.

'Enough to put you off barbecues for life,' Ed said, trying to do what was humanly impossible; breathe out without breathing in.

'You don't improve with age,' Sam smiled and pointed at the oil drum. 'Looks like he's been tied up. Fell forward when the ropes burnt through.'

She paused, looked at what was in front of her, and remembered Albert Szent-Gyorgyi's words – "discovery consists of seeing what everybody has seen and thinking what nobody has thought." 'There's a couple of pieces behind the oil drum,' Sam said.

Ed put the domestic that had broken out when the call-out came to the back of his mind...another argument about work, another slanging-match about how he spent more time with Sam Parker than he did with his wife, another torrent of abuse culminating in their latest hot topic. Ed resisting retirement, especially after a stabbing that meant six months' sick leave and almost cost him his life, had given Sue Whelan a shiny new stick when she wanted to give him a verbal beating.

'There's a strong smell of petrol in the pit, broken glass, and an oily rag,' Julie said.

'As in petrol-bombed?' Sam said.

'Possibly. Do you want the lab out?'

'Yes.' Constrained budget or not, the scientists were a necessity. 'Any ID?' Sam asked.

'There's a wallet. Over there on the floor.' Julie nodded towards it. 'His driving licence is in there. Jeremy Scott, providing it's his.'

Sam wiggled her toes. 'It's a start, but the only way he's getting identified to the Coroner's satisfaction is by dental records.'

They want us to know who it is, Sam was thinking.

Why? Giving us a starter for ten. He's not been burnt to hide his ID.

'The driving licence would make him 78,' Julie said.

Sam looked at Ed. 'Name mean anything to you?'

'Not right now, but I've only been awake about forty minutes and my brain's too busy fighting the smell to concentrate on a name... If the druggie had the where-with-all to ring us that suggests he hadn't started main-lining and he's not so skint he's had to exchange his mobile for drugs.'

'How did he get here?' Sam said.

'Don't know,' Julie told her. 'He'd gone before I arrived.'

'He wouldn't have walked out here would he?' Sam said, stamping her feet. 'Not at this time. More likely he scored his gear and got dropped off here.'

'Could have bought his drugs here,' Ed said. 'Or he was dealing from here.'

'Possibly.' Sam looked at the charred body again. 'What sort of people set fire to someone?'

'Over the ages, plenty,' the well-educated voice boomed out.

Sam spun round.

Jim Melia, the Home Office Forensic Pathologist, stepped towards them plate by plate.

'Burnings at the stake started from the feet up and hordes of people turned out to watch.'

'We've become a bit more civilised since then Jim,' Sam said. 'How are you?'

'I'm fine.'

He peered into the pit.

'But I wouldn't make too much of a thing about being more civilised. Burnings may not be state legislated anymore, but the human capacity to inflict pain on his fellow man has never diminished. Most people keep it in check because they don't want to end up in prison, but that doesn't make them incapable of inflicting it. Just look at ISIS.'

'A psychologist as well now Jim,' Ed said.

'A mere observer of life Ed, in all its faults and failings.'

'Julie, there's not much more for me here,' Sam told her. 'We'll get away. Let me know when you're done and we'll see you at the mortuary. See you soon Jim.'

Outside Sam fumbled in her pockets for her cigarettes.

See what everybody sees…

'This is really well planned Ed. Worryingly well planned. Look around. Middle of nowhere. No cameras. Set on fire in a pit. They must have known it was there.'

She lit up.

'And if they didn't bring the rope, they must have known it was here. Same as the oil drum. They couldn't chance that they'd just find something to tie him to. And the milk bottle, the petrol, the rag to light, if it was a petrol bomb. All had to be brought here.'

She shook her head slowly as she smoked the cigarette.

'This lot aren't amateurs. They knew exactly what they were doing.'

'How many do you reckon?' Ed said.

'More than one, probably more than two. He's got to be transported here, tied up. At least three.'

'Three psychos. Marvellous.'

Ed was sitting in Sam's freezing office, overcoat collar turned up, pen in hand, listening as she paced the room. The corridor outside was in darkness and the heating was off. Estates Management didn't consider the Murder Team being called out at all hours when they set the central heating timer.

'Get Bev out. She can make a start, fire up HOLMES,' Sam said.

Ed raised his eyebrows and smirked at the accidental pun.

Sam gave him a look and spoke again.

'No point in calling anybody else out. Let them come in at eight. It'll be a long day. I want to speak to the druggie. Get Bev to make some initial inquiries about this Jeremy Scott.'

She opened a desk drawer, took out a bottle of Jo Malone perfume, and sprayed her neck and her clothes.

Ed burst into a coughing fit. 'Bloody hell you're choking me.'

'Better than smelling like a coal fire. Jeremy Scott. His address will be on his licence. If it is him, 78-year-olds tend to notify DVLA when they move so the address should be current.'

She put the bottle back in her drawer.

'We'll need to get round his house,' she said. 'See if there's a Mrs Scott. If not we'll need a door-to door team to check on the neighbours, see when he was last seen.'

She took a mouthful of tea from the mug getting cold too quickly on her desk.

'Then it's associates, lifestyle, habits...the usual victimology. Jim'll not be able to give us a time of death but it hasn't just happened. He wasn't smoking.'

'Wasn't drinking either the boring bastard,' Ed grinned and Sam smiled.

Black humour was often the only way to deal with the things they saw.

'This will be a hard slog. To all intents and purposes he may as well have been in the open air. Always the most difficult to detect…' Sam said.

She and Ed knew the statistics. 80% of killers who murdered their victims in buildings were caught. Only 20% of those who killed in the open were ever captured.

Sam continued. 'This morning get someone to plot the nearest CCTV cameras. It's a long shot but he hasn't walked there. If we know where the cameras are we're good to go if anyone's seen him getting into a vehicle. See if he owns a car. If he does, where is it?'

She sat down and put her head in her hands. 'Burnt alive. Jesus.'

Ed shrugged: 'If he was burnt alive.'

'Jim'll be able to tell us that when he examines the lungs and whether there are any other injuries,' Sam said. 'If there aren't, that's a hell of a way to kill somebody. Tie them up and firebomb them. The location, the planning, taking the petrol...that's plenty of premeditation.'

She turned on her desktop computer.

'After that, there's not a lot can be done for now; victimology, forensic at the scene. We'll take it from there.'

CHAPTER FOUR

Ed called Bev then drove Sam into Seaton St George.

The warmth of a twenty-four operational police station was a marked contrast to the cold of Headquarters but the comfort didn't last long.

The two detectives gagged in unison when they opened the door of the tiny interview room by the front desk.

Curtis Brown was shivering next to a radiator, the stench of urine and faeces radiating from him like a chemical weapons attack.

Sam rubbed her watering eyes.

'Curtis. I'm DCI Parker and this is DS Whelan.'

'We've met,' Ed said.

Curtis Brown nodded.

Neither detective sat down, both preferring the relative safety of the open door and life-saving air stream.

'Sorry to keep you waiting,' Sam said. 'It must have been a shock for you.'

Another nod.

'We just need to ask a few questions then you can go. If you feel you need some professional help to talk through what you've seen tonight then we can put you in touch with people.'

The counsellors are going to love you Ed thought.

'I'm okay. It's not the first time I've seen a stiff.'

Sam's eyes were drawn to Curtis' teeth, and in that department he was a white one short of a snooker set.

'Okay. But if you do, Ed will give you his card.'

Ed put his hands in his trouser pockets. *Cheers Sam.*

'I'm okay. Look will it take long? I've got things to do,' Curtis said.

'Not long…We're not going to search you,' Sam told him, turning her head towards the corridor and taking a deep breath she hoped more than expected was discreet. 'We just need you to tell us what happened tonight'.

If someone had dropped a packet of itching powder down Curtis Brown's clothes he wouldn't be scratching anymore than he was now.

'Scored some gear. Went into the old garage to shoot up and saw the stiff. That's it. Listen will I have to go to court? I don't want to go to court.'

Ed took a deep breath, put his hands on the desk, and leaned towards Brown.

'You listen Curtis, I don't suppose anybody who works at any court wants you in their midst, but we all have our crosses to bear.'

Ed reckoned he could get one more sentence out before he needed to breathe. Burnt bodies and heroin addicts. He'd be living with the smells for weeks.

'You will have to make a statement and more than likely go to court but if you don't want to help, maybe I'll wonder if you're the one who killed that man.'

Ed stepped back, stuck his head out of the door and sucked in air. Discretion could go fuck itself.

Curtis rocked on his chair and clasped his hands as sweat broke out on his brow quicker than a fat businessman grunting on a prostitute. 'I never done nowt.'

'Then make a quick statement to Sergeant Whelan and you'll be on your way,' Sam flashed white teeth at Ed as she pushed past, liking the look when he realised the next terrible minutes of his life would be spent in the firing-line of Curtis Brown's ruined mouth.

Maybe I should try for promotion again, Ed thought sourly.

He went to the front desk, scanned the labels on the tall metal cabinet, pulled open two drawers and grabbed a witness statement frontice page and a couple of continuation pages.

He took a breath that would have impressed a free diver and walked into the interview room.

Ed had long ago come to realise there was something about being in a small confined space with a heroin addict. It wasn't just the unholy smell; eventually you became immune to that. It was the addicts themselves, the endless shaking, the dirt-grey pallor of their skin, the gaunt and sunken features of a face robbed of hope and a body starved of anything worth having.

Looking at him now, Ed knew Curtis needed a hit.

'Curtis, just tell me what you saw, how you got to the garage and then you can be out of here.'

The eyes stared back at him from sockets as deep as ocean caves.

'Look I know you're in possession,' Ed pushed. 'You went there to shoot up. I'm not helping you by taking your wrap away. Just tell me what happened.'

Curtis was silent then made his decision.

'I went to the garage to score. I rang my dealer and he said that's where he'd be. I cycled. It's miles man. Just went inside and I saw that thing. Burnt. Stinking. Scared the shit out of me. I ran man and rang your lot.'

'And I appreciate you did that Curtis,' Ed told him. 'Did you see anyone else there, other than your dealer?'

'No.'

'Did you get there before...'

'I was there before Deano, yeah.'

Curtis looked down and muttered 'shit' under his breath.

'Dean Silvers?' Ed was straight onto it.

'I'm not saying.'

Curtis pulled up the collar of his soiled summer-weight jacket, his fingers yellow with nicotine.

'Okay, so Dean comes in a car?'

'Yeah, I mean no, I'm not giving his name,' Curtis glared. 'Pulled into the garage, turned his headlights off. He didn't get out of the car. I bent down at his window, felt the warm air. Will this be much longer?'

'No. Soon as you finish.'

'I bought a tenner-bag. Him and his mate drove off. That's it.'

'Who was his mate?'

Curtis looked down at the floor again, thrust his hands in his jacket pockets, and buried his neck in the collar. 'I'm not saying.'

'Last thing Curtis,' Ed said. 'Where are you living at the minute?'

'Why?'

'In case I need to see you again.'

'Why?'

'Curtis I can search you and lock you up if you'd prefer.'

Heroin addicts like Curtis were nothing if not pragmatic...always act in your own interests, keep your loyalty level at zero and only think as far ahead as the next hit.

'On the streets but there's this squat,' Curtis said when he realised silence wasn't his best tactic. 'I'm there most nights.'

'Address?'

'How should I know? It's not like anybody's sending me letters.'

Ed banged the table. 'Curtis.'

'Blue door, old house, big house, on Station Road.'

'I'll find it. Do you want a cup of tea? Sandwich? You could do with knocking something into you.'

'I just need to go man,' Curtis scratched his head.

'How's your mother?'

'Don't know.' His knees were moving faster than pistons in a car engine.

'Shall I give her a message?'

Ed watched Curtis Brown shake his head. 'No point.'

'She's still your mother even if she did kick you out. Can't blame her. Not with you nicking things every time her back was turned.'

'Can I go now?' Curtis stood up.

'How many other times have you bought drugs at that garage?'

'That was the first time.'

'We need to get you to hospital,' Declan said as Pixie Carlton sat in the caravan's dinette, a cup of tea in his left hand.

Declan had left the A1 and parked on the first out of town retail park he had come across.

His wife had bandaged Pixie's right hand and dressed him in some of her husband's clothes. The red checked shirt was too wide and too short; the jeans, too big around the waist, finished closer to his knees than his ankles.

'I'll be fine,' Pixie said, droplets of sweat falling like the start of a cloud burst as shock and a burning temperature took their toll.

'What's your story then?' Declan said, leaning against the cooker, rolling a cigarette. 'Bollock naked, beaten to a pulp. You don't sound the type. Too posh.'

'It's a long story.'

The four women, Declan's wife, daughter and two granddaughters, were squeezed around the dinette. They stared at Pixie but said nothing.

'It's a story that you should tell us, especially if me stopping for you has put my family in danger.'

Pixie looked up at him and put the tea on the table.

'You're in no danger. If they'd wanted to kill me they could have done.'

He winced as the pain from his hand played pinball with every nerve in his body. He took a deep breath.

'They wanted to teach me a lesson and remind everybody else what happens if you cross them. Dumping me on the A1 was just Mat's idea of a laugh.'

'Mat Skinner?'

Pixie's head jerked in surprise. 'You know him?'

'Piece of shit just like his father,' Declan said. 'How did a well-spoken young man like you get mixed up with that scum?'

Pixie had found himself asking the same question on a daily basis.

'God I wish I'd never set eyes on them. I'm an estate agent. Met them when they were looking to increase their property portfolio, got chatting and eventually I got the courage to ask about buying some coke. Nothing heavy at first but I ended up supplying my mates...'

'And you stole from them. The Skinners,' Declan interrupted.

'Sort of.'

'Not the brightest.'

'I know.'

Pixie dropped his head, a big man broken but not looking to blame anyone but himself.

'Who's at home?' Declan asked.

'Nobody,' Pixie told him. 'Live alone. Rented.'

Declan's wife stood up.

She told him that was enough talking, said Pixie needed a hospital and needed it now.

'C'mon then,' Declan said. 'Listen son if the police come round I'd prefer you don't mention us.'

'I won't. I don't even know your name.'

'That's how I'd like to keep it.'

Instinctively Declan held out his right hand. Pixie moved his own on reflex but only for a moment. The pain bent him double.

'What's the sketch with Curtis?' Sam said, as Ed walked into her office.

Ed grimaced: 'Apart from scratching and my clothes stinking of piss?'

Ed brought Sam up to speed with Curtis' statement and

his slip about Dean Silvers.

'It was Silvers who suggested the garage for the meet,' he said, pulling out a chair and sitting down. 'We can't rule out dealers or users being involved. The MO would suggest dealers rather than users but a user like Curtis could have seen something. I'll go and see his mother later, see if she can shed any light.'

'You know her?' Sam asked him.

'Went to school with her. She was a magistrate.'

'Jill Brown?'

'That's her,' Ed said. 'Decent woman. Her husband died years ago. Cancer. Curtis had been no bother until then but that's when he went off the rails. He just got in with the wrong crowd. It happens.'

Ed reached into his inside jacket pocket and took out a blister pack of pain killers.

'You okay?' Sam's eyes flashed concern.

'I'm fine. Just getting a bit of gip from my neck.'

'Do you need to go home?'

Sam had wanted Ed to return to work on restricted duties, to ease himself back after the stabbing but he wouldn't hear of it.

'It's just because I'm cold,' Ed pushed the pack and took out two tablets. 'I'll be fine.'

He popped the tablets into his mouth and washed them down with a slurp of tea.

'Since his mum finally kicked him out Curtis has been locked up a few times for shoplifting,' Ed said. 'That's about his level, like most of them, that and stealing from their own.'

Sam stood up and asked Ed to head over on a fact-finder to Jeremy Scott's home as a priority.

'No point in us both going,' she said. 'I'll have a chat with Bev.'

CHAPTER FIVE

The Avenue was one of Seaton St George's most exclusive streets, the grass verge and mature trees separating the footpath from the pothole-free wide road. Ahead, Ed saw the revolving yellow lights of the council gritting machine moving at a steady pace. He pulled up outside The Willows. He knew plenty of the houses in this street were home to senior figures in the local authority.

Wouldn't do for the big wigs to put up with potholes and ice. They'd have council workers scraping the frost from their windscreens if they could get away with it.

Ed had gone from interviewing Curtis Brown to this rarefied world in twenty minutes.

He walked up the gravel path, stones slick with ice crunching under his feet. A few lights were on in some of the houses, people preparing for their working day, a day starting considerably later than Ed's.

A light shone through the small stain glass window in the top of the door. The front room lights were on, curtains drawn. He knocked on the freezing cold door, his knuckles stinging against the wood.

Nothing.

He knocked again.

Still nothing.

Ed walked down the side of the house, opened a trellis gate and stepped into the back garden. The lawn was short, the grey paving-stone patio covered in frost, the plants cut back.

He peered through a wooden-framed window, single glazed and misted by a patch of frost on the inside. Ed was looking at the kitchen, the light on. He could make out freestanding units which seemed tidy enough before his gaze rested on the dark grey worktop next to a stainless steel sink and drainer. The pork pie, cut into precision quarters, and a delicately-sliced tomato on a blue plate looked like a surgeon had dissected them.

Again no one answered when he knocked, the room silent as a still-life.

He completed a walk around the perimeter of the house. On the front drive was a Jaguar XJ6, an older model with windows frosted. A PNC check confirmed Jeremy Scott was the registered keeper.

An old woman appeared by the fence next to the Jag. Her white hair perfectly complemented the frost, although her once white quilted dressing gown was now the colour of slush on a busy town centre road. 'Can I help you?'

Ed glanced at his wristwatch. Just gone 6am. He wasn't expecting to see anybody so early

'I'm trying to get in touch with Mr Scott.'

'Are you family?'

'Police.'

Ed flashed his warrant card.

'Is he alright?'

'That's what we're trying to find out Mrs?'

'Miss… Miss Cully. Jayne…with a 'Y'. Is he in trouble?'

'We're just trying to locate him Miss Cully. Have you known Mr Scott long?'

'We're neighbours.'

Ed made a show of stamping his feet and rubbing his hands.

'Look it's cold. Do you mind if I come into your house? Perhaps we can have a cup of tea.'

'Tea? With a gentleman? That'll be nice. Long time since I've had tea with a gentleman.'

Jayne Cully turned and tottered back towards her side door, leaning heavily on a shiny black stick that was the straightest thing about her. Ed noticed one of her worn slippers was red and sheepskin-lined, the other black and plain.

She was already at the kettle as he stepped into the kitchen.

'So Miss Cully.'

She shuffled around to face him with the speed of a jewellery box marionette on a drained battery, facial expression to match. 'Who are you?'

'I'm the policeman you were talking to outside.'

Her face was vacant. 'Policeman? Where's Johnny?'

Ed sighed and felt a jab of sadness and anger.

Jayne-with-a-Y was clearly suffering from some type of dementia, another decent person left to fend for herself until she had to go into a home, the house in which she'd probably spent most of her life sold to pay for her care.

Ed made himself a mental note...give everything away so when your time comes you've got no assets.

'Do you know who lives next door Jayne?'

'Mr Scott.'

'On the other side of Mr Scott?'

'The Greens.'

'Thanks Jayne. I'll pop round later.'

He figured there was no point waiting for the tea. Jayne with a 'Y' was only making a cup for one.

'Thanks for calling round,' she told him. 'I'll tell Johnny you called.'

Ed went back to his car and put on the radio. No point in going back to the nick but it was too early to knock on the neighbour's door. He listened to the news. At least all those late night phone-ins with the world's sad and lonely ringing for a chat had finished.

He leaned back against the headrest and remembered an all-night static surveillance, where and when he wasn't sure but long before the end he'd decided he'd rather tackle piles than listen to any more sob stories.

It was just after 7am when he spotted movement in the Greens' house.

Ed walked up a gravel path even crunchier than Jeremy Scott's and knocked on the door.

'Mrs Green?'

'Sorry, no,' the woman, late middle-age, pearl buttoned cardigan over long patterned skirt, mousey short hair unflattering above a round plain face, was puzzled.

'I've just been speaking to Jayne next door and she said...'

'Ah, poor Jayne. Lovely lady. Is she alright?'

'Yes she's fine, Mrs?'

'Lescott. Deborah Lescott. We bought this house off the Greens over twenty years ago. Jayne's memory is going, bless her. Comes to all of us I suppose, everybody living longer. And you are?'

'Ed Whelan. Detective Sergeant Whelan.'

He produced his warrant card for the second time that morning. At least with criminals you rarely needed to show your ID; most already knew who you were and those who didn't guessed in a heartbeat. Something about 'the look' was an instant give away.

'It's your neighbour Mr Scott I'm trying to locate. Does he live alone?'

'He does,' Deborah Lescott said with an edge. 'Keeps himself to himself…unless he's complaining about something.'

'One of those is he?'

'My late husband used to say he had a face that could curdle milk. Complained our bushes were too high, the barbecues were too smoky, cars were parked wrongly on the road. One of the most obnoxious men anyone could ever meet. Has something happened?'

She sounded hopeful.

'That's what we're trying to establish,' Ed told her. 'Is he married?'

Deborah Lescott gave a condescending smile.

'I don't think marriage ever interested him. I don't want to sound a gossip, but he was, well,' she looked left and right, like a spy from a stage farce, and lowered her voice. 'You know, camper than a row of tents.'

Ed bit his lip and nodded. Imagine saying that at an in-house diversity course? A definite case of goodbye course, hello disciplinary hearing.

'When did you last see him?'

'A few days ago. Would you like a cup of tea Sergeant? I can put the kettle on. It's too cold to be stood at the doorway, and if I can help?'

'Thank you.' Ed was in no doubt that she would get two cups out of the cupboard.

He followed her down the hallway into the kitchen, mentioning Scott's lights were on and his car was on the drive.

'Could he have popped out?' Ed asked.

Deborah Lescott reached for the kettle with one hand and turned on the cold water tap with the other.

'Possibly, but I haven't seen him and I don't think his car's moved in a while.'

'Is that unusual Mrs Lescott?' Ed leaned against the units.

'Please, it's Debs. Yes it is now I come to think about it, but I just thought, well…you know…actually I haven't given it a second thought until you asked. He wasn't the type of neighbour you kept an eye on. A widow either side of him and he kept an eye on neither of us.'

She dropped teabags into the cups.

'Everybody else is quite friendly and I pop into Jayne's when I have time, drop off a sponge cake or some scones.'

'As a matter of interest, who's Johnny? Jayne called me Johnny.'

Debs poured boiling water into the cups.

'I hope you don't mind but it just seems easier than making a pot…Johnny? It's her brother. He died years ago.'

Ed took the cup Debs held towards him, his fingers burning before he could get it safely onto the worktop.

Debs told him a home-help came to Jayne Cully's twice a

week and Ed made a note to ring social services. She might need more than that.

'Has Mr Scott lived there long?' he asked now.

Debs took a quick sip of her tea.

'Longer than us,' she said. 'He used to be a teacher at a boarding school in the south, so the Greens told us, but that was years ago.'

She opened a cupboard door.

'Biscuit?'

'Lovely,' Ed thanked her and asked about Scott's family and friends.

'I haven't seen anyone calling,' Debs told him. 'I don't know if that's because he has no family or whether they have nothing to do with him. He really wasn't a nice man. Always writing letters to the Seaton Post complaining about this and that, moaning about the council, local GPs, bus services, and of course, the police. That man must have filled the paper.'

Ed said he knew the type, finished his tea, and thanked her.

'If we need anything else we'll be in touch,' he said.

Moments later he was back at Scott's front door. He didn't expect a reply but knocked anyway before pushing down on the handle.

Ed found the unlocked door swinging open onto a hallway colder than his wife's shoulder. He shouted into the silence, at the same time glancing automatically for post on the floor. There was none. Ed walked to a door on his right, wood-stained to the point of being black, pushing it open and stepping into a living room where warmth replaced the hallway's chill.

Ed felt he had stumbled into the set of a television show from the seventies; the brown and gold swirled patterned carpet fighting the red velour settee for attention; a stacked music centre with a tape deck and radio tuner; a pre-remote-controlled TV set as deep as a wheelie bin. Hard-backed books filled the floor-to-ceiling bookcases and a polished black piano waited elegantly in the alcove next to the leaded bow window.

Heat pumped out of a gas fire and on the windowsill was a letter rack holding opened utility bills. Ed flicked through them. No red letters, each in date order.

He went into the kitchen. He had already seen the pie and tomato and was struck again by the care that had gone into the cutting. Now his eyes rested on a mug still full of tea or coffee. There was no sign of a struggle but it looked like Scott had left in a hurry.

Upstairs, the main bedroom of three had a double bed, dark wooden wardrobe and a wicker basket full of dirty clothes. A gay porn magazine was on the table next to the bed. Ed flicked through it and shook his head. Each to their own.

Back in the hall he saw a typed note on small table telling Scott he was the lucky winner of a TV but to Ed, the note looked amateurish. Nothing glossy, not even in colour, just a sheet of A4 pulled from a basic printer.

The delivery date specified Thursday 11thth December. In that case, Ed wondered, where was the shiny new TV?

Ed found a set of keys in a drawer in the same table and locked the front door behind him.

'He got in the back of a van.'

Ed looked over his shoulder. Jayne-with-a-Y was back at her fence.

'Who did Jayne? Was it Johnny?'

Jayne Cully's eyes mocked him.

'Don't be silly, Johnny's dead. No, I mean Mr Scott. I saw him walking down the path with a man then the man pushed Mr Scott into the back of the van.'

Ed walked to the fence. 'Was it a big van?'

Her face turned blank and she looked straight through him.

He waited then asked her again.

Jayne Cully knitted her brows. 'What van?'

She turned around and shuffled slowly away.

CHAPTER SIX

SAM'S FINGERS bashed away at the keyboard as she checked her inbox. Emails fell into three categories: reply, bin after a cursory look, or delete without opening.

'I've got you a bacon sarnie,' Ed said, walking into her office. 'Not that you deserve it after leaving me with Curtis Brown.'

He put the plate on her desk and sat down. 'Extra crispy seems to be the order of the day...ha ha.'

Sam opened the white baguette, peered at the pink rashers and translucent rind. 'It looks disgusting.'

'I know,' Ed nodded, taking a bite of his own. 'It tastes better than it looks, though. I got in the canteen early. Another hour under the lamps and it wouldn't even be bacon anymore. This is the mouth-watering non-nuclear option.'

'Cheers.'

Sam pulled the rind off the bacon, spun her chair, threw the rind into the bin and put what was left of the bacon back in the bread. She bit into the sandwich.

'You're right,' Sam said, chewing slowly. 'Anyway, updates.'

Ed brought her up to speed on his visit to Scott's and the neighbours.

'I'm going to check out the company who said he'd won a TV,' Ed told her. 'What time's the PM?'

'Half ten.'

'No sweat. Oh by the way. Can you do me a favour? Get in touch with Vulnerable Adults. See if we can do anything for Jayne Cully. She needs more help than she seems to be getting and she'd be easy money for the rip off merchants. I'd hate to see her taken for a ride.'

Back at his desk Ed examined the flyer.

Congratulations Mr J Scott.

You have won the annual Christmas Postcode Prize Draw.

To claim your prize of a 52" Flat screen TV be at home between 4pm and 6pm on Thursday 11th December when one of our couriers will call. Please have proof of identification.

Ed looked at the registered address for the company on the bottom of the page and noted the listed telephone number.

A phone call to the Intelligence unit in Nottingham confirmed his suspicions...the area code was wrong; the trading estate didn't exist.

He walked into Sam's office, waving the piece of paper like Neville Chamberlain at Heston Aerodrome in 1938.

'This is fake.' Ed said. 'And it may have told us when Scott went missing.'

Sam decided to add two questions to the door-to-door team's list, one asking if anyone had seen a suspicious van in the area at any time over the last few days; the other if they had noticed any callers to Scott's house.

'I don't want to be too specific about the TV,' Sam said. 'It might be a wild goose chase and I don't want the door-to-doors concentrating on the TV at the exclusion of everything else.'

She stood up and moved her plate onto the top of the filing cabinet.

'Look at that,' she grimaced at the pool of cold, grey fat. 'My stomach'll be all over the place.'

'I know,' Ed said. 'It's enough to convert you to Islam.'

Sam's eyes locked onto Ed's, her look as cold as the grease on the plate.

'Your mouth will really drop you in the shit one day,' she told him. 'You'll say something in the wrong company.'

Ed held up his hands.

'It's a one-liner, not a racist slur.'

'And we all know the law,' Sam was serious. 'It's not necessarily what you mean, it's how others perceive it.'

Ed's shoulders dropped.

What the hell has happened? How did we ever get to this?

'I'm pleased I was a young lad when I was,' Ed said, meaning it. 'When you could have a laugh without somebody kicking off or stoking it up with Professional Standards.'

Sam moved towards the door and reached for her coat.

'Times change,' she said. 'Come on, it's PM time.'

Dean Silvers sat on a wooden bar stool drinking coffee, a white t-shirt tight around muscular tanned arms and head shaved clean above his huge neck. Dean loved three things in life...bling, his RS Focus, and himself, not necessarily in that order. Today was a big day, the day he decided it was time to move up from street dealer to major player.

The barmaid was in early, cleaning last night's mess, getting ready for opening time. She was another east European but he didn't know her name; he couldn't keep track of the staff these days.

'I got a visit last night from Mat Skinner,' Harry Pullman said, leaning over the bar, resting thick forearms with fading Fred Flintstone and Top Cat tattoos between the real ale pumps.

'Accused me of skimming, the cheeky twat. I remember

when he was just a snotty-nosed kid. God help us when he takes over from his old man.'

He wiped his thick black-framed glasses with a bar towel.

'Mat Skinner couldn't run a bath,' Dean said. 'Luke will take over, provided they're still in business.'

'Keep your voice down,' Harry's whisper was snare drum tight. 'These walls have ears and they're not all friendly.'

Harry adjusted his glasses. They looked tiny on his huge bulldog head.

Dean watched the barmaid walk down the stairs behind the bar into the cellar. 'How much does he know?'

'Billy? Nothing really. I just need to be more careful.'

'What pisses me off is that he takes all the rewards and none of the risks,' Dean picked up his mug.

'You planning a take-over?' Harry asked, his tone teasing, almost taunting.

Dean Silver looked over his shoulder and back at Harry Pullman.

'You know his suppliers, the system for his distributors...'

'Sounds like you've got it all sorted,' Harry polished a pint glass. 'One big problem though. Billy Skinner and the Apostles.'

'Let's just say they weren't a problem anymore,' Dean pushed. 'Then what would you say?

'Big market for whoever had the balls to take them on,' Harry conceded. 'But ask yourself why they're still running the show? Then check what you've got in your Calvin's.'

Dean finished his coffee as Harry walked around to the punters' side of the bar and joined him.

'CID's swarming around Bill O'Grady's old garage,' Harry said. 'Found a body.'

Dean Silver's arms grew tense, the muscles twitching.

'That fucker Curtis Brown better not drop me in it.'

'Forget that little smackhead,' Harry said. 'One word and it'll be his last.'

John Elgin sighed at the sink full of dirty dishes, food stains, crumbs and empty packaging covering the benches, the air coated with the stale smell of cigarettes. Twenty-odd years ago this kitchen was show-house new, chrome fittings gleaming, sink sparkling. Now, like his wife, it was an unloved, shabby wreck.

He sponged his pink tie and patted his shrinking stomach - the high cholesterol warning had sparked a low fat diet and lower lager intake. He opened the grubby fridge and saw more stains than food...half a bottle of rose wine, a piece of mouldy cheddar harder than concrete. He took out his yoghurt and blueberries.

Two more empty wine bottles by the door told him his bloated wife would be in bed until noon. Thank God for Pussycats. Thank God for…what did they call them?'

He conjured up an image of the two lithe young women and smiled. What were their names? He nodded when he remembered. Zara and Chloe.

He spooned the yoghurt into his mouth and contemplated another visit to Pussycats tonight. Billy Skinner was always a good host.

A blueberry burst in his mouth as he pondered whether Zara and Chloe found him attractive. He never paid them; they said they'd enjoyed it for what it was.

He looked in the wall mirror and stroked his pencil thin moustache. Maybe he should check out a tanning salon, give himself a bit of colour. He'd looked like a ghost next to the girls.

The ringing mobile interrupted his mental rerun of their time together, the caller ID telling him it was a private number.

'Councillor Elgin speaking.'

'John. It's Billy Skinner.'

'How have you got my mobile number?'

'You left it in your jacket pocket when you were entertaining Zara and Chloe,' Skinner's voice was friendly, pleasant. 'Easiest thing in the world for one of them to pass it outside and have someone ring one of our numbers.'

'That's theft.'

'We didn't steal your phone we put it back,' Skinner laughed. 'Can you steal a number? Anyway, business. I need a favour.'

John Elgin felt a creeping panic in the pit of his empty stomach.

'I'm in no position to grant favours, and certainly not to you.'

'Not to me?'

The voice that had sounded harmless was suddenly laced with aggression.

'Who the fuck do you think you are?' Skinner snarled. 'You come into my establishments, avail yourself of all the facilities, accept them for free, on-the-house so to speak, and then give me the bum's rush when I ask for a favour.'

John Elgin's forehead was suddenly leaking a sickly sweat.

'What do you want?'

'That's better John.'

There was a pause. Elgin waited, the beginnings of a headache thrumming like a drum roll at his temples.

'I want a few planning applications approved, new licensed premises.'

'I can't do that,' Elgin spluttered. 'There's a committee...'

'John, John.'

Skinner's speech was slow, precise, a teacher explaining to a child.

'Listen. You enjoyed yourself the other night. We enjoyed watching you.'

John Elgin dropped onto one of his kitchen chairs. His hands were shaking.

'There's no such thing as a free lunch John,' Skinner said. 'You had your fun. Now it's pay-back.'

'But I can't.'

'You will,' Skinner's voice was mild again. 'You don't want your Pussycat performance going on the Internet do you?'

The shaking in Elgin's hands had spread to the rest of him.

'What do you mean?'

'All those mirrors in the Green Room,' Skinner turned the knife. 'Cameras, John, cameras. You get turned on and so do they.'

Councillor John Elgin, the factory worker who had talked his way up the political ladder, was speechless.

Billy Skinner laughed into the stunned silence.

'I knew you'd understand,' he said. 'I'll be in touch to give you a list. Let me down and you'll be going viral on YouTube faster than you dropped your fucking trousers.'

Elgin heard the line click and stared at the mobile in his trembling hand, the sound of Skinner's laughter still rippling through his head.

Was there really a film?

The sickness in his stomach told him he couldn't chance it.

And there was no way he could allow it to get out.

CHAPTER SEVEN

THERE WAS something grimly unique about the sight and smell of a burned body. Victims left lifeless by knives, bullets and beatings often looked like they were sleeping but this one did not, a blackened, shrivelled thing with a smoke-heavy stench that thrashed even mortuary disinfectant into submission.

Sam winced at the gunshot-like-crack that echoed around the room as the dentist used bolt croppers to force open the jaw. She looked at the dentist, a young man used to taking impressions to repair the living not identify the flame-blackened dead.

Bev had traced Jeremy Scott's dental surgery by a ring-round process of elimination. Sam felt sorry for the dentist. Maybe the senior partners had tricked him into doing it; he was the building site apprentice sent to buy a tin of tartan paint or the bubble for a spirit level. A piss-taking reception, Sam feared, awaited him back at the surgery.

Two hours later and they had their confirmation. The body was Jeremy Scott and he had been very much alive when he was set on fire.

Sam stepped outside. The fresh air was welcome, but sometimes the smell of death hung around you for days. She felt she would be tasting this one for weeks.

Opening the passenger door, she spoke to Ed.

'We need that house to house team out there,' Sam said. 'Let's see if we can get a definitive last sighting of Jeremy Scott. If it is something to do with that television prize, somebody has put a bit of time and effort into it. How has a retired schoolteacher landed an enemy like that?'

She was still talking as she fastened her seatbelt, telling Ed to get Bev working on the victimology.

'I want next of kin, associates, habits and beliefs,' Sam rattled off. 'We won't go public with his name until next of kin have been notified but there has to be something in his background. Retired teachers don't normally attract that sort of enemy.'

Jill Brown's mouth dropped when she opened the front door, her fingers instinctively tightening around the handle.

'There's nothing to worry about Jill,' Ed said. 'I've seen Curtis. Just thought I'd pop round.'

Jill relaxed her grip, her knees bent just enough to notice and she blew out hard.

'Thank God. I dread your lot knocking on my door, and when I saw you…'

'I didn't mean to scare you Jill.'

'I know Ed. Come in, come in, how was he, Curtis?'

She was already walking down the hall of her 1930's semi. Ed followed her into the kitchen.

'No better, no worse Jill to be fair. He'd found a dead body.'

'Oh my God, one of his friends?'

She turned away, gripping the Belfast sink with both hands and shaking her head.

'Listen to me, talking about his friends as if everything's normal. Talking about his junkie mates is what I mean.'

She flicked the switch on the kettle. 'Where did it all go wrong Ed?'

They had known each other since school and Ed could

close his eyes and see her back then, giggling and pretty and safe from the things that would soon enough unfold.

'Lot easier wandering around the school yard looking for somewhere to smoke and hoping for a snog than bringing up kids,' he said gently.

'A lifetime ago,' Jill poured hot water into two mugs. 'Who did you want to snog anyway? Mandy Reeve?'

'She was bonny,' Ed smiled. 'There was Mandy, Evie and you, the three everyone fancied, including a few of the girls I suspect.'

'Was that even around in our day Ed?' Jill paused, thinking about it. 'I never saw anything but whatever way you go...anyway I'm sure you didn't come around here to talk about all our yesterdays.'

Ed felt a dart of sadness as he put the past away, the image of the schoolgirl he wanted to kiss suddenly gone.

'No. I was just wondering when you last saw Curtis?'

She brought two mugs of tea and sat opposite Ed.

'He came round wanting cash a few months back,' Jill told him. 'He normally surfaces when he wants money. I made him have a bath then took him into town. I bought him some new clothes and a mobile.'

'Probably the one he rang us on when he found the body,' Ed said. 'You haven't asked about it.'

Jill stared at her tea and then back at Ed, her face drawn.

'I'm not sure I want to know. It could be him next Ed. Any day I think the police will be at the door telling me he's gone, dead in the gutter or some squat.'

She sipped her tea and made no effort to dry the tears that began to flow.

'This wasn't an addict Jill,' Ed said, a hand on her arm. 'He found a dead body in a garage. It'll be in the media soon enough. The body was burned.'

Jill's eyes opened wide.

'Oh my God and you think Curtis has something to do with it?'

'I doubt it,' Ed told her. 'It's just if he visits and mentions it he may tell you more than he told us. He may remember something.'

'And you want me to tell you?'

'Something like that.'

'No problem. Do you know who it is?'

'Not yet, not for sure,' Ed said. 'It might be a guy who lives in The Avenue though.'

Jill's eyes snapped wide again.

'Really? Small world.'

'Why do you say that?'

'I used to take Curtis there for his piano lessons.'

'Private tutor?'

Ed remembered the shiny black piano in Scott's house.

'That's right,' Jill said. 'Curtis was quite good. Not a prodigy or anything, but decent. He hated it though. Any excuse not to go. Maybe I shouldn't have pushed him, but at the time...'

She turned away from Ed and finally wiped her eyes.

'Can you remember his name?' Ed asked. 'The teacher?'

'Why?'

'You know me, ever the detective, asking questions just seems to be habit. No reason other than that.'

'I can't,' Jill said. 'It was years ago. Curtis would have been 11 or 12 and he only went for a few months. Seemed a nice enough chap from what I can remember.'

John Elgin ordered a pint of lager. Fuck the diet. Harry Pullman appeared as he took his first mouthful.

'Councillor Elgin. To what do I owe this surprise?'

'Drop the 'councillor' bit Harry,' Elgin said, wiping the foam from his mouth. 'I've got enough on my plate without your sarcasm.'

'Hey, just having a laugh with an old mate. Two pints of whatever John's drinking sweetheart.'

The dark haired barmaid nodded and went to the Peroni pump.

'What's up then?' Harry Pullman said, leaning against the mahogany and resting his foot on the bar's footrest. 'More bother with the other half?

Elgin took a long pull on the Peroni already in his hand and closed his eyes as he drank.

'Everything,' he said. 'Oscar, the grandbairn, and now Billy Skinner.'

'Skinner?' Harry spat out the name. 'What's he done now?'

John Elgin gulped more of his pint, hand shaking and the glass rattling lightly against his teeth.

'I think I'm in the shit.'

Harry paused, picked up his own pint, sipped, and put the glass back on the bar.

'Can't be that bad can it?'

Elgin looked down, face slate grey and sallow.

'Let's sit down,' Harry said and led the way to a quiet corner away from the bar, the seats against a wall and a view of anyone approaching.

Harry leaned in close. 'What is it? You've obviously come in here to tell me.'

'Skinner wants me to pull some strings to get his new planning applications and licences through,' Elgin's voice was barely there.

Harry shook his head. 'And he's got you in his pocket how exactly?'

'Don't use that phrase,' Elgin said. 'I'm not corrupt, I've just been a fool. He reckons he has a tape.'

Elgin drained his first pint and reached for the second. 'Jesus, if this gets out Harry…'

'I have no idea what you're talking about John.'

Elgin glugged his way through half of the lager.

'He says he's got me on tape having sex with two of his girls. Says he'll put it on YouTube if I don't play ball.'

'And you obviously have had sex with two of his girls?'

Elgin nodded.

'Where?'

'One of his rooms. The Green Room.'

'Have you seen the tape?'

'No, but I've no doubt he's got one. Why would he lie?'

'People like Billy Skinner can't lie straight in bed but I wouldn't be surprised if you're right,' Harry said, keeping his voice low. 'I've seen the cameras. He uses them for his homemade pornos then flogs them under the counter. Looks like with you he saw a chance for a little bit of blackmail.'

'Jesus...'

'So you don't want to go to the police?' Harry said.

'What do you think?' Elgin sounded broken. 'I'd have to tell them about the tape. They'd go to see Skinner. He'd deny it, but upload it anyway, and who can trust the police not to leak it?'

'So what's your thinking?' Harry asked. 'I'm guessing you've got something in mind.'

Elgin drained his pint then watched Harry raise his arm and signal to the barmaid for another Peroni.

'These applications are going to be approved,' Elgin said. 'I can approve them for Skinner in exchange for the tape but what's to say he won't be back wanting something else and telling me he's got copies or…'

'...Or?' Harry waited.

'Or I tell you his plans and you step in and seek planning permission.'

A small light blinked on in Harry's head, not big or bright but an instant reaction, a chance acknowledged.

For now he kept the faint glow to himself.

'And how do I do that exactly?' Harry said now. 'Billy Skinner's not just going to let me take over.'

Elgin shrugged: 'He's your problem. But if a problem's removed…'

Harry looked at the councillor and marvelled again at the human being's inbuilt drive for self-preservation.

'Finish your pint,' he told Elgin. 'The special's lamb hotpot if you're hungry.'

DC Bev Summers walked into Sam's office.

'I've traced Jeremy Scott's nephew,' she said. 'I think he might be the only relative. Certainly he's the only beneficiary in Jezza's will.'

Sam laughed. She had a mental picture of Jeremy Scott and 'Jezza' couldn't be further from the mark.

'Where does he live, the nephew?'

'Conifers,' Bev said. 'No answer on his home phone, but he's at work in town. I've spoken briefly to him on his mobile.'

'You have been busy.'

'All hail the electronic age,' Bev mock curtseyed. 'We're meeting him in twenty minutes. He'll be on the pier. Said he would rather speak to us in the fresh air.'

'Does he know?'

Bev shook her head.

'He knows something's up just from getting a police call out of the blue but nothing yet,' Bev said. 'We're meeting him at quarter-past-one and it's not fair to keep him waiting.'

Bev drove through the light traffic.

'I saw Gone Girl last night, Ben Affleck and the lucky Ms Rosamund Pike.'

'Any good?' Sam asked.

'Yeah and there's something about going to the pictures by yourself, especially when Mr Affleck's up there.'

Sam swivelled to face her: 'I thought you were seeing that Colin bloke?'

'Not anymore,' Bev said. 'Nice lad but bored your tits off. Give me Ben anytime. Or Rosamund come to think of it. Or even both at the same time.'

Sam smiled. 'Jesus Bev!''

'Ha you'd love it,' Bev smiled back. 'But maybe Ben wouldn't quite make your dream team. Maybe it would have to be Rosamund and a more mature type, maybe a certain DS we both know...'

Sam still hadn't thought of a comeback by the time they pulled up behind a Nissan Leaf and watched Alistair Scott climb from the driver's seat.

Introductions over as they walked towards the pier, Sam judged the time was right.

'Alistair I am sorry to have to tell you that your uncle, Jeremy Scott, is dead,' she said. 'We've launched a murder investigation.'

In Sam's experience - and she had broken grim news many times - her words were often met with silent shock not weeping and wailing. The tears came later.

So Alistair Scott's reaction, wordless and blank, wasn't anything she hadn't expected.

'Fancy a coffee?' she said. 'The Surf Shack sells decent stuff.'

Alistair nodded and finally found a voice.

'I suppose there's no mistake? It's definitely Jeremy?'

'It is,' Sam said. 'Sorry.'

Bev walked ahead and ordered three coffees.

'Were you close Alistair?' Sam asked.

'Not really. I saw him all the time when I was a kid, less so after my parents died. He was my dad's younger brother. Murdered where? In his house?'

'No, not at his house,' Sam said. 'I'll get a Family Liaison Officer to sit down with you and tell you everything, but that will be better done in the comfort of your home. Do you have to go back to work?'

'No that's the beauty of being your own boss.'

'What is it you do?'

'Property developer,' Alistair said. 'Build houses, find estate pubs that are closing, buy them up and sell the land to supermarkets, you know Tesco Extra, Sainsbury's Local, that type of thing.'

'Okay,' Sam told him. 'In that case we'll have this coffee and then Bev can go home with you. She can be your Family Liaison Officer. Do you have children?'

Alistair took the coffee from Bev.

'Thanks. Not living with me. There's just me at home; too many hours, too many temptations. Not sure why I'm telling you this.'

'It's okay,' Bev told him. 'We're cops. See it all the time in the CID.'

'What can you tell me about your uncle?' Sam asked now.

'Not a lot really. He wasn't one of life's loveable characters, bit of a misery in truth. My mother never liked him. Music teacher, retired and as I'm sure you know, a suspected child molester although he was acquitted at court.'

CHAPTER EIGHT

Pussycats was never at its best during the day...no light show, no music, no shadows to hide the stains on armchairs and carpets, no painted nails and slender legs caressing the golden poles, the only women in the place carrying mops and buckets.

Billy Skinner was sitting in the back office, a take-away cup of good quality coffee in his hand. He despised instant more than Marge's spaghetti.

'So what about Harry Pullman?'

He looked at the three of them over the rim of the cardboard as he sipped the black liquid.

Mat spoke. 'We had a word. He shit it he did.'

Mark and Luke looked at the floor.

'What do you mean, we had a word?' Billy asked.

'Said we thought he'd been skimming.'

Billy put the cup on his desk, sat up straight, and asked his next question like someone conducting a job interview.

'Did you speak to the lads on the door?'

Mat puffed out his chest and glanced at his brothers.

'Went straight to the organ grinder,' he said. 'No point speaking to the monkeys.'

Billy slammed his fist hard against the desk, the sudden

impact sending the cup jumping and a river of coffee rolling across the surface.

'I told you to speak to the doormen first,' his voice was a blade. 'See if they'd noticed a drop in punters. But oh no, you know fucking best, dive straight in like the Neanderthal you are. Fucking idiot. And what did he say?'

Mat opened his mouth.

'Don't bother answering.' Skinner stood up and leaned across the desk, hands pressing into the black leather top. 'Let me guess.'

He glared at Mat. 'He said no.'

'Well, yeah he did.'

'So what's your next move Einstein?'

Mat stared at his father.

Billy Skinner sat back down. 'Luke, what do you reckon?'

The youngest son knew his father would push him for an answer; saying nothing wasn't an option and besides if Mat had listened to him and Mark he wouldn't be in this position.

'Well?'

Mat turned his head and stared at his brother.

'If he is skimming, he knows we're onto him now,' Luke said. 'He can do one of three things - run, bluff it out or take us on.'

'Don't be fucking stupid,' Mat said.

Billy was shouting again, his soaring blood pressure turning his face the colour of Ribena.

'When I want your opinion I'll ask for it.'

He pulled open the top drawer, picked a cigar from a box of Cubans and carefully trimmed the end with a metal cutter. Leaning his head against the back of the chair, he lit up and blew a plume of smoke towards the ceiling.

His eyes returned to his sons.

'I've known Harry Pullman for forty years,' he said. 'We went to school together. He's always been loyal, but do not underestimate him. That nephew of his is ambitious. You could learn from him Mat. He works for what he can get, not like you, expecting it all on a plate. Ambition is a good thing.'

He inhaled on the cigar and spoke as he let smoke drift with the words.

'Uncontrolled ambition is not, it's dangerous.'

His boxer's neck and head were engulfed in thick, aromatic smoke. 'So what do you reckon we do then Luke?'

'Nothing.'

'Are you stupid,' Mat snapped.

'Get out!' Billy yelled, pointing at the door. 'Make yourself useful. Go and help with the cleaning or something.'

Mat clamped his mouth, clenched his fists, and stormed out.

His father was losing it, going soft. There was no room for sentiment in this business even if you had known somebody for a lifetime.

'Okay,' Billy said once the door had stopped reverberating against the frame. 'Carry on.'

'As I said, do nothing,' Luke said. 'I'll go and see Harry today. Apologise for Mat's behaviour. Tell him that wasn't why we were there. Mat just got it into his head.'

'Mat won't like that,' Billy interrupted.

'Tough,' Luke went on. 'He's got us into this mess.'

Billy looked at his son and liked him.

'Your mother always said I was successful because I never made decisions based on emotion,' he said. 'I always planned, always tried to think of every angle. Hotheads never win the day and your brother's a hothead.'

'We're still looking into his background,' Sam had said, trying to hide her shock.

She felt blindsided, stunned when Alistair told them how the sex allegations went back years to Scott's time teaching at a boarding school he thought might have been in Hampshire.

'He left under a cloud,' Alistair was saying now, his gaze across the promenade and towards the sea. 'In the end he was acquitted in court but his career was finished from the moment he left that school. He moved back up north after the trial. I don't think anybody knew about it up here. Certainly my parents never said anything. Well you wouldn't would you?'

Alistair sipped his coffee, watching two gulls spiralling in a dog-fight high above the grey water.

'He became a private tutor giving music lessons and lived off that and the money my aunt left him when she died,' Alistair said. 'She was from money.'

Scott's wife had stood by him, convinced he was innocent and had felt vindicated when he was cleared.

'She died not long after the trial and he sold up, pocketed a fortune,' Alistair said.

Sam lit a cigarette, her mind racing with the possibilities the story had opened.

'Can you think of anybody who would want to harm your uncle,' Sam asked.

Alistair Scott finished his coffee and shook his head.

'No idea,' he said. 'He was an old man but I haven't exactly kept in touch.'

Dean Silvers watched the waves rolling liquid dark towards them, salt air on his lips and the lulling sound of water lapping against the pier legs below. He had loved the sea since he was a kid and still felt its call, an invisible force pulling him wide-eyed to something awesome and endless. The fact the Victorian pier was a good place to talk freely was a bonus. Police would struggle to keep any surveillance mission covert here, still less plant bugs that could conquer the winter roar of the North Sea.

He'd seen the two women detectives drinking their coffee but he was sure they hadn't seen him. And if they had, so what? He had no idea who the man was they were talking to; probably another cop by the look of him.

He watched a white yacht with white sails rise and fall on the swell and imagined a couple on board, a chart laid out to their next destination. Were they only out for the day or at the start of a bigger adventure? Deacon Blue and their song Dignity flashed into his mind. He'd have a yacht one day. The only difference between him and the bloke in the song was he didn't pick up litter and he wasn't going to work for twenty years saving his money.

In the words of another song by a band he couldn't quite remember, he was moving on up. Take over from Billy Skinner and he wouldn't have to wait long.

'So do you think Elgin will come good?' he asked.

Harry Pullman was standing next to him, an uncle enjoying some time with his nephew if the cops on the promenade ever got round to asking.

'Can't think of any reason to doubt him,' Harry said. 'He came to us. He's in a hell of a state.'

'What was the grandson bit about?'

'Oscar, a canny kid,' Harry told him. 'Elgin reckons the lad was touched up by a couple of faggots at some sports club.'

Silvers' body stiffened and he jerked his head away from the white yacht making good headway towards the horizon.

'Fucking nonces. They been sorted?'

'Not yet. John doesn't want to go to the cops. What would be the point? A 10-year-old's word against two blokes. No witnesses. No forensic.'

'That's how they get away with it,' Silvers leaned forward and rested his forearms on the railing. 'What's he going to do about it? Scum like that need sorting.'

Harry said wheels would soon be in motion, that he'd told Elgin they could probably help.

'Well give me the nod,' Silvers stood up straight. 'Beating a couple of nonces is always good for the soul. Anyway, Elgin, do you think there's a tape?'

Harry said he was 100% sure, said no way Skinner would have passed up the opportunity.

Each stood in silence, watching the distant yacht and the white tipped waves.

'So we take out Skinner and get the tape and in return

Elgin hands the new licences to us,' Silvers said. 'Sounds easy.'

Harry Pullman, deep in thought, was no longer focused on the yacht. It was a full minute before he spoke.

'It needs to be funded Dean,' he said finally. 'Billy Skinner's got a lot more cash than us. How the hell can we buy the places he's turning into wine bars and clubs?'

'I've been thinking about that,' Silvers said. 'If something happens to Billy, Mat will go after anyone and everybody. Kick an angry dog and it bites everyone. He would probably come after us but he'll go after others as well. He'll cause such a shit-storm there'll be coppers breathing down every neck that's not broken.'

Dean's knuckles tightened around the black handrail, his whole body taut and primed for a fight.

'Nobody will want that,' he went on. 'They'll not just stand by and let him. He'll get himself killed and Luke will want to broker a deal, especially if John Elgin gets his magistrate and police mates to start kicking off about the licences they already have.'

Harry let it play out in his head.

'Sort out Billy and everything else falls into place, is that it?'

Silvers nodded as Harry turned his head to face him.

'Do you have any idea what stakes you're playing for?' Harry said now. 'You'll have one shot at this and even then there are no guarantees. Get it wrong and you're a dead man. Me as well.'

Overhead, the gulls were back, shrieking into the heavy sky.

Silvers watched them and smiled, breathing in deep.

'But get it right and we move up in the world,' he said.

CHAPTER NINE

Sam left Bev with Alistair, rang Ed, and got a lift to The Avenue to meet him.

He was leaning against a wall as she walked towards him and listened in silence as she repeated Alistair Scott's story. 'Bloody hell you're not thinking of making all the victims TIEs are you?' Ed said when she had finished.

Sam laughed. 'What like a TV drama? Trace, Interview, Eliminate. No chance.'

They were nice words, good for TV crime shows, but scriptwriters had no concept of the criteria that had to be set to eliminate people, never mind the huge amount of work involved.

'It's why Sue never lets me watch them,' Ed said. 'All I do is shout at the screen. I know it's only fiction but being in the same room as reality shouldn't be that hard. I'm sure they just hear a conversation or a phrase that sounds good and run with it.'

Sam's immediate plan was much more practical - more research on Jeremy Scott and use the media to help with the digging.

A retired teacher bound and burnt alive was news. The fact that teacher had walked on child sex charges only upped the ante.

'Let's start thinking about the press,' Sam said. 'Get our strategy right and they can help us here.'

She looked around and saw the long-wheel based white police Ford Transit in the road, eight uniforms walking up and down the driveways or standing at doors talking to residents. Each officer carried a clipboard and Sam's prepared questionnaire.

'How's the door-to-door going?'

'Plenty of them at it but nothing as yet,' Ed told her. 'SOCOs are inside Scott's house.'

Sam nodded, looking at the smaller white SOCO van parked behind the Jaguar on Scott's drive.

'Anything?'

Ed told her there was no sign of forced entry, no blood traces, and nothing out of place.

'It's as if he just walked out of the house,' Ed said. 'The fact I found the door unlocked makes you think he was expecting to walk back pretty much immediately.'

'What about the van?' Sam said, scanning the houses.

Ed said the only witness so far was Jayne Cully and she seemed confused, to put it mildly.

Sam searched her coat pocket for her cigarettes.

'That doesn't mean the white van wasn't here, though. We just need to find someone else who saw it.'

The allegations, Sam told herself. They have to be the trigger.

She looked around the street. No press with cameras, no members of the public with mobile phones pointing in her direction. She lit the cigarette.

There was no CCTV around the garage and picking out the van on cameras covering the town would be a lottery shot without at least a partial number.

'Nobody we've spoken to so far got a flyer saying they'd won a TV or anything else so that's probably how they got him to the van,' Ed said. 'But why leave it lying around for us to find.'

Sam drew deeply on the cigarette as Ed went on.

'Maybe Jayne-with-a-Y disturbed them. Let's be right, if

they'd seen she clocked them they'd want to get away pronto. They won't have known she's got dementia.'

Sam looked past his shoulder and shook her head. 'Look at that.' Ed turned around and smiled. Seven uniforms were standing on the pavement, each holding a mug of tea, a large round lemon drizzle cake on a plate balanced on top of the garden wall.

Debs Lescott waved towards them.

'Seems like you've got a fan,' Sam teased.

Ed raised his arm. 'Come on. She's bound to have saved some for me.'

Sam gave him the eyebrows up.

'And if you're really lucky she might have kept some cake for you as well.'

Ed walked ahead and made the introductions as Sam joined them.

'Debs this is DCI Sam Parker.'

'Pleased to meet you,' Sam extended her arm. 'And on behalf of the officers, thanks for the tea and cake.'

'As long as there's some left for us,' Ed said, winking at Debs.

'Of course there is. Come on. And it's no bother.'

Debs made three mugs of tea and cut three large slices from a huge Victoria Sandwich cake.

'All this activity has upset Jayne,' Debs told them. 'She keeps telling me about Jeremy being pushed into a white van. She seems adamant.'

Ed bit into the moist sponge, wiped crumbs from the corner of his mouth and spoke as he chewed.

'I believe her.'

'You do?' Debs asked, startled.

'I do,' Ed took another bite. 'I know she gets confused and her memory's failing but that doesn't mean she's wrong.'

Debs dragged her eyes from Ed and cut another half brick from the sponge.

'How refreshing Ed,' she said as she worked the knife. 'Plenty wouldn't have believed a word. More cake?'

Sam looked at Ed and was giving him the eyebrows again when his text alert sounded.

'Excuse me while I check this.'

Now it was his turn with the eyebrows. The text was from Sam.

Grab your coat. You've pulled. Smiley face.

He kicked Sam's ankle.

Brown leaves blew in the wind, traffic rumbled beyond the black railings, but Adam Best's ears were tuned into something different; the sounds of children squealing as they chased each other on the grass, the noise of rusted chains as the swings flew ever higher.

Adam liked children, enjoyed watching them, and there was nowhere better to watch than in a park on a Friday afternoon when school had just finished, even if darkness was descending.

Some of the young boys wore football strips: the pale blue of Manchester City, the dark blue of Chelsea, the white of Real Madrid, all proof that tomorrow's glory supporters were ready-in-waiting. As a boy himself Adam had followed Southampton before he realised it was more fun supporting a team who won something more than once in a generation. Some of the girls wore smart brown jodhpurs and waterproof country tops, ready to go to their ponies and riding lessons.

Adam Best cut a less polished figure, brown hair needing a wash, blue suit jacket worn at the elbows and a hem coming loose from chocolate-brown chinos. The pristine white of his Stan Smith trainers made the rest of the ensemble shabbier still.

A tall man, well-dressed and like Adam in his late-fifties, sat on the opposite end of the bench. 'You're a regular here aren't you?'

Adam tugged down on his black Adidas baseball cap.

'No law against it is there?'

'None at all friend,' the stranger shuffled closer. 'Just

wondering what sort of guy sits in the park every afternoon when school's turning out.'

'Spying on me are you?' Adam looked away.

'You stick out that's all,' the stranger said. 'Stick out to the sort of people looking for your type.'

Adam turned his head and looked into the man's brown eyes. 'My type? What's that then?'

'We know your type.'

Adam stood up and began to walk away but in a moment the stranger was at his side.

He gently took hold of Adam's elbow and eased him round to face him.

'Don't rush off friend. We're kindred spirits. I've seen you in here every day for a fortnight. I know why you come.'

The stranger bent slightly until his mouth was almost touching Adam's ear.

'Same reason as me,' warm breath came with the whisper.

Adam stepped backwards, almost stumbling.

'Leave me alone,' the voice a whine. 'I know what you're doing. Just get away.'

The stranger moved closer again, arms slightly outstretched and palms up.

'You think I'm one of those vigilantes,' the stranger seemed amused. 'Like the do-gooders who pretend to be young girls online? Organise a meeting and then hand the man over to the police. That's not me, friend.'

'Then maybe you're the police,' Adam said, looking the stranger up and down. 'Just leave me alone.'

Adam turned away but the man grabbed his elbow again and squeezed.

'Let's go for a cup of tea and have a chat. I'm not what you think. I just want to get to know you better. I know we have similar interests.'

Adam wrestled his arm free but stayed a pace away from the stranger, eyeing him with a mix of tentative hope and straight up suspicion.

'You think I'm going to hurt you?' The stranger smiled. 'Why would I do that in front of all of these children?'

He looked around as if to emphasise the point.

'Look, we'll just go to the café here in the park,' the man seemed to sense Adam's indecision. 'Plenty of people about, plenty of witnesses to make sure you stay safe.'

Adam looked down at the ground and spoke just above a whisper. 'I don't know.'

'Come on,' the stranger told him. 'What harm can it do? Two friends going for a cup of tea and if you don't mind me saying, you don't seem to have many friends.'

Adam didn't look up. 'I've just moved into the area.'

'All the more reason then,' the stranger said cheerfully. 'Come on. I'm buying.'

Adam sat close to the window on the red plastic chair. The tall man placed a mug of tea in front of him.

'Where's that accent from then?'

'South,' Adam said. 'I needed to get as far away as possible. So what do want from me?'

The stranger sitting opposite emptied brown sugar from a sachet into his coffee.

'I want you to be honest. Then we can go from there.'

Adam looked into his own white mug, milky tea almost to the brim. He picked up a spoon and began to stir. He didn't take sugar but he wanted to buy himself some time. As a prop the spoon would do. He took a deep breath.

'I was falsely accused,' he said.

The stranger moved a steady hand and pressed it lightly on Adam's wrist.

'Go on,' he said. 'Tell me.'

As Adam talked he seemed more and more at ease, telling the man how he had been a tennis coach when one boy, a junior with a promising future, claimed Adam had molested him, the police all too ready to believe, the whispers all one way.

He had been speaking for many minutes when he realised they still hadn't exchanged names.

'Adam Best,' he said, offering his hand.

'Julius Pritchard,' the man's skin dry and warm. 'Come on. Let's get a proper drink. My car's just round the corner.'

They walked in silence, Adam head down, cap peak pulled low. He looked up when he heard the beeping of the car being unlocked and slid onto the black Nappa leather of the 7 series BMW.

'Nice car,' Adam said, working the seat belt.

Julius smiled, started the engine and put the automatic into drive. 'So did you go to court? Maybe I read about it.'

He looked over his shoulder and pulled out into the traffic.

'No court in the end,' Adam said, looking at the dashboard controls. 'But it fucks up your life. Everywhere you go you think people are staring at you, that shop assistants don't want to serve you. Then when they painted those disgusting words on my door, I knew I had to get out.'

Julius glanced his way. 'Where are you living now?'

'Rented flat,' Adam said. 'Nothing special, but it'll do.'

Julius negotiated a set of traffic lights, turned left and moved the powerful BMW to the 40mph speed limit.

'And what do you do with your time then, when you're not in the park?'

'Read,' Adam told him. 'I like the classics, transport myself back in time, imagine what it must have been like to live in Dickens' day. Children knew their place then.'

'I read them myself,' Julius smiled. 'Love them. Read them over and over, again and again.'

Adam shuffled in the seat. His next question needed to be asked and he hoped he'd read Julius Pritchard right.

'What did you mean in the park when you said the same reason as me?'

Julius glanced at him.

Adam looked back, relieved to see Julius' fingers hadn't tightened around the wheel, that the question hadn't changed his mood or got his back up.

'I go to the park because I like young boys,' Julius told him. 'What about you?'

Adam shrugged: 'They're alright I suppose.'

Julius suddenly braked hard, pulled the wheel, and swung

the car into the kerb. This time his fingers were clenched and his voice was edged with anger.

'Look if you're not going to honest then there is no point in continuing this conversation,' the heat bubbling under the surface. 'We're both wasting our time and I for one am not prepared to do that.'

They stared at each other in the charged silence, Adam's expression like a free-running acrobat unsure he could make the leap from one high wall to another.

He inhaled deeply, held his breath, and dropped his head as his words came in a whisper.

'Yes I like young boys.'

Julius slipped the BMW back into drive and pulled smoothly away. 'Wasn't so hard was it?'

He patted Adam's thigh then touched a button on the steering wheel, the car filling with classical music.

Adam slipped down the seat, closed his eyes and listened to violins rise and fall like graceful fountains.

CHAPTER TEN

THIS TIME JAYNE CULLY poured hot water into three mugs, enough for the people in the room.

Ed carried them to the table, Jayne following, leaning heavily against her black stick as she dropped into the hard chair.

Ed looked around. Jayne obviously lived in this room; TV on, TV Times magazine on the small occasional table next to the chair, an indicator as to how she spent her days.

Later in the day than his last visit, the room was stifling, the gas fire on full blast. The rest of the house was Baltic cold.

Sam unbuttoned her coat.

'Terrible thing about Jeremy,' Jayne said. 'All of those police looking for him. Do you think he's still with the man in the van?'

'I don't know Jayne, do you?' Sam asked.

'I don't know. You're the detectives, not me.'

'What did the man in the white van look like Jayne, can you remember?'

Jayne was quiet for a moment, eyes closed.

'I saw his face,' she said. 'He was tall. Distinguished type. Like an army officer. Back rigid straight, like my father. He was in the Guards.'

She looked away, Sam watching her eyes flicker and glass

over, distant memories suddenly vivid.

'What else can you remember Jayne?' Sam said.

'Oh everything,' she smiled. 'How smart my father looked. His shiny boots.'

'What I meant Jayne,' Sam pressed gently, 'was what else do you remember about Jeremy and the white van?'

Jayne blinked. 'They walked down the path. That's when I saw them. I was at my front door looking for milk. Jeremy seemed quite happy.'

She smiled again and paused.

'They were talking as they walked down the path. Jeremy always locked his door even if he was cutting the grass but he didn't lock it this time.'

She stopped and shook her head.

'That's why I thought it was strange when Jeremy got to the van. Why hadn't he locked his door if he was going somewhere?'

Sam nodded an encouraging smile of her own.

Jayne was talking more quickly now, her voice getting high with excitement.

'The distinguished chap was behind him, the van doors were already open, and when Jeremy looked inside the man pushed him in. Then the doors were slammed, the distinguished chap rushed to the driver's seat and they were off.'

Jayne took a breath and stared into the mug. 'That was it.'

'Can you remember which way they drove off?' Sam asked.

'Left.'

'Did you see any other men Jayne?'

'Just that one with Jeremy.'

'What about any other neighbours in the street?'

'I don't think so,' Jayne's eyes looked glazed. 'Will they find him? Jeremy?'

Sam left the question unanswered and glanced at Ed.

They drank their tea in the heat and the silence and had just passed a 'time-to-go' nod when Jayne spoke again.

'I've seen him before you know. The distinguished chap.'

Sam and Ed stared at her.

'Do you know who he is Jayne?' Sam asked.

'No, but I know him. He used to be on the television.'

'An actor?' Sam said.

'No, on the news I think. Ask Johnny. He'll know.'

Sam told her not to get up when they said their thanks and goodbyes.

'He was a fine looking man you know?'

'Who was?' Sam said, pausing at the sitting room door.

'My father.'

'What do you think?' Ed asked when they were back in the car, engine running and heater turned up full.

'Jayne? Lovely woman but as a credible witness...'

Sam and Ed both knew Jayne Cully would never be allowed anywhere near a witness box.

'And yet,' Sam said now. 'I don't think she's making anything up. I think she saw something, or at least she believes she saw something. We just can't be certain what or when.'

Sam lit a cigarette, opened the window a fraction, and inhaled deeply.

'As for the here and now, the white transit can be a line of inquiry but on the back burner. We need someone else to have seen it. Then Jayne's distinguished chap shortens in the betting.'

The tap on the passenger window made them both jump.

Darius Simpson, the reporter from the Seaton Post, was bent down with his face almost touching the glass.

'Hi Sam. What's happening?'

She was relieved to see Darius was alone. No snapper to record her cigarette.

'There might be a press con tomorrow. The press office will give you a heads up.'

Darius looked hurt.

'Come on Sam. There are SOCOs up at O'Grady's garage, SOCOs in that house,' he nodded towards Jeremy

Scott's, 'and uniform knocking on doors in the street. Something's going on. I just want an early heads up. Get started for tomorrow's edition.'

Sam knew Darius and knew the press. They had space to fill and would always find a way. Stonewall them and you had no control over what ended up in the headlines.

'I'll get something sorted and put it on the voice bank,' Sam told him. 'It's only going to be a holding statement for now though, so don't go building your hopes up.'

Darius ran his hand through his blond mop. He would need more and the voice bank, the rolling update of incidents pushed out by the police press office, gave him nothing every other journo couldn't share. The Holy Grail was always an exclusive.

'It's a body or a missing kid,' he told Sam. 'What else would you be here for? Kidnapping maybe? Are the house and the garage linked?'

Sam shook her head. Darius Simpson was still shaking his when she and Ed drove away.

The Snooty Fox was about ten miles south-west of Seaton St George. Julius pulled onto the car park of the country inn, famed, the billboard promised, for its home cooking and craft ales.

'A friend of mine owns this,' he said.

Adam walked towards the pub, white walls, window-frames painted eggshell blue, a large fox on the swinging illuminated sign dressed in waistcoat, breeches and black riding boots.

'First port of call for the Boxing Day hunt,' Julius said, following Adam's eyes and flipping open a soft pack of Marlboro.

'Bet the 'save the fox' brigade love this place,' Adam thought aloud, still staring at the sign.

Julius lit a Marlboro. 'Let's just say there's been a couple of minor skirmishes over the years but nothing a quick clip with a riding stick can't remedy. Scum just wanting to spoil people's fun. Nothing to do with the damned fox. All about class and envy.'

They were standing by the entrance porch, a terracotta plant pot by the door, cigarette ends overflowing from it.

'You hunt then?' Adam asked.

'Man and boy. Not just foxes now.' Julius laughed, an exaggerated laugh, contrived, the type loud-mouthed bores have an annoying habit of making.

He flicked the barely smoked cigarette into the plant pot. 'Come on. Let's get a drink. Hope you're a real ale man, not one of those lager louts.'

Adam followed Julius and imagined him as a young boy at his first kill, cheeks covered in fox blood.

The pub had a stone floor, mahogany bar, and low-beamed ceiling. The single frosted pump for the Heineken Extra Cold looked as out of place as granny knickers on a street prostitute.

'Two pints of your finest landlord,' Julius shouted, as the door swung shut. 'Cornelius, this is Adam.'

The stocky, ginger haired barman thrust out his thick forearm towards Adam and shook hands.

'Cornelius' family have owned this pub for over a hundred years,' Julius said. 'Used to own all the land around it too, before his great-grandfather had to sell up. Preferred chasing skirt to working the farm. Stand in here long enough you'll count more gingers than you can throw a stick at.'

Cue more too-loud laughter.

'Nice place,' Adam said, as he raised the glass to his lips and contemplated names. He didn't think he'd ever met a Julius before and he was rock solid certain his path had never crossed a Cornelius. These two would have had it every day if they'd gone to his comprehensive.

Adam would have preferred the lager but didn't want to offend Julius.

There were two other customers, sat at opposite ends of the bar, and neither seemed thrilled to see Julius.

Adam tried not to stare; it was like a ginger's day out.

'James, Steve,' Julius said.

Both guys at the bar turned, said 'Julius' in unison, and went back to their pints.

'Let's grab a seat Adam.'

Satisfied there were no CCTV cameras, Adam removed his cap as they walked to a copper-topped table in the corner of the room. *Christ even the tabletops have a touch of ginger.*

'So,' Julius said, raising his glass. 'Do you work?'

'Hardly. I was a tennis coach all my life. What job will I get?'

'Hence the trainers.' He nodded towards Adam's shoes.

Adam looked down. 'Yeah Stan Smith was my hero back in the day. Most people who wear them now don't know who Stan Smith was. Bloody tragedy. What a player.'

'About jobs,' Julius said, leaning closer. 'I may be able to help you out there. It won't pay much but it will be cash in hand and won't screw up whatever benefits you get. My associates and I will just say you are volunteering.'

Adam pushed himself into the back of the bench seat, his nose rebelling at Julius' sickly sweet aftershave. 'Volunteering for what exactly?'

'We run a five-a-side league, under 11s to under 13s.' When he smiled Adam noticed his uneven teeth. 'You don't need me to draw you pictures.'

Adam didn't respond immediately, didn't want to appear too keen. 'What kind of league?'

'Six until nine every Thursday on those floodlit Astroturf pitches,' Julius told him. 'We hire the whole place. Shots and Saves.'

'Sounds expensive.'

Adam grimaced as he sipped the pint...no head, no bubbles, and a taste like something a tramp had washed his feet in.

His father had always told him there was no such thing as a bad pint of beer, just that some were better than others. Well 'King of the Others' was lurking in his glass.

'It's very cheap actually,' Julius was telling him. 'We know the owner.'

Adam stared at Julius over the rim of his pint glass.

'And I would do what exactly?'

'Help out, referee, sort out results. We have about eight teams most Thursdays.'

'What about DBS checks?' Adam asked.

Disclosure and Barring Service checks were now mandatory for a whole host of things. Volunteering with children was one of them.

Gingers one, two and three looked their way as Julius launched another laugh.

'Seriously?' He shook his head. 'We get kids coming from the sink estates, parents who don't give a shit about them, parents who can at least pretend someone is taking an interest in their offspring while they piss their money up the wall. They don't give a toss about DBS. Anyway, you said you didn't go to court.'

'I didn't.' Adam sipped more beer. He didn't want anybody doing any checks on him. 'So what about you? What do you do?'

Julius told him he was a web designer who worked from home and volunteered at a hospice a couple of times a week, helping with fundraising.

'Well you must be DBS checked,' Adam said

'I am and I'm clear, which is how I expect to stay,' Julius told him. 'Solid upstanding citizen.'

'So why involve me?'

'I knew what you were,' Julius said. 'We are always looking to recruit new members, because let's face it we can all learn through experience, and you may have different experiences to the rest of us.'

Julius got to his feet. 'Drink up then.'

'Why?' Adam's face creased with unease. 'Where are we going?'

'Just a call on a friend,' Julius said. 'May as well drop by and introduce you to him before I go home.'

'And what's at home?' Adam asked.

The smile showed the crooked teeth.

'A wife and two kids.'

CHAPTER ELEVEN

Sam and Ed were sat in her office, empty crisp and sandwich packets on the desk, the fluorescent strip lighting bright against the early evening darkness outside.

'I hate this time of year,' Sam said. 'I really think there's something in this SAD.'

'What?'

'Seasonal Affective Disorder.'

Ed rolled his eyes. 'Jesus does everything have to have a fancy title these days? Just this week I've read about Waste Management and Disposal Technicians, bin men in my day, and a Transparency Enhancement Facilitator. Do you know what that is?'

Sam's eyes were as wide as her smile. 'Enlighten me.'

'A bloody window cleaner.'

Sam burst out laughing. 'Shut up you old goat.'

Paul Adams, the newest member of the team, came into the office. 'You wanted to see me boss?'

Sam briefed Paul on Jeremy Scott.

'Ring Hampshire and see if they've got anything,' she told him. 'I know it's late and Force Intelligence's probably shut, but see what you can find out. Try the media down there as well. See how you can access the archives.'

Paul was watching and listening, nodding occasionally.

'I want to know everything there is to know about our Jeremy Scott,' Sam told him. 'Always remember the old adage Paul. The more we know about the victim, the more we know about the killer.'

'Leave it with me boss.' He turned and walked away.

Sam watched him go then turned to Ed.

'I want to see Curtis Brown again. He had piano lessons off someone in The Avenue. What if his teacher was Jeremy Scott?'

'Hans, this is Adam', Julius said.

Hans van Dijk was standing in the doorway of a 1920's three storey terraced house; the huge front door looking like a fresh coat of black gloss was applied every time someone went out.

'Pleased to meet you.'

Adam fought down a laugh. The guy should have been called Rupert. He followed the bright yellow cords and red jumper and their 60ish owner down the tiled hallway.

'I've got some decent Malt,' van Dijk said.

There was no trace of an accent, but Adam presumed the university professor look-alike must be Dutch or maybe South African.

The living room was large, three plugged-in air fresheners locked in battle with stale pipe smoke, the lavender just getting the better of the cherry-flavoured tobacco.

White floor to ceiling bookshelves, crammed with books, filled every alcove. The carpet was probably older than Hans. The five armchairs, an eclectic mix of fabrics and colours, were around a large wooden coffee table, its thick carved legs drawing the eye to the stronger, less worn colours of the carpet underneath the table. That table hasn't been moved in years, Adam thought, and there's no settee. Does that mean he doesn't like people getting too close, physically or emotionally? That he valued his personal space?

Hans looked the type of guy, intelligent, studious even, to know the answers to those kind of questions.

Whisky tumblers filled and passed around, Hans placed an old Johnny Walker pot jug with water in it on the table. 'Help yourself gentlemen.'

Adam poured a splash of water into his drink and took in the old TV and video recorder, museum pieces in the flat-screen age.

'Hans' family originate from Utrecht, but he's been over here for decades,' Julius said. 'Lectures at the university.'

'What's your specialist subject?' Hans stared at Adam, one leg crossed over the other, holding the glass which was perched on his knee.

'Tennis, or at least it used to be.'

'Interesting,' Hans said. 'Adam would you excuse us a moment. There's something I need to show Julius in the kitchen.'

Hans followed Julius from the room and across a short hall and closed the kitchen door behind them.

'Who the hell is he?' Hans demanded, face burning red, his backside leaning against the wooden bench.

Julius shook his head in wonderment at the gleaming Belfast sink in the corner, the whole room spotless.

'Something smells nice. What is it? I can definitely smell garlic.'

'Italian,' Hans muttered. 'Never mind that. Who is he?'

'Calm down,' Julius smiled. 'He's kosher. He sits in the park every day watching the little lovelies. What do you think he does that for?'

Hans brought the crystal to his lips and downed the drink, saying nothing.

'You're paranoid, that's your trouble,' Julius said. 'I approached him. He's a tennis coach who got arrested but didn't go to court. Young boys.'

'So you just embrace him do you?' Hans broke his silence. 'Bring him into the inner circle so to speak.'

'Just like I did with you all those years ago,' Julius was still smiling. 'Now come on, let's get back to our guest. He's got a sporting pedigree that could come in useful, especially in the summer. He could teach the boys tennis.'

Adam was studying the bookshelves when the two men walked back into the room.

'So Adam,' Hans said pouring another whisky. 'Julius tells me you're into young boys.'

Adam stood motionless, not even a flicker from his eyes.

He watched as Hans walked to the TV unit, opened the rosewood drawer and selected a tape.

He looked over his shoulder and waved the cassette.

'Home movie,' Hans said. 'Nothing too heavy, just a guy with a young boy. Ancient now, but still watchable.'

He put the tape in the player, turned on the TV, and watched the snow blizzard static quickly replaced by a grainy film.

'Thought we might get to know each other a bit better,' Hans said. 'As we are all friends together it seems...'

'Bloody hell Hans,' Julius shook his head.

Hans stepped away from the screen and unfastened his belt.

'It's okay,' Adam said, 'I understand. You can't be too careful. I'd love to, really, but I'm at that age when some of us have problems and I haven't got any, err, assistance with me right now. Sorry.'

'Pity,' Hans grunted, stomping to the video player and turning the film off.

Ed pulled the steering wheel to the right, veered across the road and came to a screeching halt outside a general dealer's store. He pressed the button for the electric windows, damp evening air filling the car.

'Get in Curtis.'

Curtis Brown, cigarette gripped between his lips, bent down and peered into the car.

Ed returned the stare. If the eyes were the gateway to the soul, Curtis' were the doors to nowhere.

'It's DS Whelan,' Ed said. 'We spoke at the police station this morning.'

Bloody hell was that just this morning?

A flicker of recognition; Curtis opened the back door and climbed inside.

Ed left his window open despite the chill. Sam opened hers all the way but a diffuser the size of a phone box and a gallon of Chanel No5 wouldn't have won a fight with the ripe aroma.

Ed pulled away.

'Where we going?' Curtis said.

'I just need to ask a couple of questions Curtis,' Ed told him. 'We were on the way to your squat when we spotted you at the shop.'

Ed glanced in the rear-view mirror.

'By the way I saw your mam. She sends her love. I didn't realise you played the piano.'

Sam looked over her shoulder and watched Curtis sit bolt upright, his knees squeezed together and body stiff. Ed had hit a nerve.

'Who were you going to be? Elton John or Billy Joel?' Ed said.

Curtis turned his head and looked out of the window.

'I don't even know who that last bloke is.'

'You don't know Billy Joel?' Ed grinned. 'The Piano Man?'

He started to sing the first couple of lines of the song.

'I hope he sounded better than that,' Curtis said.

Ed made a mock-hurt face into the mirror.

'Nothing wrong with my singing.'

All three were laughing as Ed pulled into the yard at Seaton St George Police Station.

Curtis eyed the yard gloomily. 'I'm not going to be here all night am I?'

'Hopefully not,' Sam told him. 'Let's just get out of the car, stand here, and you and I can have a cigarette. Don't let anybody see you though. You're not supposed to smoke here.'

Curtis offered Sam one of his cigarettes, the box trembling in front of her.

'Thanks Curtis but I prefer these.'

She lit a Marlboro Gold.

'Curtis,' Sam said, inhaling smoke. 'Your mum told Ed you went for piano lessons somewhere on The Avenue.'

She studied him, waiting for a response, a once good-looking lad now in his mid 20s, 6 feet tall and probably weighing less than 8 stones.

Curtis' whole body shook as he blew smoke upwards.

'Long time ago. I didn't like it but my mam kept pushing me. I used to think she was doing it just to get rid of me for an hour.'

'Can you remember what they called the teacher?' Sam pushed.

Curtis looked down and allowed smoke to drift from his mouth and nostrils.

'I thought you wanted to talk to me about the body, not some piano teacher from years ago.'

'Humour me Curtis,' Sam said. 'You never know, I might be thinking of taking up the piano myself.'

Curtis looked at her.

'It was Scott...Jeremy fucking Scott,' he said at last. 'And I hope you play better than he sings.'

CHAPTER TWELVE

ADAM LEANED against the wall of the floodlit five-a-side pitch and scanned the blank membership form Julius had given him. He noted the parental permission dotted line and wondered if they knew what they were agreeing to.

The form did specify that no child would ever be left alone with one adult. That sounded good in principle and looked reassuring on paper but when everyone involved had a taste for young boys it meant nothing.

The only people protected were the perpetrators themselves; the word of two adults against one child, a child that probably already had issues at school and with the law.

Earlier Julius had given him the tour...a glassed reception area where a young woman in a yellow polo shirt bearing the centre logo sat at a computer screen; CCTV coverage in the corridors; a couple of vending machines selling energy drinks and bars; changing rooms with showers but understandably no cameras and so the obvious place for the 'sexual assault zone'.

Upstairs was a bar with sliding patio doors to a balcony overlooking the ten five-a-side pitches and at the end of the corridor, the manager's office.

Adam considered the potent combination: alcohol, vulnerable young boys and predators.

He was on the balcony, watching the youngsters on the pitches below, when Julius tapped him on the shoulder.

'What do you think then?'

'Seems well organised.'

Julius looked upwards, smiled, and shook his head.

'It's that alright, but I meant the latest crop?'

Adam stared back to the noise and movement on the busy pitches.

'They seem nice kids.'

Julius puffed out his cheeks.

'Adam, we each know what we are. Let's cut the bullshit. Anyone caught your eye yet?'

Adam looked straight head and didn't answer.

'Look there's a party next Friday night after the football,' Julius told him. 'A couple of the older boys are coming, you know, drink and cigarettes, a little cocaine. Hans has organised it. Are you up for it?'

'You sure Hans won't mind?' Adam sounded doubtful. 'He didn't look too happy when I couldn't join in the synchronised wank.'

Julius's laugh this time was genuine and throaty, a nod to his ambivalence towards tobacco health warnings.

'Quality…synchronised indeed.'

He laughed again. 'Are you up for it then?'

'Yeah okay,' Adam couldn't stop his own small smile. 'What time and where?'

'We'll meet here then we'll walk,' Julius said. 'Hans will transport the boys. He'll text me the location as we walk.'

'All a bit cloak and dagger,' Adam looked back to the boys below. 'Doesn't he trust you?'

'It's called being careful,' Julius said quietly. 'That way we keep out of prison.'

'Feeling better than you were this morning?' Harry Pullman asked as John Elgin walked to the bar.

He glanced around. The place was busier but not packed,

the customers a mix of older couples in winter coats and a younger crowd dressed for summer. Typical north east.

'How's Oscar?' Harry asked as he pulled a pint of Peroni.

Elgin watched the glass turning golden.

'Withdrawn, upset, hurt,' he told Harry. 'Everything you'd expect him to be. He doesn't want to report it though and his parents don't want to force him. Meanwhile, the two fuckers responsible walk around without a care in the world.'

Harry put the pint in front of Elgin. 'People like that always get what's coming. How did anyone find out?'

'He just blurted it, poor kid,' Elgin reached into his pocket for change.

Harry shook his head. 'On the house.'

'Cheers.' He drank the crisp lager, froth attaching itself to his moustache. 'He only went to the football because his parents thought it might get him off the iPad for five minutes. Always been a bit of a loner our Oscar.'

He drank some more and had another look around.

'But he's never liked football,' Elgin went on. 'Why they sent him there I'll never know. The bastards who abused him are called Julius and Hans. If I could get my hands on them.'

He swallowed three mouthfuls of Peroni, enjoying the cold rush in his throat.

'A man in your position is better keeping his hands clean,' Harry told him. 'Leave dirty work to dirty hands. What about his dad?'

Elgin put his glass on the bar top and wiped his mouth.

'Iain?' he said sourly. 'Don't be daft. Not everyone from Glasgow wants to fight. Drink maybe, but not fight. Iain couldn't punch his way out of a paper bag.'

Harry stepped away to serve a couple further down the bar and picked up Elgin's empty glass when he returned. He swapped it for a fresh one and held it under the Peroni tap without asking.

'As I said, they'll get what's coming to them.'

'You believe that Harry?' Elgin nodded his thanks for the new pint and put a £5 note on the bar. 'I think they'll get away with it and while I say nothing, the next kid's getting lined up.'

Harry took the money.

'You can't say anything. Oscar and his parents would never speak to you again. They've trusted you with the information. They don't expect you to spout off about it.'

Harry let his words sink in before continuing. 'Something will turn up. Trust me. Down the Astroturf you said?

Elgin nodded, hunched over the bar and stared into the pint glass. It was becoming a habit, the pint and the staring.

'Now about these licences,' Harry was saying now. 'We'll need more info.'

'What do you need to know?' Elgin said without looking up. 'I just want Skinner off my back.'

Harry spoke to the top of his head. 'John, it's not that simple. It's not going to happen overnight.'

Elgin dragged his eyes from the glass, told him the applications didn't start to kick in until January, that there was time enough.

'That's good, but we need to know the premises he's eyeing up,' Harry said. 'We'll need to sort out some backers. He's got more cash than us. It won't be easy.'

'I never said it would be, but it'll make you rich Harry.'

'And for that we'll always be grateful,' Harry said. 'Goes without saying if this comes off, drink, food, girls...always on the house.'

This time Elgin met his eyes.

'On the house is what got me into trouble with Skinner.'

'But he uses people,' Harry said. 'Forgets what side his bread's buttered. We're not like that.'

Elgin dropped his gaze back to the glass and the gently bubbling lager.

You're all like that. Out of the frying pan…

'Jeremy Scott's dead,' Sam said.

Curtis Brown stubbed out the cigarette with his left foot and pulled another from the packet.

'Fucking great,' he lit up. 'No good ever came from his life.'

'What do you mean?' Ed joined in.

Curtis shook his head and spoke as he let out smoke. 'Nothing mate.'

'Curtis we know what Jeremy Scott used to do with young boys. The body you found.' Sam stopped and fixed her eyes on his. 'The body was Jeremy Scott.'

Curtis' cigarette hand started shaking. 'What are you saying?'

Sam studied him. 'I'm saying the body was your old piano teacher.'

'No, what are you saying?' Curtis demanded. 'I did it?'

'Did you?' Ed's voice was neutral.

'Fuck off.'

Sam stepped in front of him. 'Look at it from our point of view Curtis. We know what Scott was.'

'Do you? Do you?' He shouted. 'You have no idea. Every week my mother dropped me off there.'

He flicked the cigarette away and immediately lit another. His eyes filled and his cracked voice fell to a whisper.

'Every week. She may as well have wrapped me in fucking Christmas paper.'

He inhaled and stared at the ground.

'Shall we get a cup of tea?' Sam said, touching his forearm.

Curtis was still shaking his head when Sam's mobile rang in her pocket.

She took out the phone and saw Bev's name on the screen. She answered, listened, and typed a quick text to Ed before returning the mobile to her pocket.

Ed read the message.

Neighbour of Jayne's saw Scott walking towards a white van. No reg.

'Sure you don't want to get that cuppa Curtis?' Ed said.

'No. Once I'm in there you'll try and stick this on me.'

'Curtis...'Sam said.

'I knew it was him,' the voice loud and raw. 'Knew it was that bastard when I saw him.'

'Calm down Curtis,' Sam said, voice soothing, melodic. 'How?'

Curtis looked at her.

'I saw them taking him in,' he said. 'I recognised him when they dragged him out of the van.'

Sam glanced at Ed, the breakthrough glance of hundreds of investigations, the here-we-go-glance, the detectives' heroin hit.

'Curtis we need to go inside and talk about this. Get it on tape.'

A nod.

'We need you to take your time and describe everything you saw.'

Curtis stared at the ground and mumbled. 'You can watch it.'

The walk through the town centre for a pint was Adam's idea, one for the road. Julius agreed but said Hans was expecting him, so one it would be.

Ahead of them, two masked gorillas holding pints of lager staggered in the busy street, another stag party on a bender. Julius put his hand in his pocket when he felt his mobile vibrate and glanced at the screen.

Don't be too long. Hans.

Julius, head bowed, read the message and smiled. That man even had to use correct grammar in text speech.

'Alright gents?' one of the gorillas slurred.

'Fine mate,' Adam answered.

Julius was slipping the phone back in his pocket when a rubber mask was rammed onto his head and strong arms manhandled him towards a Ford Transit parked at the kerbside.

Men were singing a loud and tuneless version of 'who's

getting married in the morning', the noise blocking out the groan as the van's back doors were flung open, flakes of rust from the unoiled hinges dropping onto the road. His arms and legs were pinned tight, restraints were snapped around his wrists, and he was thrown into the air. Whatever he landed on wasn't concrete but it was hard.

'Fuck!' he shouted.

An engine started and the transit shuddered into life.

'Adam!' Julius shouted. 'Adam. Are you there?'

The doors slammed.

'What the fuck's happening?' Adam's voice sounded panicked but close. 'Is this down to you? Some sort of initiation ceremony?'

'I'm fucking sure it's not,' Julius screamed.

The van moved; no wheel spins, no harsh acceleration.

'Hey,' Julius shouted.

No one answered.

'Kick the panels Adam,' Julius said, lashing out with his heels. 'Scream for help. Somebody will hear us and call the police.'

Adam kicked at nothing and when he spoke he sounded resigned more than frightened.

'Julius calm down,' he said. 'What's the point? Nobody's calling the police. Anyone watching would just think we were part of the stag party. It's a joke. This lot'll get bored and drop us off somewhere. So long as they haven't set out to get you.'

Julius went quiet and still.

'Nobody's out to get me, but this van's travelling. We're on a fast road here.'

He rolled onto his back to take the weight off his arms. 'What the fuck is all this about?'

'You tell me,' Adam said.

They lay in silence, the journey lasting no more than ten minutes before the van stopped and the doors were opened.

The mask was ripped off Julius' head, his eyes struggling to focus, another figure on the floor of the van next to him, wrists cuffed and a gorilla mask on his head.

Two gorillas stood at the back doors. 'Phone,' one of them demanded. 'Where is it?'

'Trouser pocket,' Julius said, still on his back.

Should I have lied?

They each grabbed an ankle and dragged him towards them. One of the masked men checked his pockets and took the phone. 'Code?'

'One-nine-seven-eight. Look can we go now? You've had your fun.'

'Get out.'

Julius did what he was told, dropping his legs over the edge and jumping the short distance to the ground.

'What about my hands?'

'They're fine for now.'

CHAPTER THIRTEEN

THEY WERE BACK in the same interview room but this time Sam and Ed weren't in a hurry and both of them sat down instead of standing in the doorway.

'You okay doing this Curtis?' Sam said.

Curtis nodded.

'Curtis we'll talk after this, talk about professional help, that sort of thing. You don't need to carry this around with you by yourself. Remember you did nothing wrong all those years ago.'

Another nod from Curtis.

He pressed play on his screen, put the phone on the desk and spun it around so that the two detectives opposite could watch. A white van was already parked in front of the garage, a tall man, the driver, walking to the back doors. Jayne Culley had described a man with a straight back and a military demeanour and this guy fit the bill. There would be no joy identifying the face. The mask, like something from the old Spitting Image puppet show, would see to that. The doors were opened, two other masked figures jumped out and there was Jeremy Scott, hands tied behind his back. Scott dropped to the floor and whilst the footage was soundless, he was talking until the driver punched him in the face and the others dragged him facedown into the garage.

'Did you record any more Curtis?' Sam asked, looking at him.

He shook his head. 'Too scared. I could hear screaming and I saw them all walk out.'

'Then what happened?' Sam said.

'The masks were off by then,' Curtis told them. 'They put them in one of those things strikers on the picket lines light to keep warm, you know like a dustbin on fire.'

'A brazier?' Ed said.

'I don't know the proper name,' Curtis shrugged. 'Then they took off the boiler suits and burnt them as well.'

'Can you remember what they looked like?' Ed pressed him.

'Not really and I don't want to.'

Curtis started clawing at the back of his right hand like a demented cat scratching a piece of carpet.

'I saw what they did to him and he fucking deserved it but no way the same thing's happening to me.'

His hand suddenly stopped.

'And anyway,' Curtis almost smiled. 'Why would I want to help you catch the people who killed that bastard? I only showed you what happened so you couldn't fit me up for it.'

'Curtis I don't want to accuse you of withholding information,' Sam said. 'I really don't.'

'I can't get accused of anything because I have a bad memory,' he shot back. 'So I remember the driver was tall, the others were medium and when they took their masks and overalls off I was too frightened to look at them.'

'What about your bad memory this morning?' Ed said. 'Why didn't you show me the film then?'

Curtis glared. 'I just wanted to get out, get myself sorted.'

Sam stood up and walked out of the room. Ed followed.

'Look we're all tired,' she said, rubbing her eyes. 'We've got more than we had before we picked him up. '

Ed leaned against the dirty magnolia wall.

'You know, years ago these would have been painted regularly, but not now,' he ran his hand lightly over a stain. 'Private Finance Initiatives saw to that. Costs a fortune just to change a light bulb now. Paint a wall? Cheaper to use Michelangelo.'

Sam face was weary but she smiled.

'At times I have no idea how your mind works,' she said, meaning it. 'We've just had a huge breakthrough and you're moaning about PFIs and paint.'

'It's called sleep deprivation,' Ed smiled back. 'It's gone nine and we've been here since two this morning. I'm probably hallucinating.'

John Elgin knew his heart-throb days were over, but he still had a way with women; at least he did by the time he was on his fifth pint and the girl he was talking to was willing to have sex for money.

After last night's disaster in Pussycats he should have walked away. His inner voice was screaming 'beer in, brains out' but he never moved.

She was medium height, early twenties, ink-black hair cut in a bob; bright red lipstick mesmerising when she spoke, all brown eyes and white teeth when she listened.

He asked the usual and got the same back. She called herself Tara, had a boyfriend but it was nothing serious, went to university to do history but dropped out when she got homesick. Elgin guessed some of it might even be true.

He ordered another Peroni and bought her a gin and tonic. He paid on his card then instantly regretted it. More ammunition for his wife when she demanded to see the statement.

Harry tapped him on the shoulder. 'Listen, I'm just popping out to give our Dean a hand with something. Won't take too long.'

He handed Elgin a key. 'For the flat. It's empty. Feel free. If the key's not behind the bar when I get back I'll know you're still up there. Take as long as you like.'

'That's good of him,' Tara said, as Harry strode to the front door. 'I'll just pop to the loo.'

Elgin turned his head, put the fresh pint to his lips, and gazed at her slim legs perform a solo waltz between the little round tables. He knew he should leave, just walk out there and then, but black leather mini-skirts and stilettos always seemed to vaporise the what-he-should-do warnings.

He gulped the lager, put his foot on the brass rail, and waited. He'd deal with any fallout later.

Elgin watched the toilet door swing open and watched her walk towards him, fresh lipstick lighting a smile straight from a toothpaste advert. His eyes travelled down her body as she got closer, his thoughts moving on rapidly from dental hygiene and make-up.

Outside he ushered her to the external door, glanced behind him as he slid the long key in the lock, and pushed the handle down when it clicked open. He stepped over the threshold, pulling Tara inside, and locked the door behind them. He made sure he was watching as she climbed the stairs.

A huge wall-mounted TV dominated the sitting room. On the coffee table was a laptop, its screen split into four separate views - the car park, the till behind the bar, and the front and rear of the big open plan bar.

Elgin sat on the red leather settee and stared at the screen. Tara flopped next to him and rubbed the inside of his thigh. He eased her hand away, sat forward, and stared at the image on the top left, a 7 Series BMW with189 GBH as a personalised plate. GBH. Billy Skinner's car, the prick. But who was in the front seats? And why were they here?

Elgin wanted to zoom in but didn't know how and was worried he would lose the picture altogether.

'What is it?' Tara asked him but he said nothing, just stared at the screen.

A moment later he watched the car doors open. The driver was too tall for short-arse Skinner. His psycho eldest son? Maybe. The driver walked to the boot, opened it, and looked inside.

Elgin scrolled through his contacts. He didn't have Harry's mobile.

'Should we go out?' Tara sat forward.

'And do what exactly?' Elgin snapped. 'Just sit tight.'

His eyes flicked across the laptop's split screen. There was nothing unusual on any of the other cameras.

Where were Harry and Dean?

A second man joined the driver at the boot. Elgin was convinced now the driver was Mat Skinner. The two men bent forward, reached inside, and when they straightened each held what looked like a pick-axe handle in their right hands, dangling by their leg.

They speed-marched across the car park and pushed open the door to the bar.

'That's Mat Skinner,' Tara said. 'Fucking creep.'

Elgin's eyes darted to the two inside cameras.

Mat was through the door first, the pick-axe in both hands and raised above his head. Elgin watched the screen as men and women scrambled to get out of the way. Mat strode behind the bar, while the other man stood guard by the door; nobody was leaving and nobody was coming in. The barmaid cowered in the corner but knew better than to argue or phone for help.

Elgin didn't need sound. His imagination heard the glass exploding as Mat swung the pick-axe repeatedly at the bottles, glass flying everywhere as the stock was wiped out in a series of savage blows, the pick-axe moving at a speed a baseball pro would have admired.

Less than two minutes later Mat Skinner marched out, his accomplice following.

Elgin switched his gaze back to the car park camera and watched them throw their pick-axe handles into the boot and drive off.

His eyes flicked back to the now deserted bar. A bomb scare couldn't have cleared the place as fast. The barmaid had her mobile in her hand.

'Now what?' Tara said.

'Give it ten minutes.' Elgin told her. 'If Harry's not back, we're out of here…and how do you know Mat Skinner so well?'

Hans opened his gleaming black gloss front door. He was expecting Julius. What he got was a punch in the mouth by a full-size gorilla.

Falling backwards over the hall table, he was aware of hands spinning him around and shoving him downwards. His stomach and face crashed into the Victorian ceramic floor tiles and a knee dropped onto his back. His arms were grabbed and cuffed. Dragged to his feet, breathless, nose dripping with blood, two gorillas grabbed his collar and dragged him backwards out of the house, his heels scraping along the floor.

No more than thirty seconds after he opened the door, Hans van Dijk was hauled into the back of a van where a gorilla dropped onto his chest.

He had no idea what was happening. If he had signed up in a moment of madness to sample Special Forces training at the sharp end it might have made some sense. It was too violent to be some sort of prank and too slick for a parent acting the vigilante.

'What the hell?' he shouted.

Another punch to the face was followed by a local accent that sounded like it had been practising pure aggression for years. 'Shut the fuck up.'

He lay in silence, concentrating on keeping his bladder intact and his churning bowels at bay. Ten minutes later he was bundled into a large disused building, a factory of some sort.

Julius was hanging upside down, his feet bound by rope tied to a metal girder.

'Hans,' he screamed, 'Hans, help.'

He started to swing like Harry Houdini trying to escape from a straitjacket.

'What do they want?' Hans shouted. 'What the fuck's going on?'

He was pushed to the floor, feet bound in thick hemp rope and then yanked skyward towards the beam.

A gorilla approached.

'The boys are safe now,' the voice was cold. 'No more five-a-side games, not with you lot anyway.'

Hans van Dijk could feel the blood rushing to his head, Julius still struggling close by.

Behind them they heard a voice, jovial and light.

'Alright lads? How's it going?'

They kicked their legs against the rope and shook their shoulders, breathing hard as they twisted themselves in vain to see who had asked the question.

They both thought they recognised the voice. Their brains just couldn't process it.

CHAPTER FOURTEEN

It was almost 9.30pm as Sam pulled onto her drive, locked the Audi and walked into the house.

What a day.

The lights and the heating were on but that was down to electric timers not a human touch.

She asked Alexa, her Amazon Echo friend that had been delivered a week ago, to play the Beach Boys' Pet Sounds. It was an album that she and Tristram often played through the cockpit speakers when they chartered a yacht.

Too tired to eat, too tired to sleep, she went to the wine chiller and picked out a bottle of white: Chateau Montelena, a Californian Chardonnay.

She had first come across it when she watched the movie Bottle Shock starring Alan Rickman and now it was a favourite. The wine had been victorious in the 1976 Judgement of Paris, beating some famous Burgundian Chardonnays in a blind tasting.

She took off her shoes, put her coat over the door, and popped the cork, pouring generously into a large Riedel glass. Then she sat at the kitchen island and burst into tears.

Her head dropped, her forehead clammy against the cool of the granite, and her sobs drowned out Brian Wilson's finest hour. Salty tears ran into the corner of her mouth, reminding her of the sea, of blue skies and snapping sails, of Tristram suntanned and smiling and alive.

Her stomach tightened, her cheeks tingled.

Get a grip Sam.

She lifted her head and looked around. Everything perfect, nothing out of place, everywhere as smart and stylish as a show-house but without a soul. She sipped the wine, a hint of ripe lemon on her tongue.

This should be her sanctuary. It shouldn't be somewhere she dreaded, a dead space that gave her nothing that mattered.

'Alexa, play Mr. Candyman by Sammy Davis Junior.'

The Beach Boys had been a bad choice. God might or might not know what she was doing without Tristram. Sam knew all too well.

'Fucking yachts,' she said to herself.

She downed the wine and poured some more.

Was this it now? Years of loneliness stretching out in front of her? Nothing more than the latest gizmo for company. She rubbed her eyes.

Sam Parker. Another lonely Jayne Culley in waiting but please God without the dementia.

John Elgin walked into the now empty bar, the barmaid mopping at a mixture of broken glass and liquid. 'Did you get hold of Harry?'

'I tried his mobile and Dean's,' she said without pausing the swishing motion of the mop. 'Both went straight to voicemail.'

Tara was leaning against the bar. Elgin noticed she was as far away from the door as possible. Sensible girl.

'Was anything said?' he asked.

'Nothing,' the barmaid told him. 'That crazy bastard just walked in and started smashing everything up. Never said a word. Harry's going to go ballistic.'

She walked downstairs into the cellar, returned with a

bottle of gin and a couple of tonics. She found three unbroken spirit glasses on the tables, abandoned by customers in their rush to leave, washed them and poured three large measures.

Tara downed hers in one and slid the glass back towards the barmaid.

'Did you know them?' Elgin asked.

'Mat Skinner smashed the place up. I don't know who the other one was.'

'Geoff Mekins,' Tara said. 'Another dick.'

Elgin looked at her. 'You never told me how you knew Mat.'

Tara glanced at the barmaid.

'I'd tell him fuck all,' she said, pouring another shot for Tara.

'Me and a few girls deliver packages for them,' Tara shrugged. 'It's how I know Harry.'

The door opened and Billy Skinner walked in. Luke was behind. 'What the fuck just happened here?'

Silence.

John Elgin broke it. 'Your Mat.'

'So the word was right,' Skinner's eyes moved around the devastation. 'An associate from the old days rang me. Did our Mat say anything?'

'Ask her,' Elgin said, pointing at the barmaid. 'We weren't here.'

Skinner looked instead at Tara then turned back to Elgin, shaking his head.

'You must have a cock like a teenager.'

Skinner moved his gaze to the barmaid. 'Well?'

'He never said a word. Just walked in, came behind the bar and smashed it up with a baseball bat or something. His mate stood at the door.'

'Who was he with?' Skinner's eyes narrowed.

'We think it was Geoff Mekins,' Elgin told him.

Skinner said nothing, the uneasy silence stretching until he spoke again.

'Give Harry my apologies. Our Mat wasn't doing this under my instructions.'

Skinner took out a roll of twenties and threw them on the bar.

'That should replace the stock and pay for the damages and leave a little left over. Tell Harry I'll deal with it.'

The Skinners walked out.

'Are you two in a rush to get away?' the barmaid asked once the three of them were alone. 'I've had enough of this.'

Elgin looked at Tara. 'We can wait until Harry gets back can't we love? We've got two glasses and a bottle.'

'And a load of cash,' she said.

'Don't even think about it,' Elgin was serious. 'Billy Skinner will know exactly how much is in that stash.'

He turned to the barmaid. 'Yeah you get yourself away sweetheart. We'll wait for Harry.'

'What the fuck?' Julius said. 'You!'

He had barely got the words out before Adam karate kicked Hans in the ribs, taking his breath in a rush, Hans' face twisted in pain.

'That's for asking me to watch kiddie porn and wank,' Adam yelled.

Hans whimpered like a wounded dog as the rope swung back and forth.

Julius' voice was quiet, trembling: 'Adam. For God's sake, what's happening here?'

'A kiddie fiddler's court, that's what happening.'

Two metres away Hans was swinging more slowly.

'I told you not to trust him,' the whimper now a wild growl. 'I fucking told you.'

Adam kicked him again. A crack, like a popgun at the fair, echoed around the abattoir. 'Shut the fuck up.'

Hans had no alternative. He couldn't breathe let alone speak. At least one rib had gone.

Adam bent down and looked into Julius' upside down eyes. 'You see Julius, someone I know and like...'

'Please stop this Adam.' He started to sob. 'I've got a family…they'll be worried…they'll report me missing.'

Adam slapped him across the face. 'You should have thought about your family before you started interfering with other people's.'

Adam straightened up. 'Now where was I? That's right. So it transpires that my friend knows you had a 12-year-old perform a sex act on you.'

Adam pointed at Hans who was groaning quietly. 'Him as well.'

He returned his eyes to Julius, now hanging limp and silent.

'Nothing can put right what you've done,' Adam told him. 'My friend couldn't possibly let animals like you just walk away. What would people think?'

A gorilla handed Adam a cigarette.

'You know my friend has always had a thing about religion. Not the actual beliefs themselves, more why men follow them, die for them even.'

He started pacing back and forward in between the captives.

'What made young noblemen leave England and all their privilege for the Crusades? What makes a Jihadist strap a bomb to their chest and blow themselves up?'

He stopped next to Julius. 'Funny thing religion.'

He gave him a gentle push and started pacing again.

'Anyway, about my friend,' Adam said. 'You might say he is firm but fair. Even though he knew what you two were, he insisted as always on proof.'

Adam shoved Hans as he passed, both bound men moving now almost gracefully like pendulums in an obscene clock.

'My job was to get that proof.'

Hans finally spoke, his words shaking between shallow breaths.

'You've got your proof,' he said slowly. 'What happens now? This has already gone too far.'

'Patience Hans,' Adam told him, and pushed both men gently again.

'Getting the proof was easy. I knew who you were, Julius. The boy pointed you out. I just sat in the park and hoped you'd approach me.'

'Idiot,' Hans grunted.

'And the bonus was you introduced me to Hans, a perfect match for his other attacker, right down to those ridiculous red trousers.'

He flicked away the cigarette.

'My name's not even Adam and I can't play tennis to save my life.'

He allowed himself a moment of satisfaction, a simple plan perfectly executed.

'So about religion,' he stood before them. 'The police will get a tip-off. They'll come to this place and they will find you, find you prepared Halal so to speak.'

Adam took out a knife, grabbed Hans' scalp and slit his throat.

He turned as Julius began to scream.

'Someone had to go first.'

CHAPTER FIFTEEN

Saturday 13th December

'I'M GETTING TOO old for this,' the taller of the two said, snipping the wire fence surrounding the compound, 'and my hands are bloody freezing.'

They'd chosen 4am specifically. Patrolling cops were hopefully having a cup of tea somewhere warm, preferably the station five miles away, and the mobile security guard had done his last drive-past ten minutes ago.

Dark clothing, ski masks and gloves helped them blend into the blackness of the open field, the sky heavy with low cloud above them. The problems would start on the other side of the fence with the floodlights blazing.

'We need to run like we are twenty again, confuse anyone watching the CCTV tomorrow,' the tall one said, pulling at the newly-cut hole in the mesh fence. 'On three...'

They sprinted towards the storage unit, pressed their backs against the yellow roller-shutters, and dropped their hands to their knees, bending forward to gulp in air.

It was all about speed now. The bolt croppers snapped the padlocks but in the adrenaline rush they pushed too hard on the roller-shutter door, the corrugated steel flying upwards and rattling against the top of the frame.

They froze and had listened to seconds of blissful silence before their ears were blasted by an explosion of noise.

The siren was directly above them, the piercing screech so loud it was physical.

They dashed inside, gave themselves moments to adjust to the darkness and settled on what they needed.

One pressed 'send' on his mobile and a pre-prepared text pinged into cyberspace.

The high-pitched whine of a Ford Transit engine at its limit came seconds later, then the smash and crash of metal against metal as the van rammed its way through the seven feet high gates, sending them clattering onto the concrete.

Alongside the open shutter the van's front end nose-dived, tyres squealing and smoking, and the gearbox crunched into reverse. The van raced backwards into the storage unit, the driver out of the cab and flinging open the back doors before the rubber of the back wheels had stopped smoking.

'Move it,' he shouted, glancing at his watch as he ran back to the driver's seat.

Four items were placed in the back, the two black-clad figures jumped in, and the van roared off, back doors swinging against their hinges before they were slammed shut.

It was less than four minutes since the fence had been cut. They raced away into the open countryside, slowing down and stopping at a pre-selected lay-by on a quiet country lane, the driver out in an instant to remove the false plates.

'So you've got him identified then?' Sue said, bent down, loading the washing machine.

Ed wiped toast crumbs from his chin and picked up a mug of lukewarm tea from the kitchen bench. 'Yeah we have.'

Ed didn't know which hurt the most. His head from lack of sleep or the stab wound scar on his neck.

Sue turned the dial, pressed 'on', and stood up to face him.

'Motive?'

Ed shook his head.

Jesus, let me pull myself together woman.

Ever since he'd involved her in the investigation into the missing Asian girl she'd thought she was the new Clarice Starling. She had even started reading true crime books.

Water flowed into the washing machine.

'As we'll tell the media we're following a number of lines of inquiry.'

Ed took his suit jacket from the back of the chair, put it on and straightened his tie.

'Which is code for you don't know who's done it,' Sue told him.

'Just like every murder inquiry in the beginning,' Ed headed for the door. 'This one's no different. I'll see you tonight.'

'I'll make a chicken curry. It'll be in the pan if you're late.'

On the plus side, involving her in the investigation had at least given her an insight into his world and she had been slightly less aggressive towards his long hours. Slightly. It still didn't stop her being moody and short-tempered, especially if she got Sam into her head.

He walked to the door, hoping the 'S' word didn't come up.

If Sue discovered Sam had chosen the multi-coloured Paul Smith scarf she'd likely tie it around his neck and throttle him. To throw her off the scent, he would wrap it himself. It would be the usual dog's dinner but Sue would recognize his hopeless handiwork. She might just be convinced the scarf was his idea.

Driving to HQ he turned his mind to Curtis' video. He may have shot it but that didn't mean he wasn't involved. Ed thought it was a little too coincidental. Curtis just happened to be at the garage when his abuser was brought there to be executed. That said, any interview with Curtis about the abuse would have to be sensitive.

'Morning,' Ed said, walking into the HOLMES room. 'Anything new?'

'Not really,' Bev answered, looking up from her computer. 'Usual shit through the night. Few drunks locked up, the usual once a year Christmas party idiots. Oh and a strange one, highways depot turned over, two road signs and a couple of portable traffic lights stolen.'

'Strange is right,' Ed said, as he walked to the kettle.

Bev answered the desk phone a minute later, put her hand over the receiver, and called to Ed.

Ed took the phone. 'Ed Whelan.'

'It's Jill Brown. Sorry to bother you but Curtis has shown up. He's in a state. Can you pop over?'

'Give me an hour Jill.'

He handed the receiver back to Bev.

Bev looked at him, all sarcastic smile and wide eyes. 'So who's Jill? Didn't want to give me her name.'

'Nobody you need to worry about.'

Bev opened her mouth to respond, but the door burst open and Sam stormed in.

'Grab your coat Ed, two more bodies.'

Everybody looked up from their desks.

'Anonymous call,' Sam said. 'Bev, get hold of Peter Hunt and cancel the press conference. Then get all staff back here on stand-by.'

Bev nodded.

Ed put on his long overcoat.

'I'll update you as soon as I know what we've got Bev,' Sam told her. 'Get onto the control room. Speak to the call taker who took the phone call. I want one of ours to take a statement off them. If there's any problem with the control room Inspector let me know.'

'Where to?' said Ed, walking towards her.

'The old abattoir.'

Dean Silvers pulled up outside Scaramangers, slammed the van door and walked across the car park.

Harry Pullman was in the cellar watching the CCTV recording.

'Let's have a look,' Silvers said, wearing nothing but jeans and t-shirt despite the snow flurries.

Harry hit play.

Silvers watched Mat Skinner march across the car park, Mekins with him, then studied the images from the car park and inside the pub.

'I'd have sent him back with that bat rammed up his arse if I'd been here,' Silvers finally took his eyes from the screen. 'You spoke to Billy?'

'He came round last night when I was still out and rang this morning. Full of apologies. He reckoned Mat did it all off his own bat, pardon the pun. I'm not sure Mat would make that call without Billy's say-so.'

'Either way something has to be done now,' Silvers said. 'You put the call into the police?'

'All done,' Harry told him. 'We'll make a move but not yet.'

'How's John?' Silvers asked.

'Upstairs in the flat with Tara. Been there all night.'

Silvers smirked.

'Will you go and restock?' Harry asked him.

He counted out £400 from the stack of £20 pound notes Billy Skinner had left. 'That should keep you going.'

'Why would they smash their own stock?'

'Simple,' Harry told him. 'Shows they can do what they like. We're next if Mat gets his way.'

'Like fuck. No point waiting for them. We'll hit them first.'

They heard the door open and walked upstairs to the bar, the barmaid not due for another half hour.

'A pint if you please landlord.'

'As I live and breathe, Detective Superintendent Reynolds.'

'Retired.'

Harry looked at his watch.

'Bit early, even for you Ray. Not even eleven yet. How's tricks?'

The two men shook.

'You know, plenty of time on my hands,' Reynolds said. 'Just thought I'd grab a pint. None of that lager shite. Pint of hand-pull. Preferably a milk stout saying as it's winter. That's if you've got anything. You seem short on the optics.'

'This is my nephew Dean,' Harry told him. 'He's just going out to restock.'

Silvers nodded at Ray.

'The last time I saw you, you were riding a three-wheeler.'

'People grow up Mr. Reynolds,' Silvers started to walk out. 'Nice to see you.'

'So what happened?' Reynolds was sat on a bar stool, bent forward, and sipping at the creamy white head of his stout.

'Mat Skinner smashed the place up, fucking idiot.'

'Why?'

'Cos he can. His dad's apologised, said Mat was acting off the reservation so to speak but…'

'Nobody moves without Billy's say-so,' Reynolds finished for him.

'That's about the size of it. Much planned for Christmas?'

Reynolds eyes lost a little focus.

'Not really. It's a time for family and I haven't really got one. Wife dead, almost two years now, and no kids more's the pity. I'll just have a quiet day.'

Harry dried his hands on a white cloth. 'What about your sister?'

'Lorraine? She's invited me to stay. Lives in York now but she's married to an arsehole who grates on me and their young ones aren't much better. Rather stay here and fly solo.'

'Well we're open for a couple of hours on the lunchtime if you fancy it.'

'I might just do that.'

Ray Reynolds turned his head as the door opened and saw the look of shock on the new customer's face. 'Bloody hell John.'

John Elgin approached the bar. 'Alright Ray.'

They shook hands.

'Aren't you going to introduce me to your friend?' Ray said.

'Tara, Ray. Ray, Tara.'

'Do you fancy a drink love?' Ray asked.

'I've got to go,' Tara said. 'Arranged to meet my study group later this afternoon, but thanks anyway.'

'Mine's a Peroni,' Elgin said.

Tara walked out.

'Still like them young then?' Ray said.

'Man needs a bit of fun sometimes, no harm in that.'

'No harm at all as long as your missus doesn't find out.'

'Anyway what you doing here?' Elgin said.

'Catching up with an old mate.'

'Didn't know you had any.' He looked at Harry, nodded at the bar devoid of stock. 'All sorted?'

'I was telling Ray. Billy said it was nothing to do with him. Mat was acting off-piste.'

'A likely story,' Elgin said and raised the glass to his lips. 'Cheers.'

'Are you totally off your head?' Billy Skinner shouted, standing behind his desk in Pussycats, hands on the leather inlay and leaning towards Mat who was stood to attention before him.

'Were you coked up?' Billy's face was crimson. 'Snorting with your faggot mate?'

The office door crashed open. Mat jumped and looked over his shoulder.

Mark and Luke each gripped a handle of a wheelchair, Stuart McFadden behind them with a pick-axe handle pointing at the ceiling.

Slumped forward in the rolling chair, held in place by a makeshift seatbelt of nylon rope tied around his chest, was Geoff Mekins. His face was pulped and caked in dried blood, his wrists bound to the arms of the chair.

'My God,' Mat shouted, raw emotion contorting his face as he spun around and stepped forwards.

'Don't you fucking move,' Billy hissed, a sovereign-ringed finger pointing at Mat. 'If you weren't my son you'd be in a chair next to him but rest assured your stupidity has cost this puff his life. Thank your mother it hasn't cost you yours.'

He nodded at McFadden who brought the pick-axe crashing down on Mekins' right forearm. The crack echoed like a dry twig snapping beneath a heavy foot.

'Bastard,' Mat screamed but never moved.

Geoff Mekins groaned from the pit of his stomach, no fight left in him. If he were a dog, a caring owner would put him to sleep. Mat Skinner's lover would die but a humane send-off wasn't in the script of his short and painful future.

Billy spoke to Mark and Luke. 'Keep him in the basement until it's dark then sort out our friendly fisherman.'

Mat whispered 'bastard,' the word almost lost in a raking sob as tears slid down his cheeks.

Billy kept looking at his other two sons.

'And make sure he's conscious when you weigh him down and throw him overboard.'

He turned to face Mat. 'You might want to start shagging birds. They'll not talk you into the kind of stupid stunt you pulled last night. Now fuck off and don't even think of touching lover-boy on the way out.'

CHAPTER SIXTEEN

Ed drove through the gates and nodded at the young uniform cop standing just inside them. For once they had beaten SOCO to the scene.

Edmundson's abattoir had been closed for years, a decaying building with broken windows, rotten doors and lead stripped from the roof. What remained still stunk of animal flesh.

'Enough to turn you veggie,' Sam said. 'Imagine them all coming here, slaughtered and cut up.'

'Thc veggies?'

Sam sighed. 'Lack of sleep hasn't dulled your wit.'

Behind them they heard an engine and turned to see the white SOCO van pull onto the car park, Julie Trescothick behind the wheel.

'May as well get suited up,' Sam said.

White paper suits on, the three of them went into the building.

Hanging upside down from a metal girder were the bodies of two men. Blood had pooled on the concrete floor directly below their heads, their faces white, drained of any colour.

'The video is on its way,' Julie said.

'That's fine,' Sam nodded. 'We won't touch anything.'

The metal girder looked out of place.

'That's new,' Ed said. 'You can tell by the welding and anyway, the scrappers would never have left it.'

Sam looked at the floor where in front of the pools of blood two leather wallets, one brown, one maroon, were neatly laid out.

'Same again,' Sam said. 'The killers want us to know who these guys are. Don't want us wasting time on ID.'

'And this time they want us to know they're paying for something,' Ed said, pointing to a piece of paper stuck onto the girder between the bodies.

The child-like handwriting was reddy-brown and the message brief…

GUILTY.

'They weren't going to run out of ink,' Ed said, nodding at the blood on the floor.

Sam told Julie she wanted the wallets as soon as they could be moved.

Back outside the gates she lit up.

'This is getting weird,' Sam said through smoke. 'Two this time, another disused building, more evidence of planning, especially if you're right about that girder being new.'

Ed put his hands in his pocket. 'That should be easily sorted. Just get a welding inspector off the Expert Witness Register. They'll be able to tell how old the welds are, and how good they are.'

'Good shout,' Sam nodded. 'Get Bev on that but ID is the big thing here.'

She answered her mobile, the call from Bev.

'That's fine. We're on our way back now.'

She turned to Ed. 'Councillor Elgin just walked into Seaton nick saying his grandson wants to make a complaint of sexual assault against our two friends in there. Question is how the hell does he know anyone's dead?'

'I got an anonymous phone-call into my office. My secretary put it through to me.'

John Elgin was in the front office interview room with his daughter and grandson. They sat in the only three chairs.

'Oliver told me last week what was happening,' Elgin said. 'That one of the men was called Julius. He couldn't remember the name of the other one but it sounded Dutch.'

'Dutch?' Sam said.

'Thank the Premier League for allowing kids to guess nationalities from names…I wanted to report it immediately but he didn't, understandably.'

Oliver looked younger than his 13 years, undernourished even, the black-framed spectacles dominating not just his face but his whole body. He had not looked up since Sam and Ed walked into the room.

'If Oliver is prepared to tell us what happened I'll arrange a specialist interview in a room nicer than this,' Sam said. 'Oliver?'

The young boy nodded without looking up.

'Don't worry Oliver,' she told him. 'You've done nothing wrong or anything to be ashamed of.'

The boy nodded again.

'Mr. Elgin, would you come with me please? Ed can you put the call in?'

Sam walked outside. The icy wind numbed her head, by her calculation a Force 4 on the Beaufort scale.

'Mr. Elgin, who rang you?'

'I have no idea.'

'But why ring you? They must have known about Oliver. So who have you told?'

Elgin looked offended.

'Chief Inspector it seems to me you are implying I had something to do with the death of those animals.'

'Did you?'

'Absolutely not and I resent the implication.'

Sam leaned closer to him. 'And I resent having the piss taken out of me. Make sure you're not doing that. For the last time I'll ask you again, who called you?'

'I have no idea,' Elgin snapped. 'Now with your

permission I'd like to go and sit with my daughter and grandson.'

After he had gone, Sam considered going into the CID office but thought better of it. The briefing could wait another ten minutes. A walk in the cold would clear her head. She ambled along the High Street, sidestepping the people who stopped suddenly when something caught their eye in a shop window.

Was Elgin involved? Was the anonymous call a lie? But if he had ordered retribution why had Scott been killed? There was no suggestion Scott had ever abused Oliver. Maybe someone wanted to ingratiate themselves with the councillor, Sam considered.

Jill Brown answered the door, her voice quick and quivering. 'I had no idea Ed.'

Her red cheeks and swollen eyes indicated Curtis had told her everything.

'No wonder he never wanted to go,' Jill sounded tortured. 'I was leaving him with a monster.'

Ed's voice was calm and full of easy authority.

'Let's go inside Jill. It wasn't your fault anymore more than it was Curtis'.'

Curtis was sitting in the front room. He spoke the second he saw Ed.

'I wanted to tell my mam everything before I told your lot. I needed to speak to her first. It all came back to me and I wanted to tell her, but I'm not sorry he's dead. Those blokes did the world a favour.'

Ed wanted details, starting with how long Dean Silvers had left before the van turned up.

'Not long,' Curtis said. 'Five minutes.'

'Could Dean have been one of the three men?'

'Don't know.'

'Is all this necessary Ed?' Jill said. 'He's been through so much.' 'You rang me Jill,' Ed faced her. 'What do you want me to do?'

'Keep Curtis out of all this. He's vulnerable, an addict. I don't want him to go to court.'

Ed could sympathise but he had to be straight, make it clear Curtis had found a body, never mind that the corpse was his abuser.

'I can't keep him out of this even if I wanted to,' Ed said. 'You of all people should know that.'

'Will it all come out Ed?' Jill's eyes were pleading.

He understood her concern, but telling her what she wanted to hear would come back and bite him.

'Probably,' Ed told her, the best he could do. 'We'll need a statement off Curtis telling us what he saw at the garage, how he videoed it. Then, if he wants, he can tell us what Scott did to him, but that's his call. We'll not force him to speak.'

'Right listen up.'

Sam marched towards the front of the room, the silence from the detectives immediate.

'Two victims...Julius Pritchard and Hans van Dijk. Family Liaison are with Julius' family now, Hans has no family according to his employment records at the university. I want to know who they were, what they were, how they were connected to each other, how they got to the old abattoir.'

Sam paused for effect.

'This was a premeditated murder, well planned and meticulous in its execution. These two guys were strung up, upside down and had their throats cut. Above them in blood was written 'GUILTY'.'

She looked around at the staring faces.

'Guilty of what? There's a suggestion of sexual abuse, but that's all it is at the minute, a suggestion.'

'Is it linked to Jeremy Scott?' Paul Adams asked.

'Too early to say, but there are glaring similarities. Isolated locations, locations that must have been identified prior to the victims being taken there. There's work needed around that Bev.' Sam sat on the edge of a desk.

'See if anyone has noticed anything unusual in those locations over the past few days, especially vehicles. We know Scott was taken there in a Ford Transit, but what about these two? Let's find out where Julius and Hans were last seen and who they were with. Remember the golden rule, the more we know about the victims, the more we know about the killers.'

'More than one boss?

All eyes turned to look at the young detective standing at the back of the room.

Sam smiled. 'Can't imagine one person kidnapping and stringing someone up alone, never mind doing it twice. We are looking for more than one. We know there were three people involved in Jeremy Scott's abduction and murder.'

The door opened and Ed walked in.

'Looks important but can it wait?' Sam said.

Ed shook his head and came to the front of the room.

'Curtis Brown's heard on the grapevine one of the victims of our two string-ups is the grandson of a councillor.'

Sam was underwhelmed: 'Not something we don't know already.' 'Absolutely,' Ed said. 'But that's not what's spooked Curtis. He's heard the councillor's connected to the one and only Billy Skinner. He's terrified he's given us a video implicating the family.'

CHAPTER SEVENTEEN

Pixie Carlton trudged towards the caravan on a field high above the sea, the Mercedes parked alongside. The car looked older than he remembered.

He fished in his wax jacket for more painkillers. His left hand to that point in his life had been used for nothing other than natural balance; even using his left pocket was alien to him.

The bruising on his back, like the swelling to his face, would eventually go, but he'd have to adjust to one hand without fingertips, what he'd heard called a 'life changing' injury.

He used the bend in his right arm to grip the plastic bottle of Fanta orange, unscrewed the lid with his left hand and washed down the painkillers. Putting the top back on was too much effort. He lobbed the bottle into the hedgerow. He looked up, dark clouds moving at speed towards the sea, and smiled. His deceased parents, both ardent environmentalists, would have done their nut, but needs must.

Declan Doherty answered his knock at the caravan door dressed in pinstripe trousers and maroon braces over a washed out, white singlet vest.

'You're a sight for sore eyes,' Doherty grinned. 'Last time I saw a bandage like that was after Appleby Horse Fair when some dozy bastard dropped a paving stone on his hand.'

Pixie smiled. 'Never tried riding a horse carrying concrete.'

Declan stepped outside laughing, his bare feet immediately wet from the grass, and slapped Pixie's back. His laughing stopped when Pixie doubled over, shrieking in pain.

'Bloody hell I'm sorry young man.'

'It's okay,' Pixie whispered, rasping for breath and standing straight.

'Who is it Pa?' his wife shouted from somewhere inside.

'The young lad from last night.'

The caravan bounced into life, the sound of stomping feet mixed with high-pitched shrieks.

'Give us a shout when you're decent and I'll bring the lad in for a brew.'

Declan looked at Pixie. 'You caused quite a stir amongst my girls.'

Pixie reddened.

'I didn't mean any offence and I haven't come to impose,' he said. 'I've just come to say thanks, you know, for what you did for me last night, and to return your clothes.'

He handed a carrier bag to Declan.

'Don't mention it and I didn't mean to sound offensive when I said you caused a stir.'

Doherty's face beamed. 'It was really funny watching them all stare at the same place.'

He looked at Pixie's crotch and laughed again.

'Even the wife was turned on.' Declan winked. 'You did me a favour there son.'

Pixie managed a weak smile and stepped back. He didn't need another back slap.

'We're all decent,' a shout came from inside.

'You look as if you could do with a brew,' Declan turned and opened the door. 'The missus will read your leaves afterwards. See what lies ahead.'

Pixie followed him into the caravan and immediately looked down at the carpet, his cheeks burning. The women wore more make-up than clothes, the lace night dresses on the granddaughters tight and revealing.

All the women were keen to hear about Pixie's treatment. Tea was drunk, the hospital account given and everything dissected before Declan suggested a walk.

'Listen son you need to lie low for a while,' Declan said as they walked away from the caravan towards the cliffs. 'You seem decent. The Skinners are not. If the fancy takes them they'll do you again just for a laugh.'

Pixie chewed his lip, the colour drained from his face.

'Do they know where you live?'

Pixie looked up, locked his eyes on Doherty. 'That's where they picked me up.'

'Rented you said?'

'Yes.'

'Get your stuff and get the hell out of there.'

Pixie realised it was the smart move but where would he go?

'Where to?'

'You're the estate agent,' Declan said. 'You tell me.'

The stumps on Pixie's right hand felt like they were on fire. He wished he'd opted for the sling.

'It's not that easy,' he told Declan. 'You need references, a bond.'

Declan said he wouldn't know, had never had to pay rent.

'You done much camping?' he asked Pixie.

'As a kid.'

'I've got a tent in the van, old but still waterproof. You can camp here with us. We'll be around for a week or so. The Skinners wouldn't dare come here and in a couple of days there'll be more of us arriving. Go home, get your things and buy a sleeping bag.'

'Why you doing this?' Pixie was touched.

Doherty's face darkened, something frightening filling his eyes.

'Because I fucking hate Billy Skinner.'

'How does Curtis know that?' Sam said, jumping away from the desk, thoughts moving as fast as a racehorse out of the stalls.

'You know this place,' Ed said. 'Not many secrets but we're not always privy.'

The rest of the officers in the briefing room were trying to play catch-up.

'That opens up another can of worms,' Sam told Ed. 'I can see why Skinner would want a local councillor in his pocket, but would he kill for him?'

'Skinner himself, probably not, but there's plenty would do it for him,' Ed said. 'And if Elgin's the councillor in question and Skinner thought it would earn him extra brownie points, it's more than possible.'

Ed pulled out a chair and sat on it while it was still rolling.

Sam was back at the desk, leaning against the edge, facing the room.

'We need to trace the anonymous call to Elgin, if it was ever made,' she said. 'He's certainly got enough motive.'

Dead men couldn't argue their innocence, Sam knew, but if the allegations were true, they had three paedophiles, all of them taken out execution-style.

She looked down at Ed who was writing in his blue hard-backed A4 notepad.

'Raise an action,' she said. 'I want to know if there's any link between these three, however long ago. Like everyone else in this room I don't like coincidences.'

'I might be able to help there ma'am,' one of the Intelligence Unit detectives spoke up.

Sam looked at him. She nodded for him to continue.

God I hate being called ma'am.

'Julius lives with his wife and two kids, both under ten.'

Nobody raised an eyebrow. They were dealing in facts, not emotions.

'Works from home; self-employed web designer. Kids go to private school. He volunteers at a hospice.'

'Very public spirited,' Sam said, walking towards the window. 'Always a cloak to hide behind.'

'We've got nothing on him,' the detective continued. 'But Jackie Mason, Sergeant Mason, remembers the name from about 15 years ago. Locked up on suspicion of flashing to a young boy. Jackie was custody officer. He can't remember much else, not even the arresting officer.'

'Okay,' Sam said. 'Let's ask around the nick see if anybody else recognises his name or the others. Leave it open ended. Just get something on the daily briefing asking for Officers Reports from anyone who has had any dealings with him or knows if anyone else has had any dealings with him, however historical. Do it for all three victims.'

A few in the group shook their heads.

Sam picked up on it immediately, moved away from the window, and stood almost to attention.

'Whatever else they might have been, they were all victims of a horrible death. Some of you might be thinking they got what they deserved but our job is to find their killers. Understood? The day we turn a blind eye we may as well turn the lights off and go home.'

The nods told Sam she had made her point.

'Right, let's get cracking.'

Another camera flash had Sam blinking again.

Telling the press about one execution would have got their attention; briefing them about three guaranteed a hungry full house.

Saturday or not, all the media channels and major newspapers were present, TV crews as always trying to hog the best spots in the crowded room.

'So I have a number of appeals today,' Sam said. 'Firstly has anybody seen any suspicious behavior around the disused buildings that used to be O'Grady's garage or Edmundson's abattoir…people, vehicles, anything?'

Sam paused to allow her words to sink in.

'I am also interested in anybody who may have come into contact with the victims or knows anything about them. I want to build up a picture of them and their habits and I'm appealing for help in that regard.'

More camera flashes.

Sam watched the assembled throng writing their notes, the print reporters no doubt in shorthand. They tended to be old school.

'Finally I want to hear from anybody who saw a white Ford Transit in the vicinity of The Avenue last Thursday. Thank you.'

With plenty of seasoned operators among the press corps, the rain of questions was never likely to be less than a heavy downpour.

Sam would have expected nothing else. She was ready.

'Are all three deaths linked Chief Inspector,' a reporter from one of the nationals fired first.

'As you would expect that is a line of inquiry we are following,' Sam said. 'Nothing, as yet, has been ruled in or out.'

'So is there a serial killer in our midst?'

The question, shot from a tabloid hack who knew the ropes, had 'give us a headline' in 10ft tall letters. It was also a moment where Sam needed to watch her step.

'I can't say that at this time,' she answered smoothly. 'Yes there are similarities in the killing sites in that they are disused buildings on the edges of the town but it really is too early to suggest the same person or persons is responsible.'

'But it is a possibility?'

Here we go, Sam thought.

'In life everything and anything is a possibility, but as I've just said it is too early, far too early, to suggest these deaths are linked.'

It was the best and safest response but Sam knew she would be reading 'Is A Crazed Serial Killer On The Hunt?' headlines tomorrow.

'Were the victims known to the police?'

'That is another line of inquiry,' Sam said. 'I'm sure you understand that we are at the early stages of the investigation. As soon as I have more information I will let you know.'

A young woman wearing a Sky zip up and, Sam noticed, beautiful drop earrings, raised her hand.

'Jeremy Scott was known to the police, albeit many years ago and albeit in Hampshire,' she began. 'He stood trial on charges of child sex abuse. Does that give you some idea of the killer's motive?'

Another tricky one but a question Sam knew would be coming.

'He did, but as you quite correctly point out, that was many years ago and he was acquitted…to link his death to him being cleared is again premature at this stage.'

Drop earrings held her pitch and fired again when she had Sam's eyes.

'Julius Pritchard and Hans van Dijk were running a junior football league,' she said. 'Perhaps their interests in young boys may be a factor in their deaths.'

Like any good journalist, she had done her research. Sam was impressed.

'I do not want to speculate,' she answered, the theme unchanged but now reinforced. 'I deal in facts. Speculation and what may turn out to be unfounded allegations help nobody, least of all the newspapers which make them. Speculation is a dangerous thing for all of us.'

Sam hoped the response would end the line of questioning.

Every journalist, she expected, knew the case of a high-profile murder suspect hung out to dry in sections of the national press in the days after his arrest. The man was innocent, no charges were brought and a handful of major media names found themselves paying him significant sums for libel. The fallout had left a mark.

As the questions moved to safer ground…how many officers were involved in the enquiry, had causes of death been established, was there an appeal hotline...Sam knew she had been right.

Harry Pullman was lying on the settee watching Sam Parker's press conference go live on one of the 24-hour news channels, Dean Silvers on an armchair close by.

'What gets me is who gives a fuck about a few nonces?' Dean said, tugging the ring-pull and feeling lager spurt onto his fingers. 'They'd be better off catching these dirty bastards when they're at it not the ones who sort them out.'

He put his legs on the coffee table.

'Look at her, appealing for this and that. Waste of time and money.'

Dean took another mouthful of lager as Harry sat up.

'Billy Skinner,' Harry said.

'Told you, take him out, sit back and watch the fireworks,' Dean shrugged. 'Mat won't know where to start and when he finally starts somewhere, it won't be with us. He'd never believe we had the balls.'

'Luke might though,'

'Doubt it,' Dean tipped the can again, belched softly. 'He'll want to cut a deal. Mat will be running around like madman's shite but not Luke.'

Harry said: 'You seem sure.'

Dean downed the lager, crushed the tin, and wiped his chin.

'I've spoken to them all at some time,' he said. 'Luke's smart, Mark's thick and Mat's an arsehole. Likes one or two as well.'

He sniggered.

'I heard Mat's marrying Geoff,' Harry said. 'Not that Billy's taken with the idea.'

'Would you be if I minced in here and said I was marrying a bloke?'

'Would make no odds to me,' Harry told him. 'Live and let live. So Luke's our man?'

Dean reached for another cold can at his feet, condensation running like summer rain to a damp patch on the floor.

'He's the brains so he'll want allies when it kicks off. We need to be sure we're in that band of brothers.'

CHAPTER EIGHTEEN

ED WAS STANDING with his right hand on a desk, bent over looking at a TV screen, when Sam walked back into the HOLMES room.

'Everything okay?' he asked.

'Fine,' Sam said, exhaling loudly. 'The Assistant Chief pulled me in the corridor after the press conference.'

'And?'

'The usual. Do you need more resources? How's it going? What are your lines of inquiry? Are the deaths related? How much are you spending?'

She paused, rubbed her eyes. 'But all roads lead to Rome. In this case Rome being how long will it take to get it sorted?'

'In that case,' Ed emphasised the word 'case', 'you might want to look at this. Rewind it Paul.'

Paul Adams hit a button and the TV monitor brought up a black and white image.

Ed pointed at the screen. 'There's Julius Pritchard.'

Sam bent down for a closer look and saw Julius walking along North Road. 'Who's he with?'

'Just watch for now,' Ed said.

Sam saw two men in gorilla suits grab Julius and force a mask on his head before one of them opened the back doors of a Ford Transit.

'Freeze that.'

Paul Adams hit a button.

Sam peered closer. 'Are they cuffing him?'

'Difficult to tell,' Ed said. 'We've watched it a dozen times but it looks like they've used something to restrain his wrists. Maybe cable ties. The quality of these cameras isn't getting any better, sadly. '

'Go on Paul.' Sam said, as she watched Julius thrown unceremoniously into the van. 'Ooh, bet that hurt.'

'No doubt,' Ed moved his eyes off the screen. 'Pretty gentle though when you think what was coming his way at the abattoir.'

Sam stared at the screen again as the two gorillas got into the back of the van.

'Rewind it Paul,' Ed said. 'Now watch closely Sam, but don't look at Julius, watch his mate this time.'

Sam locked everything onto the other figure.

'There,' Ed said, pointing at the screen.

Paul froze the footage.

Sam stared then under her breath whispered: 'Shit.'

'John Elgin speaking,' the mobile shaking in tandem with his hand as soon as he heard the voice on the end of the line.

'Councillor Elgin, star of stage, screen and CCTV,' Billy Skinner laughed. 'Not the biggest boy the girls have seen but certainly willing, for a more mature gentleman anyway.'

'What do you want?' Elgin's voice was laced with sour unease.

'Easy tiger,' Skinner serious now. 'I've got a new proposition. I've just negotiated the purchase of the old abattoir.'

'What, where those two bastards were killed?' Elgin's stomach felt like it was in a fast descending lift.

'Killed?' Billy Skinner was as calm as the sea on a still day. 'Don't do those upstanding citizens a disservice. They were doing us all a favour. I thought you'd be pleased the kiddie-fiddlers were dead.'

Does he know? Does this bastard know everything?

'You there John?'

'I'm here.' Elgin dropped into the armchair and rubbed his brow. 'What's this got to do with me?'

'Seems the owners are keen to sell,' Skinner told him. 'Hoped they'd make good apartments when they'd secured planning permission.'

'They failed twice.' Elgin exhaled, looked up at the ceiling and shook his head.

'They'd get it eventually,' Skinner paused. 'Anyway they've had a change of heart now, didn't fancy posh apartments being nicknamed The Slaughter House.'

The sinister laugh made him sound like the bad guy from a black and white pot boiler.

Elgin shivered: 'Why are you telling me this?'

'It'll be one of the first jobs on your list,' Skinner said. 'A new club. I'm going to call it Angels, a small tribute to whoever gave it to those two sacks of shit.'

'It'll never get through,' Elgin started. 'The police will object for sure and…'

'No excuses John.' Skinner's voice had changed, still conversational but Elgin could feel the aggression radiating down the connection. 'Would you like me to send you a copy of the tape? Or perhaps your lovely wife would like a preview before it hits YouTube?'

Another burst of laughter. 'I'll be in touch.'

Elgin dropped the mobile and slumped into his chair, a tidal wave of acid rising in his throat.

He took the stairs two at a time, barged through the bathroom door, and put his head in the toilet bowl. He hated the colour, 1970's avocado green. He hated it more when it reeked of disinfectant, his eyes watering as he vomited yellow bile.

He pushed himself up and saw an old man staring back in the vanity mirror, the eyes as lifeless as a dead fish, the forehead clammy and lined. He ran the cold tap and splashed icy water on his face.

The smell of the heavy pine disinfectant in the small room was harsh. The smell of his own fear was even worse.

He gargled cold water, spat it out, and squeezed toothpaste onto his brush with a shaking hand.

'I'm better than this,' the words said out loud bounced back from the mirror.

Elgin had been smart enough to make a mark, smart enough to put a blighted childhood behind him and survive.

He would survive now. He would find a way.

He began brushing his teeth slowly, rhythmically, and watched something flicker in the haunted eyes, something take hold and grow.

This time the voice was only in his head but every word burned like a flame.

Fuck you Skinner. Fuck you.

Like John Elgin, Mat Skinner stared into a small vanity mirror and felt alone. He was in the bathroom of the three-bedroom static caravan that had been the perfect bolt hole for him and Geoff…a sea view, a site that was open all year, and most importantly, anonymity. Mat filled his cupped hands with freezing cold water and soaked his face until it was numb then walked into the lounge, the water running down his bare chest. He picked up a bottle from the coffee table, stared out to sea through the rain splattered patio doors, and drank. Three mouthfuls had him spluttering, his throat on fire. He didn't like whisky but it was Geoff's drink of choice and this was his bottle. Staring at the waves thrashing against the lighthouse rock, he hoped whoever was taking Geoff to sea drowned as well. Certainly they needed to pay.

Mat had already known where he stood in the family. Even the proverbial blind man could see Luke was the favourite, the one his father always turned to for advice, the one he really trusted.

Mat took another mouthful.

The last desperate days had just hammered it home.

He was the oldest. He should be being groomed for the top job, but even his mother thought he was a hothead who was too wild to safely run the show.

Yet today, Mat knew, he had been worse than weak.

He'd walked head-down past Geoff's pleading eyes, walked past without a second glance, without begging for the life of someone he loved.

Some boss he'd make.

Mat had been on the boat many times, watched men already beaten to a pulp plead for their lives as their feet were manacled to a rope and rock; watched them try to shake free, heard the splash when they were thrown to the waiting water miles from shore.

Now it was Geoff's turn and he'd done nothing to stop it.

Mat wiped his eyes, took another slug, and dropped onto the settee. His shaking hands managed to light a cigarette and he blew smoke towards the flecked oatmeal carpet, suddenly remembering lino-floored caravans of his childhood, before statics the size of bungalows.

Contrary to what his father said or believed, Harry Pullman was ripping them off. A lifetime as an ant in their organisation, what the police now referred to as a 'crime family', enabled Harry to understand the real size of the Skinner pie. Now he had decided to take a bigger slice.

But his father was right about the nephew, Mat conceded. Dean Silvers was nothing if not ambitious.

He walked to the cupboard above the gas cooker and hunted for the unregistered Pay-as-You-Go mobile. He scrolled through the contacts list, found the pre-programmed number for Scaramangers, and hit the call icon.

As soon as the call was made he'd go for a walk and drop the mobile into the harbour.

The risk he was taking carried the ultimate price. A Skinner or not, if what he was about to say ever got out he'd be taking a one-way trip on a trawler.

CHAPTER NINETEEN

'LET'S SEE IT AGAIN,' Sam ordered.

She watched the footage and there was no doubt.

As soon as the mask was forced on Julius' head, one of the gorillas slipped another mask to the unidentified man alongside him. He took off his black cap, pulled the mask over his own head and then helped the others throw Julius into the back of the van.

'Where did the other gorilla go?' Sam said.

'The van's picked up on a speeding camera,' Ed told her.

'If you're telling me that, we've obviously got the film.'

'We have,' Ed said. 'All down to Paul.'

'Good work Paul,' Sam said. 'We got a photo of the driver?'

Paul handed Sam a blown up photograph. She stared at it. 'Not much chance of identifying him is there?'

'Not unless they're teaching gorillas to drive,' Ed said. 'But it's not all bad.'

'We've obviously got the number plate,' Sam turned to Paul.

'We have,' Paul told her. 'But it should be on a Range Rover. One of ours.'

'What?' Sam's jaw dropped. 'The cheeky bastards. So what's the good news?'

'Watch the gorilla who passes the mask to his mate.'

Paul replayed the video and Ed pointed at the screen.

'This one on the inside of the path. Look at him. Look how straight he walks. Remember how Jayne Culley said the man she saw at Scott's was ramrod straight, like he was on a parade ground?'

Sam stared at the screen. 'Same with him.'

'Exactly,' Ed said. 'Now look at where Julius is. He's walking on the inside. When they grab him he's got nowhere to go. He can't run onto the road because he's boxed in.'

'Deliberate,' Sam said.

'I would say so. But look,' Ed pointed again. 'There, they grab him right next to the van. This has been choreographed like a dance routine.'

'And our mystery man with Julius is pulling the strings,' Sam said.

'Would fit,' Ed agreed. 'Now watch it all again and count the gorillas.'

Paul hit play and Sam focused once more on the screen.

'Two on the path, a mask handed to Julius' mate makes three, and then military gorilla goes out of sight, probably to drive the van.'

She stood up straight. 'Three. The same number as Curtis filmed getting Jeremy Scott out of the van.'

They watched the now frozen screen without speaking.

'Jesus,' Sam broke the silence. 'We've got a gang of vigilante serial killers on a mission.'

'Where the fuck is he then?' Billy Skinner, sat behind his desk in Pussycats, his face redder than a curry-from-hell eating champion.

Luke, standing next to Mark, said he had no idea.

Skinner pulled a cigar from his drawer and rolled the No. 2 Montecristo between his thumb and index finger.

'How's the faggot in the cellar?'

'Unconscious,' Luke said. 'We'll gag him before we put

him in the boot just to be on the safe side. Boat's ready. Just waiting until the tide's right.'

Skinner tilted his head and sent smoke rings towards the ceiling. 'Good,' he said. 'Never liked that fucker anyway.'

He puffed his cheeks, pursed his lips, and let his thoughts drift between his eldest son and Marge.

She would go ballistic when she found out what they had done to Geoff Mekins.

Luke read his father's thoughts.

'Mat will be in bits at first but then he'll be raging,' he said. 'When he's like that there's no telling what he'll do.'

Skinner pictured his eldest son, the cold fury that coursed through him like a black river below a wafer-thin surface.

'You think he'll come after me?'

Luke stared at his father. 'That would be a big call, even for him. I don't think so but…'

Skinner folded his elbows, placed them on the desk, and leaned towards his sons. 'But what?'

'That's not to say he won't send someone else,' Luke told him.

Skinner leaned back, more smoke rings drifting gently apart on their way to the ceiling.

Who could Mat contract?

A million and one people, Skinner realised; wannabees looking to muscle in; hired help if the price was right; even one of his own would switch horses if Mat convinced them he could win.

Billy Skinner spun around in his chair and faced the wall, his back to his sons.

'Mark,' he said. 'Give us a minute.'

Mark stood without a word and walked out, closing the door softly behind him.

Luke would be the boss and he had no problem with that. He knew his place and was happy there.

Skinner waited for the door to close, sucked long and slow on the cigar, and turned back to face Luke.

'Mat's a fucking loose cannon,' Skinner spat out. 'I should

never have listened to your mother, never let him lose himself with that faggot Mekins.'

He rose, walked over to the oak unit against the wall, and picked up a photograph in a brushed chrome frame. He held it close to his eyes and studied it, him and his three sons, young teenagers then, stood on a riverbank fly-fishing. Marge had taken the picture.

'God knows I tried hard enough, gave him some responsibility, even threw a couple of girls his way,' Skinner said, his tone frosted with sadness. 'What did I get back in return? A queer for a son with more than wild hair up his backside.'

Luke had listened to his father, judging the moment to step in and speak.

'What do you want us to do?' he asked now.

Skinner gave the order with a look not words.

'Your mother can never find out,' he said when Luke nodded once.

'Sort the faggot downstairs first. Then find Mat.'

Don't miss your lover-boy too much, son. You'll soon be reunited.

Harry Pullman, beige sweatshirt and matching fleece bottoms, looked more like a gym rat than a pub licensee. He put the mobile in his sweat pants, walked to the end of the bar and sat on a wooden stool.

'A strange day son,' he said to Dean Silvers who was sipping on a Diet Coke.

'What's up?'

Harry looked around. No-one was close enough to overhear. 'Just had Mat Skinner on the phone.'

'You what?' Silvers stiffened his back like a weightlifter ready to clean and jerk his personal best.

Harry leaned closer to Dean. 'He wants to talk. Something's happened. I don't know what, but he was quiet, upset, not like him.'

Dean's fingers had tightened around his glass, Harry worried it would shatter any second.

'Calm down,' he told him. 'Let's just see what he has to say. He wants to meet. He's got a caravan up the Northumberland Coast.'

Dean stared into his glass, death grip relaxing. 'Could be a set-up.'

Harry shrugged.

'I don't think so,' he said. 'Told me his dad and brothers don't know about the caravan.'

Dean looked doubtfully at his uncle. 'And you believe him?'

Harry didn't pause, his mind already made up.

'Enough that me and you are going to drive up there now,' he told Dean. 'Get a shift on and finish your drink. We'll take my car.'

They were about to leave when the bar door opened.

John Elgin walked in, sober and clean-shaven and wearing a navy suit that had miles on the clock but was still pretty decent. The brown Paisley tie, though, was a fashion statement too far.

Harry Pullman turned towards him. 'If you scrubbed up for Tara, she's not here.'

'That tie looks like something you'd shit after a kebab,' Silvers said, grinning.

Elgin felt himself getting red. 'I'm off to a planning meeting…'

'On a Saturday teatime?' Harry shot him a 'like-fuck-you-are' look.

Elgin moved a stool close to them and waited until the barmaid was at the other end of the bar.

'I thought you might like to know Billy Skinner has bought the old abattoir.'

'Where the two beasts were found!?' Dean jumped in, his voice loud enough to have a few of the punters turning heads their way.

Harry hissed for him to either shut the fuck up or at least drop the volume.

Elgin got back to his news.

'Buy's only just happened by the sounds of it,' he said. 'He was straight onto the owners as soon as the bodies were found. Guessed they might be having doubts about converting a double murder site into top end apartments for professionals. He was right.'

When Elgin told them Skinner wanted to make the abattoir a bar called Angels as a tribute to the killers, Harry couldn't stop a bark of laughter.

'That's Billy Skinner all over,' Harry said. 'Credit where it's due John, you're very well informed. So what do you want us to do?'

Elgin loosened his tie, told them what they did was their call, that he was just giving them the heads up.

Harry Pullman stood and glanced around again. 'You still after that tape, John?'

Elgin nodded like a naughty toddler hoping his mother was about to forgive him.

'Why not save yourself a load of chew and just tell that pig-ugly wife of yours that you've been shagging?' Harry said. 'What's the worst that'll happen? She'll leave you and by Christ, that's a win-win situation.'

Silvers laughed but Elgin ignored him.

'It's not that easy,' Elgin told Harry. 'Out of spite she'll contact the council and the local rag. I'll be ruined.'

Harry looked at Dean, then back at Elgin, serious now.

'Better than taking on Billy Skinner,' leaving it hanging there.

Elgin pushed himself off the stool and moved his head closer to them.

'I'm not taking on the short arsed twat,' he said quietly. 'That's your job if you want it. I have to get the planning applications through and that's the same shit whether it's for him or you.'

Harry thought losing your reputation but waving bye-bye to a wife like Elgin's was the deal of the century, but then some people were strange.

'What time's your meeting?' he said now.

'Thirty minutes,' Elgin backed away from them. 'Why?'

Harry nodded. 'Me and Deano need to pop out but we'll be back by eight. Let's have a chat then. You never know, Tara might call in later.'

Harry winked but Elgin didn't notice. He was watching Dean Silvers smirk.

CHAPTER TWENTY

'OKAY,' Sam said. 'Get the image of Julius' mate enhanced but I don't hold out much hope. He's deliberately keeping his head down and his baseball cap's pulled low. Who else knows about this?'

'Other than the guy looking after the speeding cameras, nobody,' Ed told her.

'Paul, go and tell him not to breathe a word,' Sam said. 'If he's already told anyone else he'll have to track them down as well and tell them to keep their mouths shut. If I hear of anybody discussing this after...' Sam checked her watch, 'twenty minutes as of now, I'll have them doing career development in the worst poxy job I can find and as far from their home as I can manage.'

'Okay boss.' Paul stood up.

Ed followed Sam into her office and sat opposite her.

Sam opened her drawer, pulled out a couple of Mars bars.

'Okay let's think about it.' She lobbed a bar to Ed. 'There are a few new lines of inquiry springing up from that CCTV footage.'

'Trace and interview three gorillas,' Ed said, grinning as he ripped open the black wrapper.

Sam smiled back. 'Apart from the bloody obvious. See if

that van's captured on any other cameras, speeding, CCTV, anything. How the hell have they got the number plate?'

Sam stood, bit into the Mars, and paced the room.

'You can't just walk into Halfords without any documentation and ask them to make a plate up, so how have they got them?'

She chewed the chocolate and kept pacing.

'Next. Who was Julius with? Let's make some inquiries at the football thing he runs. Maybe the kids have seen his mate there.'

She stared out of the window, took another bite.

'Hans wasn't there when Julius was snatched, so when and where do they get him?'

Sam sat, put the last of the bar in her mouth and dropped the wrapper into the waste bin.

Ed chewed, waiting for Sam to speak.

'Let's do door-to-door around Hans' house. We now know when and where they got Julius so let's set the time parameters two hours before and two hours after that. Establish if any of Hans' neighbours saw anything suspicious in that four hour time window.'

Ed raised his eyebrows.

'What?' Sam asked.

'Time window? Really?' He leaned back into the chair. 'I've told you before about speaking that management shite. Talk like the tossers and your credibility's gone. We can just about cope with back-burner, but time window? What's next? Take that off-line, park that, run that up the flagpole.'

'Alright, alright,' Sam grinned. 'I apologise.'

'Don't get brainwashed, speak English,' Ed said. 'It's why the rank and file can relate to you. You're one of them.'

He leaned forward.

'You know what I overheard the other day in the corridor? It's my new favourite. Punch a puppy.'

'What?'

'Punch a puppy. Means do something that's despicable but good for business. You couldn't make it up.'

'Jesus. Right, I want to sort out another press appeal …'

'To launch the 'punch a puppy' campaign?'

Sam raised her hands and showed Ed her palms. 'Okay you've had your fun at my expense.'

She dropped her hands.

'I want to ask for witnesses who saw the gorillas. Maybe someone saw them without their masks getting out of the van, because let's be right they won't have walked far from that van. Why bother? They knew exactly what time their target was going to be there. All the 'friend' had to do was press send on a pre-typed text and the job's done.'

'Never mind walking like the military, this is military in the planning,' Ed said.

Sam put her elbows on the desk, cupped her palms around her chin.

'Would the driver draw attention to himself by driving around in a gorilla mask before the abduction?'

'Possibly,' Ed said. 'They've got the balls to be driving around on plates from a police vehicle.'

Sam pushed her chair away from her desk.

'Let's check CCTV on the off-chance. I'm not sure they'd be looking to draw any attention to themselves before they had to. At least we've got an image of his so-called mate. That's a start.'

Sam was cut short by her office phone ringing. Bev was on the other end of the line.

'Uniform have just attended a shout to a burnt out Ford Transit up the Zinc Road, near the old sea coal depot.'

'Bollocks,' Sam said. 'Notify SOCO. Get them up there to do their stuff.'

She put the handset down and told Ed about the van.

'Suggests it's served its purpose,' Sam said. 'Or they've got a replacement.'

Sam and Ed walked heads bowed through the downpour and ducked under the blue police tape, the water dropping onto their backs, their trousers already sodden, and the howling wind driving the rain into their faces.

The burnt out shell of a Ford Transit seemed to strangely fit the industrial wasteland where a decaying chemical plant and stubborn wildlife lived side-by-side, partners in some perverse eco pact.

The white foamed waves of the North Sea boiled against the black sky. Sam stared at the dark water and shivered as the wind chill ripped through her clothes. She always thought of the seas and oceans as timeless. That they were treacherous and without pity she knew all too well.

Julie Trescothick walked towards them, carrying something in her left hand.

'Present for you.' She handed Sam a polythene bag. 'Left near the van.'

The bag, still sealed, contained what appeared to be a brand new, unworn gorilla mask, the mouth hole with the ridiculous rubber teeth a mocking grin.

'Now they really are taking the piss,' Sam said.

She looked along the wind-battered beach. In the distance a landscape photographer, huddled under a huge golfing umbrella, peered into a camera lens atop a tripod.

Sam thrust her hands into her overcoat pockets and wished all she had to worry about was a weather photograph for the local news, even if the light was fading fast.

She didn't turn around when she spoke. 'Do we know where it was stolen from?'

'Yes, the VIN plate survived,' Julie said. 'Stolen from a boatyard in Hamble about four weeks ago. Not reported for a week as the owner was yacht racing in the Isle of Wight.'

Sam continued staring out to sea. She had sailed out of Hamble herself into The Solent and across to the Isle of Wight.

Her throat grew tight as she remembered berthing in Cowes Yacht Haven with its direct access onto the High Street; Tristram at the helm, her jumping onto the jetty with the mooring lines and tying bowline knots; the short walk to

The Anchor Inn, standing at the bar her body still swaying, legs still at sea.

She breathed deep, rubbed her eyes and turned around.

Ed walked around the van and stopped at the bonnet: 'Never imagined you yachties being white vans types.'

Sam moved closer to Ed, past caring about the rain. 'I never expected ageing, bald detectives to drive old VW camper vans, but there you go, takes all sorts…So were the thieves just lucky, or did they know the owner was going to sea for a week?'

Ed bent down and examined the dented front of the Transit but Julie told him it would be impossible to even roughly estimate when the damage had been caused, the fire having burnt the paintwork to the metal.

Ed stared at the driver's headlight then walked to the passenger headlight, looking at it closely.

Thank God the brigade saved the lights, he thought.

'Julie, get somebody to remove the headlights before it's towed away,' he said. 'Bag and tag them.'

'Thanks Julie,' Sam told her. 'We'll catch up later.'

Ed strode after Sam and the shelter of the car.

'Could they have watched him load up his boat?' Ed asked, turning the ignition, setting the heater to maximum.

'If they were in the yard, marina, whatever, anyone could see him victualling the boat and…'

'Vicking what?'

'Victualling,' Sam repeated. 'Loading the boat with food and supplies to you.'

'Aye aye captain'

Sam punched his arm. 'Less of the sarcasm, it doesn't suit you. I can't help it that I sailed.'

She rummaged in her handbag for a tissue and wiped her face.

'Christ I'm wet through.' She shivered and rubbed her thighs. 'Is the blower on full blast?'

Ed turned the fan up. 'It is now.'

Sam sat back into the seat, wishing like her Audi's it was heated.

'Why not just nick a van from up here?' she said now. 'It's a hell of a trek down to Hamble. Six or seven-hour drive. I've done it.'

She couldn't see the gang buying the van after it was stolen, too slick and switched on to involve someone else.

'They'd never risk getting bubbled,' Sam said, slipping into the police slang for being grassed or turned over by an informant.

She put her hands in front of the vent. What had her grandmother told her about putting cold hands on hot radiators? Something about chilblains? Sam would take her chances.

'It just doesn't add up,' she said. 'There'll be thousands of Transits between here and Hamble.'

Ed turned on the wipers and watched the rain.

'Least on a Saturday this weather's good news for the house-to-house teams,' he said as the blades and the zigzagging rivers of rain water did battle on the windscreen. 'Loads of people at home. Only daft buggers like us are out in it.'

Sam hunted her mobile from her handbag, hit speed dial, and reached Bev for updates.

Ed switched on the headlights, turned the car through 180 degrees, and was silently relieved his fingers and cheeks had finally defrosted.

'Cheers Bev,' Sam was saying. 'We're on our way back.'

Ed tuned the radio to TalkSPORT and waited for Sam to bring him up to speed.

'A neighbour saw two gorillas manhandling Hans down his path,' she said. 'They know he's a university lecturer so just thought it was some student prank.'

Then Sam suddenly remembered the Transit's headlights and asked Ed why they might be important.

'When we watched the CCTV I never saw any damage to the front end of that vehicle, probably because we weren't looking for it, but I distinctly remember both headlights being on.'

'Point being?' Sam said.

'There might not be a point,' Ed turned on the fog lights. 'But the makes were different when I had a look at the burn out. One was a genuine Ford headlight, the other a cheaper copy.'

'Good spot,' Sam was impressed.

Ed smiled, remembering the countless hours he had spent bringing his 1972 VW Camper van 'Doris' lovingly back to life.

'When you've been involved in restoring a vehicle you notice these things,' he told Sam. 'We can check with the owner. See if he damaged the vehicle and whether he replaced the nearside headlight. If he didn't, the gorillas did and they'll have had to buy it somewhere, hopefully locally.'

Sam was about to respond but Ed turned the radio up as the anchor announced a live update for Newcastle United.

Another goal and now 4-1 down at the Emirates to Arsenal, Santi Carzola riling the partisan commentator with a piss-take 'panenka' penalty, dinking the ball over the Newcastle goalkeeper in the 88th minute.

Ed hit the off button and grimaced.

Bloody football, as someone once said.

Ed's phone call to the registered keeper of the Ford Transit told him what he needed to know…it wasn't damaged when it was stolen; both headlights should be originals.

'So our killers have probably damaged the van and then replaced the headlight,' Sam said, looking up from her computer. 'Unusual.'

Maybe they didn't want to steal another van, didn't want to risk getting pulled by uniform for having a light out, Ed told her.

'Not that there's enough cops on the street these days to pull anyone.'

Sam wondered again how Ed could keep his anger-level so high and for so long.

'Any reports of Transits being involved in an RTC?' she asked, reaching into her handbag and taking out an oat bar.

Ed crossed his legs, leaned back, and eyed the snack with a mixture of hostility and suspicion.

'Always been good old-fashioned RTAs to me,' defiance in his voice. 'Road Traffic Accidents. No need to change it.'

'Jesus,' Sam gave him a weary smile. 'They're Road Traffic Collisions on the system so…?'

'Nothing there,' Ed told her, suddenly heading for the door. 'But give me a couple of minutes. I've just had a thought.'

Five minutes later he was back, carrying two mugs of coffee and speaking on the move.

'I remembered a message on the overnight log from this morning,' he said. 'Two sets of temporary traffic lights and two roadwork signs were stolen from a compound. The gates had been knocked off their hinges and there were glass fragments scattered on the ground.'

He put one coffee in front of Sam and sat down holding the other.

'So what's on your mind?' she asked.

Ed slurped the coffee and muttered 'bollocks,' the drink so hot it blistered his tongue.

'We believe the van belongs to the killers,' Ed said. 'That's purely and simply because there's a new gorilla mask next to it, still in its original packaging.'

Sam was silent, watching and listening.

'We can compare the glass fragments left at the depot to the glass in the original headlight and hopefully get a match.'

Sam stared over the rim of her mug, blowing on the coffee so she didn't repeat Ed's mistake, and asked if the glass had been recovered.

'It's getting sorted now,' Ed told her. 'If it is the same glass, why bother replacing a headlight if you're going to burn out the vehicle? Doesn't make sense.'

Sam stood and paced the office.

'If they've replaced the light they could have only done that this morning once the shops were open.'

Ed nodded and took a hesitant sip from his mug.

'So why within hours are they burning it out? What's happened that's made them alter their plan?'

Sam drank while she walked, working it through.

'If they replaced the light, that suggests they still needed the van,' the pieces falling into place. 'They had to burn it out so now they need to steal another! Get onto Control Room. Tell them we want to know about all stolen vans.'

Ed picked up the phone, said he was on it.

Sam leaned her back against the wall, thinking aloud again.

'What else have they got planned? What the hell are they going to do with the traffic lights?'

Ed had just replaced the receiver when the desk phone rang, Sam signaling she would take the call.

Ed stood up but she motioned for him to sit back down.

'Can I send an officer to see you,' Sam was saying. 'Okayyy…'

Ed picked up on the way Sam stretched out the word.

'Tomorrow?'

Sam looked at Ed, raised her eyebrows.

'See you then.' She put the phone on the cradle and grinned at Ed. 'Fancy a trip to Hampshire tomorrow?'

The short and sensible answer, Ed knew, was 'no.'

An away day to the other end of the country would go down like a £5 prostitute once Sue found out. Make the trip on a Sunday and he'd be in a full blown shit storm.

'Why?' he asked, dreading the answer.

'That was the headmaster from St Augustine, Jeremy Scott's old school,' Sam said. 'Wants to talk but he'll only talk to me. He has some information about Scott.'

Ed dropped deeper into the chair, the situation sinking in.

Whatever he said, tomorrow he was going to Hampshire.

How to the hell do I break that little zinger?

'More likely wants to keep the school out of it,' he grumbled, an air of resignation descending like smog.

'But we'd have gone to the school at some point,' Sam was

button bright, a long road trip hands down better than another day solo in the ice palace. 'May as well get it done.'

Ed sighed loudly, more for Sam's benefit than his.

The head had asked for Sam personally. If Ed was a betting man he'd take odds on he had something worthwhile to say.

CHAPTER TWENTY-ONE

Ed was driving through a downpour, windscreen wipers working overtime.

The destination was ciggie-break central.

'Thought you weren't bothered about smoking in the office on a Saturday?'

He glanced at Sam as he stopped his VW Golf at a junction.

'Bev's out and about with Paul,' Sam told him. 'May as well catch up in the park and have a smoke at the same time. Besides, it's Never Wright on duty today, and you know what that little shit's like with his anti-smoking agenda.'

Ed scowled, picturing Inspector Mick 'Never' Wright, a pedant with a nose so brown it looked varnished.

'Still got his wife under house arrest?' Ed moved off. 'Or does he trust her again?'

According to the in-house rumour-mill, Wright had discovered his wife had been having an affair.

Sam's grin was so wide the corners of her mouth almost met at the back of her neck. 'Still under house arrest according to Bev.'

'It'll be killing him,' Ed said. 'Was she shagging in their house?'

'Apparently.'

Ed imagined Wright fitting covert cameras around his home, remote monitoring on his laptop and checking his wife's mobile every chance he could get.

'Most intelligence gathering he'll have ever done,' he told Sam, who sniggered like a schoolgirl. 'Not that 'intelligence' and 'Never' belong in the same sentence.'

Ed indicated and turned left into the car park.

Paul Adams was huddled under a black Ping golf umbrella with Bev Summers, the hood of her Berghaus pulled over her head, cigarette poised.

'Standing in the rain just for a tab,' Ed said, shaking his head as he drew alongside.

'How did you get on with the call to Elgin's office?' Sam asked, getting out of the car and popping the button of a retracting brolly she had grabbed from the back seat.

The bright red canopy barely covered her head.

'And they say size doesn't matter,' Ed said, wiping rain off his shaved scalp.

Sam stuck her tongue out at him.

Bev blew smoke, said a check had confirmed Elgin's account of the call.

'Made from a phone box on the outskirts of town,' Bev said. 'No cameras for miles. Julie Trescothick's arranged to get it fingerprinted, but, her words not mine, don't hold your breath.'

'Okay,' Sam mentally ruled out usable prints. 'Anything from the house-to-house around Hans' place?'

She took the pack of Marlboro from her pocket, balanced the tiny umbrella under her chin, and sparked-up the cigarette.

Bev shook her head, rain filling the creases in her waterproof like miniature rock pools.

Sam turned to Paul: 'Does everybody know the score about the CCTV and the snatch on Julius?'

'Nobody will say a word,' Paul told her.

Satisfied, Sam smoked for a moment in the silence, the only sound the rat-a-tat of rain on the umbrellas.

'Me and Ed are going to the football pitches to see if the

CCTV picked up Julius and this so-called friend,' she said at last. 'You two check how we're doing with the number plates on the Transit, see if there are any more sightings on CCTV.'

Harry tapped the stop/start button on the Jaguar XF, still marvelling at how the automatic gear knob dropped elegantly into the centre console.

The caravan had raised decking, patio chairs and a table pulled close to the double white UVPC doors, the Northumberland coast less than a hundred metres away.

Harry got out of the car and inhaled the fresh sea air.

Seahouses was a place he'd visited often…a walk along the sandy beach, his favourite fish and chips in a polystyrene box, mushy peas, salt, and so much vinegar it made his eyes water.

Head down he walked towards the door. Had it been daylight he would have seen beautiful Bamburgh Castle and Holy Island. Now all he saw was Mat's Porsche.

He looked at the number plate, the last three letters GBH, the same letters as his father's BMW.

Prick.

Mat opened the door. Harry climbed the steps and walked into the caravan, Dean following.

'Sorry about last night,' Mat said, as Harry and Dean sat down on the sofa.

The caravan smelt like a whisky vat.

'You haven't called us all the way up here to apologise,' Harry told him straight out. 'So cut the crap and say what you have to say.'

'Drink?' Mat asked, sitting in the armchair opposite, reaching for the bottle of Scotch on the glass-topped coffee table, hand shaking like a wedding groom about to make his reception speech. 'Driving,' Harry said, settling into the settee, 'and he's my insurance in case other people turn up, so he doesn't want a drink either.'

He nodded at Dean.

Mat threw his head back and drained the newly poured shot in one.

Harry took in the puffy eyes, the reddened cheeks. The hair-trigger aggression that normally surrounded Mat Skinner had gone, exposing him for what Harry thought he really was…all piss and wind surrounded now not by his father's reputation but scatter cushions, tie back curtains, and two bronze Greek God table lamps with red shades.

'I haven't asked you here to fight,' Mat said. 'I know you were skimming…'

Dean bolted upright, a sprinter a fraction ahead of the starting gun. 'You cheeky twat!'

Harry put his outstretched arm in front of him, said settle down, said let's listen to the man.

'Geoff's dead,' Mat said, voice flat, empty.

Harry and Dean exchanged 'what the…' glances as Mat Skinner's body suddenly shuddered.

'Beaten half-to-death on the say-so of my father then thrown off a boat to finish him. Why? All because of what happened at your pub.'

Harry stared at Mat, in no rush to speak. When he did, he spoke slowly and picked his words. 'Whatever's happened to Geoff Mekins, it's not down to us.'

Mat reached for the scotch and poured himself a shot that would have put an elephant on its back.

'I know that and that's not the reason you're here,' he said. 'I'll never forgive my dad for Geoff. Mark and Luke went along with it, didn't fight my corner. They're nearly as bad.'

He drank long and slow.

Harry crossed his outstretched legs, watched but said nothing. He had no idea where this was going and although he didn't feel under threat, he knew better than to drop his guard.

Mat drained the whisky, licked his lips, and said: 'I'm looking for a partner.'

He glanced at Dean then back at Harry.

'Two partners I suppose. I'm taking over the Skinner empire.'

There was a stunned three second pause before Harry burst out laughing.

'You?' He shook his head. 'Taking over? How in the hell are you going to do that? Everybody knows the old man's lined Luke up for that job.'

Mat clenched his fist but that was the only movement.

'Things change.'

Harry leaned forward.

'I will have that drink after all,' he said. 'Just a small one though, touch of water.'

CHAPTER TWENTY-TWO

THE MANAGER of Shots and Saves had the squat muscular frame of a football full back; thirty something, sandy haired, and a former Premier League academy prospect who never made it beyond semi-pro.

Sam was directly behind Charlie Grey as they walked along the narrow corridor and up the stairs. She glanced at his firm buttocks

in the spray-on white shorts, her nose twitching at the smell of liniment seeping like invisible smoke from his tanned legs, a smell she'd loved ever since her father took her to watch the local pub team.

His small office housed a desk, a black swivel chair, two green plastic guest chairs and a huge screen computer that looked as out of place as an abacus in a university mathematics faculty.

Sam sat on one of the green chairs. Ed stood, fearing the flimsy looking plastic would collapse under his weight.

'Julius and Hans hired three pitches every Friday night. Seemed sound blokes to me,' Charlie said.

Ed tried to hide his disdain. Firstly, the man was clearly no judge of character and secondly, nobody involved in football should wear green sweatshirts; they belonged to Brian

Clough, his football management idol, and should have been retired with the legend.

Sam looked at Charlie, a brief image of his chest with the green sweatshirt removed flashing through her head.

'When people book pitches, what do they get?' she asked him, her head back in investigative mode.

'A seven-a-side all-weather pitch and a private dressing room with showers.'

He looked directly into Sam's eyes and smiled.

Christ he knows what I'm thinking.

'So, how many pitches do you have?' she asked.

'Twelve.'

'So twelve dressing rooms?'

'Correct.'

'And the CCTV cameras cover everywhere?'

'With the exception of the changing rooms,' another smile, 'for obvious reasons.'

Grey had already been told in a phone call to get Friday night's footage ready for the detectives.

'It's in another office,' he said. 'If you just wait here please.'

Ed waited until he'd left. 'Do you want to make it any more obvious?'

'What?'

'What?' Ed said. 'Put your bloody tongue back in.'

'You jealous?' Sam teased him.

Ed blushed, kicking himself he had made anything of it.

'Don't be stupid,' he said. 'I don't want to see you get hurt that's all.'

'Why?' Sam gave Ed a look. 'Sometimes a girl has to fall down and pick herself up.'

You could pick me up when I fall…

The door opened before Ed could speak.

'All sorted,' Charlie said.

'How many cameras do you have?' Ed asked more sharply than he meant, following Grey out of the office to make sure Sam wasn't directly behind him.

He is jealous!

'Two on this corridor, one at each end.' Grey pointed them out, each positioned above the door.

'So the corridor's covered.'

'Yeah, there's a camera in the bar upstairs and that's it.'

Grey led them into a windowless space, more a cupboard than a room, too small even for chairs. He bent down towards the video machine, pressed play, and a small TV monitor flickered into life.

Julius and the unknown man could be seen walking into the building. Julius was easily identified. The other man, head bowed and a baseball cap pulled down across his eyes, was not.

'Any more?' Ed asked.

'Yeah, you see them leaving.'

He fast-forwarded the tape but the result was the same - the mystery man kept his face hidden.

'Did anyone speak to them?' Sam asked, not looking away from the screen.

'I did,' Grey said. 'They weren't here long. Went onto the balcony I think, then left.'

'What did you say to them?' Sam pressed.

'Just, 'alright Julius'. His mate didn't speak.'

'What did he look like, his friend?' Sam asked him.

Grey squeezed his eyes closed and rubbed his nose.

'I never took much notice of him,' he said. 'Taller than Julius, medium build.'

He shrugged his shoulders and gave another smile.

Ed stared at him until the smile disappeared.

'Did the camera in the bar pick them up when they went onto the balcony?' Ed said, the sharpness this time absolutely intended.

Grey told them the camera had been broken for a couple of weeks, that they hadn't got round to a repair.

'Can we take the tape?' Sam asked.

Grey's hesitation belonged to a man who didn't know the answer, didn't know whether he had the authority to say yes or no.

'We'll take the tape,' Ed made the decision for him. 'If your boss has a problem he can ring. Thanks for your time.'

'My pleasure,' Charlie said, taking the card Ed offered but looking directly into Sam's eyes, his grin broadening.

Ed waited until he and Sam were outside, out of earshot of anybody else.

'I thought you'd be keen to give your card the way you were drooling over him.'

'I told you,' Sam serious this time. 'Pack it in.'

The walk back to the car was done in an awkward silence.

Ed opened up, slipped the key in the ignition, but didn't turn it. 'Julius' mate didn't want to be captured on camera did he?' he said, playing back the footage in his head. 'Talk about surveillance conscious.'

Sam lit a cigarette and asked Ed to start up so she could open her window.

He turned the ignition key, still thinking about the shots from the centre, then the footage of Julius' abduction.

'I can't put my finger on it, but the way he walks, our mystery man.'

He pulled away slowly.

'I've seen that walk before.'

Mat walked past the breakfast bar, ran some water into a glass, and poured whisky into it.

'I want my dad to die a slow death like Geoff,' he handed the glass to Harry. 'Mark and Luke will follow me.'

'I doubt that,' Harry sipped the scotch.

'Then they'll follow him.'

Harry glanced at Dean, then tugged at his earlobe, a show of bafflement for Mat's behalf.

'You'll forgive me if I don't get too excited, Harry said. 'I love Seahouses but I've driven all the way up here to listen to a fairy story. That island in the distance,' he nodded to the north, 'is called Holy Island not fucking Fantasy Island.'

He pushed himself off the settee. 'Come on Dean we're off.'

Mat's expression showed neither surprise nor anger.

'Wait,' he said. 'I'm the one out on a limb here. There's nothing stopping you going back and telling my father about this conversation. He doesn't even know where I am, doesn't know we have this place. I'm the one taking all the risks so at least you can hear me out.'

Harry stopped, looked at Dean again and sat back down.

'I know the business inside out,' Mat told them. 'My father might want Luke to take over because he's got the brains, but I know how everything runs…the clubs, the drugs, the girls. There's nothing I don't know. You two could be my right hand men.'

Harry's mind was starting to race, a chess player suddenly fearing a wrong move.

'And why would we want to do that?' he said, elbows on knees, chin in the palms of his hands, a show of calm on the outside.

'Forty per cent of the take,' Mat made his pitch. 'Forty per cent of everything.'

Harry tried, unsuccessfully, to calculate 40% of Billy Skinner's empire. He couldn't. It was too big to contemplate. He felt like he'd taken a punch to the gut.

'Why us?'

'My father's trusted you since you were kids,' Mat told him. 'My mother would understand why I would go to someone like you for advice, an older head if you like.'

'So how and why does your father get killed?' Harry was still so thrown he would have struggled to spell 'fuck me.'

'The how's not important now,' Mat said. 'The why's easy enough. A man like my dad? My mother's lived for years terrified someone would take him out. He's had plenty taken out himself. And some of our people favour me over Luke.'

Dean Silvers had listened in silence, as stunned as Harry but already working the new landscape in his head.

Now he spoke for the second time since he'd stepped into the caravan.

'You'd seriously kill your own father?'
Mat poured himself another malt then held Dean's gaze.
'Don't think he wouldn't do it to me.'

CHAPTER TWENTY-THREE

'THERE's shepherd's pie in the oven,' Jill Brown shouted. 'I'll be down in a minute.'

She looked in the bathroom mirror, checked her hair and make-up, brushed down the short black pencil skirt and tottered down the stairs on stiletto heels.

Getting dressed up had been an effort this time.

'How you've been?' she said, walking into the kitchen. 'It feels like weeks since I've seen you.'

He gawped at her before answering.

'Busy and stressed,' he said. 'What about you?'

She placed her arms around his neck and opened her mouth; two tongues danced a brief, fierce tango before she pushed him away. 'Food first,' she forced a smile, a finger on his lips. 'Did you bring the wine?'

Councillor John Elgin took two bottles of Sainsbury's House Pinot Noir from the orange carrier bag on the kitchen floor. Harry Pullman hadn't believed a word about any planning meeting but his wife had swallowed the story.

'Still splashing the cash,' Jill said, taking a bottle from him, eyeing the label, and twisting the screw cap.

'I only had twenty quid on me,' Elgin told her. 'I didn't want to risk my debit card. She watches my spending like a hawk.'

'Any excuse.' Jill poured the wine. 'The police were here yesterday. Old school friend actually.'

'An old flame?' Elgin leered, slapping her left buttock.

'No, although he said he used to fancy me.'

Elgin slapped her backside again, a little harder this time.

'Did you then? For old time's sake?'

Jill Brown said no she certainly had not; there had never been any old times.

'Only teasing,' Elgin took the glass Jill held towards him. 'Was it Curtis again?'

And at that moment the damn burst.

She threw her arms around his neck, spluttering and gulping for air like someone plucked from the sea, her sobs sudden and savage.

'What is it?' Elgin said, pulling her head into his chest, his other outstretched arm placing the glass on the bench, wine dripping from his wrist.

Her whole body shook, words beyond her, only Elgin's arms keeping her standing on jelly legs.

He held her for what felt like long silent minutes.

'Curtis was abused by his piano teacher.'

The words, like the tears, had come without warning.

'I used to drop him off at a monster's and now the monster's dead and Curtis was there when he was killed,' the nightmare delivered in bursts, rapid speech handing over to hitched breaths and back again in a jerky relay. 'Ed said he didn't think Curtis was involved but I don't know whether to believe him or not.'

She gulped in more air.

Elgin stroked her hair. 'Slow down.'

He passed her a glass of wine, his speech tender. 'What did this Ed say?'

Her eyes stared at the floor, her quiet voice now mirroring Elgin's.

'Just that the man who used Curtis had been killed,' she said. 'I didn't even know. How can a mother not know? Why was he so frightened he couldn't even tell me?'

Elgin took hold of her hand.

'Sometimes it's hard to tell your biggest secrets,' he said. 'Guilt…fear…anger...look this will come as a shock.'

She arched her back, leaned away from him, and looked into his eyes, her own still wet and glassy.

Elgin swallowed hard. 'He told me.'

Jill rocked back, put the glass down and gripped the bench so hard her knuckles were white

'He told you?' her voice loud with shock and hurt. 'When?'

'Last time he was here.'

Jill jumped to attention, rage and realisation lighting a fire.

'I'm sorry.' Elgin instinctively stepped backwards. 'I asked him how things were going. Didn't get much out of him at first.'

'Didn't get much out of him?' Jill shouted, clenched hands to her head.

'Look I was just trying to help,' Elgin was like a tightrope walker starting to wobble. 'I just told him how much stress he was causing you.'

'How dare you!' Jill screamed. 'What gives you the right?'

Elgin was falling, all right. It was only a question of the landing.

He took another two steps backwards. 'I've said I'm sorry.'

Elgin felt the edges of the wall unit jab into his shoulder blades and realised he couldn't back up any further.

He was relieved to see Jill seemed to be breathing slower, more controlled, and took a deep breath of his own.

'That's when he said you'd caused him a lot of problems,' Elgin was aiming for honest but understanding. 'He blurted it all out and made me promise not to tell you.'

He was thinking about an embrace when Jill hurled the glass towards the wall unit behind him and launched herself in the same direction, the punches starting before the glass shattered and peppered them both.

'You bastard!' she shouted, pummeling his chest with her

fists. 'What gives you the right to keep that from me? How do you think that makes me feel you bastard?'

He grabbed her wrists and pulled her into him, grateful it was red wine not blood dripping from his head to hands. 'I did what the kid wanted me to do.'

He bear-hugged her, squeezed her against him. The more she squirmed, the tighter he squeezed.

'Look I've said I'm sorry and I mean it,' Elgin sensed the storm begin to blow itself out. 'And it wasn't as if it had just happened. It was years ago.'

Jill sighed and he felt her body relax.

'I thought he might talk to me again about it, but if I told you, betrayed his trust, there's no way he'd speak to me again,' Elgin said.

Finally she made to move away and he let her, watching as she wiped her eyes, walked up to the sink, and splashed cold water on her face.

She spoke into a blue hand towel that muffled her words.

'It's my fault,' she said. 'He was just a boy and all the time that monster…'

This time the sobs came quietly and passed more quickly, Elgin watching, staying quiet.

He waited before he took her hand, his voice low.

'You're not to blame,' Elgin said. 'The only one to blame here is Scott and he's dead now. He died a horrible death…'

She sniffed. 'Good.'

Elgin watched her bend down at the oven, and open the door to a burst of steam.

'God you look good in that skirt and heels,' Elgin couldn't help himself.

She stood up, glass dish in her hands, the towel against the hot surface.

'Jesus John do you really think I'm interested in that now?'

'Sorry,' Elgin tried to look embarrassed. 'You know me. The Martini Man…anytime, anyplace, anywhere.'

He smiled the weak, half-hearted smile a man gives a woman when he knows he's out of his emotional depth.

'Well don't,' Jill was putting the shepherd's pie on the bench when the doorbell sounded.

'Expecting company?' Elgin asked.

Jill was already speed walking towards the hallway, saying: 'It might be Curtis.'

She yanked open the front door, her next words delayed a fraction by her surprise.

'Ed…I wasn't expecting you.'

CHAPTER TWENTY-FOUR

Harry Pullman drove south on the A1, cruise control set to 50mph. He burped loudly, filling the car with the regurgitated smell of fried fish, vinegar, and diet Pepsi.

'Shouldn't have gone for large cod,' another small belch hot on the heels of its big brother.

'Can't we go any quicker?' Dean said, tetchy. 'And that stinks.'

Harry told him the road was heavy with speed cameras, last thing they wanted was a careless ticket, the police finding out where they'd been once Skinner was dead and the murder squad was busy.

'Why would they look up here?' Dean said. 'Mat just told us nobody knows he's got the caravan.'

'They'll know when we give them a tip-off.'

Dean swiveled sharply in the passenger seat and stared at his uncle, an unspoken 'what?' in his wide open eyes.

Harry pulled out to overtake a slow moving lorry, waited until he was passed before talking again.

'You might have plenty ambition but you'll have to start using your loaf if you want to be a shark in the same pool as the Skinners,' Harry said. 'Time to shape up.'

Dean swallowed the rebuke, shuffled in his seat, gazed out

of the passenger window at the passing fields. He knew he was missing something.

Harry glanced his way. 'Do you seriously think we're going to go into business with that washed-up head banger? He'll lose the lot in six months. If he kills his dad and his brothers someone else will move in, take him out. I don't care who he's got on his side. Those with a bit of nous will be in Luke's camp. We side with Mat we'll be fucked.'

Dean gave it some thought, realised it made sense.

He turned to face Harry. 'So what do we do?'

Harry had been thinking on the hoof since Mat dropped his offer, figured it would all need fine tuning, but reckoned the way forward was pretty clear.

'We might sit back and let Mat take care of his dad, let him tell us who he's got on his side,' Harry said. 'Then we go to Luke, tell him the deal Mat offered us, tell him where the caravan is and leave him to sort Mat out. Hopefully we'll get cut in, nowhere near what Mat's offering but it'll be a much safer bet.'

Dean had to confess he was impressed. 'You fly twat.'

'Self-preservation Deano, self-preservation,' Harry smiled. 'And of course a chance to move up in the world.'

They passed the turn off for Alnwick, drove half a mile in silence, their respective cogs turning as fast as the wheels.

'What about John Elgin?' Dean broke it. 'He wants that tape but you never even mentioned it to Mat.'

Harry judged it hadn't been the time or the place.

He told Dean: 'That's the least of our worries at the minute. We're playing for high stakes here. If we can pull this off we'll negotiate with Luke for the tape. We've already got Elgin in our pocket. He'll not be bothered who we're in bed with as long as he gets the tape. I'm sure Luke will be ok with it.'

He adjusted the climate control before continuing, the powerful car becoming stuffy and over warm.

'Remember, we'll have saved Luke's life, saved Mark's life, and told them who killed their father,' Harry said. 'Then with

Elgin grateful for the tape, all the planning shit will sail through.'

Harry was liking it more and more.

They would be loyal to Skinner's memory, loyal to Luke and the family, loyal to John Elgin.

'Everyone's going to love us,' he beamed.

CHAPTER TWENTY-FIVE

'CAN I HAVE A QUICK WORD,' Ed said.

'Well it's not really convenient,' Jill told him, bending forward, using both hands to brush the front of her skirt.

Make-up, tight skirt, stilettos. No shit it's not…and feel free to look up. Your blushes are burning my legs.

'It won't take long.' Ed side stepped her and walked into the house. 'I just want to tell you about Curtis.'

Ed was following the smell of food when he found John Elgin in the kitchen.

'Mr. Elgin. How are you?'

Short of being naked and tied to the table, Elgin couldn't have looked more uncomfortable.

Ed held out his arm and shook Elgin's limp hand. 'Whelan. Ed Whelan. Detective Sergeant.'

Ed glanced at the broken glass, the still intact stem a crystal icicle in a sea of what he presumed was red wine.

'This was the policeman I was telling you about,' Jill had caught up.

Elgin was pulling himself together, one authority figure meeting another, *mano a mano*.

'The one who fancied you?' he spoke to Jill but looked at Ed.

Ed smiled: 'A long time ago Mr. Elgin, a long time ago.'

Note to self – Jill's a gossip.

'Jill, can we speak in private?' Ed said.

She told him she was okay with him speaking in front of Elgin, who nodded.

Ed said that was no problem.

'You might want to talk Curtis into having some counselling,' he said. 'He'll need to make a statement about what he saw at the garage and it's bound to come out that Scott abused him. You know how this works. Let's say we charge someone with Scott's murder…we couldn't keep something like that away from the defence.'

Jill sat down on a stool. Elgin, like Ed, remained standing.

'Are you suggesting Curtis killed that monster?' Her voice was ice.

'No but a defence barrister could adopt that tack,' Ed said. 'And we couldn't keep Curtis' alleged abuse…'

'Alleged!' Jill shouted. 'I can't believe you Ed.'

'I'm only trying to prepare you,' Ed spread his hands. 'I'm trying to help Curtis here, being level with both of you.'

Jill let out a long breath.

'I know how disclosure works but right now I can't remember the act.'

'Criminal Proceedings and Investigations Act,' Ed answered for her.

'All material that might reasonably be considered capable of undermining the prosecution case or assisting the case for the accused must be disclosed. I doubt very much the CPS would withhold Curtis' knowledge of Scott and their background.'

Jill nodded, knowing he was right, knowing it herself.

'Look I can see you're busy and ready to eat,' Ed said now. 'I'll let myself out but think about the counselling. Nice seeing you Mr. Elgin.'

Back at his car Ed ducked behind the wheel, lungs immediately overwhelmed by the fog of cigarette smoke.

'Bloody hell Sam, open the window.'

'Turn the ignition on then Sherlock,' Sam told him. 'It's hard without the key.'

He started the car and hit the buttons for all four windows. If there had been one to drop the windscreen he would have hit that one, too.

'She was entertaining Councillor John Elgin,' Ed said, playing up a rasping cough Sam chose to ignore.

'Entertaining as in entertaining?'

Ed grinned: 'Unless the short skirt and high heels are her scrabble uniform.'

'Jesus.' Sam considered another cigarette but thought she better wait a while.

'Looks like there'd been an argument,' Ed went on. 'Nice looking shepherd's pie on the bench but a broken wine glass on the floor and looking at the splatter pattern on the wall unit and floor, it hadn't been dropped.'

Sam pictured the scene. 'So all set with food, wine and shagging kit before something happens?'

'Yeah and probably not long before I went in,' Ed said. 'The place is spotless so she's not going to leave broken glass lying around long.'

Sam said she would never have put them together. Ed slid the car into gear, glanced in the rear-view mirror, and pulled away.

'If Curtis knows who his mother's entertaining it might explain how he knows which councillor the Skinners have in their pocket,' Ed said. 'The man's on more committees than enough.'

He closed the windows, reached forward, and turned the fan onto full as Sam tried to take a cigarette discreetly from her pack.

'We know Elgin's grandson's been abused,' Sam said, the cigarette still half-way out of the packet. 'Curtis just happens to be at the garage when the man who abused him is delivered for execution. Curtis' mum and Elgin…it's the first link we have to all three deaths.'

Ed was about to say the link wasn't the strongest when Sam's mobile rang and she answered with a 'Hi Bev.'

Ed glanced at her when she'd finished.

'All the parts shops close at lunchtime on a Saturday so

we're stalled on the headlight,' Sam told him. 'But a Ford Transit's been stolen from Hartlepool and that girder you spotted at the abattoir…newly fitted.'

John Elgin sidestepped the punters in Scaramangers and ordered a large whisky on ice. His early evening plans had been ruined by Ed Whelan's unexpected house call.

Jill had got changed into a sweatshirt and jeans as soon as Whelan left, confirmation absolute that sex was off the agenda. He had made his excuses, apologised again for not telling her about Curtis, and told her he'd call around in the next few days.

His relationship with Jill had been going on for years. He enjoyed spending time with her but he was shackled to his wife; his professional reputation and the spoils that went with it more important to him than his personal life. Besides, there were always younger outlets if you were prepared to pay.

Harry Pullman passed him the drink.

'On the house,' he smiled. 'Give me two minutes and I'll come round your side of the bar.'

Elgin raised the glass and looked around at the other customers, eyes settling on a group of men at the opposite end of the bar, middle aged and laughing loudly at something the tall one had said.

Elgin knew him…Detective Superintendent Ray Reynolds. Retired.

Reynolds saw him looking, nodded in acknowledgement, and Elgin forced a smile.

There are times he frightens me more than the bloody Skinners.

Elgin looked away, downed his drink and ordered another. The slap on his back made him jump.

'Good meeting?' Harry said beside him, the question loaded.

'Jesus Harry, you scared the shit out of me.'

'Me? You're amongst friends here.'

Elgin looked again towards Reynolds. 'You sure about that?'

Harry followed his glance and smiled, said Reynolds was sound, that Elgin shouldn't believe everything he might have heard.

Reynolds looked over and nodded at Harry.

'He knows we're talking about him,' Elgin said, uneasy.

Harry told him to relax, told him he was getting paranoid.

'He's just a widower out having a few drinks with mates,' Harry said. 'Let me get you another.'

Elgin took the drink, his third in not many more minutes. 'What about my proposition?'

'Not now,' Harry said. 'Haven't I told you about these walls? Tomorrow. Besides look who's here.'

Elgin turned to see Tara walk into the bar.

Sam peered out into the darkness where the snow flurries had given way to drizzle in the headlights, listening as Ed talked it through, the oddness of repairing the van then torching it, the new girder, the strength or otherwise of the possible connections in the case.

'You want me to lead when we get there,' she asked now.

'May as well,' Ed peered through the windscreen, hating the conditions.

He kept thinking about Elgin, the man having to keep tight hold of his bowels when Ed walked in.

'Let's run through it again then,' Sam was saying. 'What do we know?'

Ed let it roll out, see just where they stood.

'Elgin's grandson's abused by Pritchard and van Dijk… Elgin's shagging Jill Brown…Scott has abused her lad Curtis…Curtis is at the scene of Scott's execution…Elgin's God knows where but could be the one in Skinner's pocket… and if he is, what's Curtis got to worry about? Elgin could keep the Skinners on-side.'

Ed felt like a man wandering around a maze in the pitch-black at midnight.

'Unless they find out about Curtis' video on his phone,' Sam said, grabbing the door handle as Ed almost missed a junction and had to turn sharply.

'That still bothers me,' he said, mouthing 'oops' in Sam's direction. 'Curtis just happened to be there when the man who abused him years ago is brought there to be killed.'

Like every other decent detective, Ed was no fan of coincidence.

'He puts Dean Silvers there but that could just be bullshit,' Sam said. 'And I'm not sure Dean's got it in him. The Skinners on the other hand…'

Ed said okay, they were bad news no question, but there was no connection apart from Curtis bricking it about some councillor being in a gangster's pocket.

Ed peered out of the passenger window. Almost every house in the street was blinking and glowing, enough twinkling lights and flashing Santas to confuse a pilot.

'Seventy-five's on your side,' Ed said.

Sam strained to see the numbers on the doors, counting up until she said 'there' and pointed at a house.

'The one with Rudolph in the garden minus his nose bulb,' she said.

Ed pulled up in front of an Edwardian semi-detached villa. The green gate was well oiled; the path to the front door split the well-tendered lawn.

Ed was behind Sam who shook her head slowly, another family whose Christmas would never be the same again.

She raised her fist to the oversized door and noticed the fairy lights stapled to the doorframe were switched off.

'Here goes then.'

CHAPTER TWENTY-SIX

Luke and Mark Skinner, dressed in salopettes and dark blue waterproof jackets with the hoods pulled up, held onto the side of the small trawler, bodies swaying and the taste of salt on their lips.

'There's something about the North Sea on a pissy night,' Luke said.

'Yeah,' Mark tightened his grip. 'Terrifying's the word you're looking for.'

They both stared into the eerie blackness, their eyes straining to see the onboard lights of the tankers in the distance and the navigational lights of the cardinal buoys. They couldn't see much more than Geoff Mekins and he was blindfolded.

That their boat displayed no lights was an offence against COLREGS - the International Regulations for Preventing Collisions at Sea - but given their human cargo a breach of the sailor's highway code was worth the risk.

The noise of the engine and the bow cutting through the waves helped drown out Mekins' moaning.

He was curled up in the foetal position on the deck, shivering like a missionary with malaria, hands tied behind his back with thick oily rope; sodden jeans and t-shirt providing neither warmth nor protection.

'Much further Findus?' Mark shouted. 'It's fucking freezing.'

The expression on Jimmy Rhodes' weathered face - or at least the sliver you could see above his thick grey beard - didn't alter. He was used to Mark thinking his mickey-taking was somehow amusing. He'd gone to school with Billy Skinner, done 'jobs' for him for years. It was Skinner's money that had bought the boat a lifetime ago. Putting up with Mark, the family's weakest link in Jimmy's book, was a price he had to pay. Living solely from the sea got harder every year. The cash-in-hand he picked up from Skinner for his special services put food and a bit more on the table.

'Another half hour should do it,' he shouted from the wheelhouse.

Geoff Mekins couldn't see but he wasn't deaf. The rattle of a chain being dragged across the deck, Jimmy's thirty minute warning…he knew what was coming. He tried to scream but his vocal chords made as much noise as a snapped guitar string.

Luke bent down, yanked Mekins' head up by the hair and started coiling the old anchor chain around his upper body.

Unable to move his arms, Mekins thrashed his legs until Mark kicked him hard on the shins.

Jimmy Rhodes stared ahead through the wheelhouse window. He'd seen it all before.

Luke pushed Mekins backwards so that his spine was flat against the deck and coiled the metal links around his legs. Ankles bound, Luke ran the remaining metal up to his chest, padlocked two of the links together and checked the tautness.

Satisfied with his handiwork, he stepped back and leaned against the side of the trawler. Mekins was ready, another whose race was almost run.

'Get ready to sleep with the fishes,' Mark said, his voice lyrical like a pantomime baddie.

In the wheelhouse Jimmy shook his head…Mark and his bloody Godfather quotes. How many times had he heard that one by now? Six? Seven? He was losing count.

Same script. Different cast.

He adjusted his brown peaked baseball cap and reached for his pipe.

Georgie Mills, the Family Liaison Officer, opened the door.

'Alright boss. She's in the front room. Granny's here, her mother-in-law.'

'Kids?' Sam said, stepping into the hall.

'Two. Granny's keeping an eye on them.'

Ed closed the door behind him.

'We'll follow you,' Sam said. 'Introduce us and we'll take over.'

Georgie turned around and walked into one of the rooms off the hall. 'Linda, the boss is here.'

Sam and Ed entered a room of high, primrose yellow walls, white, deep skirting boards and a white alabaster ceiling rose as old as the house. Lamps were everywhere, all off, subdued lighting replaced by bright white light from the five-bulb close-fit ceiling centre light. Heat bellowed from the wood-burner, glass door open, the flaming logs reminiscent of a particular breakfast cereal as they snapped, crackled and popped.

Linda Pritchard pushed herself up off the chintzy floral patterned sofa; tall, voluptuous, long black curls drawing people towards her emerald eyes. Closer examination would reveal a slightly offset nose from a historical fracture but few ever noticed.

Her two young girls, who had been sitting close either side of her, clearly didn't want her to move.

'Please, there's no need to stand up. I'm Sam Parker, the officer in charge of the investigation.'

Linda extended her arm and offered Sam a limp, clammy hand. She forced a smile, giving Sam a glimpse of teeth - Christmas snow white.

'This is Detective Sergeant Ed Whelan.'

Linda nodded, emerald eyes down.

Sam continued. 'I am truly sorry that we have to meet in these circumstances.'

If being in charge of the Murder Team was the pinnacle of her career, meeting the bereaved was the nadir.

Sam sat on an armchair. Ed, still stood by the door, stepped aside as a silent, slightly stooped woman ushered the two girls out of the room. The grandmother. Ed guessed neither child was older than nine. Linda was probably mid-thirties, a lot younger than her husband.

Sam was perched on the edge of the chair, hands in her lap.

'I cannot begin to understand what you are going through Linda,' she said. 'I have sat in this seat many times, but I have never sat in yours.'

Linda Pritchard stared at the swirls on the red carpet.

When she spoke it was barely above a whisper, but the broad northern accent seemed out of place amongst the wood panelled walls.

'Who would do such a thing? Why? Julius was a family man. He'd never abuse children. To even suggest it is sick.'

Sam glanced at the tall white Christmas tree, lights off, a fallen bauble unreturned to its imitation branch. Never had a symbol of joy looked so out of place. The second line of 'Deck the Halls' flashed through her mind. *Not in this house.*

'Linda, rest assured we will do everything we can to bring the people who did this to justice.'

Linda fidgeted with her hands. Sam watched the beautifully manicured nails, salon perfect, scratching the palms.

'I know you will have already been asked this, but is there anyone you can think of who would want to harm Julius?'

Linda shook her head, wiped her eyes with a handkerchief.

Sam glanced around the room. Family photographs were everywhere; on the sandstone fire surround, in the glass fronted unit, on the recessed windowsill. Each showed Julius, Linda and their two children, similar poses, different locations…cities, beaches, mountains…clothing changing to match the climate.

Ed and Sam turned to face the 'excuse me' from the door. Grandmother had reappeared minus the children. 'Might I have a word before you go?'

'Of course,' Sam said.

The old woman turned and walked away.

'Take no notice of her,' Linda said, something flashing in her eyes. 'Julius is her only child, the prodigal son. She's always been difficult…you know the type…you're not good enough for my son, he could have done so much better than you.'

Sam made a mental note. Linda Pritchard didn't look like she took shit from anyone.

'Did you ever meet Hans van Dijk?'

'No. I know…'

She stopped, sniffed, and rubbed her eyes.

'I knew they did the football together, but I never met him. Not easy with young children. One of us always stayed in with the kids. I can't remember the last time we went out together. Can't remember the last time we did anything together, even late at night.'

Sam stored away the hint of domestic unrest. 'How long had they been doing the football?'

'Oh I don't know,' Linda said. 'A few years, but I still don't…'

Linda wiped her eyes again and bit her bottom lip. 'I won't believe they were abusing children.'

Sam knew from experience that abusers could lead the most complete double lives.

'I understand and of course there's no evidence of that at this time,' she said now. 'Linda the purpose of our visit is to introduce ourselves. Georgie will be your point of contact. If you need to speak to me for whatever reason let her know and I'll be round to see you.'

'Thanks.' She didn't move.

Sam stood and followed Ed into the hall.

Granny appeared, her large ears, free from the thinning

grey hair, looked like they'd been designed for evesdropping. She wasted no time on pleasantries.

'If you're in charge,' she pointed a wrinkled finger at Sam, 'you can tell the papers if they want to make libelous accusations about my son I will see them in court.'

Feisty and a fighter, Sam thought. She probably did tell Linda she wasn't good enough.

'All my son did was to try to make the lives of those children a little better,' her hands were trembling with anger. 'Their own parents didn't give two hoots, to suggest because some madman has slaughtered Julius and his friend that they are…I won't even say it.'

She glared at Sam and spat out the next words.

'Warn them off young lady. My husband, like my father, was a respected member of the judiciary and I still have family friends in high places.'

Ed chose his words carefully.

'Your son didn't fancy the law then?' he asked.

Her response was soft, tender almost.

'Julius was a delicate child,' she said. 'Rough and tumble was not his thing. He was very shy and being away from home, unable to cope emotionally, his academic work suffered. Besides he always wanted to help others, hence the football team and before that the youth clubs. A natural response if you were bullied.'

Or a paedophile, Sam and Ed thought in unison.

Granny looked up into Ed's eyes as she took a step towards him, her chin level with his chest, the anger back.

'So no, he didn't, as you so eloquently put it, fancy the law.'

Ed wiped the fine mist of her projectile spittle from his chin.

'He settled on starting his own business in computers,' granny was saying now. 'There wasn't much money in it but he was always happy and he made a little extra at the university. '

She paused, contempt twisting her face.

'That's how he met Fanny Adams in there,' she nodded

her head to the living room. 'She was in a class he was running.'

'Here?' Sam said. 'Seaton St George Met?'

Granny nodded again and stepped back from Ed, composure regained.

'He could have done so much better,' she said. 'I arranged all sorts of dates for him, nice girls from good families, but he went for the supermarket check-out girl twenty years younger. Looks like butter wouldn't melt but don't be fooled. She's pole-axed more men than a common cold. Poor Julius couldn't keep up with her and her…needs. No man could.'

Sam and Ed exchanged a glance.

'He told you that?' Sam said.

Granny smiled without an inch of warmth or humour.

'He didn't need to,' she said. 'You could see it in his face.'

Ed looked at the polished bannister rail curving up the twisting staircase towards the stained glass window on the half-landing, the runner rugs on the hall floor so thick they seemed ankle deep.

'Family money before you ask,' Granny said. 'I'll show you out.'

The slamming door caught Ed's trailing heel as he stepped outside.

He pressed the fob to unlock the car and didn't speak until he was in the driver's seat.

'What an obnoxious old twat.'

Sam didn't hear him, her mind processing what she had seen and heard in the house…Julius' mother hating Linda, Linda playing happy families with a thousand photographs to make sure everyone got the message.

'There's something wrong in that house,' Sam said. 'Let's get his computer tomorrow and see what we find. Meantime, we may as well bob round and see Hans' boss.'

Ed looked at his watch, hoping Sam would pick up the subliminal message.

'You think we should call it a day?' she got it loud and clear.

Ed started the car. 'We've got an early kick off tomorrow.

Hans' boss can wait. I agree there's something wrong in there and right now I want my mind to stay focused on that.'

Sam squashed her disappointment and said okay, that sounded sensible.

She said: 'Do you want picking up in the morning, save you driving in to HQ?'

Ed told her thanks but there was no need, it would be the opposite direction to where they were going. He would see her at HQ.

Jesus Sam. If Sue looked out the window and saw you picking me up at 5am…

Ed blinked and wiped his brow. What was it about Linda?

He rifled through the filing cabinets in his brain, pulling open drawers, ramming them shut. Nothing until…

'Looking for Linda'. 1988. Hue and Cry.

As the song says, he might have to wait until she finds him.

CHAPTER TWENTY-SEVEN

Sunday 14th December

Pixie Carlton, curled and shivering, stared at the faded orange canvas and the droplets of rain water ready to fall. His right hand throbbed, his back felt like the field of The Grand National had galloped over it, and he was convinced he was in the early stages of hypothermia. Pixie had never been built for rough. Now his teeth were rattling so much he swore his fillings were coming loose.

Buying a cheap sleeping bag had been his first mistake; a blue summer number, sheet thin, zero protection. His opinion yesterday was that the salesman's patter about sleeping bags and season ratings was all bluff, bluster and bullshit. He was in the selling business himself. He knew how it worked. Hadn't he described every pokey little flat on his portfolio as 'cosy.'

Agreeing to borrow Declan Doherty's tent was his second moment of rank poor judgement. Doherty's grandfather must have bought the mouldy relic at some tinker fair off Baden-Powell himself.

Rain pounded the ancient canvas, the droplets inside gathering like an invading army preparing to attack.

Even as Pixie wrestled to get comfortable enough to sleep

he knew that was never going to happen, even though the cold and the constant noise on the site had kept him awake most of the night.

Did these people never sleep? Crying kids, screaming mothers, banging doors. He would have been better off pitching his useless tent on the hard shoulder of the A1 in rush hour.

He glanced at his watch. 4.45am. He needed to pee and struggled out of the sleeping bag, numb fingers clumsy with the ancient ties on the tent flap.

It was definitely warmer and only marginally wetter outside.

Stood in mid-flow, he looked around. Two or three more caravans had arrived overnight bringing more dogs, more kids and enough Transits to start a rental company.

He watched a couple of big dogs, breed unknown, sleeping under one of the caravans and a pair of small, scruffy terriers running about yapping.

'You want a cup of tea?'

He jumped so much he peed down his pants.

One of Doherty's granddaughters, smothering a laugh with her hand.

'You're up early?' he said, his flies no easier to handle than the tent ties.

How old is she? Seventeen? Eighteen?

Pixie could see the outline of her body through the white kimono-style dressing gown tied low and loose, her tousled blonde bed hair falling past one bare shoulder. He tried not to stare.

'I heard you getting out of the tent,' the girl told him. 'Thought I'd see if you wanted a cuppa?'

Pixie looked nervously around.

'Should you even be talking to me without anybody being here?'

She laughed again, told him she was a big girl.

'My sister's getting married at the weekend,' she said. 'It'll be my turn next.'

Pixie realised he was staring where he shouldn't and snapped his eyes back to her face.

'How old are you?'

'I'll be sixteen in two weeks.'

'Fifteen! You're fifteen!'

Pixie's mouth dropped in shock and a blast of shame. His next emotion was pure fear.

Caught with a half-dressed 15-year-old on a travellers' site in the middle of the night? No one would be buying an innocent explanation, Pixie knew, and it would be something more precious than his fingers for the chop. He was just crawling back into the tent - suddenly a welcome sanctuary - when he heard 'morning Pixie' behind him.

For the second time that miserable morning his heart took a nosedive.

Declan Doherty was dressed, cheerful and very much awake.

'You're up early,' Pixie said.

'Early bird and all that,' he seemed immune to the rain and the biting cold. 'Come inside. I want to talk about Billy Skinner and his drugs.'

Pixie began to follow Doherty to his caravan, relieved the granddaughter hadn't been mentioned and his tackle was still intact.

'I don't know much really,' Pixie told him. 'And I wouldn't want you starting a battle with Billy Skinner because of me.'

Declan Doherty stopped a pace ahead of him and spun round, his eyes black ice.

'Not because of you son,' Doherty growled.

'Years ago that bastard stole my daughter.'

Ed had seen better mornings.

It wasn't even 5am, a long drive lay ahead for what might prove to be nothing more than a headmaster covering his backside, and Sue Whelan was on the warpath.

She was following him from room to room as he got ready, the questions coming at him like automatic rounds from a drive-by shooting.

'Why do you have to go?' she demanded again, Ed

realising he had heard the same question five times before he stopped counting. 'You were out all day yesterday.'

He pulled on his suit trousers. 'It's my job.'

An honest answer, Ed reasoned, but as effective as a chocolate fire-guard in the face of Sue's onslaught.

'What? Sit in the car all day, listening to her fawning all over you?' the verbal bullets flying. 'She's pathetic and you're just as bad encouraging her.'

Ed stumbled as he missed the left trouser leg. 'Look I've got a long day ahead.'

'Oh poor you,' the sarcasm biting. 'Got a long day have you?'

'Yes I bloody well have,' Ed snapped. He yanked up his zip and scanned the bedroom for his work shoes.

Sue stood quiet for a moment, rubbing her dark Asian eyes.

When she spoke again Ed was struck by the snarling hatred in her voice.

'I've had enough of this,' Sue said. 'I'm sick of her and sick of you. Deny it as much as you want but I know you're having an affair.'

Ed whipped his head to face her, shouted 'You know shit!'

He stood still, shoeless in front of the glass-fronted wardrobe and fastened his tie. Her face didn't look any happier when it was staring at his back.

'How many more times have I got to tell you,' he said to Sue's frozen reflection. 'I'm not having an affair with Sam Parker or anyone else for that matter.'

'Well you're getting it somewhere because you're not getting it from me and your whore of a boss is my favourite,' Sue raged. 'I warned her off when you were in hospital.'

Ed marched downstairs, Sue following two steps behind, the stairs giving her the height advantage, a bird of prey waiting to swoop on a field mouse.

Time for the mouse to roar, Ed thought.

He spun around at the bottom of the stairs.

'Is there any wonder I don't go near you? Listen to yourself? It's just a battle. Who wants sex after that?'

Ed stormed into the kitchen, spotted his black brogues and put them on.

Sue wasn't finished.

'You'll be getting it somewhere,' the anger still raw. 'And if I find out it's with that slut I'll be straight on the phone to the Chief Constable.'

Ed put on his jacket and slammed the front door.

I can't put up with this much longer.

Maybe he should get involved with Sam. The shit couldn't get any deeper.

By contrast Sam's house was quiet. It was always quiet. That was the problem.

'I'd rather hoped you would be here sooner.'

Ian Stirling, the bean-pole headmaster, greeted them in the school foyer wearing a grey suit as dull as his smile and towered over Ed. His yellow dickie-bow hinted at a personality, but more likely it was a distraction from a face wrecked by hard liquor. Stirling might as well have had 'alcoholic' tattooed on his forehead, the ghostly white skin with patches of red from the mass of broken veins telling a story no one could fail to follow.

His nose, a bulbous luminous glow, meant he'd be in with a chance of a one-night gig if anything happened to a certain reindeer in the next few days.

'I'll be late for church.'

Ed stepped forward, the gap between him and the headmaster narrower than was polite. The veins in Ed's neck were bulging so much they were forming an escape committee. He was in no mood for niceties, the early morning row with his wife fresher than Stirling's booze-rancid breath.

'We left the north-east at 5am,' Ed growled. 'I have sat in a car for over six hours because you wanted to speak to us. Maybe you can go to church later, maybe not, I don't really care, but I'm sure the victims of your former colleague will be grateful that after all these years somebody on the staff has finally done something for them, even if it's only missing church.'

The headmaster puffed out his ingrowing chest and glared at Sam.

Sam smiled. Stirling's aggression and intimidation might work with children but he was in her playground now.

'You should see him on a bad day,' Sam said pleasantly. 'Now if we can get on? We do have another six hour drive ahead of us.'

Stirling turned on his heels without a word.

Ed nudged Sam and mouthed 'wanker' as they began to follow.

Sam smiled, nodded in agreement.

Stirling led them into a mahogany-panelled office, bookcases covering every inch of wall space, all filled to capacity. A fountain pen sat on the green leather inlay of the desktop, the only item on the desk apart from a Tiffany lamp.

Sam and Ed sat on the maroon leather high back Milton armchairs; the type found in a cigar-smoke filled Gentleman's Club.

'You had some information for us,' Sam said, glancing at the Christmas cards on the windowsill: Victorian carol singers, churches, Dickens' London. Not a cartoon Santa in sight.

The headmaster shuffled in his seat. 'Jeremy Scott was, as you know, on the staff. I was young, probably the newest member of staff, certainly the youngest. You hear rumours… hear accusations… from the boys…'

He shook his head.

'But you did nothing?' Sam said.

'I thought they were making it up.' Stirling's eyes darted around, anxious to sound sincere. 'Jeremy was an old fashioned disciplinarian and I thought the boys were just getting their own back. He was an excellent teacher and, of course, he was acquitted.'

Ed uncrossed his legs and leaned forward in the chair, oozing as much aggression as he could without grabbing Stirling by his bird-thin neck.

'Someone felt he had to die an agonizing death.'

The headmaster blinked once and eased back in his chair.

'Can I get you some coffee?' his tone more cordial. 'As you were at such pains to point out, you have had a long journey and you're only half way through.'

Ed said no, not bothering to hide the urgency or irritation in his voice.

'So why are we here?' Sam demanded.' You haven't dragged us all the way down to tell us Scott was a misunderstood disciplinarian.'

Stirling shook his head and briefly closed his eyes.

'I am caught between a rock and a hard place,' the eyes open again. 'Whilst I want to avoid any adverse publicity for the school…'

He scratched the back of his left hand, before continuing.

'There were a couple of others who didn't go to court,' Stirling said quietly, as if someone might overhear. 'I actually thought at the time they would have been better witnesses. I had no doubt Scott was assaulting boys physically but sexually…I didn't know.'

Stirling paused, the eyes briefly closed again.

'Or perhaps deep down I did and just didn't want to acknowledge it.'

'And you did nothing?' Ed interrupted.

'Suspicion, gut feeling, as you know sergeant they aren't enough,' Stirling was on the hunt for sincere again. 'The two boys I'm thinking of didn't attend the school but Scott gave them private piano lessons at the weekends. They came onto the school site. I knew their parents. That's how I know they didn't report anything to the police. Their parents only told me after the trial.'

Sam understood where Stirling was heading, why he had invited them to the school.

'And you think the boys would talk to us now?' Sam said.

'I don't know but I thought you might want to speak to them,' Stirling said. 'One is now a high ranking military officer.'

Sam asked which service.

'They both joined the Army,' Stirling told them. 'The other is a Trooper.'

'As in SAS?' Ed said.

Stirling snapped instinctively back to the unbearable pomposity that had become part of his DNA.

'I think sergeant,' Stirling gave a superior smile, 'the correct terminology is the Special Air Service.'

Ed returned the smile with top spin, spotting his chance.

'You related to the David Stirling then?' Ed asked.

'Sorry?' Stirling's brow concertinaed.

'Founder of the SAS,' Ed said. 'David Stirling.'

The headmaster's spectral face was suddenly crimson.

'Of course not,' Stirling barked.

'Thought so,' Ed said, still smiling.

Ed was convinced Stirling would happily have caned him there and then.

Instead, the headmaster turned his eyes back to Sam, told her he would have been uncomfortable talking on the phone, that he didn't think it right to speak to anyone else.

'I understand,' Sam said. 'You obviously have their names?'

'Yes, but I'm not sure whether to give them to you now,' Stirling playing games, Sam thought.

She paused. 'I understand why you might wrestle with confidentiality and it might be we never need to go to see these two men. But we need their names just in case.'

'Just in case they've done it you mean?' Stirling shifted in his seat. 'Murdered Jeremy.'

'Every possibility has to be investigated,' Sam dead-batted with the stock reply.

'There will be some I suppose who will say he deserved it,' Stirling steepled his hands, the movement deliberate, almost religious. 'An eye for an eye.'

'And you?' Ed said. 'Do you think he deserved it?'

Stirling put both hands back on the desk, his face neutral.

'I am a Christian,' the smile thin, patronising. 'I cannot countenance violence of any sort.'

'Religion has sparked more violence than…'

Sam stepped in. A rant from Ed would be counter-productive and he was on the edge of one already.

'If we could have the names we will be on our way and you can make it to church,' she said.

Stirling opened a drawer, took out a plain piece of paper bearing two handwritten names, and thrust it towards Sam.

They followed him along echoing corridors towards the front entrance. The walls were covered with light oak boards, columns of names and a corresponding year written in gold leaf…the school's great and good, head boys down the ages, prize winners, those who had fought and died in the Great War and the conflicts that followed. Amongst the boards were framed class photographs, many in black and white.

Sam spotted the board titled 'Gregson Prize for Music' and she thought of Scott and potential victims.

She stopped and began reading the names, not expecting an Elton John on the list but maybe someone had become a name she recognised.

As she scanned the board the name of one winner caught her eye.

'Excuse me,' she said. 'This prize.'

Ed and Stirling stopped, turned, and walked back.

'What's it for?' Sam asked, eyes still on the name.

Stirling glanced at the title. 'Best music student.'

'And this boy,' Sam touched the board. 'The winner in 1983?'

Ed looked, blinked twice and refocused. The name didn't change.

Stirling's face suddenly beamed, his shoulders lost their stiffness, and even the dickie-bow looked in place.

'Everyone remembers him,' he gushed. 'A quite brilliant pianist, taught by Jeremy but gifted by God. The best we've ever produced and only thirteen when he won that.'

Ed's eyes ran further down the list. 'If he was that good why didn't he win it in the following years?'

'He left the school,' Stirling stared at the name. 'I never did find out why…'

The smile had vanished. Now the shoulders tensed and his head moved slowly from side to side.

'Oh no,' Stirling sounded wounded. 'Not him Jeremy, surely not him.'

Ed patted him twice on the shoulder, a little weight behind the contact.

'Maybe you've got your answer,' he said into Stirling's ear.

Sam finally looked away from the board, asked where the boy had gone, whether the school might have his picture.

'I should be able to look up his next school in the records,' Stirling said. 'As for a picture, there was a photograph taken each year of all the prize winners. Just find the photograph taken in 1983. They follow each other around the walls in date order.'

They had walked about twenty feet in silent procession before they found it.

The face was a lot thinner, the eyes sadder, but there was no mistaking the skinny kid staring at the camera.

John Elgin, councillor of their parish.

CHAPTER TWENTY-EIGHT

SUNDAY FRY-UPS WERE a happy but distant memory for Billy Skinner, the grease-laden full English he clean plated replaced by smoked salmon and scrambled eggs served on top of seeded bread, lightly toasted.

The breakfast tasted better than Marge's bolognaise but it was still shit, Billy reckoned. All in the quest for lower cholesterol.

'So Mekins is gone?' Skinner asked, forking egg and salmon into his mouth with no enthusiasm.

Luke and Mark were sat at the table opposite their father. Marge was upstairs in the shower.

Mark smiled. 'Sleeping with the...'

'It's about time you grew up!' Billy stopped him dead. 'We're not in fucking Hollywood.'

Mark dropped his eyes to the floor, mouth clamped shut.

Skinner wiped flakes of egg and salmon from his face and turned to Luke. 'Jimmy okay?'

'Sound,' Luke said. 'And yes, Mekins is gone.'

'And our Mat?' Skinner asked him. 'He can't have just vanished.'

'No idea,' Luke told him.

'What about you Don Corleone?' Skinner turned to Mark, glowering. 'Any ideas?'

Mark kept his head down, stared at the table, and silently shrugged his shoulders. Now was not the time for Marlon Brando lines.

'Well somebody must know,' Skinner was angry, not loud. 'Jesus. Ask around. We need him found. Your mother's going out of her head.'

He sat back. 'I'm at the cemetery this afternoon.'

'We'll come with you,' Luke said.

'No you won't,' Skinner shook his head. 'I'll be okay. I'll take Stuart. No need for you to come. You never did like your Auntie Irene.'

'Only because she wasn't an auntie and mum always said you and her were having an affair,' Luke said.

Skinner sighed, his mind on a time-trip to a destination he couldn't quite leave behind.

'It was years ago,' he said now. 'And it was more than an affair, I've told you that before. Anyway, no point in you two upsetting your mother, you've never been any other year, why start coming now?'

'Things are a bit different,' Luke said. 'A bit more dangerous at the minute.'

Skinner appreciated Luke's concern, liked the way he was looking out for him, his caution.

'I'll be fine,' he told him. 'I go there once a year. Hardly a pattern anyone's going to notice.'

Luke held his father's eyes, his voice quiet.

'Except our Mat.'

'Good morning John,' Harry Pullman raised a hand in greeting as Elgin walked into Scaramangers. 'Just.'

Elgin, unshaven but reeking of aftershave, sat at the bar. His bloodshot eyes, sallow face and creased white polo shirt hinted at a late night and a hangover for the ages.

'Black coffee…and a new head,' Elgin's throat sounded sand-blasted.

Harry was already at the coffee machine pressing buttons.

'That Tara will kill you,' he grinned. 'Should be an occasional treat not a regular work out at your age.'

Elgin watched Harry put a cup on the bar and stared through the steam at the still-swirling contents.

'Sod it you might as well give me a hair of,' he said, hand shaking lightly as he pushed the coffee away. 'You choose. A pint of something light.'

Tara was young but legal. That was the difference. Not like that bastard Scott, the way he took advantage of him and the others. They were just kids. Tara was an adult in the eyes of the law. He hadn't even reached puberty when Scott started.

It had been easy getting Curtis to open up. They both had an interest in the piano, although neither played anymore, and all Elgin had done was tell Curtis how he had been a victim of the same pervert.

What were the chances? Him and Jill's son abused by the same man all those years apart? Astronomical.

As they bared their souls it became obvious Scott had used the same techniques on Curtis as he had on Elgin and his fellow pupils. He hadn't bothered with grooming. That took time. Scott just used a full-on assault with the threat of death if they said anything, bending them over the piano stool, the pain unspeakable. That was the bastard's forte. Setting their bodies on fire but not in a nice way. Not like Tara.

'Try this,' Harry said, putting a pint in front of him. 'New brewery. Decent though.'

Elgin sipped the light coloured beer and nodded his approval. 'Any joy with the tape?'

Harry told him it was in hand, wheels were in motion.

'You'll have it this week,' Harry confident, relaxed.

He held a tumbler under the Glenmorangie optic, pressed twice, and put the double on the bar in front of Elgin. 'What you up to today?'

Pixie Carlton was laid on his back staring at the damp canvas and replaying his conversation with Declan Doherty.

He had told him everything he knew about Skinner's operation. No benefit at all in remaining loyal to him, not now. His ruined hand would always remind him what he owed Billy Skinner. Loyalty wasn't high on the list.

Doherty had told him not to worry, that Skinner and his boys would be sorted.

Now Pixie wanted out. Playing the Big-I-Am with his cocaine mates had been stupid. Getting mixed up in all of this was a plain death wish and no way was Pixie ready to meet his maker. Even thinking of the ways the Skinners might call time on his fucked-up life made his bowels go ballroom dancing.

If he'd just put the money back in time…

The ties on the tent flap were unpicked by nimble fingers and her blonde hair - brushed now - popped through the opening.

Christ she's as dangerous as the Skinners.

She looked him in the eyes. 'You still want a cuppa?'

Even a simple question sounded loaded.

'I'm fine thanks,' Pixie feeling heat on his neck.

Just leave me the fuck alone!

She inched her way into the tent and refastened the flap once she was inside.

'Do you fancy talking?'

'What about?' Pixie said, claustrophobic and clammy.

'Anything.'

She brushed his thigh with her fingers.

'I think you'd best be going,' Pixie jolted back. 'This isn't a good idea.'

'Don't you fancy me?'

'You're 15 for Christ sake!'

'Granddad will be okay about it.'

'I doubt it,' Pixie tried to imagine Declan Doherty clapping him on the shoulder, telling him it was fine and dandy. 'Anyway I'll be going in a couple of days.'

'You'll be here for the wedding won't you?' the girl trying to inch closer.

'We'll see.'

He had never been to a gypsy wedding before and was sure the other young men wouldn't want him anywhere near.

She slipped back out of the tent and left the caravan door open.

'Of course he can come to the wedding princess,' Doherty's voice carried easily.

Pixie closed his eyes and muttered 'fuck' under his breath.

Mat Skinner, head bowed, hands in the pockets of his wax jacket, ambled along the beach. He would have felt less conspicuous if he had a dog, the beach as busy as Crufts.

A tennis ball flew past his head, the oldie with the yellow sling launcher nodding an apology as he looked up, a panting Jack Russell sprinting past in pursuit.

Bamburgh Castle, the chosen location for the meet, dominated the skyline to the left.

He had changed the SIM card on his phone before he contacted his two trusted men, the brief orders to drive north of Bamburgh, double back, and wait in the small car park adjoining the beach at the end of The Wynding. The single road was narrow enough to notice anybody following.

Mat shook his head as they approached.

Twit and Twat.

He might not have a dog but these two meat heads couldn't have looked more out of place if they were wearing top hat and tails on a nudist beach.

They were identical, photo negatives in black blouson jackets, black trousers, and black shoes, each 6' plus tall and as wide as the ice-cream vans that patrolled the streets in the summer.

'Jesus, you're not working the doors,' Mat greeted them. 'Couldn't you have worn something to blend in a bit with this lot?'

He turned to look over his shoulder and swept an arm to indicate the posse of dog walkers and random beachcombers.

'We never thought,' one of them said.

'Yeah well pardon me for expecting you two to think.'

Mat turned and walked back towards Seahouses, the chastened heavies like dim but faithful Rottweilers either side.

'Anything about Geoff?' Mat asked.

Their silence told him everything he needed to know. He wiped his left eye and cleared his throat.

'There was nothing I could do about Geoff,' Mat said, voice thick. 'I only got away because my old man would have had to think of something to tell my mother if I went missing.'

Mat looked at the sand dunes, remembered rolling down them with his brothers, his mother sat on a tartan blanket surrounded by orange juice and their favourite sandwiches; chopped egg and tomato loaded with salad cream.

'We used to come here as kids….'

The Rottweilers waited for him to continue.

'He's had time to think now, come up with some shit about who killed me,' Mat let his hurt and loss fuel him for the task at hand. 'I'll get in first. Harry Pullman's got John Elgin on board so everything's sorted with the planning applications. Once we're done it'll be business as usual.'

'What about Luke and Mark?' one of the Rottweilers asked.

Mat was satisfied with the plan he had in place.

He had booked into a pub on Holy Island so he would be well away when Billy Skinner was taken out.

'Luke might suspect I'm involved but I'll be nowhere near,' Mat said now. 'I'll even FaceTime my mother, show her where I am.'

His smile didn't wash the cold hate from his eyes. Luke wasn't the only one who could plan.

'I'll make sure I talk to a barmaid until the tide's in then anyone who checks will know I couldn't get across the causeway,' Mat told his men.

He turned to face the sea, spread his arms out wide, and breathed in deep.

'The tide will be my alibi,' he said to the waves that never listened. 'I'll be out of the frame, mum will tell me, Luke, and Mark to sort out whoever killed the old man, and there'll be plenty of choice.'

Mat walked to the water's edge, staring at the Farne Islands and the cormorants diving into the sea.

'No point in you two walking too far from your car,' he turned his head. 'Everything all set?'

The Rottweilers nodded as one.

'The unfaithful bastard will be at the cemetery this afternoon,' Mat sent his words across the water. 'You know what to do.'

CHAPTER TWENTY-NINE

Ed settled back into the driver's seat. Service Station Sunday was hardly haute cuisine. The tuna sandwich, the only thing on offer without mayo, would repeat more often than 'Only Fools and Horses'.

He reached across and opened the passenger door as Sam sauntered across the car park, two coffees in hand.

'Do you want me to drive?' she said, bending down and passing him the cardboard cups.

'I'm okay for now.'

He rejoined the A34 signposted The Midlands and Newbury, shook his head, and moved into the outside lane.

'I remember a time when you hardly saw a wagon on the roads on a Sunday,' Ed grumbled. 'Now it's like a truckers' convention.'

Sam turned her head and pushed her cup into the drink holder beside the gear stick.

'That's the problem with being a miserable old goat,' her voice was teasing. 'You'll still remember pubs closing at three, shops all shut on Sundays and even the notion of a takeaway still a twinkle in Colonel Sanders' eye.'

She started to sing Dvorak's "New World" Symphony.

Ed laughed. 'Alright, alright but I'm telling you there weren't many lorries driving on Sundays back in the day.'

Sam sighed. 'It's called progress.'

'Not always a good thing,' Ed muttered. 'Mind that tuna might have tasted better in old fashioned Hovis.'

Sam turned on the radio and channel hopped through Christmas perennials and mind-numbing talk shows before she gave up.

She leaned back into the seat and closed her eyes, her mind back on the case.

Stirling told them the records showed the young maestro John Elgin had transferred to a school in Seaton St George. He was definitely one and the same.

Ed seemed to be reading her thoughts.

'Elgin doesn't look like he could set fire to a BBQ never mind a bloke, even if the bloke just happened to be a paedophile who abused him when he was a boy,' he stretched his back and wiggled his ankles behind the wheel.

Four more hours of this. I'll have to be carried out.

'But he's well connected,' Sam said. 'Even Curtis said he's scared Elgin's involved with Billy Skinner.'

The problem, both of them knew, was how far to trust the information.

Another resting in the 'unconfirmed' box was whether Elgin and Curtis knew the other had been one of Scott's victims.

Ed said it was possible but any of the victims could have been involved in his execution.

'Who'd be more capable than two military men, especially one in the Special Forces,' he said, Stirling's revelation a striking new element.

'What worries me,' Sam said, stretching her legs, 'is since we started looking into the backgrounds of Scott's known victims we've already discovered another two that never reported, three if we count Elgin. How many more are still out there?'

'More don't report than do,' Ed said, glancing in the rear view mirror and indicating to overtake yet another HGV.

Sam watched the giant wheels of the truck as Ed accelerated past, the noise and closeness making her uneasy.

'Elgin's a potential victim of historic child abuse so we need to think about how we come at him,' Sam said. 'And let's see what we've got locally before we go running all around the country chasing new victims and potentially new suspects.'

She felt her mobile vibrate before she heard the ring tone and only pulled it from her pocket after an expletive-laden fight with her seatbelt.

'Hi Bev.'

Sam listened. 'Really? Christ, the plot's thicker than Bisto…look we'll not be back until late. Keep it under your hat. We'll talk tomorrow.'

She put the phone in the centre console.

Ed glanced at her. 'What's up?'

'No obvious kiddie porn on Julius Pritchard's computer.'

'Pity but he was savvy enough with the tech to cover his tracks,' Ed said. 'So what's with the Bisto?

'An interesting document that is on the computer,' Sam told him. 'A pre-nup dated before their marriage saying his wife gets nothing if they divorce.'

'They're not worth the paper they're written on,' Ed said.

'Maybe but a family like the Pritchards, all that legal stuff in the gene pool, would just keep the case in court for years,' Sam tried to imagine just how hard Granny Pritchard would fight to stop shop girl Linda snatching the family jewels.

'But more interesting…'

'What?' Ed all ears.

'In her email box there's a nice series of photographs of our grieving widow snogging in the park.'

Ed indicated and moved out to pass another truck, Sam making a conscious effort not to look this time, saying the pictures had been taken by a retired cop turned private investigator.

'So maybe granny was right,' Ed said. 'Do we know the lucky man?'

'Seaton's resident lothario,' Sam paused for effect. 'John bloody Elgin.'

Cold, stiff and cursing his luck, the man peering over the hedgerow breathed out his own swirling fog. Thirty minutes squatting in a field would have been bad enough in the summer; in December it was a nightmare.

His thick leather gloves had given up the fight with the plunging temperature and his fingers were now welded around the binoculars. To his left, a straight road descending towards him gave an unobstructed view of approaching vehicles.

The BMW appeared in the magnifying lenses as it travelled down the hill, nothing in front of it.

He bent down, pulled open the hand-held marine distress flare and ran towards his rendezvous point. Orange smoke rose upwards, a much better means of communication than a mobile in the countryside where the signal might be a bit dodgy.

Passing the billowing smoke and fleetingly curious about the source, Helen Larney slowed as she drove towards the red traffic light. Coming to a stop she swore under her breath.

She and her 13-year-old daughter Maisy were headed for the cemetery - flowers for her mother's grave on the back seat - before heading home and tea with Helen's in-laws.

She fiddled with her wedding ring, muttering frustrations under her breath. Had she had more time to spare she might have savoured the smell of new leather as her Range Rover Sport idled behind the BMW, the first vehicle in the queue.

She glanced across at her daughter singing along to something playing through the headphones attached to her iPhone.

Always the bloody same. Never a workman in sight.

She looked at the BMW's number plate - 189 GBH - and shook her head. Years ago she dated a lad called Gary Henderson. He was the type of dick who'd have loved a plate like that.

A blur of movement to her left broke her wander down memory lane.

She jumped in her seat as two figures dressed in dark boiler suits and ski masks ran out of the hedge. They raced to the BMW, one smashing the front passenger window with a sledgehammer and yelling at the driver, the other swinging a similar hammer at the front of the car, the blows so hard the airbags exploded.

Helen hit the remote locking button, frantically searching her handbag for her phone, Maisy rigid, wide-eyed, and screaming beside her.

In the BMW, the driver had dived towards the glove-box but the hooded figure at the passenger window repeatedly punched him in the head…five, maybe six bone crunching blows, Helen couldn't keep count.

She watched the driver scramble backwards out of his seat.

By the driver's door, the second attacker spun him around, grabbed his collar and head-butted him with such force his nose exploded. A flurry of lightning fast blows with a cosh the figure was now carrying sent blood spraying in all directions.

Helen Larney had seen enough. Gasping, she put the Range Rover in reverse and gunned the accelerator but she hadn't been quick enough.

She saw a white Ford Transit van tearing towards her, tyres squealing as it skidded to a halt, its back doors alongside her window.

The two attackers were dragging the limp BMW driver by his arms towards the van as another masked figure jumped from behind the wheel, flung open the back doors, and held them as the victim was thrown inside. Within seconds all three masked men were back in the Transit and the van was roaring away, the back doors swinging wildly as Helen watched in her offside wing mirror.

The whole attack had lasted less than two minutes.

Wide-mouthed, stunned, and shaking, Helen Larney dialed 999. The driver of the BMW, who looked like he could fit in the pockets of his attackers, had never stood a chance.

CHAPTER THIRTY

Bev Summers and Paul Adams rang the bell on the stone pillar, spoke to a woman on the intercom, and walked through the electronic gates as soon as they started opening. They smiled at the fountain and the mermaid as they approached the front door. Marge Skinner was waiting.

'What's happened? Has he been in an accident? They wouldn't tell me anything on the phone, just that I had to wait for you.'

'Can we come in?' Bev asked.

'Yes but tell me what's happened.'

'Let's go and sit down,' Bev said.

They followed Marge into a large split-level room with a pool table on the upper level. Luke and Mark were leaning against it; both dressed in cream chinos, Luke wearing a white v-neck t-shirt, Mark with a pastel coloured cashmere jumper draped across his shoulders.

Marge put a cigarette between her trembling lips and had to spark the lighter three times before her shaking hand got close enough to connect. 'Please.'

Bev and Paul, like everyone else in the silent room, remained standing.

'About thirty minutes ago a man driving your husband's car was attacked and abducted,' Bev said.

Marge's hand shot to her mouth and she dropped onto the sofa. Luke and Mark jumped to attention, Mark demanding 'where!' just as Marge was crying 'who by?'

Now Luke stood relaxed against the pool table, legs outstretched, hands inside his pockets, annoyed that he had shown emotion by snapping into a rigid stance.

'Mother, Mark,' his tone controlled. 'Let the detectives continue. Officers…'

Bev sat next to Marge.

'Were you expecting your husband to be driving his car this afternoon?'

Marge nodded.

'Do you know where he was going?'

'No.'

Paul was watching for any reaction from the sons. Their initial shock suggested they had no idea about the abduction.

'There were flowers on the front passenger seat.'

'Bastard!' Marge shouted.

'Mother,' Luke said quietly. 'Where he was going is irrelevant.'

'Actually we think it is,' Bev said. 'This wasn't a spur of the moment attack.'

'What do you mean?' Marge asked, dabbing her eyes with a tissue she had taken from the sleeve of her blouse.

'Whoever it was driving your husband's car...'

'It was dad.' Luke hadn't moved and his voice still had no trace of emotion. 'They'll find out anyway, so we may as well tell them.'

Marge nodded.

'Years ago dad had an affair,' Luke said. 'The woman died whilst they were still involved. It's the anniversary of her death today. He never misses, hasn't since…'

'Alright Luke,' Marge stopped him. 'They don't need to know the ins and outs about that cow.'

'How long has she been dead?' Bev asked, looking at Luke.

'Twelve years,' Luke thinking how fast that time had gone

by. 'He goes every year. Puts flowers on her grave at the exact time she died. Just before ten past three.'

'Is that well known?'

'I bloody hope not,' Marge said, stubbing out the cigarette in the onyx ashtray. 'I'm feeling a big enough fool sticking by him without the world and his wife knowing about it.'

'Luke?' Bev asked.

'It wasn't a secret and I see where you're going,' he told her. 'Would people know where and when to ambush him? Yes I suppose they would. You know as well as I do, nothing's secret in this world. So what happened?'

Bev stood. It was bad enough the sons were on the raised area without her adding to their height advantage.

'He stopped at traffic lights, temporary lights, and that was where he was attacked,' she said. 'He was driven away in a Ford Transit.'

Luke plucked a fleck of lint from his chinos and glanced at his brother.

'It wasn't just good luck that the lights were there I take it?' Luke said.

Bev understood why all the police intelligence had Luke taking over once Billy Skinner stepped down…not only could he keep whatever emotions he was feeling in check, he was tack sharp.

'The lights hadn't been put there by any agencies,' Bev confirmed. 'We believe they were put there by his abductors.'

'Fucking hell,' Mark said.

'That's enough,' Luke stared at his brother then turned back to Bev. 'I presume by asking who was driving you haven't found anybody yet.'

Bev nodded. 'Where's your other brother?'

'Why?' Luke asked.

'Well you're both here and I know you don't live at home.'

'Who told you that?' Luke interrupted. 'Your sources are not as good as you think. Let's hope they're good enough to find my father.'

'So where is Mat?' Bev pressed.

'God knows.' Luke told her. 'He's a big boy and I'm not his keeper.'

Marge was fumbling for another cigarette, hands still shaking.

'I haven't seen him and Geoff for…'

'Mother!' This time Luke's voice was pulled tight, anger barely under the surface. 'The detectives aren't interested in Mat, they're here about dad.'

Bev moved on but she knew something was wrong.

'Can you think of anybody who would want to kidnap your father?'

'Are you fucking serious?' Mark shouted.

Bev watched Luke's right leg tap his brother's shin.

Only one person doing the talking…

'I don't know if we can help you officer,' Luke again. 'Any businessman makes enemies. My father was no different. Half the time you have no idea who those enemies are.'

Bev upped the ante but not the level of her voice.

'Most businessmen don't tend to make the type of enemies who plan an ambush, smash the windows of your car and beat you senseless before dragging you…'

Marge yelped like a tiny puppy accidentally trodden on.

'…before dragging you into the back of a waiting van.'

Bev let the statement hang in the air.

'You might want to give my question some serious consideration. It might be the only way you see your father again.'

When he came around Billy Skinner was lying face up on a metal workbench. Panic and adrenalin kicked in. He pushed his back against the cold surface, bucked upwards but couldn't move.

Freezing…

The coldness confirmed his nakedness. Cable ties dug into his ankles and wrists, the nylon ropes around his legs, torso and neck were tight but not life threatening. Through puffy eyes he could just about make out the corrugated ceiling twenty feet above.

'Fuckers!' he shouted. 'Cocksuckers!'

His head was pounding in the silence.

Skinner sensed more than heard movement behind, straining again against the bindings.

A man's voice, gentle as a therapist but without the empathy.

'Good afternoon Mr. Skinner.'

Skinner shouted again: 'I have no idea who you bunch of cocksuckers are but you better untie me before your worst fucking nightmares come true.'

'You're going nowhere William,' monotone man said calmly.

Skinner pushed his back hard into the workbench but it was useless. His throat felt like it had been peeled and he could taste blood. His words were quieter this time.

'What do you want? Money?'

A small laugh; a polite stage cough.

'You haven't got enough money to get yourself out of this situation William.'

The quiet voice was driving Skinner mad. He went back to shouting.

'Be a fucking man,' he yelled. 'Show yourself you bottleless wanker and stop calling me William.'

'Calm down, William,' another laugh, more natural this time. 'You'll give yourself a heart attack.'

'Fuck you!'

'Nobody can hear you, that's why we didn't tape your arrogant mouth,' the voice getting closer. 'Besides we've got some of your product for you to try so we'll be needing your nose and mouth.'

Skinner thrashed against the table, foam at his mouth, white saliva running down his chin. His body, stiff with aggression, was still tied fast. Breathless he continued his tirade.

'My lot...my lot will come after you...come with everything they've got.'

The quiet, invisible voice seemed amused.

'Really William? I'm shitting it. Your lot couldn't win an arse kicking contest against a group of one-legged men.'

A quicker movement now and monotone man appeared at Skinner's side.

Billy Skinner had never been easily shocked but now he gasped, eyes as wide as the swelling allowed.

'You?' he said, in disbelief. 'Are you fucking insane? Do you expect me to talk?'

Monotone man shook his head and smiled, recalling how Skinner loved James Bond, remembering the words of Auric Goldfinger.

'No Mr. Skinner, I expect you to die.'

CHAPTER THIRTY-ONE

'JESUS HOW MANY IS ELGIN SHAGGING?' Ed said, overtaking another lorry.

Sam reached for the bag of toffees, unwrapped one for Ed, and then popped one in her mouth.

She had decided to see Elgin the next day, tackle him about Jeremy Scott and Linda Pritchard.

'He might say nothing but at least he'll know we know,' Sam said. 'He's not short of motives for all three murders.'

They knew already two of the dead had abused Elgin's grandson, the other his lover's son. Now it looked as though Elgin himself had been a victim.

'Why wait so long though?' Ed said. 'It was years ago.'

Sam was unwrapping two more toffees.

'Who knows?' she passed one to Ed. 'Maybe hearing about boys close to him being abused tipped the balance, maybe he didn't have the connections before, maybe...and this is a possibility...maybe he didn't know Jeremy Scott was in Seaton, maybe he just found out.'

That's an awful lot of 'maybes', Samantha

Ed chewed on the toffee, recalling something Scott's neighbor Debs Lescott had told him, how Scott was a serial complainer, forever on to the council or the local press.

'Remember that big hoo-ha a while back about a

planning application to open a pub on the Avenue,' Ed said now. 'It didn't get the nod but it did go before the planning committee Elgin sits on and I'm sure I read in the Seaton Post the meeting was packed.'

Sam gave it some thought.

'Could be something as daft as Elgin finds himself in the same room as Scott and recognizes him,' Sam said.

Add a 'could be' to the 'maybes' whilst we're at it…

Her phone rang and she took it from the centre console, Bev Summers again. Sam leaned back into the headrest and listened then sat upright when it was her turn to speak, her words a stream of orders not conversation.

'Fast Track Actions,' she told Bev. 'Witness statements, especially from this Helen Larney. Leave the daughter for now. Check the field where she saw orange smoke. CCTV on the roads back into town, see if we can pick up the Transit.'

Ed glanced at Sam, eyebrows raised at the mention of a Ford Transit van.

'Identify the traffic lights,' Sam went on. 'See if they were the ones stolen the other day. Who's the Senior SOCO at the scene? Good. Get Julie to liaise with Firearms and make the gun safe. Anything else give me a call. Update me in an hour. Cheers.'

Sam disconnected.

'Billy Skinner's been abducted.'

'Fucking hell!' Ed so surprised he let the car drift, the boom-boom-boom of the wheels over the hard shoulder cat's eyes putting his attention back on the road.

Sam gave him the details, told him there had been a gun in the BMW glove box but Skinner hadn't had a chance to use it, that Skinner had been on his way to the cemetery when he was taken.

'What's the date?' Ed had seemed lost in thought.

'14th,' Sam told him.

Ed glanced at Sam and nodded towards the toffee bag between her feet.

'I know why he was going to the cemetery,' he told her. 'It's the anniversary of Irene's death. He goes every year.'

'Irene?' Sam said, wondering how many more characters, dead or alive, would end up in play.

'His mistress years back,' Ed told her. 'The love of his life some reckon. It's no secret he takes flowers to the cemetery for her every year.'

Sam shook her head. *How do you know all this stuff?*

'So he's on his way there,' she said. 'Stops at some temporary traffic lights...'

'The ones that were stolen?' Ed nipped in.

'Probably,' Sam remembered the toffees, reached down for the bag. 'Fancy a quick cup of coffee?'

Two minutes later Ed was pulling into the service station car park, plenty of spaces even near the entrance to the shops and cafes.

'Who's got the balls to take on Billy Skinner,' Ed wondered aloud, switching off the engine.

'Time will tell,' Sam told him. 'And Bev's got it into her head that Mat Skinner's missing as well.'

Two men appeared either side of Billy Skinner, each with a half brick of cocaine in plastic bags, Skinner shouting 'wait!' as they ripped them open.

An avalanche of white powder descended on his face while fingers gripped his nose. Skinner had two options...hold his breath or swallow the snow. The result would be the same either way.

Marge Skinner was standing in the kitchen, a half-finished gin and tonic in one hand, cigarette in the other.

'I'm really worried about our Mat,' she gulped at the drink. 'I can't get hold of Geoff either. Both their mobiles go straight to answer phone.'

Luke and Mark stared at their mother and said nothing.

Marge began to wail as loudly as a lifetime of smoking would allow. 'What if they've got Mat as well?'

A coughing fit whose raspy origins lay somewhere in the bottom of her lungs sent her rushing to the sink, Luke and Mark looking away as she spat into the plughole.

Flushed and still wheezing, Marge returned to her drink, picked up the bottle of Hendricks, and filled her glass to the brim.

Fuck the tonic.

She took a huge gulp. 'Who's behind this Luke?'

'No idea,' Luke shook his head. Best not to tell his mother he thought it was Mat.

But who was helping him? Mat knew his father would be going to the cemetery, but stealing traffic lights? Making sure their father's BMW was first in the queue? That was way beyond Mat's planning capabilities. Wasn't it?

'I used to tell him that cow would be the death of him.' Marge lit another cigarette. 'But who'd go after your dad in broad daylight. And why wasn't Stuart McFadden with him?'

'Leave Stuart to me,' Luke said, a plan already forming in his head.

'We might get a phone call,' Mark got their attention.

Marge's eyes, wide as flying saucer sherbet sweets, blazed at her middle son.

'Why would we?' She loved all her boys equally but Mark wasn't the sharpest, she knew that. 'Nobody's in the kidnap and ransom game. Did your father ever ask for a ransom? This is about taking us on. Us!'

She hit the sink with the palm of her hand.

'Who the fuck do they think they are?' she shouted before gulping the gin, willing herself to calm down, the booze helping. 'Your father played this game for years. Now someone's doing it to us. But who?'

Luke took a thick blue glass from a tall cupboard, walked to the sink, and used the cold water tap.

'We need to protect our assets,' he said as the glass filled. 'If mum's right this is only the start. Whoever's behind it knows we'll come after them so they'll be ready. I'll increase all of the security at our clubs and I'll have two lads in here.'

Marge eyed the remaining two fingers of gin in her glass and the Hendricks bottle close by.

'I don't want anybody here,' she said. 'I've never been involved in your father's business.'

She lit another cigarette.

'You're involved because you're his wife,' Luke said, all patience gone. 'Let's just do it for a couple of days and see what happens.'

Mark's mind was on Stuart McFadden, hating him more than normal, the smart arse forever in their home, eating their food.

'If McFadden's involved I want him sorting Luke,' Mark said. 'Sorting slowly.'

Luke was watching his mother, concern struggling to break through his emotional dead space.

His mother wanted Stuart dead. She'd thank him for sorting that.

But she was already so worried about Mat she was vulnerable. If Mat got to her first, she'd believe anything and everything he told her.

It was a very big if…

Harry Pullman wiped his hands on a grubby bar-towel and pulled a pint for the man on the stool.

'Quiet today,' the customer said. 'Seen more life in a tramp's vest.'

Lone drinkers were scattered around the place, some reading tabloids, others staring into their pint glasses, nobody saying a word.

An old man with long fingernails the colour of coal was engrossed in a paperback that looked like it had spent a long, battered life being read down a mine.

Harry sometimes felt like a librarian with an on-licence.

'Definite touch of the Moon Bar about it,' the customer was saying now.

He responded to Harry's quizzical look. 'No atmosphere.'

Dean Silvers burst through the door. Some jumped at the interruption; everybody looked at the cause of it.

Dean, head wet with rain, was as excited as a toddler in a ball-pool and just as breathless.

'He's only gone and done him,' he shouted.

'Who?' Harry said, 'and keep your voice down. Done what?'

The drinkers went back to their pints, newspapers and books. No one needed reminding who owned this pub. They knew better than to get involved.

Dean hurried behind the bar, his voice quiet but still fast with adrenaline.

'Billy Skinner. He's only gone and done him.'

'What are you on about?' Harry said.

'The filth's everywhere…'

'Watch your mouth boy,' the man on the stool cut in.

Silvers turned, his face reddening quicker than a gas fire.

'Sorry,' he muttered. 'No offence Mr. Reynolds.'

Ray Reynolds took a mouthful of beer and wiped his mouth. 'Apology accepted. Now continue. Sounds interesting.'

Dean looked at his uncle. Harry nodded.

'The car's near the cemetery, Billy's BMW,' Dean told them. 'Right next to some traffic lights that weren't there when I went past earlier. Cops everywhere…armed cops, cops in those white suits. The doors of the car are open, the passenger window's broken, and the airbags have gone off.'

'You seem to know a lot,' Ray said.

Silvers tapped his head: 'Photographic memory.'

'Surprised the police let you get close enough to take a photograph,' Reynolds grunted.

'What's that supposed to mean?' Silvers bridling, ex cop or not.

'Nothing. Continue.'

'That's it,' Silvers said. 'They've obviously done Billy.'

'Who has?' Reynolds said.

'Somebody,' Silvers suddenly wary, reluctant.

Reynolds still had his pint in his hand but now he put it back on the bar without taking a drink.

'When you came in you said 'he's only gone and done him' not 'somebody'. So who's the he?'

'Come on Ray,' Harry said, sensing the danger. 'You're retired.'

Reynolds kept his eyes on Dean.

'Just professional curiosity, Harry. We tried for years to nail that bastard. So who exactly is this he?'

Dean Silvers looked like a man who had already said too much.

CHAPTER THIRTY-TWO

Sam was driving now, the wheels running down the miles on the A1, the home stretch.

Ed's lungs felt like he'd inhaled every drag of Sam's cigarettes and his clothes stunk of tobacco, but she could blow smoke over him all day if he could just get his 6'5" body out of the car. His backside was numb and his legs were as rigid as speed camera poles.

'So run past me again what Bev said in the last service station,' Ed said.

He'd missed the phone call, racing to the loo then telling Sam the tuna sandwich had gone through him 'like a Porsche.'

Sam hadn't laughed. Sometimes, Ed knew, he just got things wrong.

Now she repeated Bev's update, the traffic lights had been identified as the ones stolen from the Highways Depot.

'Got to admire the planning,' Ed said.

Sam reached forward and closed her air vent.

'No sign of the van on CCTV,' she said. 'A spent marine distress flare was found in a field. Looks like that was used as the signal to activate the lights.'

'How easy are they to get hold of?' Ed wouldn't have known where to start.

'Any chandler will sell them.'

'Any what?' Ed looked at Sam as if she had switched to Swahili.

She sighed, explained it was a shop that sold things for boats.

'You can buy them off the internet as well,' she went. 'Before you ask they have a shelf life of about four years and orange smoke is the daylight flare.'

A Black Rat zoomed past, blue lights flashing, the Roads Policing Unit driver, hands positioned on the wheel in the classic ten to two, concentrating on the road ahead.

'Another one late for the card game,' Ed deadpanned.

Sam watched the rear end of the BMW opening up an ever increasing gap.

'We might be able to trace whoever sold the flare but it's probably a long shot and certainly there are no prints on it. Julie reckons it's been wiped clean.'

Ed wiggled his toes, a futile effort to ease the stiffness in his legs. 'If you go to the extent of stealing traffic lights you're not going to be daft enough to leave prints.'

'Exactly,' Sam agreed. 'So who do you think is behind this?'

Ed unwrapped two toffees, passed one to Sam, and slipped the other into his mouth.

'If you're asking do I think any of the local crews would take Billy Skinner on, no chance, not without outside help,' Ed said. 'But if Skinner's upset someone from Newcastle, Leeds, wherever, anything's possible.'

Ed stopped and shook his head, nostrils twitching and throat tightening despite the toffee he was still working on.

Only Sam Parker could suck on a sweet and a cigarette at the same time.

'But why would he do that?' Ed got back to Skinner. 'He's never done it before, he's not exactly struggling, and if he wanted to expand he'd have done it when he was younger.'

Ed couldn't put it together, the pieces not matching the picture.

'What about his sons?' Sam said, blowing out more

smoke. 'Maybe one of them has rubbed up the wrong people.'

Ed knew The Apostles brought different talents to the party, although plodder Mark's was hazy at best, absolute loyalty Ed's best guess. Luke was ruthless, Ed had no doubt, but calm and smart when it mattered, more difficult to read. Mat was the open book, the hothead who did first, thought later. If someone had lit a fire for the Skinners, Mat would be odds on the one with the matches.

Ed shook his head.

'It just doesn't make sense, unless…'

He stopped, closed his eyes, and let the new thought take shape in the silence before it vanished as quickly as it had arrived. 'Unless what?' Sam brought him back.

'Unless it's somebody in their own group.'

Sam's expression told him she would need convincing.

'It would have been inconceivable ten years ago, even five years ago, that somebody would take Billy Skinner on, someone local at least,' Ed working through it as he spoke. 'But he's getting older and as you so often like to remind me, nothing stops for progress. If the enemy's from within, someone close, even the sons, they'll have been hiding in plain sight.'

Sam was still struggling to picture Billy Skinner letting it happen, dropping the guard that had kept him where he was for so long.

'Why are you so surprised?' Ed watching her. 'Remember Aisha?'

Ed instinctively stroked the scar on his neck, the memory of the knife attack that almost killed him running like an ice river down his spine. 'Just because it's family doesn't mean it can be ruled out.'

They drove without speaking, tiredness and the noise of the tyres on the road lulling them both.

They reached Ferrybridge, the end finally in sight and the carriageway now three lanes, the outside closed to the HGVs.

Sam waited for Ed to make some comment but he stayed

silent as she accelerated, powered down her window, and flicked her latest cigarette away.

'We've had no intelligence about a potential gang war have we?' Sam said, glancing Ed's way again.

'No,' the reply slow, the voice dry. 'And thanks, I was asleep there.'

Sam said oops, sorry and, well, what did he think; why was the grapevine so quiet?

'If it was to settle a score or even a proper outside takeover you'd expect to get a whisper at least,' Ed stretched the best he could in the confines of his seat. 'But if it's all inside Skinner's own set up…'

They both knew an inside job was fraught with danger for the one looking to take the head of their own snake. The element of surprise was inevitably their trump card; that relied on lips staying sealed.

'So if it's the sons…and this just stays between us two… are we thinking all of them?' Sam kept their kite flying. 'Luke stepping out of his dad's shadow or Mat taking him on?'

Ed was only sure Mark could be ruled out for any solo coup.

'He can probably find his mouth with his fork if the light's on but you wouldn't send him to the corner shop with a note.'

Sam smiled. 'Not leadership material then?'

'Oh, I don't know,' Ed kept his face straight. 'He would probably fit nicely in our wonderful corridors of power. They could all go to the corner shop together. Make sure they made it back safe.'

Mathew Skinner was an altogether different beast, moved by impulses he seemed unable or unwilling to control, the wild man charging around in his own red mist.

'Feels he should be the one to step up when Skinner retires,' Ed said. 'But the craic has Billy handing over to Luke come the day.'

But could Mat plot a successful take over; plan something like the traffic lights grab from the compound and a precision job like the ambush?

Ed couldn't see it: 'If Mat's involved he's getting help.'

A team effort by all three brothers was something neither Sam nor Ed were happy to rule out.

John Elgin pushed open his black metal garden gate and walked past his postage stamp sized Astroturf lawn; they'd lived in this house, a council house, for thirty-odd years.

He preferred to live amongst those he represented, show he hadn't forgotten his roots unlike some pompous clowns on the council.

His socialist principles notwithstanding, he bought the house under the Right to Buy Scheme, using some of the discount to have a new kitchen fitted. Was that really twenty years ago?

At least Tara made him feel young again, if only for a few hours, and he felt a warm glow even now just thinking about her.

After pulling himself round in Scaramangers he'd taken a long walk by the sea, a chance to clear his head and prepare to face the music.

His own personal she-devil had been in bed when he got home last night, snoring like a bull elephant with bronchitis, the room reeking of booze and body odour. He couldn't sleep in the same bed. Not that he wanted to, especially after Tara.

He'd gone to the spare room and was already up and out before his wife woke, or more accurately to Elgin, came round.

Now his warm glow thawed faster than an ice cream in a microwave as he crossed the threshold.

Her voice, loud enough to wake the dead, boomed from the sitting room like biblical thunder.

'Where've you been you arsehole and what fucking time did you get in last night?'

He heard her grunt and wheeze, pictured her heaving herself up on bingo wing arms, his sympathies with the long suffering settee.

Her bulk filled the door.

'Come on then,' the walls shaking, cider fumes almost visible around her like an aura. 'Where the fuck have you been? Another one of your little slappers?'

Elgin muttered 'out' and backed towards the front door.

She charged at him, deceptively quick over the short length of the hallway.

'What do they call this one?' shouting on the move, the distance closing.

He grabbed her podgy wrist as she threw a windmill right hander, the motion half turning him round.

'Another one of your slappers?'

She was swinging her wrist from side to side trying to break free, saliva flying from her wet lips.

'What time did you get in?' she screamed.

Elgin pushed her away, wiped something moist from his cheek, and said 'fuck this' before he turned and walked out.

CHAPTER THIRTY-THREE

MOST OF THE lights in Police HQ were out but they were burning in the HOLMES room.

Ed got out of the car, bent over and rubbed his thighs. His knees were aching, the side of his neck on fire.

'You alright you old crock?' Sam said. 'I keep telling you to take it easy.'

Sam flicked open a packet, lit a Marlboro, and leaned against the bonnet. 'Wonder how they're getting on with Skinner?'

'Your guess is as good as mine,' Ed said, now standing straight, raising his right knee to his chest.

'Camping in that van of yours looks well and truly over,' Sam watched him stretching. 'You better think about cashing it in.'

Ed looked hurt.

'Sell Doris? Be like selling a child.'

Selling the wife… now there's a thought.

Bev walked towards them, head down as she lit a cigarette.

'No sign of Skinner,' she told them. 'Media are all over it, as you'd expect. Never seen so many out on a Sunday. So much for you seeing me tomorrow.'

'He's dead,' Ed raised his left knee to his chest and winced. 'It's just a case of waiting until his body turns up.'

Bev looked at Sam. 'Who's rattled Mr. Aerobics' cage?'

Sam smiled. 'He's done nothing but whinge for the last hour about how stiff he is.'

'A bit stiff are we Ed?' Bev said with a smile. 'Need a hand with anything?'

'I'll let you know,' he said. 'Nice to see the PC Brigade haven't infiltrated the entire police force…yet.'

'Service,' Sam corrected him.

'Yeah right.'

Sam inhaled the cigarette.

'Not much we can do tonight,' she said. 'Skinner could be anywhere. Any sign of Mat?'

'No,' Bev said, flicking ash onto the car park.

Ed planted his heels on the ground and started rocking back and forth on them. 'Could be with his father.'

'What the two of them snatched?' Bev said.

'Or Mat's the one who snatched Billy,' Ed said, still rocking.

Sam gave Bev an update on their trip to Jeremy Scott's old school, the revelations about John Elgin drawing a 'bloody hell' and the hurried lighting of another cigarette.

'Look we'll regroup tomorrow,' Sam said now. 'Get everybody away home Bev but keep the school thing to yourself. We'll tell everybody in the morning.'

Bev turned and walked away, a teasing 'night night stiffy' to Ed over her shoulder.

He looked beat, Sam thought, and not just physically.

You should be coming home with me.

'What sort of reception will you get?' she asked him.

Ed shook his head and puffed out his cheeks, knowing nothing good would be waiting.

'Probably a two-sandwich buffet,' a weary grin at Sam's puzzled expression. 'Cold-shoulder and tongue. Just a question of which will be first.'

Shoulders slumped he turned and walked away.

'See you tomorrow.'

'Ed,' Sam hesitated. 'Fancy a drink?'

Ed stopped and turned around and thrust his hands in his pocket. 'You know what, I do.'

At another house on another street he pressed the bell on the front door, hoping for a different reception.

Jill Brown wasn't wearing her short skirt and heels but she didn't try to punch him.

'I wasn't expecting to see you so soon,' she smiled. 'Trouble with you know who?'

She stepped aside.

'The usual,' Elgin walked into the kitchen. 'The only time she's not drinking is when she's in a coma.'

Jill Brown felt for him but her sympathy was tempered. She had been telling him for years to leave, that people would understand, that he was the only one who could make it happen.

Easier said than done was Elgin's usual response.

'You got any beer in the fridge?' he asked now.

She brought him a bottle of Flag Porter, a favourite from the small Darwin Brewery in Sunderland, worried it was too cold.

Elgin told her the beer would be just fine.

He took the small bottle with the galleon on the label and followed her into the sitting room, Jill muting the TV and sitting down.

Gas flames danced around the coal effect fire, the only light from the small table lamp and the curved TV.

He sat next to her. 'Anything good on?'

'Nothing special, just channel hopping,' Jill sounding uneasy. 'Look I'm sorry about yesterday. It was just…it was the shock.'

She picked up the half full glass of red wine that was on the carpet. 'To think I took him there. No wonder he went off the rails.'

Elgin took hold of her hand, told her to stop blaming

herself, that Scott had all the blame on his back.

His eyes glanced at the TV, the news, what looked like a car wreck.

'Turn that up,' he said.

On the screen was a damaged BMW, windows out, airbags inflated.

Elgin realised it must be a recording not live - it was still daylight.

'What is it?' Jill said.

'Shhh'

The voice of the reporter filled the room.

'The police have made no statement as yet but we understand that as the car,' the camera zoomed in on the BMW, 'stopped at these lights,' the traffic lights came on the screen, 'masked men launched a violent attack and abducted the driver, making off in a Ford Transit van.'

The item over, Elgin muted the TV and drank from the Porter like a man finding a standpipe in the Sahara.

'What is it?' Jill asked.

'I think that was Billy Skinner's car.'

Elgin slouched into the settee and closed his eyes. Harry had been as cool as the proverbial cucumber this morning. Was this what he'd meant by 'wheels in motion', a mobile abduction? He took another pull on the Porter, eyes still shut.

Out of the frying pan John, out of the frying pan.

But as long as Harry kept his word and got the tape…

'You alright,' Jill's voice jolted him. 'You look like you've seen a ghost.'

Elgin forced a smile: 'I'm fine…just you don't expect people getting kidnapped in broad daylight. Not in Seaton St George anyway.'

Jill got up and headed for the kitchen, speaking over her shoulder on the way.

'Play with fire you get burnt,' she said. 'And Billy Skinner's played around fires all his life.'

Elgin closed his eyes again and wondered where the flames were heading next.

Stuart McFadden had seen the news bulletin, but unlike Elgin, he wasted no time sitting around. He took a coke from the mini-bar and drank it as he walked to reception.

He was just another faceless guest but if he was on the in-house CCTV, he had a cover story…hotels and prostitutes not exactly an unknown mix.

She had left immediately by the fire escape stairs, glad of the money but wondering if she had done something wrong.

Timing was everything now, Stuart knew.

Mat Skinner hadn't been seen since Geoff Mekins was tied up and beaten.

Luke would be holding it together, trying to work it all out, to find out where Mat was, what he was doing. Mark would be Nero, watching as their empire burned, and Marge, genuinely grieving, would be seeking solace from the bottle.

No doubt Mekins was fish food now but Mat would be like a rabid dog. And everybody knew the best way to deal with that kind of animal.

Stuart jumped into his car. Plenty were likely to think Mat was behind the snatch on Billy Skinner and now was the time to strike.

Game on.

He headed north out of Seaton St George. He knew exactly where he would find Mat. As Skinner's most trusted employee, the man Billy paid to be his in-house gatherer of intelligence, there was very little he didn't know.

But that didn't mean he shared everything.

Some gold was best held in reserve; only reveal the nuggets when maximum impact was anticipated.

It had been months ago when Geoff Mekins, crying because Mat had his eyes on a new cock, needed a listening ear. Stuart had built his life on being a listener.

Mekins droned on for about half an hour, sobbing, shaking his head, declaring his love for Mat, even though Mat had spent the previous night chatting up some young blond guy.

Stuart's grandmother had always told him good things came to the ones who waited and now his wait had proved worthwhile.

Mekins told him how hard he'd worked to make the caravan special, a place to escape. He'd even chosen the selection of paperbacks.

It only needed Stuart to be sympathetic, nod in the right places, before Mekins disclosed the caravan's location.

Stuart found it in the early hours one morning when he suspected they were there, just to make sure of Mekins' story. Mat's car provided the confirmation.

Now as he drove north up the A1 his thoughts weren't consumed by how he would kill Mat. That was easy. One bullet, two tops. His mind was preoccupied with getting rid of the body after it was done.

A sea disposal had long been the Skinner family's preferred choice but Stuart didn't have access to a boat, and while Mekins told him once they had an inflatable with an outboard motor for fishing trips, he didn't fancy lugging the body into one of those unstable things.

An empty mineshaft would have been ideal, but as far as he knew there were none left. All of the old mines had been landscaped, the headstock wheels born during the Industrial Revolution airbrushed off the horizon.

What he couldn't do was leave the body with a bullet in the head to be found by the police or the Skinners. After he'd killed Mat he would vanish, but only temporarily. He'd make some calls and prepare for a takeover. He knew he could count on Harry Pullman and his nephew Dean. The Skinners were on borrowed time and he had no intention of being caught on the wrong side of a gunfight.

Parking on the outskirts of Seahouses he took a rucksack from the boot, and put on his walking boots and waterproofs. What was more natural than a hiker in Northumberland, rucksack and tent on his back?

He didn't know if there were any CCTV cameras, but keeping your head and face obscured wasn't a problem.

The handgun in his waistband was a risk but how many cops would be up here on a Sunday night?

He made his way up the hill overlooking the site, lay down on the wet grass and took out the binoculars from his bag. They weren't brilliant in the dark, but they were better than nothing.

He scanned the site and found Mat's silver Porsche parked away from the caravan. There were no lights on in the caravan, but there were no lights on in any of them. He didn't even know if the site was open.

He pressed the binoculars tight against his eyes.

Well I'll go to the foot of our stairs.

He grinned. Maybe he didn't need the gun. Maybe he didn't need to dispose of the body.

The caravans were in darkness, but Lady Luck was shining. He smiled, focused on the entrance gate and watched the two-staggers-forward-one-stagger-sideways progress of someone pissed-up.

Mat Skinner, chest pointing at the ground, was weaving across the site like Bambi on ice. He swayed as he put one outstretched arm against the caravan door. Three times he tried to put the key in the lock, finally opening the door on the fourth attempt.

Stuart McFadden knew from experience that Mat would be in a coma in ten minutes but it was best to wait. He figured two hours should mean everything was quiet. McFadden popped the headphones into one ear, climbed into his sleeping bag and put his phone on shuffle.

Golden Slumber, the Elbow cover-version, filled his head.

He smiled at the night sky.

Mat Skinner's slumber would be permanent.

Monday 15th December

Ed gripped the door handle as he swayed: drink, lack of food and lack of sleep, a dangerous combination.

Outside the taxi driver tapped his horn.

Sam moved unsteadily past him towards the front door.

Ed grabbed her wrist, pulled her towards him. Their mouths locked on each other's before their eyes reacted to what was going on.

In the end McFadden gave it three hours before he made his move, darting across the site head kept low, each stride taking him closer to the caravan. Standing outside he could hear deep snoring. He climbed the few steps onto the decking.

McFadden took his rucksack off his back, fished inside and found what he was looking for, a small screwdriver and a yellow duster.

He wrapped the duster around the blade - no point leaving striation marks for the forensic team - and forced open the patio doors.

The police would never establish how long the doors had been damaged, even if they were still capable of being examined. Both owners would be dead and nobody else, to McFadden's knowledge, knew the caravan even existed let alone made visits.

He stepped inside, smiled at the snoring and turned on his head-torch. He saw scatter cushions, statues of Greek Gods with lampshades on the top of them. He crept towards the open plan kitchen and turned on every gas ring on the cooker.

The snoring was rattling around the caravan.

Dead to the world and you soon will be.

He closed the patio doors behind him, not tight but tight enough, and walked away.

Mat wouldn't die of carbon monoxide poisoning, not with LPG gas, but he was a creature of habit, Stuart knew. As soon as he woke he would reach for his cigarettes like every other certified chain smoker and then…BOOM!

Mat dead, problem solved.

The police would establish the pub he had been in, find a

witness or two who recalled how pissed he was, possibly find the hob in the debris and discover the gas rings turned on.

The presumption? A drunk who forgot to switch them off and blew himself up when he sparked a cigarette.

No tears shed by the police.

Job jobbed

CHAPTER THIRTY-FOUR

SAM TURNED on the car radio, glanced in the mirror and shuddered. She looked as bad as she felt; pale eyes like the proverbial piss-holes-in-the-snow, cramps in her stomach. The price of too little sleep, too many cigarettes, and too much wine. She was furious with herself for putting the washing machine on when she was half-cut. The new red t-shirt had ruined the whites, delivering a garish collection of pinks when she went to unload.

A dodgy washing moment she could handle. But that kiss? She was furious with herself. It was passionate, electric, and exactly what she didn't need. Not while Ed was still married, still living in the marital home, still with Sue. Thank God he'd got in the taxi.

She changed down to first gear and swore under her breath. She hadn't got out of second for the last mile, the roundabout a never-nearing mirage on the horizon. Another day, another miserable rush hour and every prospect of an awkward silence with Ed at journey's end.

Maybe get a take-away tonight, Sam thought, mentally changing topic. She imagined a Chinese or something fiery from the new Indian she had been waiting to try. She could already smell the spices as she turned up the radio.

Police in Seahouses are investigating an explosion on a caravan park. An eyewitness described hearing a huge explosion at around 7am this morning and rushed outside to see the remains of a holiday home on fire.

It appears that one caravan has been totally destroyed and those nearby damaged. It is not yet known if anybody has been injured.

Police and the fire brigade are on the scene and we understand that the few visitors on the site have been evacuated as a precaution.

There will be more on this breaking story in our next bulletin.

And now the weather…

Sam turned the radio off. She already had enough on her plate.

Harry Pullman was shaving in front of the bathroom mirror, luminous blue blobs of fallen gel bright against the grubbiness of his white sleeveless vest.

His feet stopped tapping as Fleetwood Mac's 'Go Your Own Way' ended and his head jerked towards the radio, the blunt razor nicking his top lip.

Police in Seahouses…

The white towel matched his vest in terms of colour. He pressed it against his lip and dashed into the bedroom, pulling on a shirt and jeans before working again at the trickle of blood.

All he could think about was Mat and his caravan. Was it Mat's? If it was, who was behind it? Luke? Someone else?

He sat on the edge of the bed, lit a cigarette, and put the packet and lighter next to his Samsung Galaxy on the bedside table. He needed to think and was still sitting like some Rodin mickey-take when his mobile danced a Northern Soul slide across the MDF.

He glanced at the screen. Number not recognised.

'Hello?'

'That you Harry?'

McFadden.

'Yeah,' Harry said.

'You heard?'

'Heard what?' Harry believed in playing dumb. It always served him well.

'Billy's been snatched. Mekins is gone and now Mat's been killed.'

'Where are you?' Harry said.

'Phone box just outside Berwick.'

Berwick? North of Seahouses. What's your game?

Harry didn't respond, inhaled on his cigarette.

'We need to talk, Harry.'

'What about?'

'What happens next.'

'What's happened to Mat?' Harry said, trying to work out where this was going.

'Caravan explosion. You not heard it on the news?'

'The news never mentioned anyone being dead.'

'They will.'

'When do you want to talk? Harry said. 'And where?'

A pause, the noise of traffic and a distant siren on the line.

'Soon as but away from Seaton. How about Berwick?'

'You must be joking,' Harry almost laughed. 'If Mat's dead in a caravan in Seahouses…how do you know he's got a van up there anyway? First I've heard of it.'

'Long story,' McFadden swatted the question away.

Harry said he was happy right where he was; no way was he going further north than his front door.

'Meet me here in the pub,' he said. 'Nothing suspicious about that.'

Stuart McFadden wasn't sure.

'Think about it Stuart,' Harry said, rummaging under the bed for a pair of socks. 'You're up in Berwick for whatever reason. If Mat's in that caravan it'll look a lot more iffy if you're in that neck of the woods rather than down here. Why are you up there anyway?'

Harry already knew the answer.

There was only one way Stuart McFadden could know Mat was dead and it wasn't that he'd heard it on the grapevine. The Marvin Gayes of Seaton St George wouldn't be up yet let alone singing.

'Harry, the Skinners are finished,' McFadden beginning his move. 'Billy snatched and that's down to Mat. Revenge for Mekins.'

'Mekins?' Harry said. 'What's happened to him?'

'Billy ordered it after the shit Mat and Mekins pulled at your gaffe,' McFadden told him. 'Mark's like a rabbit in the headlights. Luke won't be able to pull this together. Either somebody in Seaton takes over or outsiders come in.'

Harry said McFadden was jumping to a lot of conclusions but yeah, they should meet, he would listen to whatever was on his mind.

Harry checked the time. 8am. 'See you about eleven then?'

Stuart McFadden said he was on his way.

Harry pulled on his socks. He needed to make a few calls.

'Do you want to explain that?' Sam said, throwing a photograph at Elgin, the embrace with Linda Pritchard not lacking in passion.

They had brought him to Seaton police station and after some huff and puff he came quietly. Whatever reception Ed had faced at home last night, or whatever had happened this morning, it hadn't affected his mood. When they had met at the nick that morning the silence Sam feared had never happened. Ed had spoken straight out.

'Listen,' he had said as soon as Sam shut the passenger door, turning to face her from the driver's seat. 'Last night. It was what I wanted, it's just with Sue…'

Sam had found a smile, said she understood, and that wasn't drink the devil's own work.

And that was it, at least for now, their world one second out of kilter and next spinning on its old familiar axis. Sam would later acknowledge her relief was shaded in disappointment.

Now in the interview room, John Elgin's adam's apple

moved around his throat like a golf ball spinning in a cup. 'How dare you spy on me!'

Typical politician, Sam thought. Back to the wall so go straight on the attack.

'No-one's been spying on you Mr. Elgin, at least nobody from the police, but now this has come into our possession it is quite interesting don't you think?' Sam with a light touch, polite even.

Small blisters of sweat spread across Elgin's brow.

'Please tell me you haven't dragged me here to talk about an innocent little cuddle…'

'Mr. Elgin,' Sam interrupted, leaning towards him, voice a little sharper now. 'I'm not interested in whether it was an innocent little cuddle or not. What interests me is that the woman you're cuddling is the wife of one of your grandson's abusers.'

Elgin's tongue ran around the inside of his mouth.

Sam sat back. 'How long have you been on cuddling terms with Linda Pritchard?'

'It's not what you think?'

'What is it then?'

Elgin rubbed his eyes and sighed.

'That poor woman was trapped in a loveless marriage. She knew what her husband was… his words trailed off.

'Yet did nothing to stop it,' Sam said, not a question but a fact.

Elgin threw his shoulders back and raised his voice, happy to be back on the attack.

'What could she do? Report it to your lot! That would have got her a long way. You only became interested in her husband once he was dead. We all know what happens to uncorroborated allegations of sexual abuse and besides, nobody had made a complaint to my knowledge.'

Sam wanted background, wanted Elgin to calm down and talk and maybe let his guard down.

'When did you meet Linda?' she asked him.

Ed had picked up the photograph and was staring like it was a masterpiece in an art gallery.

He wasn't interested in the cuddle. What was it about Linda Pritchard?

'Just answer the question,' Ed said, still locked on the snapshot.

Elgin sighed: 'About four months ago at some meeting.'

'Which one?' Sam asked.

'I don't know. I go to a lot of meetings.'

Ed finally looked away from the photo.

'Surely not that many where you meet a future cuddling partner,' he watched Elgin go red. 'Where did you meet?'

Another sigh, heavier this time, Elgin looking at the ceiling, sitting back in the chair, his body language reaching for an air of indifference

'Travellers Group Meeting. Linda is interested in their…plight.'

'And did you know then that her husband had abused your grandson?' Sam said.

'Of course not! What are you suggesting?' Elgin pushed against the table and was on his feet. 'Oh I see. I'm like a foreign agent on a mission. Get close to the wife, get close to the husband.'

'Sit down John,' Ed said, leaning back into his chair, stretching his legs and putting his hands behind his neck. 'You're making the place look untidy.'

Elgin's defiance lasted five unconvincing seconds before he sat back down.

'Why didn't you tell us you knew Jeremy Scott?' Sam said.

The swift change of direction - deliberate on Sam's part - did its job. Elgin was unnerved.

'What?' He floundered, head shaking. 'I don't know him.'

Sam leaned in close again.

'John this is getting tiring and I am starting to wonder why you feel the need to continually lie.'

Elgin sat in silence, nerves jangling like wind-chimes in a stiff breeze.

'Yesterday I went to your old school. Not the one here.'

She paused, allowed Elgin to digest her words, waited for a reaction.

Elgin stared at her.

'The one in Hamble. St Augustine,' she told him.

This time she got a reaction. Elgin couldn't have looked more shocked if Sam had plugged him in and hit the on switch.

'What?' he barely managed the word.

'We spoke to one Mr Stirling, the head now but a young teacher in your day. He told us you were pretty good on the piano.'

Elgin was breathing hard, looking for the escape hatch.

'I have no idea what you're talking about.'

It was Ed's turn to jump to his feet.

'Throw him in the traps,' looking straight at Elgin. 'I'm sick of listening to this shit.'

Sam rose slowly to her feet.

'You might be right,' she said, an air of something close to boredom on her face. 'What do you think, John?'

Elgin's resolve left him so quickly he swore he heard it snap, his head dropping in the same moment. 'Could I have a glass of water please?'

Ed sat back down. 'How about a cup of tea? Sugar?'

'No sugar. Just milk.'

By the time Elgin was sipping his third cup he had told them everything about his time in the clutches of Jeremy Scott.

Sam and Ed had listed to many an adult relive a childhood ordeal but it didn't get any easier.

'You have no idea what it was like,' Elgin said now. 'You can't have, not unless you were abused. The stale smell of cigar smoke before and then that mix…semen, piss, blood…I can still smell it now. It's with me wherever I go.'

They watched Elgin bow his head and clear his throat, another victim wrongly carrying the guilt.

'You've got to remember back then children weren't often believed,' Elgin told them. 'The schools themselves, the institutions where it was happening, society as a whole, they all have to take some responsibility for that culture.'

He lowered his voice.

'The school didn't abuse me but they let it go on. My mother told the headmaster…'

He paused, lost in the memory of the nightmare.

'Guess what happened? Nothing. The reputation of the school was all that mattered.'

He wiped his left eye and fell silent, the tiredness bone deep.

Sam offered Elgin a break but he wanted to go on, to get it over with and get out.

'You were a boarder at the school?' Sam raised her eyebrows.

Elgin nodded. 'That's right. I was six when I went there and left when I was about thirteen.'

'I'm puzzled, Sam told him. 'Please don't think I'm being rude, but boarding school and all the fees I imagine go with it, but you live in a former council house.'

Elgin took a deep breath and explained.

He grew up knowing his grandfather had been a wartime 'spiv' in London and a good one, good enough to buy a small shop in a wealthy area of Southampton when the fighting finally stopped.

Ration coupons meant there was still a thriving black market and Victor Elgin sold more goods under the counter than he did over it.

By the time John Elgin was born to a single mother, his grandfather owned mini-markets, clothes shops and even a couple of small hotels. Victor idolized him and he wanted for nothing, nothing until he found the courage to speak about Jeremy Scott.

'My grandfather refused to believe that a man of education and standing like that would abuse young boys,' Elgin remembered crying at his grandfather's reaction.

Stop telling tales boy!

'All he wanted was for that school to get me to university, get the start in life he never had. He always had notions of me being an officer in the Royal Navy.'

Elgin wiped his eyes, his hands shaking as picked up his cup.

'I think he fancied me being the First Sea Lord.'

He sipped on the tea.

'When my mother said my happiness was more important than his idea of my career it all kicked off. Things were said between them and wounds were opened that never healed.'

Elgin never saw his grandfather again. Victor had married a secretary a third of his age who inherited everything when he died.

'My mother did her best for me,' Elgin said. 'We moved up here to make a fresh start but it was hard. Mum was used to having a private income. Up here she ended up spending the rest of her life working in shops. Ironic really.'

He shook his head, took another deep breath.

Elgin might have left a nightmare behind but his rebooted childhood still wasn't easy, his accent and his manner making him an easy target for bullies in a very different kind of school.

But Elgin was proud he had come through, learned to fit in and pushed his old life as deep down as it would go. He had even spent hours working to lose his accent.

'You adapt to survive,' he said, while Sam and Ed sat in silence, letting the story go.

'I reinvented myself. I'm still reinventing myself...a Labour councillor living in a council house, a man of the people. Can you imagine if the press found out I went to boarding school, that my grandfather was a spiv who made boatloads of cash? They'd have a field day.'

When he fell silent Sam waited to make sure he had finished before she asked him another question, asked whether his wife knew the truth about his past.

For the first time something different flashed in Elgin's eyes.

'Stupidly I told her before we got married,' unmissable regret in his voice. 'Now she has a hold on me for the rest of my life. You saw my name on the prize winners' board down there. So could anyone else who looked.'

Sam watched Elgin and felt his pain. Her husband may have died prematurely but child abuse always seemed to be on a different level, victims moving with their dreadful secrets in a world that was oblivious.

'How did you feel when you found Jeremy Scott was dead?' Sam asked quietly.

Elgin looked at her, only hatred on his face now.

'How do you think I felt,' he spat out the words. 'I would pay to dance on his grave and piss all over it.'

'And your relationship with Jill Brown?'

Elgin shook his head, bemused. 'Why?'

'Come on John,' Ed joined in. 'You're abused, your grandson's abused. Jill Brown's son's abused.'

Elgin never looked away as the tears came.

'He's my son too.'

CHAPTER THIRTY-FIVE

Scaramangers was like a half-forgotten church on a wet Sunday morning - empty save for a few older souls scattered around, lonely and lost in their own thoughts.

Harry sometimes listened to the woes of his congregation but today he wasn't up for the Barman's Confessional. Too much going on.

So the sight of Ray Reynolds walking through the doors almost gave him a migraine on the spot.

'Pint of your finest landlord.'

Harry picked up a glass and stepped towards the pumps.

'Another early start Ray, it's becoming a habit. It's not a weekend now you know.'

Reynolds tossed him a look.

'Who are you, my mother? Just grabbing a quick one before the Pensioners' Party.'

Harry passed him a pint. 'On the house.'

'Cheers.' Reynolds raised his glass and gulped, heard Harry asking him where was the party?

'The Ship,' Reynolds said. 'They've hired it out. Closed to the public for the afternoon.'

Harry was hoping another customer would get him off the hook, even for a minute or two.

What are you really after you nosy bastard?

'Any more thoughts on your boss going missing?' Reynolds asked him. 'You know, after Dean's memory suddenly came back.'

Here we fucking go…

'He was excited Ray, shouting his mouth off like young lads do.' Harry was squirming but doing his best. 'He knows as much as I do, which is nothing. You know me. Keep my head down. You just having a solo one before the party.'

'Couple of the other lads might come in,' Reynolds glancing behind him when he heard the door.

Stuart McFadden, walking to the bar, seemed calm enough, relaxed even.

'How are you, Mr. Reynolds,' the greeting easy, respectful.

Reynolds said he was sound and then got right to it.

'What's happened to your boss then?'

He put his glass to his lips and waited.

'Your guess is as good as mine,' McFadden told him. 'He'll turn up. Pint of cooking Harry.'

They always referred to non-premium lager as 'cooking lager.'

'Oh I think you can guarantee he'll turn up,' Reynolds said, the hint of a smile. 'What state he'll be in is anybody's guess. But you know what they say, live by the sword.'

McFadden turned to face him.

'Probably best you don't overstay your welcome,' McFadden said, picking up his glass. 'Lots of people aren't happy about Billy being snatched and if they thought you were gloating…'

Reynolds put his glass on the bar and stood up straight. 'What would they do? Have a go at me?'

If McFadden was intimidated he was hiding it well.

'Mr. Reynolds all I'm saying is that you're out of the game now,' the tone considered. 'Don't try and come back into play. It'll only end in tears.'

'I hope that's not a threat Stuey.'

He smiled when McFadden's grimace showed he'd hit a nerve. He knew McFadden hated being called Stuey.

'And as you're buying,' Reynolds said, 'I'll have another

beer, just to make sure I do overstay my welcome. Can't have people thinking I'm running scared. Especially from plastic gangsters like you and your cronies.'

He turned to face Harry Pullman. 'Same again landlord. Stuey's in the chair.'

Harry pulled a pint and passed it across the bar.

Reynolds took a slow, single sip. 'On second thoughts Harry, that tastes like shit. Not your fault. Maybe the pint had an allergic reaction to the person who bought it.'

He looked at his watch.

'Best be off. Places to go, people to see. Cheers Harry.'

Reynolds walked away from the bar, pushed open the door and shouted 'see you later Stuey.'

He didn't turn around. He knew McFadden would be raging.

Sam walked along the pier, coffee in hand. She needed to be alone, out of the office, process the information that was bouncing around her head.

The sea air always cleared her head like a vapour rub eased congestion. She smiled. Three things cured every ill as far as her mother was concerned: Vicks, Germolene or a good night's sleep.

At the end of the pier she leaned against the railings and watched a yacht half-a-mile-out sail by on a starboard tack. The white sails look well-trimmed, the yacht making good progress through the water. She sipped the coffee, wondering who was on board, where they were headed. Could she really do it again?

Maybe I can, maybe…

She thought about John Elgin. Started off with a life of privilege, wealth and future all mapped out, then everything snatched away because he had the audacity to be abused. He even had to watch his grandfather use his money to destroy his mother.

Sam stared into the water and shook her head at the rank injustice.

Elgin's revelation he was Curtis' father had been a gob-smacker, Elgin only finding out himself later in life. When Jill Brown had discovered she was pregnant she had chosen to end their affair and tell her husband the child was his.

For Elgin to learn he had a son and that his son had been abused would have been hard for anyone to handle. To find out his son had been abused by Jeremy Scott, his own hated predator, would have sent anybody over the edge.

His grandson's ordeal at the hands of Julius Pritchard and Hans van Dijk took Elgin's story to somewhere unimaginable.

Sam shuddered and searched her pockets for the Marlboros. Commonality - the sharing of features or attributes - was important in complex investigations.

Sam knew she had them in spades with this one.

Three generations of the same bloodline, all victims of child sexual abuse. All three abusers murdered, each dying horrific, violent deaths.

She lit a cigarette.

One murder reported by a known drug user, Curtis Brown, Elgin's son. Was he really there to buy drugs? The other two reported via an anonymous phone call.

Who rang that in?

The call had been traced to a call box different to the one used to anonymously ring Elgin, if that call had ever really happened.

The more she turned it over, the more it was clear.

John Elgin was slap bang in the centre of the whole conundrum.

He had the motive big time and the connections to the Skinners and Harry Pullman. Was Elgin capable of burning a man alive? Who knows what was going through his mind when everything came out but for Sam, picturing Elgin turning Jeremy Scott into a screaming fireball of smoke and flame was a stretch too far. The Skinners, even Harry Pullman, on the other hand…

And Curtis Brown, putting himself there at the time of

Scott's death by ringing the police. Was he involved? Another with the motive box ticked but if he was involved why make the call? Double bluff?

Pritchard and van Dijk, the abusers of Elgin's grandson, strung up with their throats cut; another gangland-style punishment.

Elgin and Linda Pritchard in the park added another thread to the tangle and now Billy Skinner had been abducted, his wild son Mat possibly missing. Had the two soldiers, Jeremy Scott's former pupils and possible victims, used their military know-how to stage the slick ambush?

Sam returned her gaze to the yacht, suddenly wishing she was aboard, nothing to think about but the sails, the wind and the tidal flow, the sound of the boat moving through the water and the movement of the boom, salt spray and coffee on her lips. She stared as the yacht sailed further away, destination unknown.

She was about to discover wind and tidal flows would mean nothing where she was going.

PC Tom Evans had driven from job to job since he started at 7am.

He'd joined the police with the noble intention of helping people and their communities; instead he was permanently firefighting, helping almost nothing but response targets.

He gripped the wheel, flexed his forearms and tried to forget his hunger. Oversleeping had left him with a tough decision on his morning ritual. He'd settled for shit, shower and shave at the expense of the porridge, blueberries and scrambled eggs.

Now he was in no hurry. The anonymous call to control room about a body being in a deserted factory was inevitably a hoax, the local urchins taking the piss.

On the approach he slowed even more; the little bastards could be hiding, watching him, ready to laugh and leg it.

He drove through the two-tone matt red and rust gates

and negotiated the bricks, stones and broken green glass scattered around what was once the car park.

He'd lived in Seaton St George all his life, recalled that somewhere nearby was where the boss-man used to park his shiny red Jaguar XJ6.

That was back in the day when he was a child himself and the factory employed hundreds of seamstresses. He glanced at the sleeve of his police issue shirt, wondered whether it was made in China.

His mother and grandmother had both worked here, both made redundant the same day, their skills amounting to a big fat zero in the profit and loss column.

He got out of the patrol car, stuffed his hands in his trouser pockets and idly kicked a stone. He knew people who had left here and had never been employed again, sentenced to a lifetime of low self-esteem whilst the clothes they used to make were manufactured thousands of miles away on the cheap.

He walked through the doorway, past the rusting clocking-in- machine that still hung on the wall, no use even to the scrap metal thieves.

Stepping onto what had once been the huge factory floor he mentally heard the deafening clatter of a hundred and more machines, women's hearing left permanently damaged in the days before Health and Safety at least gave them a chance.

The sight in front of him dragged him away from memory lane in a heartbeat.

Breathless he spoke into his radio. 'PC Evans to control.'

'PC Evans go ahead.'

He remembered the ABC of radio procedure as preached by his older colleagues years ago - accuracy, brevity, clarity.

'Naked body at Spikers factory. Face covered in white powder. Deceased believed to be Billy Skinner.'

CHAPTER THIRTY-SIX

The Christmas party was in full flow and so was the beer and lager, the revellers of an older cut but not a blue-rinse perm or Velcro fastening in sight.

The back room of The Ship was bouncing, men of physical stature in suits, smartly dressed women, all discussing the good old days and how modern policing was fucked.

Ray Reynolds was holding court.

'Not a man under 5'10" in the old days, men who joined when minimum height restrictions were enforced, before the bloody PC brigade kicked off about 'heightism' and the tiny tots flooded the force.'

For emphasis he held his right hand, palm down, against his hip.

'Christ half of the latest recruits look like they could audition for fridge magnets.'

The group burst into laughter, even though they'd heard it all before.

Ray Reynolds sipped his pint and looked around. Some of the assembled throng were in their seventies, but many were in their fifties, people who joined at 19, 20, 21 and retired after their 30 years' service, all bonded by a lifetime in 'The Job'.

Through the cranked up speakers George Michael was singing Last Christmas, the four staff crammed behind the tiny bar handing over pints quicker than George's lover gave away his heart.

Ed Whelan walked in. Sam had told him to take an hour out, show his face at the party. He'd worked with a lot of them, signed up with some, and would have been retired himself by now if he hadn't left and rejoined.

'Still hard at it Ed?' Ray Reynolds shook his head. 'Bloody dinosaur like you. How the hell do you cope?'

Reynolds looked like most people would imagine a senior detective to look like; neatly cut hair, navy blue suit, red tie, shiny black shoes.

Ed shook Reynolds' hand and turned down the offer of a pint.

'I'm working. Just popped in to see a few of the old faces.'

Reynolds followed Ed's eyes as he scanned the room.

'Surprised you've got time to pop in at all, what with Billy Skinner missing.'

'Missing presumed dead,' Ed said, having to raise his voice above the racket.

'We can all hope,' Reynolds beamed. 'Sam Parker must be due another promotion.'

He raised his eyebrows. 'They didn't look like that in my day mind, more's the pity.'

Ed let that go while the group around them, hanging on Reynolds' words like backstage groupies, nodded in eager agreement.

'I'd say she deserves to step up,' Ed said. 'But who knows what goes on in the head of the Chiefs?'

'Fuck all if they're still like they used to be,' Reynolds said, the man on a roll.

The laughter could have come straight from a can.

'Anyway I'm surprised you managed to make it,' Reynolds said now. 'You've got more dead bodies than Agatha Christie. Anything on the one up at Bill O'Grady's old place?'

'Jeremy Scott?' Ed said. 'Nothing. It's like it said in the

papers. Charred body found. The only thing we kept back was the fact we believe there was three there.'

Reynolds raised his glass.

'Still on the beer then,' Ed grinned.

'You know me,' Reynolds priming another one liner. 'When I want a cocktail I'll order lager. So three? Sounds interesting.'

Ed put his hands in his trouser pockets, widened his stance.

'Three pairs of boots and three sets of dungarees burnt out in a brazier by the garage. Took the lab ages to piece them together but they seem convinced. Other than that, nothing.'

Ed shrugged his shoulders and continued.

'No sightings around his house, total dead-end at the minute. But you all know how it is, suspected paedophile found dead and it's a case of, who gives a fuck?'

Nods all round. They knew the score.

'When I saw it on the TV I thought Sam's got some job on there,' Reynolds said. 'Still I suppose for some there's a sense of justice. Scum like that deserve everything that comes their way. Sure you don't want a drink?'

Ed took his hands out of his pockets, said he was fine.

'Nothing on the two up at the abattoir?'

Ed shook his head and shrugged.

'Same story,' he told Reynolds. 'Everybody's been diagnosed with 'who gives a fuck syndrome'.'

'Let's go downstairs to the cellar,' Harry said. 'I don't trust Ray Reynolds not to come back.'

Stuart McFadden walked behind the bar and down the steps, head low.

He paused at the entrance, his eyes adjusting to the gloom. The shove in the back catapulted him forward.

'Fucking hell Harry.'

McFadden regained his balance, straightened, and turned around.

'Alright Stu.'

Harry hit the light switch.

Luke and Mark Skinner emerged from the dark corners of the cellar nearest the door.

Harry took two steps to his left and leaned against the whitewashed wall.

Luke and Mark blocked the door, the only exit unless McFadden could magically drill through walls.

With nowhere to run he stood still, faced his captors and waited.

'You've been a naughty boy Stuart,' Luke said. 'Harry here has told us all about it.'

McFadden glanced at Harry then settled his eyes back on Luke, his face blank. He needed to think quickly.

'So where's my father?' Luke said.

'Your father?' McFadden indignant. 'I don't know what shit this idiot's been feeding you, but I've nothing to do with Billy going missing. Remember, it was him,' he nodded towards Harry, 'who your dad thought was skimming. Since when did he become Mr Fucking Trustworthy?'

Luke looked at Harry and then Mark and then back to McFadden.

'Since he filled us in on your telephone call about Mat.'

McFadden felt his heart rate increase but he could still walk away from this. It would be his word against Harry Pullman's, his king 'checked' but 'mate' a long way off.

'I have absolutely no idea what you're talking about.'

McFadden tried to relax, keep his voice calm and controlled.

'Harry said you were up at Seahouses and that you blew our kid's caravan up,' Luke said.

McFadden stepped backwards and leaned against the cellar wall.

'I can't remember the last time I was at Seahouses, and I don't know shit about any caravan.'

Luke told him it had been on the morning news but

McFadden said sorry, he hadn't seen the news, hadn't made a call to Harry or anyone else, sensing he was taking back control.

'I came in here for a pint and what did I find?' McFadden said.

'What?' Luke said, watching him.

'Your man here deep in conversation with a certain Ray Reynolds.'

Luke and Mark exchanged a look.

'Is that true Harry?' Luke said.

Harry Pullman looked like a punter who realised he had been shouting home the wrong horse.

'Now hang on,' he said. 'Don't try shifting this onto me. Reynolds was in here for a pint. He's always in. And he's retired.'

'Fuckers like him never retire,' Luke said.

McFadden liked more and more where this was going, turned the screw when he saw the chance.

'How many times over the years did your dad say Reynolds must have a good informant because he was always getting close?'

Harry Pullman lunged forwards. 'You cheeky bastard!'

Mark grabbed him around the neck and pulled him backwards.

'Calm down Harry,' Luke said. 'Nobody's accusing you of being a grass...not yet anyway...but I need to see your phone, quick look at the call register.'

Harry Pullman was watching his plan unravel faster than smelly stuff off a particularly well-polished stick.

'It was an unknown number,' his voice getting ragged. 'Jesus you're not believing this fucker?'

McFadden grinned, made another move, feeling like a Grand Master going for the kill.

'Maybe Harry went to this caravan I've never heard of...'

Harry Pullman lunged forward again and this time Mark didn't stop him, the punch knocking Stuart McFadden to the floor.

Mark stepped forward and pulled Harry away, McFadden

pushing himself up, wiping the trickle of blood off his lips with the back of his hand and grinning.

'Big protests from the copper's nark.'

Harry lunged again but Mark pulled him back.

'Settle down Harry,' Luke said.

He turned his attention back to McFadden.

'So you're saying you didn't ring Harry this morning?'

'I didn't ring him.'

'And you're saying you never went to see Mat in his caravan?'

'What caravan?' McFadden told him. 'I didn't even know he had a caravan.'

Luke kept his gaze on him for seconds that seemed like minutes in the sudden silence.

'So,' he said at last, shifting his eyes, turning them on Harry Pullman. 'If Stuart didn't ring you Harry, how the fuck do you know about Mat's caravan?'

Where McFadden was cool, Harry's gaskets were blowing, his voice desperate.

'I don't know anything about a fucking caravan!'

Luke had done his own checks, been in touch with the site and confirmed a caravan there was in Geoff Mekins' name. He was surprised him and Mat had managed to keep it under wraps.

'One of you two definitely knew,' he said now. 'That's a fact.'

The knock on the door was loud. Mark opened it and two heavies, both Luke's muscle, squeezed sideways into the cellar.

'Nobody leaves,' Luke said.

The two suited men nodded and stood with their hands clasped in front of them below the waist. They looked like they could have been in church.

'So who's lying?' Luke said.

The door was pushed open again.

'Both of the fuckers.'

The owner of the voice was hidden behind the two suits but

Harry Pullman and Stuart McFadden didn't need to see a face.

The suits separated and the voice stepped between them.

'Alright Harry, alright Stu.'

It was the turn of the brothers to grin.

All three of them.

CHAPTER THIRTY-SEVEN

Ed Whelan felt his mobile vibrate, took it out of his pocket and saw Sam's name on the screen.

He stepped outside The Ship, answered the call.

'Bloody hell it sounds like you're outside a nightclub,' Sam said, picturing something more high-season Salou that Seaton St George. 'Do me a favour and move away from the door. It looks like they've found Skinner.'

Ed began walking, already sure Skinner was dead by the tone of Sam's voice.

'He was naked, tied up and covered in what looks like coke,' Sam told him. 'Anonymous call. He's up at the old Spikers factory. Did you get a lift down there?'

Ed said yes, said nothing attracted the Black Rats more than a police party.

'I'll pick you up in ten,' Sam ended the call.

Ed walked back into the pub and said his goodbyes.

'You off already?' Reynolds caught him on his way back from the gents. 'No rest for the wicked.'

Ed gave him a 'something-like-that' look, told him to look after himself, and stepped outside.

He heard the voice before he saw the owner.

'Fucking hell, Ed, it's shit when we can't even have a pint in our pub because of you retired bobbies.'

Carol Pender, Seaton St George's all-peroxide-blonde, stopped in front of him.

Ed noted the December weather hadn't been high on Carol's priorities when she chose her outfit, the short yellow leather jacket and brown felt mini-skirt a courageous call, not to mention the huge yellow-hooped earrings.

The only concession to the cold was her footwear, but that was just luck. Carol liked her black cavalier thigh high boots, liked the effect they had on the men she would catch having a stolen look.

By her own admission she needed to be eye-candy; if she couldn't get testosterone pumping through their blood what was the point?

Ed had known her and her family for years, Carol through prostitution, the male line through a compulsion to end every drinking session with a fight.

Ed thought Carol had been off the game for years. Looking at her now, maybe she had just stopped getting caught.

'I'm not retired Carol. How's things?'

'Can't grumble,' she tugged at the boots one after the other. 'You'll be busy with those three nonce murders are you? Good enough for them. Should do that to all the kiddie-fiddlers if you ask me.'

'I didn't,' Ed wishing Sam would get a move on.

Carol put her hands in the pockets of her jacket.

'Ed, you can't tell me you wouldn't do it to them if you got the chance,' she glanced around, leaned in close, and dropped her voice. 'Anyway, who the fuck got Billy Skinner? I couldn't believe it.'

She backed away satisfied nobody could hear or see her.

'Good enough for that bastard as well.'

She took a packet of menthol cigarettes out of her fake leopard fur shoulder bag, allowing the long hooped gold chain to dangle against her boots. She put the unlit cigarette to her lips. 'I mean setting up them traffic lights. How good was that?'

Ed's interest perked up.

'You've got your ear to the ground,' he said. 'Who do you think's behind it?'

She lit the cigarette, put the bag back on her shoulder, and adjusted the gold strap.

'There's nothing Ed,' blowing smoke out of the side of her mouth so it missed him. 'Plenty of people guessing, talking shit. This one's behind it, that one's done it. Nobody's got a clue. And you know yourself if nobody knows, it's usually an outsider.'

'Possibly,' Ed struck again by the way things had been kept under the radar.

'You seen Linda then?'

'Sorry?'

'Linda Pritchard, little Miss-Prim-and-Proper,' she spoke through a spluttering cough. 'My arse!'

Ed said: 'You know her then?'

Carol tapped the cigarette, tugged at the boots again.

'Course I do, not that she'd let on,' here words battled through another cough. 'So do you.'

Ed furrowed his brow, shook his head, said he had only met Linda Pritchard on Saturday.

'Some detective you are,' Carol swapped the cough for a wheezy laugh. 'Mind she's had her teeth and tits done since you knew her.'

Ed was baffled, shrugged again.

'Linda Avery,' Carol said, like a conjuror pulling silk scarves from her sleeves. 'Former escort and Billy Skinner's one time bed warmer.'

It came to Ed in a rush and he kicked himself, stunned he hadn't remembered.

'The hair,' he said. 'It's longer, darker.'

This time Carol went from cough to laugh and back again.

'Get lost,' she gasped. 'You'll have been too busy staring at her tits to notice her hair. Not that I blame you. They look good, but so they should. They're years younger than the rest of her.'

Now Ed realised what was wrong in the house. It wasn't

the family photographs or the obnoxious granny; it was the fact that a one-time escort was living in relative grandeur with descendants of the judiciary. That's what he couldn't put his finger on. It was all wrong.

He smiled. Hue and Cry were right. He wasn't looking, Linda found him.

Sam Parker pulled up alongside them.

Carol bent down, looked at Sam, and quickly stood up, brushing her skirt straight. 'Still pulling the lookers Ed?'

'She's my boss.'

Carol said 'yeah right' as Ed opened the passenger door.

'If you hear anything, give me a shout,' he told her. 'I might even get you a couple of drinks.'

'Yeah that's right up your street,' Carol shot a look at Sam. 'Get a girl pissed.'

She walked away, raised her arm and waggled her hand.

'Friend of yours?' Sam asked as Ed settled into the seat.

He tugged on the belt, clicked it in place.

'Carol? Known her years. Ronnie Pender's daughter. Rough diamond and on the game back in the day. I always got on alright with her.'

Sam put the car in gear and drove off.

'It looks like it,' the smile getting one back in return.

As they drove Ed told her about Linda Pritchard and her past, still chewing himself that he hadn't twigged.

'Can Carol be trusted?' Sam asked him. 'She looks a dangerous woman.'

Ed grinned. 'I know, trust me I know.'

'You haven't have you?' Sam said, glancing at him.

Ed kept eyes fixed on the windscreen.

'Course not. Anyway, who's at the scene?'

Sam decided it was best to let it drop.

'Uniform. Tommy Evans.'

'Tommy Evans? Young blond haired lad?'

'He's got about ten years in,' Sam told him.

'That's what I mean, young. Good lad. He'll do it by the book.'

Sam pushed the indicator stalk and turned left.

'I think he got a bit of a shock,' she said. 'Not every day a uniform finds the head of a crime family naked and covered in white powder.'

When the investigation talk stopped, the silence felt only mildly uncomfortable.

Ten minutes later the pool of vomit outside the factory told them just how shocked Tommy Evans had been.

'Everything alright Tom?' Sam asked.

'Yes boss,' his face a strange shade. 'Nothing's been touched in there.'

He sheepishly looked at the vomit. 'Sorry about that.'

Ed smiled. 'At least we won't have to recover it now we know it's yours, and judging by the consistency, you need to eat breakfast young man. You can't be viewing dead shitbags on an empty stomach, even if we all praise the Lord for their passing.'

Everyone smiled. One sentence and Tommy Evans' embarrassment was gone.

'We may as well wait for SOCO and the pathologist,' Sam said. 'You sure it's Billy Skinner, Tom?'

'It's him. I don't know if this is connected, it might have nothing to do with him, maybe it's just been left by a kid…'

'Spit it out Tommy?' Ed said.

'On the floor, near the metal workbench he's tied to. There's a gorilla mask.'

Five against two was not good odds, odds that were significantly lengthened when the two suits handed out the iron bars.

Mat and a suit rushed McFadden.

Luke and the other stormed Harry.

Harry and McFadden were both knocked off balance by the suits.

As Harry stumbled back into the wall, Luke raised the cosh and struck a crushing blow against the back of his head.

Harry dropped to the floor, already semi-conscious, blood seeping from a gaping wound.

McFadden regained his balance much quicker than a man of his age should have. He sprung back onto his feet, planted his heels against the concrete floor and adopted the stance of a boxer. But nobody in the ring ever had to defend an iron bar being swung in a vicious arc towards his jaw.

McFadden tried to jerk his head backwards away from the blow. Blocking it with his forearm wasn't an option; it would have broken any bone with ease. For McFadden it happened to be his cheek. He stumbled forward, blood rushing from his nose, and screamed as Mat smashed the bar against his collarbone, snapping it clean.

Mat hit him three times across the back each blow harder than the last, each blow forcing McFadden finally to the floor.

'You tried to fucking blow me up,' Mat was breathless, his eyes wild.

He took two steps back, ran forward and kicked McFadden in the stomach.

Harry was on the floor, groaning and trying to crawl away. Luke bent down and pulled his head up.

'So you thought you'd take over did you?'

Harry's response was barely audible. 'It was your big brother's idea.'

Luke stood up and dropped the bar, breathing heavily.

'He was hurting about Geoff, but he's still family,' Luke said. 'Came to his senses when fuck-dust there tried to kill him.'

McFadden lay motionless.

Luke turned to the suits. 'Clear the pub. Send the barmaid home. Give her a hundred quid for lost wages and seeing nothing and bring two chairs down and tie these fuckers up.'

Harry whispered: 'If our Dean comes here...'

'He won't,' Luke said, moving towards the door. 'Unless he swims better than he runs, he won't be coming anywhere.'

Luke walked back, bent down, and thrust a mobile into Harry's face.

The screen showed Dean Silvers slumped against the blue wheelhouse.

Luke used his thumb and forefinger to zoom in on Dean's face, puffed, bloody and eyes wide with terror.

'You bastard,' Harry pushed himself up onto all fours.

Luke walked away but then turned, ran and kicked him in the stomach so hard Harry's body jerked upwards, breath flying out of him faster than a kite caught in a gale.

The suits returned with two chairs and blue nylon rope.

'Pub cleared?' Luke asked.

'The lassie's doing that. It'll be clear in a few minutes.'

CHAPTER THIRTY-EIGHT

JOHN ELGIN SAT in the Jolly Roger nursing a pint of cooking and a Bell's whisky. Visits to Jill Brown and Linda Pritchard after his meltdown in the police interview had left him drained.

Why was Scaramangers shut? He needed to talk to Harry Pullman. His car had been in the car park together with a large 4x4 and a BMW. He didn't recognise them but neither looked like it belonged to a brewery rep.

What a life. Married to a battleaxe, mixed up with gangsters, and one sex tape from ruin.

Rot in hell, Granddad

He stared at his pint glass and reflected on the day.

Jill Brown hadn't been happy that he had told the police about Curtis. She seemed more bothered about what Ed Whelan thought than how the chain of abuse had affected him. It was all about her and her toffee-nosed attitude.

What will people think? How could I bring up another man's baby pretending it was my husband's?

Then he'd met Linda Pritchard in a lay-by on the outskirts of town. She'd told her paedophile-rearing mother-in-law, her heartfelt description, she needed to get out for an hour. Even without make-up Linda looked stunning.

He replayed the meeting in his head, how he had told her about the police, the photograph in the park.

'So what?' she had said. 'It makes no odds now.'

He was dumbfounded to discover she had set up the park scene herself.

'I wanted to show the bastard men still wanted me even if he didn't.'

Elgin had been gutted, felt used and foolish.

'So I was just a pawn?' he'd asked.

'You were never just a pawn John,' Linda had said, and kissed him.

When he asked how she knew Ray Reynolds it all came out.

Reynolds had given her the name of a retired cop with a good camera and she had done the rest.

Elgin swallowed the whisky.

He doubted Julius Pritchard even knew the photograph existed, Linda probably waiting to bring it into play when she thought the time was right. Her husband would know she was getting it elsewhere and, Elgin believed, men like Julius Pritchard hated that thought.

With Julius dead Linda would now own the house and receive whatever policies were in place.

Elgin picked up the lager, gulped a couple of mouthfuls, and wiped the foam from his mouth

Women really are the root of all evil...

Thinking about it, Elgin conceded he wasn't being fair. It was his own weakness for women; that was the root of his problems.

Linda, Jill, Tara, Zara and Chloe... lumped together they sounded like that 60's pop group who sang Legend of Xanadu.

Elgin closed his eyes, took himself back to school, and hummed the song.

The smell of liver and onions, carried by a young waiter, snapped him back before he could mimic Dave Dee's cracking whip.

Whatever place he was in right now, it was neither idyllic nor magnificent.

He was a long way from Xanadu. He had been most of his life.

Harry Pullman was dazed and disorientated, the gash in his head still bleeding. Strapped to the chair, head slumped forward, he realised he should have told Luke about his meeting with Mat as soon as it happened.

He had never wanted to work with Mat. Christ it was Mat who smashed up the pub.

He should never have believed McFadden either.

He feigned ignorance about the caravan because he thought Mat was dead. He had no doubt McFadden had blown up the caravan and Mat must have ran straight to Luke scared shitless and confessed all.

He had totally underplayed the brotherly bond. Either that or Luke didn't have Billy's ruthlessness. Harry knew Billy would have killed Mat. And who had snatched Billy?

Mat? Luke? Stuart?

Not Mark. He couldn't snatch a box of cereal in a supermarket trolley dash.

Harry was snapped from his thoughts by the suits carrying a desk. McFadden was untied and pulled to his feet. He tried to fight but one good arm against ten was useless.

He was pushed face down onto the desk, wrists tied to the front two legs, thighs to the back ones.

Luke ripped off McFadden's shirt.

Harry knew what was coming next. So did McFadden who was bucking like a bronco.

'Where's my father?' Luke said.

'Luke, listen to me,' McFadden told him. 'I have no idea where your father is. You should be asking Harry.'

'You tried to take Mat out last night,' Luke said. 'He saw your car so he pretended to be pissed, stayed awake and heard you come in. Then he followed you out and watched you leave. He blew the caravan up, not you, you daft fucker. So I'll ask you again. Where's dad?'

'I don't know,' McFadden screamed.

Mat bent down and pushed a plug into an extension box he had trailed from a wall socket. The iron heated quickly, sizzling when Mat spat droplets of saliva onto the steel.

'Iron Man is back,' he laughed at his own joke.

The suits pushed down on McFadden's legs while Luke and Mark pushed down on his shoulders.

Mat pressed the button, watched the steam fly, and drove the iron into the small of McFadden's back.

'Don't you ever laugh at my mother's cooking you piece of shit,' the smell of singeing flesh filling the cellar.

When the shrieking stopped Mat put his mouth against McFadden's ear. 'Now where's dad?'

McFadden was pleading. 'Luke I swear I don't know.'

'Don't tell me,' Luke said, 'he's asking the questions.'

He pressed hard on McFadden's collarbone, then stepped back to give Mat room.

'Watch your hands little brothers,' Mat said. 'Shoulders now.'

McFadden was unconscious before Mat completed the second, slow, swipe.

White suits donned, Ed and Sam followed Jim Melia into Spikers factory.

One of the Crime Scene Investigators was videoing the scene, careful not to step off the metal plates and destroy any forensic evidence that might be on the floor.

Jim stared at the thick neck, the white powder covering the face. 'Looks like a yeti in an avalanche,' the pathologist joked.

Sam smiled. She had never been keen on hairy men. Billy Skinner had grown a grey coat over his lifetime.

'Snuffed out by his own drugs presumably,' Jim was saying

now. 'I can't imagine anyone buying that amount just to kill. Just hit him over the head. Hell of a lot cheaper.'

'But not as dramatic Jim,' Sam said, Skinner's execution almost theatrical. 'He's been running the drugs trade in this town for decades.'

She stared at the body, convinced this hadn't been a gangland hit, that no cartel would waste so much money.

'This is somebody with a grudge against him, against the products he supplies,' Sam said.

Jim stood: 'A bereaved parent perhaps?'

'They wouldn't get near him,' Ed said, looking into Skinner's lifeless eyes. 'His snatch was professional, well thought out. He was brought here. Three people, presumably men…and where would a parent get this amount of coke or the bottle to break in and steal traffic lights?'

Someone's done a good number on you Billy Skinner, Ed thought, still looking into the eyes. Payback time.

'Was he a grandfather?' Sam asked, nodding towards Skinner.

'Who cares,' Ed said, 'He dealt in misery all his life. Not many will be mourning and some, as Mick and David would say, will be dancing in the streets.'

Jim looked quizzically at Ed.

'Jagger and Bowie.'

Jim nodded. 'Of course.'

'Now someone else will fill the vacuum,' Sam said, wondering if Skinner's sons or outsiders would soon be the new lords of the jungle.

Sam made to leave but suddenly stopped and turned. 'The gorilla mask,' she said. 'The only reason they've left it is to show us they're the same people who did Pritchard and van Dijk. So we need to find out who or what links two murdered paedophiles with Billy Skinner.'

'And who is going to so much trouble,' Ed said.

The boat had just left its mooring lines when Luke's mobile

rang. 'Hello,' he shouted, straining to hear above the chugging of the diesel engine.

It was his mother, distraught and crying so hard she was difficult to understand but Luke got enough.

The police had found a body they believed to be his father.

'Sit tight mum,' Luke told her. 'Me and Mark will be there in a couple of hours. Don't say anything to the cops. Let me deal with them.'

Luke put the mobile in his pocket, rested his hands on the back of the boat and stared at the trailing wake. It was one of the few things visible.

He was in charge now. He had to follow his father's cunning and ruthlessness if he was to protect the business; protect his mother. He knew what needed to be done.

He edged unsteadily to the bow, one hand always gripping something. He never suffered from seasickness but he couldn't walk about a boat like a true sailor.

McFadden, barely conscious, was curled and shivering in the foredeck, groaning low every time salt spray hit his raw, naked back.

Harry sat alongside McFadden, legs tucked under his chin, hands, bound with blue nylon rope, resting on his knees. Eyes down he stared at the deck swaying under the motion of the sea, using his ears to plot the whereabouts of the three brothers and the heavies. He knew he had no real chance of escape but he had to do something. The boat was outside the harbour now, pushing out to sea. Once they had weighed him down, he would be lost to the depths. If he threw himself overboard before the chains went on, his body could be washed up and the police might investigate. At least they'd know he was dead.

'They've found dad,' Luke said, Harry listening.

'Where?' Mat asked.

'I thought you might be able to tell us,' Luke said, his voice acid.

Mat sounded caught off guard. 'What do you mean?'

'One or both of those fuckers might have had something

to do with it, but just because you came crawling back, doesn't mean I don't think you were involved.'

Harry knew this might be his only chance.

'Involved,' he shouted with everything he had left. 'He was the fucking ringleader.'

Mat inched towards Harry. 'You lying twat.'

'Back off Mat,' Luke shouted. 'Let him speak. Call it last requests of the condemned man.'

'It was all his idea,' Harry said, spitting a loose tooth onto the deck. 'I went to his caravan with our Dean. This lying bastard contacted me. I know I should have told you.'

Harry shuffled on his backside.

'I was never going into business with him, not against you but that's what he wanted. He told me not to worry about your father. He'd sort him. Well he's done that by the sounds of things.'

Mat was shaking his head.

'Luke you've got to believe me. I had nothing to do with dad.'

Luke adjusted the hood and shoved his hands into the hand warmer pockets of his red Musto Offshore jacket. He didn't look angry but sad.

'Your problem Mat is your brains were always in your cock.'

Mat stepped towards the side of the boat and sat on the portside edge, his back to the sea.

'Look I was pissed off about Geoff,' he said. 'Yeah I might have let my mouth run away with me, but I didn't have anything to do with dad and I'm not likely to go into business with Harry fucking Pullman am I? It was me and Geoff who smashed up his pub to teach him a lesson.'

'Despite dad telling us all to take it easy with him,' Luke said. 'The way I see it, we'll never know for sure, but what I do know is that one, two or all three of you carries the can.

And throw that fucker over the side now.' Luke nodded at McFadden. 'His crying like a girl is getting on my tits.'

As the heavies moved towards McFadden, Harry rocked

forwards on his toes, sprang upwards and charged at Mat Skinner.

'Bastard!' Harry screamed, ducking his shoulder like a prop-forward and smashing him below the chin, his momentum driving both of them overboard into the freezing dark waters.

Harry surfaced first, retching and snatching breaths. He knew hypothermia would get him, but at least now he had a chance.

Mat had none. He couldn't swim.

Harry spun onto his back and started kicking towards the shore. He had less than ten minutes, probably less than five, but at least he would die in his own way. Fish food perhaps, but fish food that had put up a fight.

'Fucking hell,' Mark shouted. 'Turn the boat around.'

Luke banged the front of the wheel-house.

'Straight ahead,' he shouted at the skipper.

'No!' Mark staggering forwards.

Luke grabbed him by the lapels of his jacket, shouted into his face.

'This is already a big enough fuck up,' he said. 'Let's get McFadden overboard and get the hell out of here. Mum needs us or have you forgotten about her.'

CHAPTER THIRTY-NINE

Sam called it a night after the post mortem. Billy Skinner had head and facial injuries consistent with Helen Larney's account of the abduction but his death was down to the drugs not the beating.

She had pulled on to her drive 30 minutes later, the electric timers allowing the hall lamp to give some pretence of a warm welcome.

Now changed into electric blue velour sweat pants and top, a Les Clos Chablis was already opened and poured. Mineral and laser sharp, it masked the taste of death that always hung around after a visit to the mortuary. Sam sat on the settee, tucking her legs beneath her.

She had the TV muted, whatever was on the screen just a comforting background, and was flicking through the Royal Yachting Association Day Skipper Introduction to Navigation book. It had been a few years since she qualified as a Day Skipper, passing both the theory and practical exams first time.

Leafing through the book she realised how much she'd forgotten but the more she read, the more she remembered.

Perhaps it really was time to put Tris behind her. Nothing would bring him back and she wouldn't forget him, but putting her enjoyment of life on hold was cheating nobody but herself. For the first time in as long as she could remember Sam felt excited about something other than work.

Maybe booking herself on a short sailing voyage was just what she needed, although the North Sea even in spring was a different proposition to summer in the Med.

That said, choose the right sail school and the skippers they provided would be extremely competent.

Time slipped as she sipped and studied. At a quarter to midnight she bolted off the sofa, sprinted upstairs and scooped the washing from the basket in her bedroom. Her mother washed religiously every Monday. Sam washed whenever she remembered, usually when she was down to her last couple of blouses and knickers. The fact that today was a Monday, albeit fifteen minutes from Tuesday, was pure coincidence.

At least she was putting a dark wash in; no chance of her whites turning pink.

She took a Marlboro from the packet on the bench and watched the water fill the washing machine; was that Tristram's last memory? The rising swell of the Atlantic?

She poured another glass. No point leaving one in the bottle. Two cigarettes later and she was in bed.

Sleep didn't come immediately, it rarely did after a drink and never when she'd been thinking of Tristram.

But he wasn't on her mind when she finally fell sound.

Sam had been thinking how hard would it be to trace the buyers of metal benches and girders?

Tuesday 16th December

Ed closed the front door and walked to his car. No breakfast, not even a cup of tea. Still, no tea was better than another domestic. Sue had been asleep when he got in and she was just stirring when he dressed after his shower.

He glanced up at the bedroom window as he reversed off

the drive. She stood peering through the vertical blinds, coldness staring at him.

She was ready for round three after the battles of Sunday night and Monday morning. Last night's reprieve would be waiting for him tonight, unless he got home late again.

He rubbed his stinging, blood-shot eyes, eyes that were screaming for sleep as much as his pounding head, but in the stay-at-work-go-home-early contest, work always won.

His mobile rang. He glanced at the screen, smiled when he saw it was Jayne-with-a-Y-Culley.

'Morning Jayne. How are you today?'

'Is that you Mr. Whelan?'

Her voice echoed around the car on his hands-free.

'It is Jayne.'

'Can you come and see me. I think I saw one of the men who took Mr. Scott on the television last night.'

Ed sighed. 'Okay Jayne. I'll pop round this afternoon. Have the kettle on.'

'I will. Goodbye.'

Ed's smile was shadowed with sadness. Would she remember she called him? Would she remember who or what she'd seen on the TV? Would she remember to make two cups of tea?

Dementia terrified him. Mortality was one thing, but if the last years of your life were locked in your own little world…

So why had he missed the obvious with Linda Pritchard? Linda Avery staring at him all the time.

And that so-called friend of Julius? The one involved in the abduction. What was it about his walk? He'd seen that walk before but he couldn't place it.

Why?

For years he'd been renowned for his memory for faces and mannerisms, yet now he had failed to identify Linda Avery or the 'walker'.

Maybe he was just getting old. Perhaps all those nights on the booze in his younger days had destroyed his brain cells.

He drove through the traffic, his thoughts turning to Ray

Reynolds. He was in fine form yesterday. Great gaffer but without doubt a product of his time. He smiled again. What was Reynolds' head like this morning? No doubt fresh as a bloody daisy. The man had always been a machine when it came to drink. Could be out all hours downing pints for fun, but come the next morning he was always first in the office, always immaculate.

He rang Sam from the car park. 'Fancy going to see Linda Avery?'

'Who?'

'Linda Pritchard. Remember? Carol Pender told us about her.'

'I'll be out in five,' Sam told him.

Twenty minutes later they were walking up the path of number 75.

'Rudolph still looks pissed off,' Ed said.

'Not as pissed off as Linda's about to be.'

Linda opened the door and ushered them into the lounge. The bright ceiling lights were off but the log burner was roaring.

'Kids at school?' Sam asked.

'Yes.'

'Your mother-in-law?'

'Out for the day thank God.'

'So it's just us then,' Sam said sitting down.

'Yes.' Linda perched on the edge of the chair, one knee across the other, hands overlapped, resting on her knee. 'Any news? Have you arrested anyone yet?'

Ed stayed standing, watching Linda.

Miss-Prim-and-Proper.

'I must apologise,' Ed said. 'Please forgive me Linda.'

'What for?'

'Not recognising you?' He paused, waiting for a reaction.

'Not recognising me?' Linda looked nonplussed. 'Have we met?'

Role-playing to the end.

'Not in this lifetime but plenty in the last,' Ed told her.

Linda's face turned as red as the carpet.

Ed said: 'The hair, the teeth, many things, but it was the house that really threw me. Never in a million years did I expect to see one of the Averys in a house like this.'

Linda's puzzled expression was gone, in its place a glare and a mouth set rigid, expensive new bridge work clenched.

Ed, enjoying the moment, put his hands under the lapels of his blue Crombie and rocked back on his heels. All he needed was a gown and wig.

'Linda Avery...shoplifter, escort, Billy Skinner's moll and now to the manor born,' Ed beamed. 'Two kids, a smart house, and full makeover ending in an air of respectability.'

Miss Prim-And-Proper had vanished faster than a summer cloud burst. 'Fuck you Whelan.'

'There we go,' Ed clapped his hands. 'The real Linda's still in there. Sewer-mouth, accent from the back streets and oh goodie, you remember me. I'm touched.'

Ed sat down. 'So, tell me about John Elgin and that photograph.'

'What...'

'And before you start the bullshit we can do this in front of ghastly granny if you'd prefer.'

Linda shot to her feet. 'Don't you dare threaten me Whelan. Just because I never sucked you off like Carol Pender.'

Ed smiled and stuck out his arms palms facing upwards. 'It's not a threat Linda. It's a promise. Now do you want to sit back down and decide whether we wait for nasty nana to return? You know the one who thought her son married beneath him because you worked in a supermarket.'

Linda muttered. 'Same old bastard.'

'But unlike your good self, an honest old bastard,' Ed shot back. 'We should have sent you to A and E for an x-ray, see if there's an honest bone in there.'

Ed leaned back on the settee, stretched out his legs and said: 'So are we waiting for the sweet old soul?'

Linda glared some more and sat down.

'Probably best if we get this done now, don't you think?' Sam made the extra push.

Linda told them how she had met John Elgin at a council meeting about travellers - a part of her life she had run away from years ago but still cared about.

'What about the kiss?' Ed asked her.

'What bloody kiss?'

Ed was like a schoolmaster trying to stay patient with a mouthy pupil.

Sam stepped in. 'Linda this will get tiring if you answer our questions with another question. The one in the park.'

When the questions moved to Julius, the sham the marriage had become was soon clear, Linda telling them how she found out what her husband really was soon after their youngest was born.

'It was a total accident,' she said. 'I caught him watching some sick shit on the computer. Julius was never much into sex with me. That's when I realised why. Not like Billy Skinner. Christ he was a three meal a day man. Julius just wanted children, wanted to complete the image.'

But now he's gone, all of this is yours, Ed was thinking.

'From a caravan to this in one lifetime isn't bad going,' he told her. 'So what was your relationship with John Elgin?'

'There wasn't one.'

'Did he tell you anything about his family?' Sam asked.

'What, apart from his horrible wife?' Linda shook her head. 'He knew Julius had interfered with his grandson. How do you think that makes me feel? I'm glad he's dead and I hope he rots in hell. My kids will grow up wondering what he was like but if he'd just been convicted not killed they would have known exactly what their father was.'

Ed looked surprised: 'So you were protecting the family name?'

'I did nothing, protect or otherwise,' Linda said, prickling. 'I cuddled a distraught older man. Big deal.'

'Who took the photograph?'

Linda looked wary. 'A friend.'

'Recommended by Ray Reynolds?'

Linda shrugged. 'You're not the only copper with ex-tarts on the payroll.'

Ed and Sam stood.

'We'll be in touch Linda,' Ed said. 'Lovely to bump into you again.'

The door wasn't slammed behind them as they left but Linda did give them a send-off.

'Go fuck yourself.'

CHAPTER FORTY

'WHERE'S MAT? He should be here.'

Marge Skinner was sitting at the kitchen table, a pot of stewed tea in the middle, milk in two mugs.

The metal ashtray, taken from one of their pubs, was overflowing, the bottle of gin waiting for its neck to be tilted one last time.

Luke and Mark were leaning against the kitchen bench; the two bodyguards Luke insisted on staying at the house were busy checking the grounds.

'He knows about dad,' Luke said. 'I told him.'

'But where is he? He's the oldest. He should be here.'

Marge looked like an artist had used a scalpel to dig crevices down her cheeks and around her mouth and then drawn deep, black shadows under her eyes.

She filled the tumbler then lay the bottle on its side.

'You want to go steady mum,' Luke said. 'It's way too early for that.'

'What for?' Marge took a hit from the gin. 'Your dad's gone. What's left for me? Nothing.'

She swallowed another huge mouthful, coughed and spluttered. 'We don't even know who's behind it?

'Yes we do,' Luke said.

Marge looked up from the glass. 'Who?'

'Harry Pullman.'

Marge looked stunned.

'I don't believe it!' putting the glass down hard on the table, her voice shaking. 'Harry's been with your dad...'

Marge wiped her eyes while her sons waited.

When she spoke again her voice was filled with certainty.

'Harry Pullman's been involved with this family for years,' she said. 'Since your dad started out. Why would he turn on him now?'

Marge clenched her fists, the veins in her wrists standing to attention against her fake tan.

'He admitted it mum.'

Marge's eyes locked on Luke's. 'You've spoken to him?'

'Yes,' Luke told her. 'That nephew of his and McFadden as well.'

Marge picked up the glass and swallowed gin.

'I never liked that McFadden,' she spat out the name. 'Was he involved?'

'They all were.'

'I hope he suffered Luke, like I asked.'

'Trust me mum it's sorted,' Luke said. 'They were all plotting to take over: Stuart, Harry and his nephew Dean Silvers. Take out dad, take us all out. Here, let me put some tonic in that.'

He walked to the fridge, took a glass bottle of Schweppes, and found a straw in the drawer next to the bottle opener.

Marge nodded her thanks and lit another cigarette.

'I still can't believe it about Harry…where are they now?'

'Taken care of,' Luke said. 'There's nothing for you to worry about.'

Marge stirred her drink with the black straw. 'What if there are others?'

'Then we'll deal with it. But for now, it's sorted.'

'Mark, you do what Luke says,' Marge turned to her middle son. 'I know he's the youngest...'

'It's okay mum. I know. Luke was always going to be the boss.'

'Well until Mat returns,' Marge told them.

Luke threw a glance at Mark and walked over to his mother, putting a gentle hand on her shoulder.

'Mat's not coming back.'

'What!' She pushed herself out of the chair, gin spilling from the glass still in her hand. 'What do you mean, not coming back?'

'Not like that,' Luke reached out for the glass and Marge handed it over, watched him put it back on the table. 'Mat's fine. Stop panicking. Sit back down.'

Marge sat.

Luke knelt down, took hold of her hand.

'Dad never wanted Mat to run the business when he retired,' he said. 'He must have told you that.'

Marge stared at the floor and nodded.

'Mat knew that as well,' Luke went on. 'He doesn't want to hang around with dad gone. He texted me to say he was getting on a flight.'

Marge looked up. 'Where?'

'Him and Geoff are going to Spain to start again,' Luke said. 'Live the life. Mat wants a new start and who can blame him?

Luke knew exactly which of Marge's buttons to press.

'He takes so much shit about what he is,' Luke said. 'He just wants to go somewhere where nobody's bothered, somewhere him and Geoff can be themselves.'

Maybe it was relief, maybe it was the gin, but Marge didn't spot the holes in the story, Luke was happy to see.

She didn't even ask why Mat had never said goodbye.

'It's always been tough, bless him,' Marge said. 'Even your dad gave him a hard time about it, but as I used to say to your father, that's the way he is. What are you going to do? Disown him? And Geoff is such a canny lad.'

She sipped her drink through the straw. 'When will he be in touch?'

Luke told her Mat planned to leave it for a while, let all this settle down.

'They've got plenty of Euros and we can get more to them if they need it,' Luke said. 'All you need to know is that him and Geoff are fine. Me and Mark will sort everything else out.'

She pulled him into her, kissed his head.

'You're a good boy. What do you want me to tell the police when they come round?'

Luke stood up.

'Tell them we want them to catch whoever killed dad,' Luke said. 'A businessman kidnapped off the street in broad daylight and then murdered. Tell them it's not the wild west.'

He walked to the sink, turned on the tap, and filled a glass with water.

'Tell them that we don't know who could have done it or why,' Luke took a long drink. 'If they ask you about McFadden or Harry Pullman admit knowing who they are, but say you have no idea where they might be.'

Luke drained the glass.

'If they push it just say you never involved yourself in the business.'

Mark, still leaning against the bench, unpeeled a banana.

'What if it wasn't them? What if it's someone else?'

'I thought you said they admitted it?' Marge stared at Luke, waiting for a response. 'Well did they or didn't they?'

Luke had always been patient with his brother but there were times...

'What Mark means is anybody could have a pop at us now, so we have to be careful,' he said. 'Don't go into town without taking at least one of those lads outside with you.'

Marge nodded.

Mark knew better than to speak again, at least not until they were both outside.

He waited until they were standing by the bonnet of the car.

'What if it wasn't Harry and Stuart?' Mark said now. 'Have you thought of that? I know I'm supposed to be the thick one, but what if someone just wants us to think it was them?'

Luke moved towards the driver's door.

'It was them all right and remember you're not paid to

think. You're paid to do what you're told. We need to make sure all the pubs are working properly.'

He got into the car and was talking before Mark closed his door.

'We need to send a strong message. We don't want dad's death giving anybody ideas about skimming or trying to take over. We need to put someone in Scaramangers and then see John Elgin, see how he's doing with the planning.'

'What did you think of her then?' Sam asked.

They were pulling away from Linda Pritchard's, Ed driving.

'She would still have known enough in the travelling community to have her husband sorted out,' Ed said. 'Skinner dumped her when she'd served her uses but the travellers wouldn't be frightened to take on Billy Skinner. That might explain why Carol Pender said nobody knew anything.'

Ed fell silent, thought processes turning like the car wheels. They were still turning when the wheels stopped at HQ.

Sam opened her door and broke the silence. 'I've decided I'm going to book myself on a sailing trip.'

'What?' Ed taken by surprise. 'Good, that's great. So you should.'

Doors shut, Ed walked around the front of the car.

Bang!

He smashed his palm against the bonnet. 'Shit!'

'What the hell?' Sam gasped, heart racing.

'I want to watch the tapes again,' Ed said. 'Pritchard's abduction and his trip around the football place with his new mate. I want to watch the mate again. It's that walk. I think I've remembered who it reminds me of.'

Sam said they could kill two birds with one stone.

'Thanks to Bev we've got the CCTV from the car spares shop,' Sam told him. 'She's in the crew room.'

Sam entered the building first, Ed following as they climbed the stairs.

'And by the way,' Sam said. 'They're on a laptop. All been transferred across to make easier viewing.'

Not even Ed missed the days of rewinding and fast forwarding tapes.

They reached the second floor.

Bev was sitting behind one of the eight desks in the large office that the detectives who weren't involved in the HOLMES Room functions worked from.

'Morning Bev,' Sam said. 'What have we got then?'

There was nobody else in the office; everybody already out and about.

'Not a lot,' Bev said. 'Guy goes into the shop, buys the headlight. It's the only one sold on Saturday anywhere for miles. The quality of the CCTV is good; the chances of identifying the buyer are not.'

'Why?' Ed asked, moving behind Bev so he could see the screen.

'Keeps his head down, keeps his baseball cap low.' Bev said.

Bev tapped one of the keys. The inside of the shop came into view. Bev was right; the quality was TV-like.

'Here he comes,' Bev said, touching the screen to point him out.

Sam and Ed watched him walk into the shop, head bowed, black baseball cap pulled low and join the queue. After the three men in front were served, he propped himself against the counter.

He never looked up.

After a short conversation, the salesman walked away, presumably to the stores, and returned soon after carrying a cardboard box. The man in the baseball cap nodded, handed over a note, took his change and walked out past the people who had formed a new queue behind him.

'Would the storeman recognise him again?' Ed asked, standing up straight.

'He doesn't think so,' Bev said, without looking away from

the screen. 'You saw how busy it was the few minutes our man was in. It was like that all morning apparently. Always is on a Saturday.'

'Blue jacket, dark brown trousers, and white trainers.' Sam said. 'Not exactly distinctive.'

Ed asked Bev to zoom in on the man's feet.

Ed moved closer to the screen. 'Thought so. Stan Smith trainers. Re-released this year. They're more of a fashion statement now for the young and trendy but chummy there doesn't walk like a young gun. More likely to have worn them years ago and fancied going retro.'

Ed asked Bev to play the footage from the Shots And Saves complex.

She minimised the film they'd just watched and keyed up another.

Ed leaned forward, peering at the screen. 'Same cap, same clothes, same trainers.'

Same walk?

'Play it again Bev,' Ed said. 'Watch how he walks in comparison to the guy who bought the headlight.'

Ed walked to the window and rested his back on the windowsill while Sam and Bev studied the screen.

'See how he seems to bounce on his heels?' Ed asked them.

Sam and Bev nodded.

'But more importantly,' Ed continued, 'it's the way his arms hang loose by his sides with the palms facing backwards. Now play the one of him walking with Pritchard before the abduction.'

Ed remained by the window. He'd seen everything he needed.

'You're right,' Sam said, concentrating on the screen. 'Same walk, same cap, same clothes and as we've said before, it's as if he's surveillance trained.'

Ed rejoined them at the laptop, the last image still frozen.

'That walk's pretty unique,' he said. 'Not enough for identification granted but I knew a cop who walked like that. I just need to pop out. I'll bring you up to speed when I get back.'

'Before you go,' Sam asked. 'The cop you're talking about. Surveillance trained?'

'And then some,' Ed said. 'One of the best DCs in Hampshire. Undercover specialism...'

He paused for effect. Sam and Bev stared, waiting.

'Infiltrating paedophile rings.'

CHAPTER FORTY-ONE

John Elgin trudged through the streets, hands in pockets and head down, eyes hiding under the peak of his Harris Tweed Gold Barleycorn Baker Boy hat. He needed to speak with Harry Pullman, see if there was any progress on the tape.

He scanned the car park. Harry's car was there. The 4x4 and BMW from yesterday were not.

The pub doors were open.

Elgin quickened his step and took off his cap as he stepped over the threshold.

He'd never seen the barman before: thick neck, thick arms, hands like shovels, polished head, no more than twenty five, wearing a white tailored shirt and black trousers.

Definitely more at home in front of the door than behind the bar.

'Pint of Peroni please.'

Not even a grunt in response.

Elgin put the five pound note in the barman's hand. It looked like a postage stamp.

'Where's Harry?'

'Left,' the barman said, bending down to rearrange some glasses on the bottom shelf, like a circus contortionist in the space made tight by his bulk.

'What, for an hour or two?' Elgin asked. 'When's he due back?'

The barman stood up and leaned across the bar on his huge arms. 'Left as in packed in.'

Elgin stopped dead with the Peroni still six inches short of his lips.

'You're kidding,' nonplussed, disbelieving. 'When did all this happen?'

The barman turned and fiddled with the optics. 'You auditioning me for Mastermind? How the fuck do I know?'

He spun on his heels, surprisingly deft for a big man.

'They needed a new manager, rang me and hey-presto, here I am.'

He stretched his hand towards Elgin. 'Jason Tonks.'

Elgin's hand was enveloped in a bear's paw with a vice-like grip.

'Now, I'm here to serve, you're here to drink. I'm not here to answer questions.'

'Well you can answer mine.' Ray Reynolds walked to the bar wearing a pair of bright yellow golfing trousers.

Jason Tonks looked him up and down: 'You're either wearing those as a joke or you've just finished your Ronald McDonald shift and forgot to change. Jesus.'

Reynolds turned to Elgin. 'Alright John. Who's the comedian?'

Elgin looked at the barman. 'Jason Tonks meet Detective Superintendent Ray Reynolds.'

Tonks remained impassive.

'Retired,' Reynolds said. 'I'll have a pint of…'

He walked along the bar looking at the hand-pulls. 'Titanic Plum Porter.'

He stared at the barman. 'Let's hope you last longer than the ship.'

Reynolds smiled. The barman didn't.

'Don't dish it out if you can't take it young man. Now where's Harry?'

'Gone,' Tonks told him. 'Left.'

'Gone where?' Reynolds asked.

Luke appeared from the cellar. 'Warmer climes Mr Reynolds, warmer climes.'

Luke walked to the punters' side of the bar and sat on a bar stool. 'Do me a mug of tea, Jason.'

He looked up at Reynolds, one arm resting on the bar.

'After what happened to dad, Harry decided things wouldn't be the same so he took early retirement,' Luke said. 'Can't say I blame him. We gave him a nice package.'

He glanced at the Rolex on Reynolds' wrist.

'Obviously not as good as yours, but we can't all get police pensions. He asked me to say goodbye.'

Reynolds picked up his pint. 'All a bit sudden?'

Luke shrugged, kept the story spinning.

'Nothing to hang around for,' he told Reynolds. 'Wife gone, just him and Dean. Said he was going to London and then off, flying to wherever. Said he might try Argentina.'

Reynolds sipped his beer, nodded his approval to Jason Tonks.

'Never mentioned anything to me,' another drink, two swallows this time.

'Why would he? Once the filth always the filth.'

Luke smiled and waited for a reaction. He got none.

'Harry enjoyed reading about escaping Nazis and loved Diego Maradona,' Luke enjoying himself, seeing how far he could go. 'Argentina seems the perfect combination. He said he might go and watch Boca Juniors, Maradona's first club.'

Reynolds watched him, face blank, and raised the pint back to his lips.

'He discussed a lot with you in a few hours,' he said mildly, not taking the bait.

'He certainly did,' Luke told him. 'Strike while the iron's hot and all that.'

'Talking of irons, where's your Mat?' Reynolds licked foam from his top lip.

Luke grinned. 'Another one who wanted to travel, get away from this place.'

'Everybody seems to be flying away,' Reynolds took two

more mouthfuls of the black liquid. 'Or have they gone swimming?'

Nobody spoke.

'Word is,' Reynolds said, putting the glass back on the beer mat, 'your dad liked to see people having a splash in the water.'

The grin had vanished but like Reynolds, Luke was keeping his reactions in check.

'I wouldn't know about that Mr. Reynolds. I was just a kid when you and dad were sparring.'

He looked at his Omega. 'Now if you'll excuse me I've got a business to run.'

Luke walked back behind the bar, a look to Jason Tonks as he passed and headed for the cellar.

'Fancy a seat John?' Reynolds asked Elgin, who had watched the exchange without a word.

They chose a table in a quiet corner.

'What do you make of all that then?' Reynolds asked.

'Not my job Ray,' Elgin uncomfortable. 'Not yours anymore. None of us getting any younger.'

'Did Harry get the package you needed?' Reynolds asked.

Elgin looked around. 'Not here Ray. I appreciate the advice you gave me when I rang but the matter's closed now.'

Reynolds sighed and looked into Elgin's face.

'John you're not at one of your council meetings. Did you get it or not?'

Elgin looked away, shook his head. 'No.'

Reynolds finished his drink and stood up.

'Must dash. Catch up with you later John. Keep smiling.'

Declan Doherty fiddled with his red neckerchief as he leaned against the bonnet of his black pick-up.

Watching the youngsters chasing each other around the caravans always made him smile. Others would be arriving throughout the week with their parents and grandparents, Saturday's wedding getting closer by the minute.

He still found it hard to believe she was seventeen and all grown up.

Where had it all gone? Those years since he married in Seaton St George? It seemed one night he went to bed a teenager and when he woke he had a wife, two daughters a grandson and two granddaughters.

At 61 he had already outlived the 33% of his community who die before they're 59.

The wedding venue, booked and paid for by a friendly *Gorgio,* would be kept secret, announced only after the marriage ceremony. That was the way.

No *Gorgio* establishment wanted a gypsy wedding; no grandfather of the bride wanted its location made public and the big day ruined because the hotelier got wind of it and cancelled.

He watched the car approach and park in between the pick-ups and Mercedes, watched the police officer get out of the car.

'Morning Declan,' the policeman said.

'And a fine one at that. What can I do for you?'

'More what I can do for you.'

The men shook hands, a mutual respect going back decades.

'You'll be wanting a drink.'

'I'm fine. I don't want to keep you. It's just a quick visit.'

'Do you want to go inside?' Doherty indicated his twin-axle caravan.

'Thanks, but this won't take long. Mary O'Neil.'

'What about her?' Doherty wondering where this was headed.

'Luke Skinner's been telling everybody how he picked her up when she was in town last year, took her to one of their pubs, gave her a few drinks and then filled her with his *Gorgio* man-seed. His words not mine.'

Doherty gave it some time. 'And you're telling me this because?'

The policeman was scanning around the site, taking it all in.

'I don't know if it's true or not, but I thought you should know what he's putting about.'

Doherty said: 'In case I want to take the law into my own hands you mean?'

Now it was the policeman's turn to let a short silence speak.

'Luke might be a loose cannon now his dad's dead, but what you do with the information is a matter for you.'

Doherty spat on the ground.

'I heard about Billy,' he said. 'No loss. They're all low-life scum.'

He kicked a stone with his brown brogue boot.

'But I thank you for taking the time to come and tell me,' Doherty said. 'Better than one of the hot-heads overhearing it in the pub.'

The men shook hands.

'Enjoy the wedding,' the policeman said. 'I'm sure you'll be very proud.'

Declan Doherty nodded, smiled.

Same old fox; never misses a trick.

'And don't worry,' the policeman told him. 'Your secret's safe with me.'

Doherty watched him drive away, took the tobacco tin out of his waistcoat pocket and rolled a cigarette. Mary O'Neil wasn't married but she was one of theirs.

He put the cigarette to his lips, licked the paper, sparked-up with his trusty Zippo.

Only cheeky bastards like the Skinners would dare say something like that.

Within twenty minutes it was standing room only in his van. He had sent the women away. He spoke eloquently and despite the expected resistance he got his way.

Within an hour of the policeman leaving, four pick-up trucks, without registration plates, screeched into Scaramangers' car park.

Pixie Carlton was in one of them.

Declan Doherty had argued for his inclusion: someone who had suffered like he had deserved to be present when the

Skinners got theirs, and he wasn't so blind to see what his girls already felt for the outsider.

Had Jason Tonks checked the live-stream CCTV he would have seen what was coming...15 armed men marching across the car park en masse, aggression mixed with honour and a dose of outrage.

Pixie wasn't allowed out of the pick-up.

Pick-axes and iron bars were a sign to anyone passing by they weren't just calling for a quiet one.

When the door burst open, an Apache war cry hit the pub like a sonic boom and although they had probably never read him, what followed was straight from the teachings of military strategist Sun Tzu - subduing your enemy without fighting is the supreme art of war.

Jason Tonks' mind wasn't fast enough. He was dragged across the bar and smashed over the back of the head before his brain ordered his body to react.

One of the invaders, a tall, wiry man with black curly hair, shouted: 'We have no beef with anyone in here. Leave now. Do not speak to the police about this. Ever.'

Everyone, including John Elgin, rushed forward quicker than punters scrambling for a 'Black Friday' bargain.

Three travellers stood at the front door ushering everyone out.

The tall wiry one pulled Tonks' head up by his ear. 'You the boss man here?'

'Yes.'

'We want Luke Skinner. Where is he?'

'Out.'

'If you know what's good for you, you'll get up and walk out without looking back. Understand?'

Tonks nodded.

'Anyone upstairs?'

'No'

'On your way then.'

Tonks, still dazed, staggered past the three men at the front door.

One of the gang went downstairs and disconnected the

CCTV system while two removed the cameras. The kit would be recycled, sold in another town. They'd all get a drink out of it.

Two ran to one of the pick-ups. One grabbed a number of plastic crates; one grabbed the large jerry can.

Every bottle of spirit in the pub was put into the crates. Thanks to Mat Skinner and Geoff Mekins smashing everything up on Friday, the stock was high and the bottles full.

The floor was then doused in petrol, the biggest puddle under the window.

Booze, CCTV and men all loaded, pick-ups off the car park, the tall, wiry one stuffed a rag into a half full bottle of whisky - Irish for luck - lit the rag and hurled the bottle through the window.

He was sprinting away while the bottle was still airborne and launching himself into the nearest truck as the first explosion spread orange flames ten feet high.

The pick-up convoy sped away.

Mission accomplished.

CHAPTER FORTY-TWO

'It's already kicking off with the Skinners,' Sam said, looking up from her computer as Ed appeared in the doorway. 'Scaramangers has been torched.'

He sat down and listened as Sam filled in the details.

When she finished Ed's face was split with a grin.

'What goes around comes around,' he said. 'They've brought plenty of misery so I'm not going be crying now they're getting some in return.'

When Sam asked if he was sorted, Ed's expression became as blank as Jayne Culley's.

'You had to pop out,' Sam gave him a verbal nudge.

'Oh yeah, sorry,' Ed said. 'I just needed to sort something out at the bank. Keep Sue off my back.'

Sam nodded.

'Okay,' she said. 'This UC from Hampshire.'

'Cat.'

'Sorry?' Sam's turn to be thrown.

'Cat, that's his nickname, better than Cary.'

'You've totally lost me,' Sam said, pushing her wheeled chair away from the desk.

Ed was all patience. 'Cat, the man with two surnames, Archibald Leach.'

'I'm still playing catch-up,' Sam said, shaking her head.

'He was born Archibald Leach, same real name as his father's hero, Cary Grant.'

Sam had the look of a schoolgirl staring at a board full of algebra.

'So imagine you're at training school,' Ed said. 'Do you want to be called Archibald, Archie or Cary? He didn't want any. Someone came up with Cat.'

Sam shook her head in bewilderment. 'Because?'

Ed grinned: 'Cary Grant played 'The Cat' in the film 'To Catch a Thief' with Grace Kelly.'

Sam had wheeled herself back to the desk, silently mourning the 30 baffling seconds she would never get back.

'Talk about being off the wall,' she said now. 'That's off the whole reservation.'

Ed was still smiling.

'The name stuck. He used it throughout his entire career.'

'You're well informed,' Sam conceded.

'I was in his class,' Ed nodded. 'It was me who christened him Cat.'

Sam shook her head.

'And you know David Stirling?' Ed wasn't finished.

'Who?'

'The founder of the SAS,' Ed beamed. 'I've just remembered. His first name was Archibald.'

'Fascinating,' Sam was mentally scanning the desk for something to throw at him.

'I know,' Ed said. 'Two Archibalds in one inquiry. Anyway back to Cat. That's why the walk bothered me. I shared a dorm with him for ten weeks. Watched it day and night.'

Ed gave Sam a quick history of police training at RAF Dishforth in 1978.

Ten weeks living in a dormitory with every male member of your class: ate together, slept together, sat in class together, bulled shoes together, marched together, and you marched everywhere, Ed told her, to the sounds of a bawling retired Regimental Sergeant Major who had joined the police just to chew recruits' arses.

'Cat was Hampshire,' Ed said. 'You're mates with each

other when you're there, but once you pass-out, marching in front of your parents, all white gloves and shiny buttons, that's it. Everyone goes back to their own force.'

'Did you enjoy it?' Sam relieved sanity had returned.

Ed nodded at the memory.

'Loved it. Some hated it but I loved it, and the more they shouted and balled the more I loved it.'

Ed smiled at the memory, a time when his personal road map had barely taken him a single pace, the future still waiting for his footsteps.

'Bit different now, but I wouldn't change it,' Ed said. 'Character building.'

Sam smiled. It was good to see Ed happy.

'Did you see Cat again?'

'Years later, he was on the Regional Crime Squad,' Ed told her. 'Doing a job up here. He got in touch out of the blue. Said he was a UC but didn't talk about it for obvious reasons.'

Ed looked through the window behind Sam and gazed at the sky, his head replaying a military marching tune blasting out of the parade ground loudspeakers.

'You still with us?' Sam stared, waiting.

'Sorry I was miles away…Anyway, next thing I'm reading in some police magazine he'd been given an award when he retired for all his work with paedophiles.'

Ed remembered thinking that was a career path he would have struggled to survive.

'Dodgy work but fair play to him,' Ed said. 'I saw him once after he retired, asked him how he coped with it. He just said someone had to do it otherwise half the bastards would never be caught.'

Ed paused. He remembered asking Cat about his legends - job jargon for the personas he had used undercover.

They had been drinking whisky, Ed's nose almost twitching at the memory of the malt and its smell.

'He said he adopted a new legend for every job, obviously, but he always chose a first name beginning with 'A,' Ed remembered. 'Reckoned he found it easier, you know, with his own name being Archibald.'

'I get that,' Sam said, still not sure where this was all going.

'We could always ask Ray Reynolds about him.'

'Why?'

'Ray always said he didn't want to work on his own patch so Devon and Cornwall was out for him,' Ed explained. 'He joined Hampshire just like Cat. They probably knew each other there and if we had undercover operatives working up here in Cat's day, Ray Reynolds would have sanctioned it.'

Linda Pritchard, green Nike holdall in hand, walked into the toilets of the local department store, stepped into a cubicle and double-checked the lock on the door.

Her mother-in-law had eventually agreed to look after the children while she went to the gym but Linda had no intention of doing a workout.

And as she was a regular at the gym, the department store was a much safer option.

Linda Pritchard went into the cubicle. Linda Avery emerged ten minutes later, feeling strange in a pink furry jacket, tight white vest top, blue skinny jeans and baby pink ankle boots with stilts for heels.

Clarke Kent might spin around in revolving doors or telephone boxes but Superman didn't have to put on make-up.

Linda's heavy black mascara, black eyeliner and bright pink lipstick, completed the metamorphous.

The look had always drawn the attention of men and she knew it still worked when she stepped onto the pavement, feeling their eyes, hitting what always lay at the heart of them.

Not that getting attention in the street mattered. Her mission was more focused, an attempt to reunite the travelling family she ran away from all those years ago. It was time.

Everyone was getting older and besides, one of her nieces was getting married at the weekend.

She looked at her reflection in one of the windows. Linda Avery stared back but Linda Pritchard was only a costume change away.

Linda Avery had vanished the day she met Julius. She wasn't coming back, not on a permanent basis.

Linda shook her head at the reflection, apologised as she bumped into an old lady pushing her wheeled shopping bag.

Linda and Julius had fed each other lies, both falling for the other's deceit.

His were far worse, Linda always told herself.

Yes, she forgot to mention her traveller upbringing, the prostitution and the fact she never worked in a supermarket. She knew the lies weren't small.

But he just wanted her to add a cloak of respectability to his sickening life, a cover so he could carry on with little boys.

Thank God he was dead. No new victims.

Some small child, somewhere near here, would never know what he had escaped. The thought made Linda feel stronger.

Fate. Karma.

Julius' death certainly ticked those boxes.

Linda had no intention of leaving her children, no desire to abandon the Edwardian villa and certainly no wish to be back in the life of her childhood.

But she wanted to embrace her old world, not ignore it. She wanted to hug her parents, her sister and the nieces she had yet to meet. Whether she told them about her children, let alone introduce them, remained to be seen.

She took a taxi, knowing exactly where to go.

What she didn't know was the reaction she would get when she arrived.

Her father had telephoned her a couple of weeks ago out of the blue and she was stunned. He had traced her number through someone in John Elgin's Travellers Group, an individual who placed loyalty to the community above the confidentiality of personal information.

She had sobbed on the phone when she told him about Julius and young boys, and how she'd been dumped by Billy Skinner.

But a face to face reunion was different.

And he wasn't expecting her.

She walked up the track, wondering if she knew the mothers of any of the children playing in the distance. She smiled. The girls she grew up with were probably grandmothers.

Fifty metres.

She stopped when she saw him.

He looked older but she knew it was him.

The cigarette fell from his lips, dropping in what seemed like slow motion to the dirt.

Neither moved.

This is it. Rejection or affirmation.

His smile broke out and she had her answer, her father's 61-year-old legs carrying him as fast as they could to greet her.

She ran towards him.

They were like actors in a heart-tug movie but the tears were real, not faked for the camera. He flung his arms around her, picked her up and swung her full circle, just like he did when she was a child.

Feet back on the floor, she took a step back. 'Hello Dad.'

'Oh Elizabeth.'

He threw his arms around her again.

She had never seen him cry. She doubted anyone had seen him cry. Men like him didn't.

Not men like Declan Doherty.

CHAPTER FORTY-THREE

Luke and Mark Skinner stared, speechless, out of the windscreen as they headed up the road towards the pub.

The place was a boiling mix of yellow flames, acrid smoke and flashing blue lights.

Firefighters seemed everywhere, ladders high and water jets powering from thick hosepipes. The throb of the fire engines and tenders was a constant soundtrack. Police were diverting traffic and keeping the growing crowd behind the cordon; ambulances were stationary, on stand-by.

They parked as close as they could and got out of the car. The smell and the sting of smoke hit them and they rubbed their eyes. They saw firefighters pulling on breathing apparatus, preparing to go in.

'Jesus,' Mark said, as they walked towards the crowd at the cordon.

Luke was already thinking about revenge.

'Whoever did this will wish they were going inside that building with nothing but a fucking hankie.'

He pushed his way through the crowd, Mark close behind.

Charlie Sneddon, a skinny, ginger, low-life with a reputation for saying the wrong thing at the wrong time, didn't disappoint.

'Talk about watching your business go up in smoke.'

Luke didn't break stride. His right hand shot towards Sneddon faster than a snake strike. The punch landed flush on the side of Sneddon's jaw and he was unconscious before he hit the pavement.

'Remind me to send someone round to see that little shit,' Luke said, turning to Mark.

They stood and watched for a few minutes. Nobody spoke to them; nobody even looked their way, too scared of following Sneddon. They all knew his troubles had only just begun.

'Let's go,' Luke said. 'Nothing we can do here.'

Back in the car Mark asked: 'Is it insured?'

Luke shook his head. 'Nope. Dad didn't believe in insurance. Our name was the insurance. He always said nobody would dare attack our property.'

'Well they are now,' Mark started the car and drove off. 'And it can't have been Harry or Stuart or Geoff or Mat. So who is it Luke?'

'How the fuck do I know?' Luke shouted, the palm of his right hand slamming into the dashboard.

This time Mark shouted back. 'How the fuck do I know doesn't cut it Luke!'

He took a breath and lowered his voice. 'We need to find out. What did Tonks say apart from the pub's on fire?'

Luke pressed his head against the headrest.

'A gang of about thirty rushed in,' Luke said. 'He fought a few off, injured a couple before they dragged him out. Too many of them. They hit a few of the punters and dragged them out as well.'

'Did they speak to each other?' Mark asked.

'Not that he can remember.'

Mark stopped at the lights and stared at his brother.

'Does he know any of them?'

'Says not.'

'Recognise any of them again?'

'Nope.'

Mark had just moved off on amber when Luke's phone rang, the number withheld.

'You might want to go to Pussycats,' the slow-speaking voice said.

'Who's this?' Luke snapped into the mobile.

Silence and the call was ended.

'Pussycats quick as you can,' Luke said, voice shaking, a wash of fury and fear across his face.

'Jesus Luke.'

Mark yanked the wheel to his right, U-turned, ignored the blaring car horns and sped towards the industrial estate. The black smoke was already pluming high into the distant sky.

Again they parked as close as they could.

Same script, different location, the club already an orange inferno, windows fire blasted and flames winning the fight against the water jets.

Nobody was daft enough to do a Sneddon as they pushed through the crowd, but to one side a group of excited middle-aged women seemed to be shouting a chant in celebration.

'What are they shouting?' Luke said.

'Leave it,' Mark told him. 'They'll be the ones who protested years ago coming to gloat.'

Luke dipped his shoulder, turned his mouth down.

Mark, who had seen it all before, pulled him back by his collar. 'What are you going to do?' he said. 'Attack a group of women? Really clever.'

Neither spotted John Elgin. He kept his head down, didn't want to be seen, worried they would catch him laughing.

About time you got some grief

He had reserved his biggest laugh for the tape. No way had that survived.

'I'll ask again,' Mark said getting into the car. 'Who's behind this?'

'And I'll tell you again, I don't know.'

'Well who has your mobile number?'

'Plenty of people have that.'

'That's two places torched,' Mark said.

'I can fucking count!' Luke right on the edge. 'Just drive. I need to think, get lads at our other pubs.'

He scrolled through the contacts in his phone.

Had Mark been concentrating he would have seen the red pick-up with no number plates tailgating them, the big, green ex-army Bedford truck revving its engine, waiting to emerge from a left hand side street up ahead.

But he wasn't concentrating.

His own red mist had descended and he was driving on auto-pilot, instincts blinded. He was angry with Luke, who never took him seriously, and shaken by the arson attacks.

The ex-army truck had been used for decades to collect washed up sea coal at Seaton Carew, to the south of Seaton St George, before the council banned vehicles from the beach. Now it was on a different mission, billowing diesel fumes as it began to roll.

The Skinners heard it before they saw it and by then it was feet away from impact with Luke's passenger door.

Luke tried to throw himself sideways towards Mark but his seat belt held firm.

There was a deafening bang as the Bedford rammed the BMW side on, the air thick with the crunch of metal, glass and debris flying then crashing all around.

Behind, the pick-up had slewed across the road blocking it to oncoming traffic.

The Bedford pushed the BMW across the road as easily as a snowplough clearing a mid-winter dusting. Mark, coughing and fighting the wheel, hit down hard on the accelerator but got no traction.

The Bedford pushed the BMW against the red-bricked wall of a supermarket car park, inching forward until the wall collapsed. The Bedford backed up, hit the BMW again and finally roared away.

The pick-up followed, slowing as it passed, the faces inside laughing.

Mark was bleeding from a gash to the right side of his head where he had smashed into the driver's window. The airbag had scorched his right wrist and singed the hairs on his forearm.

Luke, dazed, was struggling to move his left arm. Blood seeped through his left trouser leg, a shard of metal protruding from it.

He shuffled in his seat, leaned forward, and searched the footwell for the ringing mobile. The impact had thrown it from his hands. He found it, picked it up.

He blinked repeatedly trying to focus. Through blurry eyes he read the screen. Number withheld.

The caller was aggressive and abrupt.

'Now fuck off altogether unless you want your mother to do a Joan of Arc.'

'So tell me more about this Cat,' Sam said, biting into a chicken wrap, the first thing she'd eaten all day.

'Not a lot more to tell really.'

Ed was sitting, elbows resting on Sam's desk.

'Hampshire. Went into CID. Worked as a DC with Ray Reynolds. He told me when we met up that time. He was never interested in promotion but said Ray wanted it from the off.'

Sam paced the office, her thoughts interrupted by the desk telephone.

'Sam Parker.'

She listened.

'Thanks for letting us know.' She looked at Ed. 'Pussycats is up in flames.'

'Bloody hell,' Ed said, sitting up straight. 'Game on.'

She chewed another bite from the wrap, swallowed, and wiped her mouth with a paper napkin.

'Who's taking the Skinners on Ed?'

'God knows. But they're hitting them where it hurts.'

Sam took a mouthful of sparkling water. 'We've got enough on our plates without this shit. Everybody in this place will be trying to link the arsons to Billy Skinner's death and pass it all onto us.'

Ed said: 'No problem if they give us more men.'

Sam stared at him, raised her eyebrows.

'You mean more officers.'

'You know what I mean,' Ed said.

'I do, but there's a way of saying it these days,'

Sam sat down, rubbed her eyes, felt the lack-of-sleep-grit scratching her eyeballs.

'So this Cat…he knew Ray Reynolds, what else?'

Ed said he didn't really know, he had hardly spoken to him since they'd left training, save the time Cat made contact.

'He got that award and he must have been on a job up here when he got in touch,' Ed said.

'Wonder what that was?' Sam took another bite of the wrap, Ed watching, feeling the hunger pangs.

'Like you he did a bit a sailing,' Ed told her. 'Quite a lot really. At training school he seemed to be racing every weekend from what I can remember, even sailed to France one weekend I think. Brought up in Hamble-le-Rice. I remember thinking what a great name.'

Sam wiped her mouth and stood up.

'Sailed the Solent then,' she said. 'Same neck of the woods that the Transit was stolen from and you said Pritchard's abductor walked like Cat.'

'That's a bit of a leap of faith,' Ed seeing it but not convinced.

'What would Cat be doing up here dispensing vigilante justice? If he was going to do it, and it's a massive if, why not in his own neck of the woods?'

'You said yourself he was awarded for his work with paedophiles,' Sam said, leaning against the windowsill. 'He wouldn't be going undercover in his own neck of the woods and he'd more than likely have Intel on ones who got away from him in the areas he was undercover, maybe peripheral players they didn't get the evidence on before the job was pulled.'

Ed had to concede it was possible but why now, why when Cat had been out 10 years or more?

He jumped up. 'Shit, I said I'd go and see Jayne-with-a-Y.'

Bev Summers appeared at the door. 'You need to see these. The background checks into Jeremy Scott.'

She put the papers on Sam's desk. 'I've gone through the court transcripts for his trial.'

'Thank God for the courts,' Ed said. 'Best record keepers in the land. Well, them and the Church.'

'Hark at our little historian,' Sam said, sliding onto her chair.

'In this case he's probably right,' Bev said. 'Look at the interviewing officer who gave evidence at the trial.'

She pointed to the relevant entry.

Sam stared at it. 'Oh my God.'

CHAPTER FORTY-FOUR

Elizabeth Doherty, aka Linda Pritchard nee Avery, was sitting in the twin-axle caravan with her parents, sister, nephew and nieces.

The years were rolled back, the years before she ran and ended up in the clutches of Billy Skinner, the years before she married a paedophile.

There were no accusations, plenty of tears and hundreds of questions. Linda listened and answered while she took in the brightly coloured interior. The caravan was different to the one she grew up in, but the garish colours, a world away from the pastels of her home, were not.

She had her own questions about their life but everyone apart from her knew the answers to those. Her questions would have to wait.

The teapot in the middle of the table was permanently full, topped-up by her mother, sister or nieces.

As word somehow circulated of her return, distant relatives formed a queue at the door.

She wanted to ask what had happened to the people of her own age. She really wanted to ask what had happened to the boy who was always pulling her at The Grabbing. But those questions could keep for later.

Her dad looked out of the window, stood up and walked outside. Nobody questioned his departure.

She looked out of the window. Doherty was in deep conversation with a dark haired man. A group were standing behind them, posing and preening, silently leaning against the four pick-ups.

A toddler ran into the caravan, shouted 'boo!'

Everyone laughed at the boy who was bare-foot and naked except for a disposable nappy and an oversized gorilla mask.

Sam and Ed travelled in silence, both thinking about Jeremy Scott's interviewing officer and the implications, if there were any.

Coolio's 'Gangster in Paradise' broke the silence.

Ed answered his phone and listened.

'Cheers,' he said, and ended the call.

He glanced at Sam.

'What?' she said.

'Traffic giving us the heads-up, he said. 'Luke and Mark Skinner have had their car rammed by an army wagon, shunted twice into a wall.'

'Fuck,' Sam muttered.

'Both carted off to hospital but the injuries aren't life-threatening, more's the pity,' Ed smiled. 'What a day this is turning out to be.'

Sam didn't share his enthusiasm.

The last thing Sam needed was an all-out gang war on her plate.

Approaching a set of lights, she grabbed the gear-stick and changed down to third with more speed and thrust than necessary.

Ed had worked with her for long enough. This was not the time for a one-liner.

'Let's get back to the beginning,' she said. 'Jeremy Scott's first, then Julius Pritchard and Hans van Dijk and then Billy Skinner.'

She slowed for a roundabout, came to a stop.

She turned and looked at Ed. 'All killed in disused buildings, all snatched with a lot of planning and now two Skinners rammed off the road.'

Ed took it on. 'By a truck who witnesses said was revving its engine at a junction as if it was waiting and the Skinners were being followed by a pick-up with no registration plates.'

Sam moved off.

'But why?' she said. 'The Skinners aren't connected with sex abuse, not of children anyway.'

'But they're all connected with John Elgin,' Ed said.

Sam looked to her right, moved onto the roundabout, Ed still talking.

'Elgin was a regular at their clubs, seemed close to them. So why kill them and how would he plan all of this never mind execute it? And involve Curtis? I can't see it.'

Ed shuffled in his seat.

Sam indicated left. 'Linda Pritchard gets dumped by Skinner then discovers her meal ticket is a paedophile. Plenty of motive there.'

'She couldn't do it, but her childhood family?' Ed said. 'Torching and torturing would be right up their street and they're in town.'

'Are they?' Sam said, edging slowly forward.

'Yep and more coming daily,' Ed told her. 'Word is one of Declan Doherty's granddaughters is getting married.'

'Word from where?' Sam glanced at Ed, irritated. 'I never hear it.'

He turned to face her.

'Sam, I've worked this place longer than you, know more people than you. I'm bound to hear things you don't.'

That was true but Ed heard things no one else in the nick picked up.

'Sign of a good detective,' he tried a smile.

Silence again.

'But what's their connection to Scott?' Sam said. 'Skinner yes. Pritchard and van Dijk yes. But Scott?'

She sighed. 'Everybody in the frame is always one body away from having the full set…unless we stop looking at people singularly.'

'Go on,' Ed looked at Sam.

'No one person is linked to them all. But if you put Elgin and Linda Pritchard together...'

'The cuddle?'

'Yes, then between them they're linked to every victim,' Sam said.

Ed saw how that would work, especially with Declan Doherty on the scene to pull it all together.

'Would he be capable?' Sam sounded unsure. 'Even the attack on the Skinner brothers?'

'Absolutely.' Ed had no doubt.

Sam wondered aloud if Doherty would try to take over Billy Skinner's empire but Ed said the travellers were too mobile.

'Their motivation would be revenge but they'd take a few quid if someone offered. Pull over at the shops will you? I'm starving.'

Sam nodded. 'Like the guy at Scaramangers?'

'Harry Pullman?' Ed said. 'Possibly but I'm not buying that bull from Luke that Harry's just gone away.'

Sam pulled into the small parade of shops. Ed was out and marching to the butchers before she'd reached for the handbrake. He emerged with a white paper bag and a mouth full of pork pie, shedding crumbs in a shower when he got back in the car.

'Bloody hell, be careful,' Sam wincing at the passenger carpet covered in pastry flakes. 'Is it nice?'

Ed nodded, mouth too full to speak.

Sam waited until he finished the first pie. A second was in the bag. 'Why don't you believe Harry's gone away?'

'Too convenient and too quick,' Ed told her. 'I think something's happened to him, and if it has, something's happened to Dean Silvers as well. Nobody would take out Harry and leave Dean. He'd go looking for them.'

Ed pulled pie two from the bag, steak and onion this time.

'And Deano's way too ambitious to walk away for a new life in bloody Argentina. He can barely speak English never mind Spanish. That whole story is a piss take.'

Ed bit into the pie, holding it on a tilt to stop the hot juice running down his fingers.

'Don't get that on the seats, I'm warning you,' Sam picturing a full valet heading her way. 'How do you know all this?'

Ed smacked his lips. 'Like I've just said. I know people.'

Sam's mobile trembled in the Audi's centre console.

Ed worked on the rest of the pie as she listened, nodded, and terminated the call.

'That caravan,' Sam said. 'The one in Seahouses.'

'What about it?'

'That was the intelligence unit. It belongs to Geoff Mekins.'

Sam shook her head, wondering how many she would need to tackle a full-on war.

Ed stared out of the passenger window, looking at the houses and chewing the last of the gravy-moist crust.

'You in a rush?' he said.

'Not particularly.'

'Fancy meeting Declan Doherty?'

Sky Sports News would have been a distraction while he contemplated his next move. Daytime TV at 3pm was not. But if you were holed up in a budget hotel where the clientele were more rigger boots and hi-viz than shiny shoes and sharp suits, Sky Sports wasn't part of the package.

He had lain in the dingy room and watched the radio alarm clock and its red digital display until 5am. He must have drifted off because he didn't wake until after 1pm.

He was still on the single bed now, the tiny TV fixed on

the wall bracket providing nothing but background noise. Time was when he'd have been in bed with the owner but they were past that stage now, had been for years.

Still, she was a good friend and he didn't have many of those left. Maybe he didn't have any.

He jumped at the two quick taps on the door but relaxed immediately. It wasn't the pre-arranged danger signal; no need for him to leg it out of the en-suite window.

En-suite? More like a converted wardrobe but it was on the ground floor and it did have a window.

The door opened and she walked in carrying a tray loaded with a metal teapot, a chipped china cup, and a plate of Bourbons.

'Thought you might like some tea.'

'Thanks.'

'What you going to do?'

'There's a problem with every plan I come up with,' he picked a biscuit while the tea brewed. 'All I can think is Ed Whelan. I need you to get in touch with him. Call the Murder Team and leave a message for him to ring you. Don't mention me. When he rings, tell him to meet you here.'

'You sure about this?'

He reached for the pot.

'No choice,' he told her. 'Out of options and nowhere to run.'

She thought about The Commitments, thought about singing the song but saw his face.

'I'll do it now then.'

She closed the door behind her.

He sat up and poured the tea. More leaked out of the spout onto the tray than went in the cup.

Harry Pullman was on borrowed time. The Skinners would come for him again, but right now they thought he was dead.

He allowed himself a small smile.

He doubled over the cheap pillow and stretched out, trying to get comfortable, still struggling to believe he was alive.

The sea had been freezing but it was also black and in the darkness the Skinners couldn't see him.

On his back and moving his legs like a breaststroke swimmer, he wouldn't have won any prizes for style but it was effective.

He kicked towards the flashing red light of the port-marker-can, a navigational buoy indicating the outer edge of the channel to vessels coming into the harbour.

On the third attempt he successfully heaved himself onto the buoy. He had probably been in the water two minutes.

The rocking marker-can and bound hands meant getting his trousers off was a task to humble Houdini but he did it. He had one slim chance at survival.

Before the navy dishonourably discharged him for desertion, Harry had learned two things during his 18-month service...hatred for authority and Morse code, more specifically, how to send an SOS signal.

Marker-cans are allowed, with certain exceptions, to flash their lights in any rhythm. Flashing a pattern that might be read as three dots, three dashes, three dots would be a statistical miracle.

Covering the red light with his trousers, Harry Pullman made the miracle happen.

That the lifeboat crew who saved him thought the SOS signal was an extension of the training exercise they'd just finished was, Harry knew, divine intervention.

Harry, covered in a medical foil blanket, had feigned shock and remained silent throughout the journey to shore. He knew he'd be taken to hospital, knew someone would notify the police, and knew he could never allow that to happen.

The Skinners had contacts everywhere, in every organisation. Reach a hospital bed and he might as well have let the sea and the darkness take him.

He had been helped into a waiting ambulance, feeling the blanket doing its job, the cold that had gripped him beginning to ease.

When the ambulance stopped and the back doors opened, the A and E entrance a glow of light, Harry saw his moment.

He stepped down as the driver went for a wheelchair, pushed the other green-uniformed paramedic to the ground and bolted.

For a dead man he was surprisingly fast on his feet.

CHAPTER FORTY-FIVE

Sam had followed Ed's directions on auto pilot, her mind full of the ruthless gang capable of military planning and execution.

Doherty would have access to enough people and no issue with vigilante justice. But military planning? Sam wasn't convinced it would be his style.

She turned through a five-bar gate at Ed's behest and slowed down. The Audi wasn't designed for rutted country tracks and the potholes in the fading light were harder to miss.

'When we pull up let me do the talking,' Ed said.

Sam rolled her eyes. 'I know. Patriarchal culture. Women should be barefoot, pregnant and tied to the kitchen sink.'

Ed laughed. 'Something like that. God those must have been the days.'

Sam playfully punched his left shoulder. 'Sexist pig.'

'Just kidding.' He looked at her and smiled.

Sam stopped the car, looked around and shook her head. 'Why do people still want to live like this?'

A woman inched her way towards them. Sam guessed she was less than thirty but with a back borrowed from an octogenarian and blue, swollen fingers that gripped a mug of something hot, more for the warmth than the drink inside, Sam suspected.

'Mr Whelan,' Doherty said, as Ed got out of the car.

The woman turned and walked away.

Doherty walked towards him, hand extended.

'How are you Declan? Long time no see.'

'You know how it is,' Doherty said. 'Just want to live a peaceful life, but not everybody wants us to have it.'

'Quite a gathering,' Ed said, looking around as another two white caravans were towed onto the makeshift site. 'Council not been round yet?'

Doherty shrugged, said by the time the council got at them they would already be on their way.

'Not here long,' he said.

'This is Detective Chief Inspector Parker,' Ed said, indicating Sam with the palm of his hand.

Declan extended his hand again.

Sam shook it. 'Mr. Doherty.'

'Such manners on one so young and a chief inspector already,' he smiled. 'Now what can I be doing for you?'

'Just thought I'd pop by and say hello,' Ed said. 'You've got a busy weekend coming up and we don't want to spoil anything.'

Declan grinned and gave Sam a wink.

'I have no idea what you're talking about Mr. Whelan.'

Ed let that go, satisfied Doherty knew he knew.

'Mind if I have a wander about?' Ed asked now. 'Police business.'

The wattage dropped a notch on Doherty's smile.

'Be my guest, but I'll walk with you,' his huge hands struggling from the pockets of his waistcoat. 'Some of the young lads aren't as friendly as me. Just because you're not wearing a uniform doesn't mean they'll not know who you are. Call it instinct.'

'That's fine.'

'Does the young lady want a cup of tea?' Doherty asked.

Sam forced a smiled, 'The young lady's fine. I'm coming with you.'

The three of them walked amongst the caravans dodging mothers hanging out washing, dogs barking, tethered horses feeding.

'Who owns the pick-ups Declan?' Ed nodded towards four vehicles, all bearing Irish number plates.

Doherty stopped. 'I can't remember, Ed. It's my age. Everyone seems to have them these days. Less and less Mercedes and Land Rovers than in my day.'

'Can you find out?' Ed said.

Doherty crammed his hands in his waistcoat pockets again. 'I could, but you'd have to tell me why?'

'I saw your daughter the other day,' Ed sneaking it in like a rabbit punch.

This time the lights behind the smile went out and Doherty stared into Ed's eyes. 'Then you'll know we have nothing to do with her. Not since she ran off and got in with Billy Skinner.'

Ed kept it short. 'He's dead.'

'I heard,' Doherty fiddled with the chain of his pocket watch. 'Good.'

'And his sons are in hospital,' Ed said.

'Even better.'

Doherty started to walk.

'Seems they were in a bad crash,' Ed walking with him. 'Pick-up involved.'

'Go and check them for damage,' Doherty told him, not altering stride, looking straight ahead.

'And four pick-ups just like those were seen at Scaramangers pub before it was torched,' Ed nodding towards the vehicles.

Doherty stopped and looked into Ed's eyes.

'Torched you say,' not a hint of unease. 'Nasty. I'd like to help but I don't know how I can.'

'Let's start with the owners of those vehicles,' Ed said, moving so close they were stood nose to nose. 'We don't want the site swarming with police do we? I've come here to keep this low-key.'

They stood in silence like gunfighters ready to draw, the moment stretching.

'There'll be no need for that,' Doherty turned around and shouted to a tall, wiry man with curly brown hair leaning against a caravan. 'John. Come here a minute.'

The man ambled over, hands in the pockets of his oily jeans, sleeveless vest covered in oily finger marks. He kept his eyes on Sam as he walked, licked his lips. The cold didn't seem to bother him.

'This is Sergeant Whelan. He wants to know who owns the vehicles. Don't argue. I've said it's okay.'

'Alright.'

Ed looked at him. 'Full name.'

'John Smith.'

It was Ed's turn to roll his eyes. 'Date of birth?'

'1st January.'

'What year?'

'Every year.'

'Ah the campsite comedian,' Ed sighed. 'What year were you born?'

'Can't say sir,' the hint of a grin. 'My mother was never much good with numbers.'

He stared at Sam, looked her up and down.

'Who owns the pick-ups?' Ed pointed towards them.

'That black one's John's. That red one's John's, that...'

'Are you saying they're all owned by the same person?'

'No,' the man enjoying himself. 'Different people, just all called John.'

'All John Smith?'

'You're good at this officer,' the grin wide and insolent as he looked into Sam's eyes and licked his lips again. 'I'm good at other things too.'

Sam took two quick steps forward, her shoulders stiff, her stance aggressive. She ignored the whisky on his breath.

'You might be the World Wanking Champion for all I care, but if you want to be a smart arse we can continue this conversation down the nick.'

John Smith blushed but not with embarrassment. Anger was belching out of him like smoke from a power station.

'And who owns the army truck?' Ed said, unable to hide his smile.

'Jo...'

Doherty stepped in front of him.

'What army truck?' he said. 'You never mentioned any army truck. Tricking people? Not what we expect from our police.'

John Smith seethed. Sam and her put down had snapped his concentration.

'We'll be on our way Declan,' Ed said. 'Have a good weekend. We'll see you later.'

Doherty the genial host was back, although the warmth never quite made it to his eyes.

'We'll be moving come Sunday so don't wait too long,' he said. 'Might see you Saturday if you find out where and want to pop by. It'll be a free bar. You and your Irish ancestry and all that.'

Ed thanked him for the offer, said he'd think about it.

Sam turned to John Smith. 'Your mother might have been shit with numbers but she wouldn't have fallen for that three card trick. Stick with the script in future. No one likes a clever twat.'

Sam walked away, Ed following, the silent stares like lasers on their backs.

'So where do you think the army truck is?' Sam said, as she slid behind the wheel. 'Burnt out?'

Ed shook his head, said they wouldn't burn out a useful vehicle unless they had no choice.

'They've not had time to get it on a ferry so my guess, it'll be in a unit somewhere,' he told Sam. 'Any damage will be getting repaired.'

Just like the Transit, Sam thought.

'Doherty was quick to jump in when you asked that tosser about it,' Sam said.

'John, or whatever his name is, was too busy trying to play

you,' Ed told her. 'That's why Declan jumped in. But we got the confirmation we needed. They've got a truck.'

Sam turned the car around, Jayne Culley the next name on their call list.

'Stop the car!' Ed shouted. 'Look.'

Two boys aged about ten were chasing a group of girls. Both were wearing gorilla masks.

Ed jumped out of the car. Sam followed.

'Alright lads,' Ed called to them. 'Nice masks. Where did you get them?

The youngsters had frozen but Doherty was watching, for the first time a darkness on his face.

'Calm down, they're only fucking masks,' he said, walking towards the children.

'Where did they get them from?' Ed holding his own temper in check.

'How should I know?'

Sam stepped closer to Doherty. 'It might be important. Do you know?'

'No idea.'

'Okay thanks,' Sam said, a plan flashing bright in her head. 'Look, can I buy them off the children?'

Doherty hesitated then said: 'Everything's got a price.'

Five minutes later Sam and Ed were back in the car, masks now on the back seat, purchased for £5 each.

'No point in seizing them and giving ourselves a load of grief,' Sam said. 'A tenner's better than needing loads of uniforms to restore order.'

Sam drove off, the Audi pitching and rolling over the track.

'And now we can see if forensics can link them to any of our scenes or victims.'

CHAPTER FORTY-SIX

LUKE AND MARK SKINNER were patched up in A and E.

An x-ray showed Luke's left arm was badly bruised but not broken, the piece of metal was pulled with some difficulty and plenty of pain from his left thigh and the wound was cleaned and closed with 10 stitches.

Mark had concussion, whiplash and eyes that were already blackening from the impact of the air bag.

Both discharged themselves against medical advice.

Marge jumped from a plastic seat in reception and ran towards them when they emerged from the swinging double doors.

'Not here mum,' Luke said, turning to protect the sling on his left arm.

Marge stopped then head bowed she followed her sons.

Luke looked around, checking the other people in reception, and stuck two fingers up at the CCTV camera.

No one spoke until they got into the small hatchback, Marge's choice instead of the showy beasts her Billy had wanted her to drive.

Her hands, shaking like an alcoholic's before their first drink, struggled to get the key in the ignition.

'Calm down mum,' Luke shouted from the back seat. He may be leader in waiting, but like children the world over, as the youngest he sat in the rear. 'We need to get home sometime today.'

Marge wiped her eye and forced the key into the ignition. 'How can I calm down?' she shouted. 'What's going on?'

The car lurched forward, chugged and stalled. Marge dropped her head, eyes closed and white-knuckled hands squeezing the wheel.

Luke pressed his nose against the window and sighed. 'Just get us home mum.'

The journey was completed in silence until Marge pulled up alongside the fountain.

She couldn't wait any longer.

'Will somebody tell me what the fuck's going on?' she screamed. Luke and Mark jumped at the sudden explosion, whipped back to boyhood for a split second, ready for a tongue lashing or worse.

Mark touched his mother's arm, told her they would talk inside.

'So what's this all about?' Marge said, as soon as the front door was closed. 'First the pubs are set on fire, then you two get rammed off the road and before you ask, there were plenty of bizzies at the hospital. Most of the bastards were just there to gloat.'

She threw her woollen coat over the kitchen table.

Luke stiffened and adjusted his sling. 'The truth is we don't know who's behind it.'

Marge ran and pushed him against the sink. He screamed out in pain.

'You said it was sorted,' she shouted, taking a step backwards. 'So it can't be Harry or his nephew or McFadden this time, can it?'

She yanked open one of the wall units, took out a bottle of Poetic Licence gin, and poured a large measure.

The fridge light threw the lines on her face into sharp focus as she grabbed the tonic. Ice and lime added she sat down with the drink.

'So who is it?' Marge said, voice tired but back under control. 'Unless it's our Mat, come back to burn down the family jewels and crash into you two. Attempted murder the police reckon.'

'There's no attempt murder,' Luke said. 'We'll not be cooperating. If the police want to crack on investigating it, fine, but they'll get nothing from us.'

'Are you stupid?' Marge glared before taking two large mouthfuls. 'Your dad's been murdered. They've had a go at you and Mark. Two of our places have been burnt down. The police won't just walk away. So you will cooperate.'

She drained the glass, the gin hit making her dizzy.

'So what are you going to do now?' the words a challenge. 'The pair of you need to get a fucking grip here and sharpish.'

Mark sat next to his mother.

'We need to see John Elgin.'

Her laugh was short and a stranger to humour.

'John Elgin!' Marge shouted. 'He's the least of your worries.'

She stood up, stormed across the kitchen, and refilled the tumbler.

Marge took a deep drink as she returned to the kitchen chair.

'I know all about the planning applications but you need to sort this first. Your dad never took his eye off the ball. It's why he lasted so long.'

She looked down at the table, lost in the moment. When she looked up at Luke her burning eyes cut through him like a grinder attacking metal; the sparks might not be visible, but they were there.

'If you've sorted your dad's killers, they must have had help and the help is still out there,' Marge said. 'So I'll ask again. Who?'

'The answer's still the same mum,' Luke told her. 'We don't know.'

He walked to the table and sat down.

'Well I suggest you find out quick,' Marge said. 'Otherwise everything your dad built up is going down the pan.'

She suddenly started to sob.

'I can't even give him a funeral yet,' snuggling into Mark when he put his arm around her. 'The police are keeping him until they've done all their tests.'

Luke thought better of telling her about the threat to burn her alive. Violence and retaliation was the world he lived in, but this was different. The rules of the game no longer applied. His mother had been threatened and he had no idea who was behind it. He was fighting ghosts and he didn't know where they would attack next.

Maybe they could all live the lie he had made up about Mat, sell and move to Spain, move anywhere where there was sun and safety. Money wouldn't be an issue.

Linda Pritchard had hidden behind the curtains in the caravan when she saw Ed Whelan. The whisper that police were on the site had moved at light speed, only taxi drivers matching travellers for the best intelligence systems in the country.

She had watched Whelan talk with her father, watched them wander off with that policewoman. She had made her excuses and left when her father returned and the police were gone.

In the public toilets on the promenade she changed back into Linda Pritchard.

John Elgin was waiting for her on the pier. It was 6.05. She was five minutes late.

'How did it go?' he asked, the two of them walking further out to sea.

'Alright with mum and dad,' Linda told him. 'Better than I expected. But Whelan showed up.'

'Did he see you?'

Linda said no but a few minutes earlier and he couldn't have missed her.

'I liked the outfit you just had on,' Elgin brought the image into his mind. 'Very…'

'Slutty?'

'Your words not mine,' Elgin said with something unpleasant in his smile.

Linda told him to forget it, there were more important things in play. 'Firstly, two of the Skinner boys were rammed off the road.'

'How do you know that?' Elgin asked her.

'Dad told me.'

'They'll be bricking it,' Elgin said. 'The pub and club burnt down. Then the demolition derby.'

He saw her quizzical look.

'I'm showing my age,' Elgin said. 'Stock car racing back in the day. Always ended in a demolition derby. Last car standing.'

He watched a shadow of impatience or irritation move over her face and felt foolish.

'Whatever it was, the Skinners must be running scared,' Linda said. 'But you're sorted. No tape to upset your lovely wife and your abuser burnt to a crisp.'

Elgin stopped and turned to face her, taking in the hair, the clothes, the makeup. Nothing sleazy from the street now.

'You haven't done so bad yourself,' he said. 'Paedo husband dead, nice house now in your name, and I'm sure there'll be a decent pension in the pipeline.'

'A husband who also abused your grandson,' Linda threw in.

Elgin gave that a nod in recognition.

'And let's not forget, the gangster who dumped you has also met his maker.'

'We'd make pretty good suspects if they linked all of it together,' Linda said. 'Just as well Ray Reynolds is retired.'

She leaned against the railings, staring out to sea, and smiled at the memory. Ray Reynolds, her knight in shining armour all those years ago. She was a gypsy runaway when he found her and helped her forge a new life as Linda Avery only for her to run into the arms of a gangster. She had started delivering drugs in a car Billy Skinner provided but was soon enough living rent free in one of his flats. Flat? Who was she kidding? It was just a shag-on-demand pad, Skinner liking to keep her close.

When he'd finished with her after a couple of years she was turfed out to make way for the next one.

She was bitter, angry and apologised to Ray Reynolds, knew she had let him down. She did try to help him with bits of information on the Skinner empire but it never came to anything. Skinner was too smart. He was surveillance conscious, a master at covering his back, and always had at least 20 SIM cards for his phone, all of them pay-as-you-go.

But now he was dead and his arsehole sons were running scared. That much she had picked up in the caravan.

'So what happens now?' Linda asked, turning her head towards Elgin.

'What do you want to happen?'

'I'm too old for games John,' she told him, meaning it. 'I spent too long on my back after that twat dumped me on the street.'

Elgin put his arm around her, pulled her into him.

'I think it's time I was honest,' he said. 'I'll take whatever shit comes my way but I want to be with you.'

She kissed his cheek and stepped away. 'You've only known me a few months and what about Jill?'

Elgin was surprising himself, something about the moment, the beat of the water, the way Linda was looking at him.

'A few months is long enough to know what I want,' he told her. 'I could tell you Jill was just about sex but I loved her, loved her for years.'

He stopped and wiped his eyes.

'But I could never be with her after what she did, all the years never knowing I had a son. I would have stood by her if she'd told me but she wanted to save face more than let the two of us be together.'

Linda saw his hurt and hugged him, said she liked that they had a future but they would have to wait while she played the grieving widow.

'People will talk if we're together too quick,' she said. 'And Ed Whelan is nobody's fool.'

They walked up the path. Ed knocked.

The hall light came on and Jayne Culley opened the door, glassy eyes blank, devoid of recognition.

Ed smiled. 'Hello Jayne, it's me, Ed Whelan.'

No response, Jayne leaning heavily on her black walking stick, looking lost.

'The policeman,' Ed said gently.

Suddenly the empty face lit up.

'The policeman!' Jayne remembered. 'Come in Mr. Whelan, come in.'

Jayne had still been confused, still walked slowly, but Ed was happy to see she wore matching slippers this time.

Dignity seemed way down any political agenda, he thought.

They followed her into the kitchen. 'Do you want tea?'

'Yes please,' Ed said.

'And your wife?' Jayne looked at Sam.

Sam and Ed glanced at each other and smiled. 'Yes she would love some tea Jayne.'

Ed watched Jayne struggle with three cups and three teabags, his shoulders slumping out of pity and anger.

It was outrageous in modern Britain, one of the planet's wealthiest countries, a woman who no doubt had played by the rules all her life was now left to God and providence.

Jayne's shaking hand passed Sam a cup.

Sam smiled and thanked her. Like Ed she'd seen Jayne forget to boil the kettle.

'It's not too hot for you dear?'

'It's perfect,' Sam said.

Jayne smiled.

Ed spoke. 'What did you want to show me Jayne?'

'Do you want cake? I've got a nice sponge cake.'

'No thank you Jayne,' Sam said.

'You had something to show me,' Ed said again.

'I did. What was it?'

'Was it about the man who knocked on Jeremy's door?'

'Yes, I remember,' she sailed across the kitchen. 'He was on the TV last night and in the paper.'

She took the Seaton Post from the bench and held it up. 'There.'

She pointed to a picture of a suited man.

'It was him,' the paper waving in an imaginary breeze. 'I told you he was a military sort of man. Take a close look at him.'

They didn't need to.

They knew who it was.

Ray Reynolds. Detective Superintendent. Retired.

CHAPTER FORTY-SEVEN

'What do you make of that?' Sam said, when they were back in the car.

Ed was sure Jayne Culley believed she had seen Ray Reynolds. Whether she had or not was a different matter.

'We've both seen witnesses describe the same event in totally different ways,' he said. 'People recall different things, not always correctly, and Jayne is...'

The words trailed away as Sam nodded, balanced her wrists on the top of the wheel and took a cigarette out of the packet.

'There could easily be an element of auto-suggestion,' she said. 'She's seen the photo and convinced herself that's the man who was at the door.'

'That's why we had to show a witness12 different photographs in an album back in my day,' Ed said.

'Exactly,' Sam agreed, conjuring up the photograph of Reynolds, the newspaper article about a convicted killer who was being released. 'But don't forget Cat and his links to Ray.'

Ed whipped his head to face her.

'Hang on Sam, there's nothing to link Cat to this.'

'Other than you saying the guy on the CCTV walks like him.'

Sam put the cigarette between her lips and lit up.

Ed said nothing. He pressed his nose against the window. Could this be down to Ray Reynolds and a bunch of vigilante cops?

'We'll go and see him tomorrow,' Sam said.

'Ray?'

'Who do you think?'

'And say what?' Ed liked Ray Reynolds, wanted him far from the frame. 'We've got a witness with dementia who saw your picture in the Post and says you were one of the men who abducted Jeremy Scott. He'll eat you alive and feed what's left to the wolves.'

Sam bridled. 'Maybe you're too close to him?'

'Maybe I am,' Ed holding his ground. 'But that ID is weak and you know it.'

Sam was about to come back when Ed's mobile rang.

He answered and listened.

'She asked for me personally?' Ed said. 'Okay, I'll be there in ten.'

Sam watched as he ended the call.

'That sounded important,' she said. 'Where to?'

'Sea View Palace.'

Sam laughed, said she thought it had been condemned or bulldozed.

'Not yet,' Ed stared out of the window. 'Why's the owner asking for me? I think I've only met her twice and that was years ago.'

Ten minutes later Sam pulled up outside a building so tired looking it could have been called Rip Van Winkle, salt-blasted paint work long missing in action, the net curtains faded sepia from tobacco smoke and time.

The Sea View Palace, like the rest of the small hotels in the curved Georgian terrace perched above the sea, had been popular throughout the first half of the 20th century, a beach escape from the coalmines and shipyards.

Now it housed contract labourers looking for cheap digs. Rooms at less than £15 per night left enough cash for beer and a fish supper from their accommodation allowance.

'Do you want me to come in?' Sam asked.

'No, it's fine.' Ed said, getting out of the car. 'If it's anything I'll let you know.'

He pushed open a wooden gate that might once have been red, walked up the path and through the door. The name-plate had begun life as brass but was now a sickly blue-ish green, the chemical reaction between the copper and the atmosphere left unchallenged since its last, distant polish.

There were no tourist plaques, no stars or rosettes. Trip Adviser wouldn't have heard of this place.

He pressed the bell on the tiny reception desk and a shoulder length peroxide blonde appeared behind him. Jeannie Jackson looked as tired as her hotel.

'Jeannie,' Ed said, as he turned. 'How are you? It's been ages.'

'Long time Ed, a long time.'

Ed saw the memory of the pretty woman he remembered. For the second time that day he felt a jab of sadness.

'You wanted to see me?'

'Not me,' Jeannie said. 'Harry. He's in the room down the hall.'

'Harry who?' Ed asked, nonplussed.

'Harry Pullman,' Jeannie told him. 'Who do you think?'

The Harry Pullman who's supposed to be on his way to Argentina?

'What does he want?' Ed's mind racing now, playing catch up.

'I've no idea, other than he thinks only you can sort out his problem.'

'Well I can't build him a new pub.'

Now it was Jeannie's turn to be lost in the dark.

He followed her down the hall, watched and listened to her knuckles giving two quick taps on the unpainted door of room 2.

Harry Pullman answered.

Ed thought he looked like shit.

'Cheers for coming,' he saw Ed look him up and down, eyebrows heading for the mildewed ceiling.

'Jeannie got me some clothes off the other residents,' Harry's explanation.

The shirt was too small, the trousers too big.

'All a bit cloak and dagger,' Ed said, walking past Harry into the room.

'Thanks Jeannie,' Harry said, closing the door behind Ed.

Ed sat on the bed. 'Is this the best you can stretch to Harry? It's an absolute shit hole. I know Scaramangers' gone up in smoke...'

'What?' Harry interrupted.

'You don't know?'

Harry's wide-eyed stare gave Ed the answer.

'Burnt down earlier this afternoon Harry,' he said. 'Sorry to be the bearer and all that.'

Harry had his back against the door.

'It's okay,' he said. 'I wasn't planning on going back.'

Ed asked again what Harry was doing holed up in a toilet.

'Shitholes are sometimes the last places people look for you,' Harry told him. 'And I can trust Jeannie to keep her mouth shut.'

'Who's looking for you?' Ed said, taking in the room's joyless decay, like something slowly dying. 'Luke and Mark Skinner for a kick-off.'

Ed gave Harry his full attention.

'Luke said you and Deano were heading for Argentina,' he said. 'Some bull about your fascination with escaping Nazis and Diego Maradona.'

'Very funny,' Harry looking a million miles from amused. 'Those bastards killed Dean and tried to kill me.'

Ed was working this on the hoof, trying to hold the unfolding story together, looking for gaps he could fill in the jigsaw.

'So what do you want me to do?' he said.

'I want to go into that witness thing,' Harry dropped next to Ed. 'You know where you get a new identity.'

Ed smiled but he was watching Harry Pullman, watching a man who was scared and playing the last ace in his hand. He wouldn't be the first frightened criminal to bring down an empire.

Ed puffed out his cheeks and slowly blew the air from them. It was becoming a habit.

Putting someone into witness protection wasn't easy and there were strict criteria to be fulfilled. Not only that, but as the police had a duty of care until the person on the scheme died, it was a huge financial undertaking.

'Witness protection,' Ed whistled softly. 'What have you witnessed to qualify?'

Harry licked his lips and leaned forward, chin in his hands and elbows on his knees.

'Everything the Skinners have got up to in the last thirty years,' he said slowly. 'The drugs, prostitution, extortion, murder.'

He had paused before the last loaded word.

Yep that could safely be said to put you at risk of serious harm, Ed thought. You're on your way to qualifying.

He stared at the peeling floral wallpaper and said nothing, waiting for Harry to continue.

'Luke and Mark Skinner tried to kill me last night,' Harry told him. 'They probably killed Stuart McFadden, they definitely killed Geoff Mekins and that twat Luke was smiling when he showed me a photo on his phone of our Deano just before they killed him.'

Ed shuffled, heart telling him to punch the air, head keeping him in check.

This might be pure investigative gold but gold that would take days of interviewing to ensure it was mined correctly.

If Harry was as good as his word he would need every bit of help the UK Protected Persons Service - all the individual Witness Protection Units now united under one National Crime Agency umbrella - could deliver.

Harry Pullman swallowed and spoke again.

'I can give you the lot,' he said. 'Even the name of the skipper who takes them out to sea when they want to get rid of somebody. Ask Ray Reynolds. He knew about them throwing people over the side, he could just never prove it.'

Reynolds popping up again

'My boss is outside,' Ed said. 'I need to speak with her.'

'Parker?' Harry sat up, looking at the door as if Sam was about to walk in.

'DCI Parker to you.'

'God if I was 20 years younger,' Harry letting something crude but exciting briefly shine in his gloom.

'Even then you couldn't have punched that far above your weight,' Ed killing it. 'You understand once you start down this road there's no going back.'

Harry sat forward and put his head in his hands.

'What's to go back to?' he said. 'Deano's gone, the pub's gone. I'd be watching my fucking back forever anyway.'

'Who killed Billy?' Ed asked.

Harry looked up, shook his head. 'No idea.'

Ed jumped off the bed.

'Enjoyed the craic Harry but I've got better things to do than hang around listening to your shite,' he said. 'You either tell me the lot, or you don't bother at all.'

Harry pushed himself up off the mattress and moved towards Ed.

'The easiest thing for me would be to feed you a load of bollocks, tell you what you want to hear, but what's the point of that?' Harry was close enough for Ed to catch the stale, sour breath. 'You'd find out sooner or later it was all crap. I'll tell you what I know, no more no less. What you do with it is down to you.'

Ed stepped backwards, Harry watching and waiting, no cards left to play.

'Fair enough,' Ed told him. 'But where's Mat? Has he gone AWOL as well?'

For the first time, Harry Pullman allowed himself a smile.

'He's missing alright,' remembering, enjoying the replay running in his head. 'Missing at sea, presumed dead. I pushed him overboard.'

Ed turned towards the door, said it was time to move.

'Why?' Harry asked, reluctant, wary. 'It's sound here. Jeannie would never tell.'

'And Sam Parker's been sat outside in a car and I've been sat in here,' Ed told him. 'If you want to do this, you do it our way or not at all, and the first thing, right now, is your safety.'

Ed opened the door.

'Move it.'

Harry Pullman was sat in the back of the car behind Sam as she sped west towards the Lake District.

They had stopped and bought him some clothes that fit - a jumper, a pair of cords, a three pack of underpants, three pack of socks and a pair of shoes. They'd kept the receipts. They didn't buy him a coat. He wasn't going out. Not yet anyway.

Harry Pullman was well known around the north east and Sam and Ed couldn't take the risk that he'd be seen with them going into a hotel or recognised by a member of staff.

Harry said he had never been to the Lake District so the likelihood of him being clocked over there was minimal. As long as he stayed in his room and didn't speak to anyone he should be fine. He would only be there long enough to be interviewed and the Skinners arrested. Once that happened he'd be moved.

While Harry had never been to the Lake District, Ed couldn't remember how many weeks he'd spent there.

He loved the whole area for different reasons. Meandering around the shops in Keswick and Bowness, walking up Fleetwith Pike and Great Gable, relaxing on the steamers on Ullswater or Windermere.

Ed suggested Ullswater. It was the first lake you came across when you travelled west across the A66 from Seaton St George. It was also very quiet at this time of the year.

The White Lion in Patterdale, nestling under Place Fell, was a typical Lakeland Inn: open fire, real ale, clean functional rooms often occupied by walkers tackling some or all of the coast to coast route, and few prying eyes. Sam knew the pub, told Ed she thought it was perfect for a one or two night stay.

Harry didn't want anyone else to interview him, insisted it was Ed. That had gone down just dandy with Sue. If staying away wasn't bad enough, the limited mobile and wifi coverage just ramped up the grief. Fortunately he hadn't had long to explain. At one point he considered letting Harry talk to his wife to validate the trip, but he thought better of it.

Sam would have loved a couple of days in the Lakes, but there was too much going on in Seaton St George and besides Sue might just turn up. Sam didn't want any repeat of the humiliating hospital scenes when Ed was injured. Sue had made it crystal clear she wanted Sam nowhere near.

CHAPTER FORTY-EIGHT

Wednesday 17th December

SAM PUSHED OPEN the glass door of the cafe, coffee fumes hitting her nose before her feet were over the threshold. The steam swooshing from the machine did nothing to ease the pounding like a steam hammer in her skull.

The drive back from Patterdale had given her a headache that refused to budge, but it had also given her time to think...time to think about the murders, time to think about the kiss with Ed, time to think about Jayne Culley and her revelation about Ray Reynolds.

She was heading to the counter and searching her bag for her purse when she glanced up and spotted Reynolds sitting at a table by the window. A large white cup was in front of him, his head was down, and the pen in his hand was hovering over the Daily Telegraph crossword.

Sam bought herself a hot chocolate and walked over.

'Morning Ray.'

Reynolds looked up over the top of his reading glasses, stood, and shook Sam's hand.

'Hi Sam. How are you?'

He looked around, something that could have been curiosity in his eyes. 'No Ed?'

'Not today.'

'Please have a seat.' He indicated to the chair next to his, folding up the newspaper. 'Surprised you've got time to pop into these places what with all the dead bodies and gang wars.'

'You're well informed,' Sam said, sitting and lifting the mug to her lips.

'I know a lot of people.'

Just like Ed, she thought, blowing across the chocolate.

'Actually I'm glad I've bumped into you,' Sam said. 'It's about Ed. I'm worried about him.'

She sipped on her drink.

'Go on,' Reynolds said, eyes darting around the shop.

'I can't quite put my finger on it, but something's not right,' Sam stared into her cup. 'He doesn't seem himself but he say's everything's fine. I just get the feeling he's not telling me something, that there's something preying on his mind.'

Reynolds tapped the pen on the newspaper, watching Sam.

'He seemed okay to me,' he told her. 'Don't get me wrong, he's had grief off Sue for years but he can cope with that. Or at least he could back in the day.'

Sam watched the pen, temporarily Reynolds' drumstick. Nothing too flash. Decent enough, but not worth hundreds.

'You might be right,' Sam said. 'Maybe I'm looking for things that aren't there, watching him too closely. He should have taken retirement like you.'

Sam asked Reynolds what it was like to give up The Job and drank her hot chocolate as he told her how things were different in his day...different society, different expectations from policing, different rules.

It could have been Ed on one of his 'good-old-days' rants.

Sam let Reynolds talk before she picked her moment, pushed the chair backwards and stood up. 'Well I best be off.'

Reynolds got to his feet, glanced around the gathering crowd at the counter and the over-worked barista, and smiled as he shook Sam's hand.

'Nice to see you,' he said.

'Ray, would you mind, in case I ever want to check in about Ed, could I give you a call? Between you and me.'

'Of course,' Reynolds still smiling.

Sam took a notebook out of her jacket pocket. 'Left my phone in the car. Needed ten minutes without it.'

'Can't say I blame you.'

'Can I borrow that pen?' Sam bent down and took it off the newspaper before Reynolds could answer.

He gave her his home phone number. 'Refuse to have one of those mobile things. Managed before they came out, still manage without one.'

Sam smiled. 'Thanks Ray.' She turned and was gone.

He picked up the newspaper and put it down immediately. She'd taken his pen.

Ed spent all day in a small hotel room with a DVD recorder and Harry Pullman. They'd told the staff Harry's wife had left him for another man, that they'd be unlikely to go out.

Harry, grieving for Dean Silvers and feeling the pressure of turning informer, looked miserable. Ed knew every hour he was away the more shit he'd get when he got home. In truth, he wasn't much more cheerful. Given their cover story, that was fine.

At 5pm Ed turned right out of the White Lion and walked towards Glenridding. He'd told Harry to chill in the room for a couple of hours and then they'd go downstairs and get something to eat.

Ed walked briskly through Patterdale and into Glenridding. He knew Ullswater was on his right but he couldn't see it, not in this light.

He walked up the driveway of the hotel, through the glass doors, past reception and into the lounge.

Sam was already in the corner by a huge window, a glass of white in front of her, a pint of ale next to it.

In daylight they would have seen the lawn sweeping down

to the shore of the lake, the surrounding fells providing an ever-changing backdrop.

'Cheers,' he said, as he sat opposite. 'How was the trip?'

'Fine,' she told him. 'Few of your favourite wagons on the A66 but no real hold ups.'

'I told you,' Ed said, jumping on it. 'More lorries than you can...'

'It was a joke,' Sam stopped him. 'Don't even go there. How have you got on?'

Ed told her they needed to move tomorrow, that Harry was getting cabin fever, even wanted to go and help in the bar.

'That's why I can't stay long,' Ed said.

Sam said she would give him a lift back when they had finished their drinks.

She sipped her wine, giving an approving nod to the excellence of the Burgundy. 'So what's he said?'

'Enough for a novel,' Ed told her. 'We've got a shed-load to do tomorrow. Get him moved and passed onto somebody else to interview. He's fine with that now but he's given us so much already you'll need a full team on it. The Skinners are finished.'

Ed picked up his pint and swallowed a couple of mouthfuls.

'There's enough to start rounding people up as soon as the staff's sorted but it'll need plenty of planning.'

Sam said she would get on it, said he had done well to get so much out of him. She didn't tell him she'd seen Ray Reynolds that morning. Twice. Twenty minutes after she'd walked out of the coffee shop she'd returned to give him back his pen.

'Wait there,' Sam said, standing up. 'I'm going to see if they've got a room here tonight.'

Ed looked up. 'Why? I don't think...'

Sam bent down and put her hands on the table. 'You're not the one who has to drive home tonight, back across in the morning and then back to Seaton again.

'I drove back last night but why? Just to spare Sue? I

know she gives you a load of shit about me but forgetting one drunken snog there's nothing going on so grow a pair and tell her, instead of expecting me to trail backwards and forwards across the country just to save you some earache at home.'

She pushed herself away from the table, turned on her heels and headed to reception.

Ed glanced at the other customers scattered around the lounge. They all looked like they'd been happily married for years and they had all cast eyes in one direction at Sam's raised voice. They hadn't missed a word.

Ed could look embarrassed or front it out. He chose the latter. He shrugged his shoulders and smiled at his new found audience. They all looked away.

Sam walked back in, grinned at the barman dressed in black who nodded and smiled, and sat down.

'Sorted,' she said.

'I'm surprised the job will sanction this place,' Ed told her. 'Must cost an arm and a leg.'

'It won't and it has,' Sam was still grinning. 'I'll pay. I'm not bothered. I've got a room with a balcony and a view of the lake.'

Sam leaned forward. She whispered but the words still seemed loud and he was worried others could hear, even if Sam was back to business.

'Does Harry know anything about the murders of Scott, Pritchard, van Dijk or Billy Skinner?'

Ed matched her, keeping his voice low. 'He says not.'

'You believe him?'

Ed answered without hesitation. 'I do. He's told me about murders going back years, told me the name of the owner of the boat who takes the Skinners out to sea when they need to dump a body.'

Ed leaned across the table, their noses almost touching.

'He's scared and out for revenge after Dean. I don't think he's lying.'

They both sat back in their chairs and finished their drinks in silence.

As they stood up Ed was tempted to wave to the watchers but thought better of it.

Outside they sat in Sam's car, engine running, heater on full.

Sam lit a cigarette. 'If Pullman isn't giving us anything to progress our murders, then tomorrow I've arranged for him to be passed onto Organised Crime.'

Ed nodded. It was the right move.

Harry knew nothing about the executions of Scott, Pritchard, and van Dijk, no idea who killed Billy Skinner, and no idea who torched his pub.

'Which brings us back to Ray Reynolds and Cat,' Sam said. 'Not torching the pub, but the rest.'

She put the car into gear and pulled away, thinking about Reynolds.

As she drove up the small incline into the White Lion car park she warned Ed not to get into a session with Harry.

'We don't want him pissed and shouting his mouth off in a small Lakeland pub,' she said.

Ed made the Scouts' sign, opened the door and stepped out.

Sam put her hand on the passenger seat and peered up at him.

'I'll get Organised Crime here by 8am for Harry. I'll pick you up at 8.15. Play your cards right and I might treat you to breakfast.'

She pulled the door shut and drove away.

Sometimes you just had to wait.

Thursday 18th December

Sam pushed her knife into one of the perfectly cooked Eggs Benedict. Ed put brown sauce around the Lakeland Full English.

Sam had been in the restaurant earlier, sweet-talked the

host into giving her a table in the window with a view of Ullswater.

Harry and Ed had just wanted coffee at 7.30am. The Organised Crime Unit were early and Harry was keen to get away.

'Too quiet here for me Ed,' he had said. 'Too much time to dwell.'

'They'll have to relocate him to a city not the sticks,' Ed said now, chewing a small piece of the spicy Cumberland sausage. 'Put him somewhere like this and he'll swing back to Seaton St George quicker than a boomerang.'

They had both seen people relocated who, for all sorts of reasons, decided living under threat in your home town was better than living anonymously where you were completely alone. Not everybody had it in them to adapt.

'I don't know whether I could do it, wherever they put me,' Sam said.

The waiter topped up her coffee.

'What's on the agenda today then?' Ed asked. 'A nice walk and a pub lunch by a roaring fire?'

Sam dabbed the corner of her mouth with the starched napkin. 'As nice as that sounds, I want to go and see Ray Reynolds. I put it off yesterday because of Harry, but I want him boxing off today.'

Ed sliced through a mushroom.

'You have an interview strategy sorted?' he asked without moving his eyes from the plate.

I might have, Sam thought.

'We'll sort it in the car on the way back across. For now enjoy your breakfast.'

CHAPTER FORTY-NINE

Ed and Sam squeezed past the Jaguar on the bungalow's driveway, ten years old but still with a showroom shine.

Ray Reynolds, in blue cords and grey cable sweater, polishing the paintwork around the offside headlight, straightened as he heard their footsteps.

'Alright Ed,' he said, rubbing his fingers against the muslin cloth. 'To what do I owe this honour?'

'Ray. You remember Sam?'

'Of course.' He walked past the bonnet, shook Ed's hand, then Sam's. Nothing in the handshake indicated he'd seen Sam yesterday.

'Come in, come in. I was just about to make a brew.'

'Car's looking well,' Sam said.

'Thank you,' pride in Reynolds' voice. 'Bought it when I retired. Still as good as new.'

'Sam's our resident petrol head,' Ed said, as they followed Reynolds into the glass porch, three empty terracotta plant pots on the floor.

'What do you drive then Sam?' Reynolds asked, bending down to swap his shoes for slippers.

'Audi A5, 3 litre Quattro.'

'Very nice.'

'And what do you grow?' Sam said, nodding towards the pots. 'Tomatoes?'

'Very perceptive,' Reynolds smiled.

He led them through a small hall into the sitting room.

'Please take a seat. Tea?'

'We're fine,' Sam said, 'but don't let us stop you.'

Reynolds left as Sam settled into the armchair opposite the settee.

The room was not what she expected from a widower: carpet, surfaces and windows all spotless, the pleasant smell of fading air freshener and furniture polish mixed with a hint of tobacco like a subtle musky aftershave.

Now who's being sexist Sam?

At either end of the windowsill were two framed photographs, both black and white: one, a young Ray Reynolds and his bride, the other, a class photograph from his police training school days.

'You sure you don't want one,' a shout from the kitchen, the noise of tea-making in the background.

'We're fine thanks,' Ed said.

Reynolds walked back into the room carrying a red mug of the 'Keep Calm Carry On' variety and a white plate with six Club biscuits. He sat next to Ed, opposite Sam.

'So,' he said, raising the mug to his lips. 'I take it this is not a social call saying as neither of you have been here in your life.'

Sam looked at him as he sipped on the tea. 'It's not a social call although I would have been much more comfortable if it had been.'

Reynolds leaned forward, put the mug on a coaster on the coffee table, and sank back into the settee. Sam looked at the copy of the Telegraph on the table, open to the crossword, the same pen across the half-finished grid.

'Spare me all the pink and fluffy stuff Sam,' he said. 'I come from a time when the job got done without consideration for all that emotional intelligence shite.'

Sam blushed. 'Very well. As you know we are investigating the death of Jeremy Scott.'

'Is that why you're sitting opposite me?' Reynolds' eyes glared. 'Recreate the interview set-up?'

There was no friendly smile.

'You were the interviewing officer when Scott was arrested for offences of child sexual abuse,' Sam said.

Reynolds sighed loudly. 'And your point is?'

'Just looking for confirmation to start with.'

'Well you obviously know, otherwise you wouldn't be here,' Reynolds picked up the mug, sipped and waited.

Sam said: 'Do you know Archibald Leach, also known as Cat?'

Reynolds stood, walked to the fire-surround, and picked up a pack of cigarettes. He lit one but didn't offer them around.

'This is going to take a long time if you propose asking me about everybody I met in my police career.'

'When did you last see Cat?' Sam said, keeping her voice neutral. She wasn't going to allow Reynolds to get under her skin, but she intended to get under his.

'Monday morning,' Reynolds answered. 'He'd been staying here for a few weeks. Left Monday about half-nine to go back home. I remember because it was the day of the pensioners' party. You were there Ed.'

He drew on his cigarette. 'Is there a point to all this?'

'If you just bear with us,' Sam said.

Reynolds blew smoke down his nose, stared at Sam.

'Listen,' he said. 'Ed rates you and I've seen how you come across well on the TV. I'm sure you'll get promoted again but sometimes you've got to forget all the shite coming from the latest management fools masquerading as detectives and just ask the questions.'

He stubbed out his half smoked cigarette in the metal ashtray on the fireplace and reached for another. He pointed the open packet towards Sam.

'Thanks.'

Sam took one and reached for her lighter.

'There you are, you're starting to build your rapport,' Reynolds said, sitting down next to Ed. 'Just forget about the

PEACE interviewing model or whatever they call it now. What was it back in the day?'

He drew on the cigarette and blew out smoke.

'Prepare and plan, Engage and explain, Account, Closure and Evaluate. PEACE. Load of bollocks. Sometimes you've just got to come out and ask the question.'

He's treating this like a game. Or a lesson.

'Bollocks? You still remember the pneumonic for it,' she said.

She watched Reynolds, his stiffening forearms a spotlight on the rising anger he was trying to hide from his face.

'What was the purpose of Cat's visit?' Sam asked, lighting up.

Reynolds leaned against the arm of the sofa and crossed his legs. 'He's terminally ill,' he told her. 'Cancer. A bloody shame really. He's riddled with it. Just like me.'

Ed snapped his neck towards Reynolds. Sam's mouth dropped.

'Only it seems he gets to check out before I do,' Reynolds' tone had never changed.

'I'm sorry I had no idea,' Sam said, thrown and scrambling.

Reynolds pulled on the cigarette and looked at the glowing end, thin smoke winding upwards.

'As I said, save the pink and fluffy stuff. I've had a good life, a good wife too. She passed. Two years ago.'

Another deep draw and a tap into the ashtray.

'All the scum contribute nothing and end up running around for years while good people like my wife and Cat die too young,' Reynolds putting feeling into it now. 'No justice in the world.'

He turned to look towards the window and smiled at the photograph.

'We had so many plans for retirement,' he said, almost as if he was talking to himself, or maybe his wife. 'She had to put up with all sorts over the years...the callouts, the late nights, the cancelled family get-togethers. I always promised

I'd make it up in retirement. The two of us planned to take up yachting. Five years in and along comes the cancer.'

Reynolds' voice was starting to break, a thin mist over his eyes, but he held it together.

Another draw and the cigarette, half smoked like the last, stubbed in the glass ramekin dish by his feet.

'We couldn't have kids,' his laugh was short, ironic. 'My fault. Low sperm count but she never blamed me. I'm not sure why I'm telling you this'

Reynolds reached for the tea with a shaking hand and stared into the mug.

'So much for being the big man,' a flash of self-loathing not pity on his face. 'No lead in this pencil.'

Sam could feel his pain, empathise with it. She was a widow. All that time working towards retirement and then, whoosh. Everything blown away.

But Sam had to move from emotion to question. 'We'll need to go and see Cat. I've got some questions for him.'

She flicked ash in the ashtray by her chair.

'You'll be lucky.' Reynolds smiling now, reaching for the iPad on the coffee table.

'Cat knew it was over,' he said. 'He wanted to do it at a time and in a manner of his choosing.'

Reynolds swiped a finger across the screen and passed the tablet to Sam.

Local yachtsman feared drowned.

The headline was from the website of a local newspaper in the Hamble area.

'We said our goodbyes on Monday morning,' Reynolds was speaking as Sam read. 'Cat drove back home and rang me first thing Tuesday.'

Sam was trying to take in the words on the screen.

A local man, 59 years old, is feared drowned after his yacht was discovered adrift on The Solent near the entrance to The Needles on Tuesday morning.

He had last been seen sailing alone out of Buckler's Hard Yacht Harbour some hours earlier.

'The sea was his life's hobby,' Reynolds said. 'Even used to take underprivileged kids sailing with him.'

Sam's eyes stayed on the screen. Buckler's Hard, where ships were once built for Nelson's navy, was a tranquil setting on the Beaulieu River and a marina where she and Tristram loved to berth. She'd told him many times if they ever bought a boat of their own Buckler's Hard would be her home.

The coastguard was alerted to a VHF radio distress call at 11.25am. The RNLI attended and found the boat empty but with no apparent problems. A search is still underway.

Reynolds had been watching her read.

'They might find him eventually but he jumped,' he said now. 'Better than waiting to die, the way Cat saw it. As for me, well'...'

Reynolds looked suddenly like a man drowning in loss.

He lit another cigarette and spoke again.

'I was just like you back in the day,' he said. 'People rated me like Ed rates you, told me how good you were the other day at the pensioners' party.'

'Why then?' Sam asked him. 'Why take the law into your own hands? I don't understand.'

Reynolds studied her, a game player once more, moving the pieces.

'Who says I have?' he said. 'What do you think? I wanted to use my last few weeks righting some wrongs, wanted justice for some long ago victims?'

Reynolds caught Sam staring at his thick, black hair.

'I didn't want chemo,' he said, blowing out smoke. 'Seen too many go through it. Might have got me some time but at what cost? Four days a week feeling shit getting it done, next day wiped out, one good day and then the last day's shit because you know it's all starting again tomorrow. No thanks.'

He worked on the cigarette and let more smoke join the rest turning the air in the room toxic.

'So what do you think you've got?' Reynolds a man used to being in control, wanting to know what Sam knew.

Ed was finding it hard to look at him. He heard Sam answer.

'As well as Jeremy Scott we're looking into the death of Julius Pritchard who was snatched from the street,' she said. 'He was in the company of a man who looks like Cat.'

'Looks like or was?' Reynolds' smile was sly, teasing.

'Looks like.'

'Not good enough then is it?' Reynolds let the smile grow and got to his feet.

Ed remained in his seat, the smoke making his eyes ache.

'Let's cut through the bullshit,' Sam said, her eyes locked on Reynolds', her expression a challenge.

Is this direct enough for you?

Reynolds sat, controlled again. He leaned forward, stubbed out the cigarette, and unwrapped a mint biscuit.

'A bit oppressive Sam,' he said. 'It's not the late seventies now you know. Were you still in nappies then?'

He bit into the biscuit.

Sam sat. Silent. Waiting.

'That was a time when policewomen made the tea and looked after lost kids,' Reynolds said. 'Before they got big ideas.'

Sam ignored the jibe.

'There are a number of things connecting you to these crimes.'

'I'm all ears,' Reynolds said, popping the last of the chocolate biscuit into his mouth.

'You interviewed Jeremy Scott years ago then watched him walk. That must have been hard,' Sam said.

'My job was always to put them before a court,' Reynolds straight batting. 'After that it was down to the jury.'

Ed turned his head to look directly at him, offended by the answer, the words nothing he would ever have expected to pass Ray Reynolds' lips.

'Then,' Sam was saying now, 'there's your friendship with John Elgin.'

'So?'

'He was abused by Scott. His grandson was abused by Pritchard and van Dijk.'

'And let's not forget Linda Pritchard,' Ed joined in.

'Fucking hell Ed. I thought you'd lost the power of speech.'

Ed ignored Reynolds' sarcasm.

'Nee Avery, previously known as Elizabeth Doherty, a snout of yours for years, informing on Billy Skinner's businesses after she was dumped by him.'

Reynolds turned his eyes back on Sam. 'Is this the best you've got?'

He unwrapped another biscuit. 'I know all of these people, so that makes me a killer?'

'Everything was so well planned,' Sam said.

'Flattery won't get you anywhere,' another cold smile. 'If you had anything you'd be asking me these questions down the nick.'

'Believe me,' Sam said. 'I've got more than enough to take you into custody.'

'And I'd sit and say nothing,' Reynolds shot back. 'You'd have struggled to get a charge back in my day, but now? Not a prayer.'

Reynolds sat forwards, narrowing the gap between himself and Sam, chess players without the board.

'Trust me I will get the evidence if you're involved,' Sam said.

'And trust me it'll never get to court,' Reynolds' eyes locked on hers.

'You wouldn't know what evidence looked like if it smacked your tight little arse. Like all modern coppers, you haven't got a clue.'

It was Sam who broke the uneasy silence that settled, Ed watching and wondering where she would move next.

'Maybe I should arrest you anyway,' letting Reynolds think about it, the consequences.

'So you lift me and then what? Try to get me charged, get me on remand, let me die there, surrounded by the scum-bags I spent a lifetime putting away,' the bitterness as biting as the smoke grey haze in the room.

'But all you were bothered about was getting them before a court,' Sam pushed.

Reynolds sat up straight and jabbed his index finger, the voice a blade.

'Don't get arsy with me young lady…And at what point do you propose cautioning me?'

'I'm just here for a chat,' Sam staying with it, refusing to let herself be intimidated.

Reynolds said: 'So what do you want? Me to fill in the blanks for you? The wannabe seeking advice from a real SIO.'

'Something like that,' Sam told him, keeping her emotions hidden, any pity for him gone.

Reynolds sat back and crossed his legs, eyes sharp, alert, Ed watching him.

He's still in this...

'What's in it for me?' Reynolds said evenly now. 'You're not seriously expecting me to talk myself onto the remand wing are you?'

Sam looked away. The rule of law sat above everything. Noble-cause corruption, whatever the reasons behind it, was no different in her world to out and out corruption. She despised bent coppers.

Sam looked at Ray Reynolds, looked at Ed, and made her decision.

'You're right,' she said. 'Maybe I don't have enough evidence to charge you now and while I might get it, it might not come quick enough.'

Reynolds listened, his mouth a tight line.

'I have no desire to put a man, retired police officer or not, on remand for the last few weeks of his life...'

Sam fumbled in her bag and found her cigarettes, tugging a Marlboro free.

'But I want to know what happened,' she went on. 'I don't want you taking it to...'

She stopped, the next words held at a mental road block.

Reynolds said it for her.

'To the grave?' He held her gaze. 'Even if I had secrets, how do I know I can trust you?'

Sam fired her lighter and held the flame to the Marlboro, the taste good as she drew in smoke.

'You'll have to take my word for it, but things haven't changed that much since your day,' Sam told him. 'A confession here, in your house, without you being cautioned, is worthless. Any brief in the land will trash it; just say your illness had made you confused, vulnerable.'

Reynolds was quiet, listening.

Sam said: 'What I want is a confession and then for you to make a written statement between now and your last day outlining what happened.'

'A quasi dying declaration?' Reynolds gave a weak smile. 'Very dramatic.'

He reached for a new pack of cigarettes and slowly unwrapped the cellophane.

'You know I always loved that Ealing Comedy 'Kind Hearts and Coronets' but the killer, Louis Mazzini, lived to regret writing the account of his murders.' He took a cigarette from the packet. 'Why should I write mine? So you can look good, Sam? So my reputation ends in shame, cut to pieces in the press?'

'So the families can get closure,' Sam told him.

Reynolds put the cigarette in his mouth and left it unlit while he unwrapped another biscuit.

'The families of nonces and gangsters,' he spat the words. 'Scum who terrified little kids and decent people. This is about you Sam. Not them.'

Ed had been watching in silence but now he spoke.

'Maybe plenty will call you a hero,' he said. 'They might celebrate what you did, certainly the victims of the ones who've been killed.'

Reynolds nodded, a gesture to a point well made, but offered another take.

'What I may, or may not have done, was not done for acclaim or kudos,' he said. 'If it was me, it was done out of a sense that the system is broken, the guilty being acquitted, some of them not even getting to trial. Summary justice dished out for the people.'

He snapped the biscuit in half and popped it into his mouth.

'If it was me, I've done you a favour,' he spoke through crumbs. 'I've got rid of Pritchard and van Dijk, who would never have stopped, and I've started a gang war that will end who knows where. Billy Skinner's dead, may he burn, Luke Skinner running around like a headless chicken, his brother Mat and his boyfriend Mekins vanished. It's quite a list. Shame about Harry...'

'Harry Pullman?' Sam said. 'What about him?'

'He's upped sticks.'

Reynolds gave Ed a knowing glance.

'We've got Harry,' Ed told him.

Reynolds picked up his mug, the brew only luke warm.

'I wasn't expecting that,' he said. 'And his nephew?'

'Don't know,' Ed answered.

Reynolds shrugged then spoke again.

'Linda was living a nightmare with Pritchard and Scott's victims at least know he went in agony. Who exactly lost here?'

He turned his head and looked at his wife on the windowsill.

'Not the good guys, that's for sure.'

When Reynolds rubbed his eyes it had nothing to do with the smoke.

Sam wanted to tell him he was wrong, that the good guys always lost when they tore up the rule book and let true justice die.

'So, what happens now?' Reynolds throwing it back on her.

'I want the names of those involved,' Sam said.

'You've got them according to your line of thought,' Reynolds told her. 'Me and Cat.'

'A witness at the traffic lights saw three men.'

Reynolds shook his head. 'You get nothing if you expect me to tip up a decent lad helping two men fulfil their dying wishes.'

'We'll find out eventually,' Sam said.

'You won't,' Reynolds digging in, determined. 'You've got nothing. No witnesses, no forensics and you'll not get me or Cat bless him tipping up anybody.'

Sam believed him but had to push. 'Was he another retired detective?'

Reynolds stared at her. 'Move on Sam or this conversation's finished.'

'What about Declan Doherty? Did you speak to him?'

'Declan's a good sort,' Reynolds answered. 'Easy to wind up. He would always buy my innuendos, but you'll have more chance charging me than you will him and his mates. Not exactly renowned for cracking in police custody are they?'

'Did you give him any masks?' Sam asked.

'No law against that is there,' this time Reynolds' smile seemed genuine. 'I gave them to him for the young ones.'

'And John Elgin?' Ed joining in, moving through the cast list.

'A weak man but decent enough,' Reynolds stood up. 'Imagine being born into a life of privilege and having it snatched away on the whim of a vindictive old twat. Considering his start in life he turned out okay. He just needs to wise up, get shot of his wife, stop shagging young girls and settle down with someone nice. Life's too short to be stuck in unhappy relationships.'

He looked at the photograph.

'I want to know why Cat replaced the headlight on the Transit and then burnt it out,' Sam said.

The detective in Reynolds understood the attention to detail, the need to close everything off.

'Maybe the people concerned felt it had been compromised,' he said. 'They might have been wrong, but better safe than sorry. They certainly wouldn't want to be caught before they sorted Skinner.'

'The number plate?' Sam said. 'Belonging to a traffic car.'

Ray Reynolds laughed. 'Someone with a sense of humour. Obviously liked the thought of taking the piss out of the Black Rats. Bit like Cat. He once broke into a uniform Superintendent's office one weekend and wallpapered it in cartoon racing cars because the Super wouldn't stop talking about his one and only trip to Silverstone.'

Reynolds smiled at the memory.

'Easy enough to get a set of plates made up the way we would for a retirement present and before you ask, supposing I knew I won't say where or by who and nobody who made them is going to admit it.'

'What about the coke to drown Skinner,' Sam asked, like ticking off a shopping list.

'Easy enough to get it off someone like Harry I would imagine,' Reynolds told her. 'Enough to do the job. Maybe Harry wanted to take over. Maybe that's why he was accused of skimming by Mat. If you've got him you can ask him, but he's old school. He's not going to drop any of his friends in the shit.'

'And Pritchard and van Dijk?'

Reynolds suddenly looked tired, seemed older.

'What about them?' he said. 'Two favours in one if you ask me. Helped out John and Linda. I still see Linda now and again.'

'Does it go beyond that?' Sam said.

Reynolds shook his head.

'Don't get me wrong, Linda is beautiful and when I helped her years ago she did offer favours in return.'

Sam held his gaze.

'But I couldn't betray Barbara then, just like I couldn't betray her memory now.'

Sam stood up. 'Can I borrow your pen again?'

Reynolds looked at Ed. 'Don't you even teach them to carry pens these days?'

Reynolds reached towards the table, lifted the pen from the newspaper and handed it to Sam.

She thanked him as she headed for the door.

'I'll be back in a minute.'

'Now what?' Reynolds said to Ed.

Ed shrugged his shoulders and looked at the ticking clock.

It was ten minutes before Sam returned with her briefcase.

Ten minutes is a long time to sit in another man's house in silence.

'Any danger I can finish polishing my car,' Reynolds was on his feet.

Sam was suddenly back in the doorway.

'Sit down and spare me the indignation and histrionics you murdering bastard.'

The words hit Reynolds like a blow, his face moving from shock to rage in a heartbeat.

'How dare you?' his voice burning. 'Don't ever speak to me like that, not in my own home, not anywhere. You'll show me the respect my rank warrants you jumped up little...'

Sam moved across the room, didn't speak until she was nose to nose with Reynolds.

'You lost that the day you started your killing spree,' she said. 'Did you seriously think I was just going to walk away? Let your number three get away with murder. You might have torn up the rule book but I haven't. Now sit down.'

Ed hadn't moved. Like Reynolds, Sam's outburst had left him stunned. Now he was trying to work out where this was going.

Sam sat down, opened her briefcase and took out her laptop.

She put the laptop on her knee and powered it up.

'Remember when computers were heavy as hell and stuck on desks?' She said it almost to herself. 'These days you can lift them in one hand and be holding more memory than you'd need in a lifetime.'

She took a silver USB from her case, held it between her thumb and forefinger, and raised it towards the ceiling.

'So much memory in one of these, too.'

Sam pressed the USB into the computer and didn't look up when she spoke, Reynolds watching her like a man in front of a magician.

'Smaller and smaller computers with bigger and bigger memories,' Sam went on. 'The mobile phone you won't have is now basically a computer.'

Reynolds' eyes locked on Sam, nostrils flaring in the charged courtroom silence.

Ed was waiting, still bewildered. Experience had taught him that Sam, like a smart defence barrister, was about to drop a bombshell.

The two men watched as Sam hit a couple of keys, listened without moving their gaze as she spoke again.

'But it's not just computers that have got smaller. Lots of technology is packed into smaller things.'

Now Sam looked up and glared at Reynolds. 'Maybe some evidence did smack my tight little arse.'

She put the laptop on the floor and leaned forward. 'Did you think it was an accident when I bumped into you yesterday?'

Ed's eyes were widening by the second.

'Did it never cross your supercilious macho mind that I knew exactly where you were?' Sam turning the screw. 'That I knew you were alone, knew you were doing a crossword?'

She waved the pen. 'With this...'

Reynolds jumped to his feet.

'Congratulations. I'm impressed. So you knew I was in the coffee shop. What a detective you are.'

His arm shot up and he pointed at the door. 'Now get out.'

Sam didn't move.

'Sit down,' it was an order, 'I'm not finished.'

She held the pen like a prize or a piece of secret treasure.

'Covert devices are tiny these days,' her voice quiet now. 'Do you know you can put a camera in a watch? Or a listening device in a pen?'

Reynolds and Ed followed her hand as she hit play on the laptop.

It was only a moment before Ray Reynolds' voice boomed from the speaker.

'Ed Whelan's got Harry. Jeannie Jackson's been on the blower.'

Sam pressed pause.

'You conniving little slag,' Reynolds spat the words.

'With the tight little arse,' Sam's response coated in sarcasm.

Ed was still trying to process what had happened, what had been in play whilst he was in the Lakes with Harry Pullman.

Reynolds turned to him.

'You had no idea what she was up to did you, you useless bastard. Ever thought she believed you were the third man?'

Ed looked at Sam, said nothing.

'It doesn't matter what I thought,' Sam said. 'All that matters is the third man is on tape.'

The silence moved in on Reynolds like the sliding walls of a tomb in a fantasy film. The cancer wasn't the reason for his rapid, shallow breathing.

'And he is,' Sam said with a smile and an air of triumph. 'I've just had a quick listen in the car. The two of you running through the murders, making sure you'd covered your tracks.'

Reynolds was back on his feet, shouting, breathing deeper, his heart pumping blood to his neck. 'Breach of privacy! You'll never get it admitted.'

Sam stood up, authority in every word. 'Get your coat and lock your car. We'll do this at the nick.'

She closed the laptop, took out the USB, and placed both back in her briefcase.

She took a few steps forwards. 'Rest assured Mr Reynolds everything I have done has been correctly authorised in accordance with the Regulation of Investigatory Powers Act. You might remember it. I learnt all about it on my looking after lost kids course.'

CHAPTER FIFTY

Friday, 19th December

NEITHER OF THEM spoke in the car.

Ed was thinking of The Eagles' song 'Desperado'. What was that line? Something about letting someone love you before it's too late?

He looked at Sam and smiled.

She was aware of him looking. She glanced at him and smiled back.

'I need some fresh air,' she said.

Fifteen minutes later she parked near the promenade.

'Let's have a walk.'

They headed towards the pier, a wind nipping at them, carrying a fine spray and the smell of the churning water.

'I need to clear my head,' Sam said.

The sea, rough white waves breaking early, was punching into the pier, the spray getting heavier.

A couple, head down, had their black Cockapoo on a short lead.

'Is there anything worse than arresting police officers, even if they're retired?' Sam said, her cheeks already numb.

'Did you seriously think I was involved?' Ed looked away as he spoke.

'No.'

Lie, Sam told herself, even though she hadn't hesitated.

Everything and anything was possible in her world.

'But,' she continued, 'I didn't want anybody on the team to know what I had planned with Reynolds. Besides, if he hadn't got in touch with Jimmy Bell I'd have been none the wiser.'

Reynolds and DC Jimmy Bell had retired about the same time.

Blind loyalty, an ingrained hatred of certain types of criminal and a vicious willingness to inflict serious pain made him the perfect recruit to Reynolds' and Archibald 'Cat' Leach's no mercy mission.

He was in the nick with a 'fuck you' attitude that wouldn't survive when the remand cell was locked behind him.

Reynolds himself was playing the dying detective card, but he had taken pride in demonstrating his planning throughout his admissions.

Both prisoners knew the covert recordings were enough to convict them.

Saturday, 20th December

The wedding was in full flow when Ed walked into the seafront hotel.

The order of the day was suits for the men and lavish ball-gowns for the women.

The hotel management had quickly contacted a local security firm who now had burly personnel positioned by the stairs and lifts. Only guests with key cards were allowed to pass.

Declan Doherty strode over to Ed. 'You found us then?'

'Not too difficult Declan. Followed the pony and trap.'

Doherty laughed, slapped Ed's back. 'A fox just like Ray. We're honoured that you've come.'

'Thanks'

'Now enjoy yourself,' Declan grinned. 'It's a free bar.'

Ed let his eyes scan the crowded dance floor.

'Who's the lad with the bandaged arm, dancing with the girl in the purple dress?' he asked as he watched the pair move together to the music.

'That girl is my granddaughter,' Declan said with obvious pride. 'The lad is another one who wasn't sorry to learn about the Skinners' change of fortune.'

The two men watched as the girl turned and wiggled her hips with something unspoken behind her smile while her partner drank from a bottle he held in his good hand.

'A lad whose starting to fancy our way of life I reckon,' Declan said, grinning again. 'Goes by the name of Pixie.'

AFTERWORD

If you enjoyed *'Angels and Apostles'* do check out Tony Hutchinson's other Dark Tides books, *'Be My Girl'* and *'Comply or Die'*.

And keep up to date with forth-coming titles by visiting Tony's website:

www.tonyhutch.com

ACKNOWLEDGMENTS

No work of fiction is ever completed without the help and guidance of a great team of people.

My first thanks are to my family for their love and support: Saphron for her encouragement, Ben for his humour and Flynn for his permanent smile. Without you guys I wouldn't write a word.

I am indebted to Cheshire Cat Books for having the faith to publish.

Thanks to Paul Jones, Head of Publishing, who is my biggest critic and continues to succinctly highlight weaknesses in the narrative.

Thanks to Garry Willey, Head of Editorial, for sprinkling little pieces of magic dust across the pages.

Without either of you this book would not be what it is.

Thanks to Adam Maxwell, Head of Digital at Cheshire Cat Books, for formatting the books ready for digital and print and always involving me in the process.

My thanks go to my son, Ben, for providing the cover photograph and of course Laura Swaddle for designing the cover.

As ever my final thanks are to you, the reader. A book that is not read is just words on a page.

29731433R00218

Printed in Great
Britain
by Amazon